A Winter
Wedding

A *Winter* Wedding

Marguerite Denise
KAYE **LYNN**

First Published in Great Britain 2016
By Mills & Boon, an imprint of HarperCollins*Publishers*
1 London Bridge Street, London, SE1 9GF

A WINTER WEDDING © 2016 Harlequin Books S.A.

Strangers at the Altar © 2014 Marguerite Kaye
The Warrior's Winter Bride © 2014 Denise L. Koch

ISBN: 978-0-263-92687-3

9-1116

Our policy is to use papers that are natural, renewable and recyclable products and made from wood grown in sustainable forests.
The logging and manufacturing processes conform to the legal environmental regulations of the country of origin.

Printed and bound by
CPI Group (UK) Ltd, Croydon, CR0 4YY

STRANGERS
AT THE ALTAR

MARGUERITE KAYE

Born and educated in Scotland, **Marguerite Kaye** originally qualified as a lawyer but chose not to practise. Instead, she carved out a career in IT and studied history part-time, gaining first-class honours and a master's degree. A few decades after winning a children's national poetry competition she decided to pursue her lifelong ambition to write, and submitted her first historical romance to Mills & Boon. They accepted it, and she's been writing ever since.

You can contact Marguerite through her website at: www.margueritekaye.com

Chapter One

Dear Madame Hera,

The other day, while taking a walk in the Cowgate district of Edinburgh, I was approached by a young man who gave me some assistance with my umbrella. Since he was very well dressed, seemed most polite, and the rain was coming down in torrents, it seemed churlish of me not to offer to share my shelter. He accepted with some alacrity, but the small circumference of my umbrella forced us into a somewhat compromising intimacy, of which the gentleman was not slow to take advantage. He stole a kiss from me, and I permitted him to take several more while we found respite from the downpour in the close of a nearby tenement. By the time the rain stopped, we were rather better acquainted than we ought to have been.

We parted without exchanging details. Alack, when he left me, the young man took not only my virtue but my umbrella. It was a gift from another gentleman, who is bound to question me

most closely when he discovers its loss. I fear he will not understand the peculiar effect the combination of rain, a good-looking young man and a very small umbrella can have on a woman's willpower. What should I do?
Drookit Miss

Edinburgh—June 1840

'I am very sorry, Mrs McBrayne, but there is nothing to be done. Both your father's will and the law are perfectly clear upon the matter. Could not be clearer, in actual fact, though if you insist upon a second opinion, I believe my partner is now free.'

'You, Mr Thomson, *are* my second opinion,' the woman said scornfully. 'I have no intentions of spending more money I don't have, thanks to that spendthrift husband of mine and that trust of my father's, simply to hear what you have already made perfectly plain. The law is written by men for men and administered by men, too. Be damned to the law, Mr Thomson, for it seems to be forcing me to earn my living in a profession even older than your own, down in the Cowgate. I bid you good day.'

'Mrs McBrayne! Madam, I must beg you...'

The Fury merely tossed her head at the lawyer's outraged countenance and swept across the narrow reception hall of the office, heading for the door. Innes Drummond, who had just completed a similarly entirely unsatisfactory interview with Thomson's partner, watched her dramatic exit admiringly. The door slammed behind her with enough force to rattle the pane of glass on which the names Thomson & Ballard were etched. Innes could hear her footsteps descending the rackety stairs that led out into Parliament Square. She was as anxious to quit the place as he was himself. It struck him, as he flung the door behind him with equal and satisfying force, how ironic it was, that they both, he and the incandescent Mrs McBrayne, seemed to be victims of very similar circumstances.

He reached the bottom of the stairs and heaved open the heavy wooden door, only to collide with the person standing on the step. 'I am terribly sorry,' Innes said.

'No, it was my fault.'

She stood aside, and as she did so, he saw tears glistening on her lashes. Mortified, she saw him noticing, and scrubbed at her eyes with her glove, averting her face as she pushed past him.

'Wait!' Instinctively knowing she would not, Innes caught her arm. 'Madam, you are upset.'

She glared at him, shaking herself free of his reflexive grip. 'I am not upset. Not that it's any of your business, but I am very far beyond upset. I am…'

'Furious,' Innes finished for her with a wry smile. 'I know how you feel.'

'I doubt it.'

Her eyes were hazel, wide-spaced and fringed with very long lashes. She was not pretty, definitely not one of those soft, pliant females with rosebud mouths and doe-like gazes, but he was nonetheless drawn to her. She eyed him sceptically, a frown pulling her rather fierce brows together. She was not young either, perhaps in her late twenties, and there was intelligence as well as cynicism in her face. Then there was her mouth. No, not a rosebud, but soft all the same when it ought to be austere, with a hint of humour and more than a hint of sensuality. He noticed that, and with some surprise, noticed that he'd noticed, that his eyes had wandered down, over the slim figure in the drab grey coat, taking a rapid inventory of the limited view and wanting to see more, and that surprised him, too.

'Innes Drummond.' He introduced himself because he could think of nothing else to say, and because he didn't want her to go. Her brows lifted haughtily in response. For some reason, it made her look younger. 'A fellow victim of the law, of his father and of a trust,' he added. 'Though I'm not encumbered with a wife, spendthrift or otherwise.'

'You were listening in to a private conversation between myself and Mr Thomson.'

'Ought I to have pretended not to hear? The tone of your voice made that rather difficult.'

She gave a dry little laugh. 'A tone I feel sure Mr Thomson found most objectionable. Bloody lawyers. Damned law. You see, I can swear as well as shout, though I assure you, I am not usually the type who does either.'

Innes laughed. 'I really do know how you feel, you know.'

She smiled tightly. 'You are a man, Mr Drummond. It is simply not possible. Now, if you will excuse me?'

'Where are you going?' Once again, he had spoken without thinking, wanting only to detain her. Once again her brows rose, more sharply this time. 'I only meant that if you had no urgent business— But I spoke out of turn. Perhaps your husband is expecting you?'

'My husband is dead, Mr Drummond, and though his dying has left me quite without resources, still I cannot be sorry for it.'

'You don't mince your words, do you, Mrs McBrayne?'

Though he was rather shocked at this callous remark, Innes spoke flippantly. She did not smile, however, nor take umbrage, but instead paled slightly. 'I speak my mind. My opinions may be unpalatable, but at least in expressing them, there can be no pretending that I have none.'

Nor, Innes thought, could there be any denying that a wealth of bitter experience lay behind her words. He was intrigued. 'If you are in no rush, I'd very much like it if you would take a glass of something with me. I promise I don't mean anything in the least improper,' he added hurriedly, 'I merely thought it would be pleasant—cathartic, I don't know—to let off steam with a kindred spirit—' Her astonished expression forced him to break off. 'Forget it. It's been an awful day, an awful few weeks, but I shouldn't have asked.'

He made to tip his hat, but once again she surprised him, this time with a faint smile. 'Never mind weeks, *I've* had an awful few months. No, make that years. The only reason I've not taken to drink already is that I suspect I'd take to it rather too well.'

'I suspect that you do anything well that you set your mind to, Mrs McBrayne. You strike me as a most determined female.'

'Do I? I am now, though it is by far too late, for no matter how determined I am to get myself out of this mess, in truth I can see no solution.'

'Save to sell yourself down the Cowgate? I hope it doesn't come to that.'

She gave him what could only be described as a challenging look. 'Why, are you afraid I will not make sufficient to earn my keep?'

'What on earth do you know of such things?' Innes asked, torn between shock and laughter.

'Oh, I have my sources. And I have an umbrella,' she added confusingly.

She spoke primly, but there was devilment in her eyes, and the smile she was biting back was doing strange things to his guts. 'You are outrageous, Mrs McBrayne,' Innes said.

'Don't you believe me?'

'I have no idea what to make of you, and right at this moment, I don't really care. You made me laugh, and honestly, after what that lawyer told me, I didn't think that was possible.'

Her smile softened sympathetically. 'It sounds like I am not the only one in need of a dram,' she said.

'Why not! I've nothing at home waiting for me except final demands and most likely a few bailiffs. Buy me a drink, Mr Drummond, and we can compare our woes, though I warn you now that mine will far outweigh yours.'

Ainsley McBrayne wondered what on earth had come over her. There had been ample time in the short walk from Parliament Square over the North Bridge for her to change her mind, but she had not. Now here she was, in a secluded corner of the coffee room at the Waterloo Hotel, waiting while a complete stranger bribed one of the waiting staff to bring the pair of them something stronger than tea.

She had surrendered her coat at the door, and her bonnet, too, for they were both wet with that soft, mist-like mizzle that was not quite rain, in which Edinburgh specialised. Her hair, which even on the best of days was reluctant to succumb to the curling iron, was today bundled up into a careless chignon at her nape, and no doubt by now straggling equally carelessly out of it. On a good day, she would tell herself it was chestnut in colour, for it was not red enough to rate auburn, and she was fairly certain there was no such thing as mahogany hair. Today, it was brown, plain and simple and the colour of her mood. At least her gown was one of her better ones. Navy blue worked with silver-grey stylised flowers formed into a linking pattern, the full skirts contrasted with the tightly fitted bodice, with its long narrow sleeves and shawl neck. The narrow belt showed off her slender waist; the crossover pleating at the neck was cut just low enough to allow a daring glimpse of bosom. It had been designed to be worn with a demure white blouse, but this morning Ainsley hadn't been interested in looking demure. This morning she had not, however, intended to take off her coat. Now, she tugged self-consciously at the pleated shawl collar in an effort to pull it a little closer.

She had been angry when she left the lawyer's office, though she should not have been, but it seemed, despite all, that she'd not managed to lower her expectations quite enough. There had been a tiny modicum of hope left in her heart, and she'd been furious at herself for that. Hence the tears. Stupid tears. If Mr Innes Drummond had not seen those stupid tears, he'd more than likely have gone on his way and she wouldn't be here. Instead, she'd be at home. Alone. Or in the company of yet another bailiff. And it wasn't going to be her home for much longer. So she might as well be here. With a complete stranger. About to imbibe strong li-

quor, just like one of the loose women she'd claimed
she would become.

Not that that was so far-fetched either, given the
state of things, except one thing she was absolutely
sure about was that she had no talents whatsoever for
that sort of thing. In fact, she had not even the skill to
interest a man if he didn't have to pay, if her husband
was anything to go by.

Ainsley sighed. Second to tears, she hated self-pity.
Giving her collar a final twitch, she forced herself to
relax. Mr Drummond was still conferring with the waiter,
so she took the chance to study him. His hair, which was
cut unfashionably short, was glossily black. He was a
good-looking man; there was no doubt about it, with
a clean-shaven jaw, and none of the side whiskers gentlemen preferred these days. A high forehead spoke of
intelligence, and lines fanning out from his eyes and
forming a deep groove from nose to mouth spoke of
experience. He looked to be in his mid-thirties, perhaps
five years older than herself. A confident man, and well
dressed in his dark coat and trousers, his linen impeccably white. Judging by appearances, money was not
one of his worries. But then, if one could have judged
John by appearances, money had not been one of his
worries either. Not that her husband had ever been at
all worried by money—or the lack of. No, that was not
true. Those sullen silences of his spoke volumes. And
latterly, so, too, did his habit of simply disappearing
when she challenged him.

Ainsley sighed again, irked with herself. She was
absolutely sick and tired of thinking about John. Across
the room, Mr Drummond, having concluded his business with the waiter, glanced up and smiled at her. His

eyes, under heavy dark brows, were a deep, vivid blue. She felt it then, what she had ignored before, a tug of something quite basic. Attraction. It made her stomach do a silly little flutter. It made her pulses skitter and it made her mouth dry, that smile of his, and the complicit look that accompanied it, as if the pair of them were in cahoots. It made her forget her anger at the injustice of her situation, and it reminded her that though she might well be a penniless widow with debts so terrifying they could not be counted, she was also a woman who had not known the touch of a man for a long time. And this man, this Mr Innes Drummond, who was seating himself opposite her, this man, she was pretty certain, would know exactly how to touch her.

'So, ladies first.'

Colour flooded her face. She stared at him blankly, horrified at the turn her mind had taken, praying that none of those shocking thoughts were visible on her countenance 'I beg your pardon?'

'Your tale of woe, Mrs McBrayne. You tell me yours, and then I'll tell you mine, and we can decide which of us is worst off.'

He had very long legs. They were stretched out to the side of the table that separated them. Well-made legs. Not at all spindly. And really rather broad shoulders. *Well built,* that was the phrase she was looking for. Athletic, even. And yes, his face and hands were rather tanned, as if he spent a deal of his life out of doors. 'What is it you do?' she asked. 'I mean—do you—are you a resident here in Edinburgh? Only, you do have an accent, but I cannot place it.'

Instead of taking offence, or pointing out that she had changed the subject, Innes Drummond gave a little shrug. 'I'm originally from the Highlands, Argyll on the west coast, though I've lived in England most of my adult life. I'm an engineer, Mrs McBrayne.'

'A practical man.'

He smiled. 'You approve.'

'I do. It is none of my business, but—yes.' She smiled back. 'What do you build?'

'Railway lines. Tunnels. Canals. Bridges and aqueducts. There is a very high demand for all these things, thanks to the steam locomotive. Though I don't actually build the things myself, I design them. And even that— Business is very good, Mrs McBrayne. I am afraid I employ a rather large number of men to do most of the real work while I spend too much of my time in the boardroom, though I still like to think of myself as an engineer.'

'A very successful one, by the sounds of it. I did not think that money could be an issue with you.'

He gave her an enigmatic look before turning his attention to pouring them both a glass of whisky from the decanter that the waiter had deposited. *'Slàinte!'* he said, touching her glass with his.

'Slàinte!' Ainsley took a sip. It was a good malt, peaty and smoky, warming. She took another sip.

'I take it, then, that money *is* an issue for you,' Innes Drummond said.

She nodded. He waited, watching her, turning his glass round and round in his hand. One of the many things she'd learned from her marriage had been how to keep her own counsel—and how to keep her own secrets. Her failures, and the trusting, timid nature that had contributed to them, made her ashamed. She confided in no one, not even Felicity, and Felicity was the best friend she had. But confiding in this stranger, what harm could it do? Whatever had brought him to Edinburgh, he wasn't likely to be stopping long. If—however—he judged her, she'd be spared the pain of seeing it. Who knew, perhaps articulating her problems might even help her see a path to resolving them.

Catching sight of her wedding band, Ainsley tucked her left hand into the folds of her gown. 'It is money,' she said, 'it comes down to money, and though I tell myself it's not fair, for I did not spend the money, I know at heart it's just as much my fault as his.'

Mrs McBrayne took another sip of whisky. 'Dutch courage,' she said, recklessly finishing the amber liquid and replacing the glass on the table before straightening her back and taking an audible breath. Innes wondered what on earth was to come, and wondered if he should stop her confidences, but dismissed this idea immediately. She was steeling herself, which meant she wanted to talk. Besides, he was interested, and it was good to have his mind concentrate on someone else's woes rather than his own for a while. He took a cautious sip of his own whisky and waited.

'I will need to go back a bit,' she said. 'Are you sure you want to hear this?' When he nodded, she smiled an on-your-head-be-it kind of smile. 'So,' she said, 'I met my husband, John McBrayne, when I was twenty. Nearly a decade ago. He was very much the gentleman, respectable, handsome, presentable, popular.' She counted her husband's assets off on her fingers. 'He was also what they call a charmer, and I was charmed. I met him at the Assembly Rooms. He was the friend of a friend. He seemed to be a man of means. Within six months, he had proposed, and I was delighted. I was happy. I was in love.' Another smile, only this one was a bitter little twist. 'John spoke to my father. My father asked me if I was sure, he told me there was no hurry, that if I wanted to change my mind—but I didn't, and I didn't think—I thought Papa was just being his usual cautious self, that's all. He was always polite to John, never said a word against him to me, and— But I'm getting ahead of myself.'

Innes swallowed the rest of his malt. 'Do you want another?' he asked, indicating her glass, and when Mrs McBrayne shook her head, resisted the urge to pour one for himself. 'Go on.'

'We were happy. I find I have to remind myself of that, but for a year or so we were happy. Then the bills started to go unpaid, and when I asked John, he told me not to worry. But I did, and when I eventually looked into matters properly, I discovered we owed a monstrous amount. My husband was furious when he found out that I knew, he told me it was a temporary situation, he told me—ach, he told me all sorts, and I believed some of it, because I wanted to. I'd never en-quired about his income until then, I had assumed my father—but there, you see, I'm putting the blame on others when it was my own fault. I should have asked right at the start. I should have made it my business, but by the time I did, it was too late.'

'You mean that by that time, your husband's debts were unmanageable?'

'I mean it was too late for me to persuade my hus-band that his debts were not only his business but mine, too,' Mrs McBrayne responded wryly. 'I think I will have another, if you don't mind.'

She was pale despite the whisky, her mouth thinned, her eyes focused inwards. When she sipped her drink, her hand trembled. Noticing that, she placed the glass carefully down. It was a common enough tale, but the way she told it was not at all common. Her feelings ran very deep. Innes was struggling to understand why.

'I told you you wouldn't understand,' she said, taking him aback by seeming to read his thoughts.

He made no attempt to deny it. 'Explain it, then,' Innes said.

'Imagine how you would feel if someone else was given control of your business. Imagine how you'd feel if they could make decisions about it over your head, without consulting you. Decisions that had consequences for you, but that you had no say in. Now imagine that at first you don't realise this is going on. Then when you do realise, and you challenge this person, they tell you that they're only doing what is expected of them. Then they tell you that you've no right to challenge them. And then they simply turn a cold shoulder. As a businessman, you can do something about it. You can even take action in court, if that person's been fraudulent. As a wife…' Mrs McBrayne spread her hands and gave him another of those bitter smiles. 'As a wife, you can choose to make both your lives a misery with constant nagging, or you can put up and shut up. What you can't do is change a thing. Not a single damn thing.'

Innes felt slightly sick. Having sworn all those years ago never to marry, he had never actually considered the state of matrimony from any point of view. Mrs McBrayne's perspective was horrible, and all the more so for the almost cool way she described it. Almost cool—for he was willing to bet that her fist was tightly clenched in the folds of her gown, and there was hurt in those hazel eyes as well as anger. He felt angry on her behalf, though he knew her husband had done nothing that society would condemn. In fact, more likely society would condone, for a man was expected to take care of his wife, and a wife—was it true, that a woman was expected simply to *put up and shut up*, as Mrs McBrayne so succinctly put it?

Innes put his glass down, and ran an agitated hand through his hair. 'You're right, if I were in such a situation— It sounds intolerable.'

'And yet I bore it,' she said bitterly. 'I wonder if things would have been different had I not. I thought of leaving him, but lack of funds made that impractical, and I would not go to my father. Edinburgh might appear to be a large town, but in practice it is not much more than a village. My leaving my husband's protection would have caused quite a scandal. Besides, I was— I was ashamed.' She glared at him as she said this. 'I was under the misapprehension that if I'd behaved differently I could have changed my husband,' she said. 'It took me some time to realise that since he would never change, then I must.'

She concluded with a small, satisfied smile that made Innes wonder how, exactly, she had changed and what, exactly, the effect had been on her spendthrift husband, but before he could ask, her smile had faded. She took a sip of whisky. Her hand was quite steady now. 'I remained with my husband, but matters between us were extremely strained. John devoted himself to myriad schemes he found to lose money, and I—I pursued a new interest of my own which was distracting and made me feel not quite so useless, but ultimately, I was burying my head in the sand. And then my father died, and his will dealt our marriage a death blow.'

'The trust?'

She nodded. 'I discovered later that John had asked him for money. Neither of them saw fit to inform me of that fact.' Her eyes blazed. 'My own father! I thought he trusted me. I thought— But there, I was wrong. Money is a matter for the man of the house, apparently.' The fire disappeared from her eyes as quickly as it had come. 'To cut a long and tedious story short, my father changed his will so that my entire inheritance was put into trust for my first child. He did not specify the sex, so at least I should be grateful for that—not that it makes any difference, since there is no child. When John found out, he...' Her voice wavered, but she quickly got it back under control. 'He was furious. He wanted to break the trust. He wanted *me* to find a way to break the trust, to use the law to go against my own father's wishes. It was not exactly conducive to marital harmony. Not that there was much of that by then. When I wouldn't cooperate—well, it seems I didn't have to, for what was mine was actually my husband's. Fortunately for my father's wishes, though not so fortunately for my husband and his creditors, the trust could not be broken. And then my husband died.'

Her voice was hard. Obviously, the love she'd felt for the man she had married was long gone. 'How?' Innes asked, wondering fleetingly if she was about to confess to killing him. There was a bit of him that would not have been surprised. A bit of him that would have approved.

'Pleurisy,' she replied. 'They found him dead drunk down in the Cowgate, out cold in a puddle. Heaven knows how long he'd been there or where he'd been before. He had not been home for three days.'

Was that what she'd meant when she implied she knew more than any respectable woman ought, about the women who plied their business in that scurrilous area? He wanted to ask, but he didn't want to distract her. Despite the sorry tale she'd told him, she was defiant, and he couldn't help but admire her for that. 'I take it then, that your husband left you with nothing?' Innes said.

'Nothing but debts. Not even my jointure, for it was to be sourced from investments that are now worthless. There is a mortgage on our house that becomes due in a month, a year after his death, and my father's trust is so watertight that, as Mr Thomson confirmed this morning, not even my utter ruin can break it. But you know, it's not even the money that bothers me. It's the extent to which I have been kept in the dark—allowed myself to be kept in the dark—not just by John, but by my father. It makes me feel about this size.' Mrs McBrayne held her thumb and index finger about an inch apart. 'That's how much of a say they gave me in my own life.'

'I am sure your father meant only to protect you.'

'Because I'm nothing but a frail female without a mind of my own?' she snapped. 'It made me wonder how many hundreds, thousands more of us poor wee souls there are out there, living life blindfolded.'

'You make it sound like a conspiracy.'

'That's because it feels like one, and not even Madame He...'

'Madame He?'

'Never mind.' Mrs McBrayne shook her head and picked up her glass, swirled the contents, then replaced it without drinking. 'I beg your pardon. I did not mean to become so emotional. I have made my bed, as they say, and now I must lie on it. Or not, for it is to be sold.' She smiled tightly. 'Like all sorry tales, this one comes with a moral. Whatever happens, I shall never again allow anyone to make my decisions for me. For good or ill, my fate will be of my own determination in the future. And now that is quite enough of me. It is your turn.'

He had a hundred questions, but she had folded her hands and her lips together, and was making a great show of listening. Innes was not fooled. Her eyes were overbright, her fingers too tightly clasped. She had taken quite a battering, one way or another. A lesser woman would have cried, or flung herself on some man's mercy. He could not imagine Mrs McBrayne doing either. He wanted to cheer her. He wanted to tell her she would be fine, absolutely fine. He was very tempted to offer her money, but she would be mortified, to say nothing of the fact that he was pretty certain she'd also see it merely as a transfer of obligation, and he didn't want her to feel beholden. What he wanted was for her to be free. It wasn't so much that he felt sorry for her, though he railed at the injustice of it all, but he felt—yes, that was it—an affinity.

'What have I said to make you smile?'

'Your situation, Mrs McBrayne, has struck a great many chords.'

'I do not see how. I don't know you, but you have told me yourself you're a self-made man and a success. Men such as you will never brook any interference in your life.'

'Actually, that's not true. Unfortunately, I know very well indeed what it's like to have someone else try to bind you to their rules, to dictate your life without you having a say.'

He was pleased to see that he had surprised her. 'What do you mean?' she asked.

'Did I not say at the outset that we are both the victims of fathers and trusts?' Innes replied. 'It's a strange coincidence, but I while you were consulting Thomson on the finer points of your father's will, I was consulting Ballard on the very same thing. I too have been left the victim of a trust fund, only my father's intention was not to protect me but to call me to heel, and unlike your trust, mine can be broken, though only in a very particular way.'

'What way, Mr Drummond?'

Innes smiled thinly. 'Marriage, Mrs McBrayne. An institution that I assure you, I abhor every bit as much as you do yourself.'

Chapter Two

Ainsley stared at him in astonishment. 'Your father's will sets up a trust that requires you to marry?'

'No, it establishes a trust to control the family lands that will remain in effect *until* I marry,' Innes replied.

'Lands?' She only just managed to prevent her jaw dropping. 'As in—what, a country estate?'

'A little more than that. I'm not sure what the total acreage is, but there are about twenty tenanted farms as well as the home farm and the castle.'

'Good heavens, Mr Drummond—a castle! And *about* twenty farms. Is there a title, too?'

He shook his head. 'My father was known as the laird of Strone Bridge, but it was just a courtesy.'

Laird. The title conjured up a fierce Highland patriarch. Ainsley eyed the impeccably dressed gentleman opposite her and discovered it was surprisingly easy to imagine him in a plaid, carrying a claymore. Though without the customary beard. She didn't like beards. 'And these lands, they are in Argyll, did you say?'

When he nodded Ainsley frowned in puzzlement. 'Forgive me, Mr Drummond, but did you not tell me you had spent most of your life in England? Surely as the heir to such a substantial property—I know nothing of such things, mind you—but I thought it would have been customary for you to have lived on the estate?'

His countenance hardened. 'I was not the heir.'

'Oh?'

She waited, unwilling to prompt him further, for he looked quite forbidding. Innes Drummond took a sip of whisky, grimaced and put the glass back down on the table. 'Dutch courage,' he said, with a shadow of her own words and her own grim little smile. 'I had a brother. Malcolm. He was the heir. It is as you said—he lived on the estate. Lived and breathed it, more like, for he loved the place. Strone Bridge was his world.'

He stared down at his glass, his mouth turned down in sorrow. 'But it was not your world?' Ainsley asked gently.

'It was never meant for me. I was the second son. As far as my father was concerned, that meant second best, and while Malcolm was alive, next to useless, Mrs McBrayne.'

He stared down at his glass, such a bleak look on his face that she leaned over to press his hand. 'My name is Ainsley.'

'I don't think I've heard that before.'

'An old family name,' she said.

He gave her a very fleeting smile as his fingers curled around hers. 'Then you must call me Innes,' he said. 'Another old family name, though it is not usually that of the laird. One condition I have been spared. My father did not specify that I change my name to Malcolm. Even he must have realised that would have been a step too far. Though, then again, it may simply have been that he thought me as unworthy of the name as the lands.'

He spoke viciously enough to make Ainsley recoil. 'You sound as though you hate him.'

'Rather, the boot was on the other foot.' He said it jeeringly. She wondered what hurt lay behind those words, but Innes was already retreating, patently regretting what he had revealed. 'We did not see eye to eye,' he tempered. 'Some would call him a traditionalist. Everyone had a place in his world. I did not take to the one he allotted me. When I finally decided to forge my own way, we fell out.'

Ainsley could well imagine it. Innes was obviously a man with a very strong will, a modern man and an independent one who clearly thrived in the industrial world. It would be like two stags clashing. She wondered what the circumstances had been that had caused what was obviously a split, but curious as she was, she had no wish to rile him further. 'Tell me about the trust,' she said. 'Why must you marry, and what happens if you do not?'

Innes stared down at his hand, the one she had so abruptly released, his eyes still dark with pain. 'As to why, that is obvious. The Strone Bridge estate has been passed through the direct line back as far as records exist, and I am the last of the line. He wanted an heir.'

'But he only specified that you must take a wife? That seems rather odd.'

'We Drummonds have proved ourselves potent over the generations. My father no doubt assumed that even such an undeserving son as I would not fail in that most basic of tasks,' Innes said sarcastically.

'You don't want children?'

'I don't want a wife, and in my book, one must necessarily precede the other.'

This time Ainsley's curiosity overcame her caution. 'Why are you so against marriage?' she asked. 'You don't strike me as a man who hates my sex.'

'You don't strike me as a woman who hates men, yet you don't want to get married again.'

'It is a case of once bitten with me.'

'While I have no intentions of being bitten for a first time,' Innes retorted. 'I don't need anyone other than myself to order my life, and I certainly don't want to rely on anyone else to make me happy.'

He spoke with some vehemence. He spoke as if there was bitter experience behind his words. As there was, too, behind hers. 'Your father's will has put you in an impossible situation, then,' Ainsley said.

'As has yours,' Innes replied tersely. 'What happens to your trust if you have no children?'

'It reverts to me when I am forty and presumably deemed to be saying my prayers.' She could not keep the bitterness from her voice. She had loved her father, but his unwitting condemnation of her was still difficult to take. 'I have only to discover a way of avoiding my husband's creditors and surviving without either a roof over my head or food in my belly for the next ten years in order to inherit, since I have no intentions of marrying again.'

'Nor any intention of producing a child out of wedlock, I take it? No need to look so shocked,' Innes said, 'it was a joke.'

'A poor one.'

'I'm sorry.'

She forced a smile. 'I do not really intend to sell myself down the Cowgate, you know.'

Innes covered her hand. 'Are your debts really so bad?'

'There will certainly still be sufficient of them to pay off when I finally do come into my inheritance,' she said.

His fingers tightened around hers. 'I wish I could be of some help to you.'

'You have been, simply by listening,' Ainsley replied, flustered by the sympathy in his look. She no longer expected sympathy. She had come to believe she did not deserve it. 'A problem shared and all that,' she said with a small smile.

'It's a damnable situation.'

He seemed much bigger, this close. There was something terribly comforting in those broad shoulders, in the way his hand enveloped hers, in the way he was looking at her, not with pity at all but with understanding. Close-up, his irises were ringed with a very dark blue. She had never seen eyes quite that colour.

Realising her thoughts were once more straying down a most inappropriate path, Ainsley dropped her gaze. 'If my father had not left my money in trust, my husband would have spent it by now, and I'd have nothing to look forward to in what he clearly thought of as my forty-year-old dotage. The money might have postponed my husband's demise, but I doubt very much it would have been for more than a few years, and frankly I don't think I could have borne a few more years married to him.'

'I confess, at one point I thought you were going to tell me you had killed him yourself,' Innes said.

Ainsley laughed. 'I may not be the timid wee mouse he married, but I don't think I've become a monster.'

'I think you are a wonder.' She looked up, surprised by the warmth in his tone, and her pulses began to race as he lifted her hand to his mouth, pressing a kiss to her knuckles. There was no mistaking it for one of those polite, social, nothing kisses. His mouth lingered on her skin, his lips warm, his eyes looking deep into hers for long, long seconds. 'You are a most remarkable woman, Ainsley McBrayne.'

'Thank you. I— Thank you.'

'I really do wish there was some way that I could help you, but I know better than to offer you money.'

'I really do wish there was a way I could accept it, but—well, there we are, I cannot, so there is no point in discussing it. In fact, we have talked far more about me than you. I'm still not clear about what happens to your lands if you remain unmarried. What does this trust entail?'

She was pleased with how she sounded. Not a tremor to betray the quickening of desire his lips had stirred, and she hoped the flush she could feel blooming had not reached her cheeks.

However Innes Drummond felt, and she would have dearly liked to have known, he took his cue from her. 'A trustee appointed by that lawyer, Ballard, to manage them, and all monies associated with them banked. I can't touch a penny of it without a wife,' he replied, 'and even with a wife, I must also commit to living for a year on Strone Bridge.'

'Is it a great deal of money?'

Innes shook his head. 'I've no idea, since I'm not even entitled to see the accounts, but the money isn't the point, I have plenty of my own. I haven't a clue what state the place is in at all. It could be flourishing, it could have gone to rack and ruin, for all I know.'

'So the fall out between yourself and your father then, it was...'

'More like a complete break. I told you, he was an old-fashioned man. Do as I say, or get out of my sight.'

Innes spoke lightly enough, but she was not fooled. 'How long is it since you were there?'

'Almost fourteen years. Since Malcolm—since I lost my brother.' Innes shuddered, but recovered quickly. 'You're wondering why I'm so upset about the trust when I've spent most of my adult life away from the place,' he said.

'I think this has all been much more of a shock than you realise,' Ainsley answered cautiously.

'Aye, mayhap you're right.' His accent had softened, the Highland lilt much more obvious. 'I had no inkling the old man was ill, and he'd no time to let me know. Not that I think he would have. Far better for me to be called to heel through that will of his from beyond the grave. I don't doubt he's looking down—or maybe up—and laughing at the mess he's put me in,' Innes said. 'He knew just how it would stick in my craw, having to choose between relying on someone else to run what is mine or to take up the reins myself under such conditions. Be damned to him! I must find a way to break this trust. I will not let him issue decrees from beyond the grave.'

He thumped his fist on the table, making his glass and Ainsley jump. 'I'm beginning to think that your situation is worse than mine after all.'

'Ach, that's nonsense, for I at least don't have to

worry about where my next meal is coming from. It's a sick coincidence, the way the pair of us are being punished by our parents, though,' Innes said. 'What will you do?'

'Oh, I'm beyond worrying right now.' Ainsley waved her hand in the air dismissively. 'The question is, what will you do? If only you could find a woman to marry who has no interest in actually being your wife, your problems would be solved.'

She spoke flippantly, more to divert his attention from her own tragic situation than anything, but Innes, who had been in the act of taking another sip of whisky, stopped, the glass halfway to his lips, an arrested look in his eyes. 'Say that again.'

'What? That you need to marry…'

'A woman who has no interest in being my wife,' he finished for her with a dawning smile. 'A woman who is in need of a home, and has no fixed plans, who might actually be looking for a respite from her current life for a wee while. You're right, that's exactly what I need, and I know exactly the woman.'

'You do? You cannot possible mean…'

His smile had a wicked light in it. 'I do,' Innes said. 'I mean you.'

Ainsley was staring at him open-mouthed. Innes laughed. 'Think about it, it's the ideal solution. In fact, it could almost be said that we are perfectly matched, since you have as little desire for a husband as I have for a wife.'

She blinked at him owlishly. 'Are you drunk?'

'Certainly not.'

'Then I must be, for you cannot possibly be propos-ing marriage. Apart from the fact that we've only just met, I thought I had made it plain that I will never—absolutely *never* again—surrender my independence.'

'I'm not asking you to. I'm actually making it easier for you to retain it, because if we get married, I can pay off all those debts that bastard of a husband of yours acquired and then you really will be free.'

'But I'd be married to you.'

'In name only.'

'I owe a small fortune. I couldn't take it from you just for the price of putting my name on a bit of paper.'

'You'd have to come with me to Strone Bridge. The clause that specified my spending a year there doesn't actually include my wife, but all the same, I think you'd have to come with me for a wee while, at least.'

'That would not be a problem since, as you have already deduced, I'm going to be homeless very shortly, and would appreciate a change of scene, but I simply couldn't think of accepting such a huge amount of money and give so little in return.'

'What if you saw it as a wage?' Innes asked, frowning.

'For what?'

'A fee, paid for professional services,' he said, 'and a retainer to be paid in addition each year until you are forty, which you could pay me back if you wish, when you eventually inherit, though there is no need.'

'But I'm not a professional.' Her eyes widened. 'You cannot possibly mean— I told you, I was joking about the Cowgate.'

Innes laughed. 'Not that! I meant a business professional.' She was now looking utterly bewildered. Innes grinned. 'The more I think about it, the more I see how perfect it is. No, wait.' He caught her as she made to get up. 'I promise you, I'm neither drunk nor mad. Listen.'

Ainsley sat down, folding her arms, a sceptical look on her face. 'Five minutes.'

He nodded. 'Think about it as a business proposal,' he said. 'First of all, think of the common ground. To begin with, you need to pay off your debts and I am rich enough to be able to do so easily. Second, you are a widow, and I need a wife. Since we are neither of us in the least bit interested, now or ever, in marrying someone else…'

'How can you be so sure of that?'

'How can you?' He waited, but she made no answer, so he gave a satisfied nod. 'You see? We are of one mind on that. And we are of one mind on another thing, which is our determination to make our own way in life. If you let me pay off your debts, I can give you the freedom to do that, and if you marry me, you'll be freeing me to make up my own mind on what to do—or not—about my inheritance.'

'But we'll be tied to one another.'

'In name only, Ainsley. Tied by a bit of paper, which is no more than a contract.'

'Contracts require payment. What *professional* services can you possibly imagine I can provide?'

'An objective eye. An unbiased opinion. I need both.' Innes shifted uncomfortably. 'Not advice, precisely,' he said.

'Because you do not like to take advice, do you?'

'Are you mocking me?'

'Another thing you're not used to, obviously.' Ainsley smiled. 'Not mocking, teasing. I'm a little rusty.

What is it, then, that involves my giving you my un-biased and objective opinion without advising you?'

'When you put it like that!' He was forced to smile. 'What I'm trying to say is, I'd like you to come to Strone Bridge with me. Not to make my decisions, but to make sure when I do make them, I'm doing so without prejudice.'

'Is that possible? It's your birthright, Innes.'

He shook his head vehemently. 'That's the point. It's not. It pains me to admit it, but I don't know much about it, and I haven't a clue what I want to do with it. Live there. Sell it. Put in a manager. I don't know, and I won't know until I go there, and even when I do—what do you say?'

'That's the price? That's the professional services I'm to render in order to have my life back?'

'You think it's too great a cost?' Innes said, deflated.

Ainsley smiled. Then she laughed. 'I think it's a bargain.'

'You do? You understand, Strone Bridge is like to be—well, very different from Edinburgh.'

'A change from Edinburgh, a place to take stock, is, as you pointed out, exactly what I need.'

'I'm not asking you to stay the full year. A few months, until I've seen my way clear, that's all. And though I'm asking you to—to consult with me, that does not mean I'll necessarily take your advice,' Innes cautioned.

'I'm used to that.' Ainsley's smile faded momentarily, but then brightened. 'Though being asked is a step in the right direction, and I will at least have the opportunity of putting my point across.'

Glancing at the decanter of whisky, the level of

which had unmistakably fallen by more than a couple of drams, Innes wondered if he was drunk after all. He'd just proposed marriage to a complete stranger. A stranger with a sorry tale, whose courage and strength of mind he admired, but he had met her only a couple of hours ago all the same. Yet it didn't seem to matter. He was drawn to her, had been drawn to her from that first moment when she'd stormed out of the lawyer's office, and it wasn't just the bizarre coincidence of their situations. He liked what he saw of her, and admired what he heard. That he also found her desirable was entirely beside the point. His instincts told him that they'd fare well together, and his instincts were never wrong. 'So we are agreed?' Innes asked.

Ainsley tapped her index fingers together, frowning. 'We're complete strangers,' she said, reflecting his own thoughts. 'Do you think we'll be able to put on enough of a show to persuade your people that this isn't a marriage of convenience?'

'I'm not in the habit of concerning myself with what other people think.'

'Don't be daft. You'll be the—their—laird, Innes. Of course they'll be concerned.'

She was in the right of it, but he had no intentions of accepting that fact. He was not the laird. The laird was dead, and so, too, was his heir. Innes would not be branded. 'They must take me—us—as they find us,' he said. Ainsley was still frowning. 'Strone Bridge Castle is huge. If it's having to rub shoulders with me on a daily basis you're worried about, I assure you, we could go for weeks without seeing each other if we wanted.'

'That is hardly likely to persuade people we're living in domestic bliss.'

'I doubt domestic bliss is a concept that any laird of Strone Bridge is familiar with. My ancestors married for the getting of wealth and the getting of bairns.'

'Then that puts an end to our discussion.' Ainsley got to her feet and began to head for the door of the coffee room.

Innes threw down some money on the table and followed her, pulling her into a little alcove in the main reception area of the hotel. 'I don't want either of those things from you. I don't want to be like them,' he said earnestly. 'Can't you see, that's the point?'

'This is madness.'

He gave her arm a little shake, forcing her eyes to meet his. 'Madness would be to do what you're doing, and that's walking away from the perfect solution. Stop thinking about what could go wrong, think about what it will put right. Freedom, Ainsley. Think about that.'

Her mouth trembled on the brink of a smile. 'I confess, it's a very attractive idea.'

'So you'll do it?'

Her smile broadened. The light had come back into her eyes. 'I feel sure there are a hundred reasons why I should walk very quickly in the other direction.'

'But you will not?' He was just close enough for her skirts to brush his trousers, to smell the scent of her soap, of the rain in her hair. She made no attempt to free herself, holding his gaze, that smile just hovering, tempting, challenging. Tension quivered between them. 'You would regret it if you did,' Innes said.

'Do you know, Mr Innes Drummond, I think you may well be right.'

Her voice was soft, there was a tiny shiver in it, and a shiver, too, when he slid his hands from her shoulders down her arms, closing the space between them and lowering his mouth to hers. It was the softest of kisses, the briefest of kisses, but it was a kiss. A very adult kiss, which could easily have become so much more. Lips, tongues, caressed, tasted. Heat flared and they both instinctively recoiled, for it was the kind of heat that could burn.

Ainsley put her hand to her mouth, staring wide-eyed at him. Innes looked, he suspected, every bit as shocked as she. 'I'm sorry,' he said.

'Are you?'

'Not really, but I promise *that* was not in any way part of the bargain I'm proposing.'

She slanted him a look he could not interpret as she disentangled herself from his loose embrace. '*That* was merely the product of too much whisky on top of too much emotional upheaval. It was like a—a valve to release the steam pressure on one of those steam engines you build bridges and tunnels for, nothing more.'

He laughed. He couldn't help it, because she was right in a way, and she was quite wrong in another, but in every way she was wholly unexpected and a breath of much-needed fresh air. 'I'm thinking that my return to Strone Bridge is going to be a source of constant emotional upheaval,' Innes said. 'We might need to do a lot of kissing.'

'You're an engineer,' Ainsley replied primly, though her eyes were sparkling. 'I suggest you invent a different kind of safety valve for yourself.'

'Ainsley, what a nice surprise.' Felicity Blair, editor of the *Scottish Ladies Companion*, greeted her friend with a warm smile, waving her into the shabby chair on the other side of the huge desk that dominated her tiny office. 'I've just been reading Madame Hera's latest advice. I am not at all sure we can publish this reply, not least because it's rather long.'

'Which one is that?' Ainsley asked.

In response, Felicity picked up a piece of paper from the collection that Ainsley recognised she'd handed in to the office a week ago, and began to read:

'Dear Anxious Miss,
Simply because you are more mature than the average bride-to-be—and I do not consider two-and-thirty to be so old—does not mean that you are exempt from the trepidation natural to one in your position. You are, when all is said and done, setting sail into unchartered waters. To put it plainly, no matter how well you think you might know your intended, you should be prepared for the state of matrimony to alter him significantly, for he will have secured his prize, and will no longer be required to woo you. This might mean calm, tranquil seas. But it might prove to be a stormy passage.

My advice is to start the way you mean to go on and take charge of the rudder! Give no quarter, Anxious Miss; let your husband see that he cannot set the course of the matrimonial vessel to suit only himself. Do not allow yourself to be subsumed by his nature nor his dictates simply because you have assumed his name. Do not allow your nerves, your maidenly modesty or your sex to intimidate you. Speak up for yourself from the first, and set a precedent that, if not immediately, will, I am sure, eventually earn your husband's respect.

As to the more intimate matters with which you are concerned. You say your intended has indicated a lack of experience, and you are worried that this might—once again, I will revert to the seafaring metaphor—result in the becalming of the good ship wedlock. First, I would strongly advise you to muster your courage and have a frank chat about the mechanics of your wedding night with a married lady friend, thus eliminating the shock of the complete unknown. Second, I would advise you equally strongly to give your husband no inclination that you come to the wedding night armed with such information, lest he find it emasculating. Third, remember, if he really is as innocent as he claims, he will be as nervous as you. But he is a man, Anxious Miss, and thus a little flattery, some feminine admiration and a pliant female body, will ensure the success of your maiden voyage.

Good luck!

Madame Hera'

Ainsley smiled doubtfully. 'I admit, the sailing metaphor is rather trite, but if I had not used it, I would have been forced to invent something else equally silly, else you would have deemed it too vulgar to print.'

'At least you did not surrender to the obvious temptation to talk about dry docks in the context of the wedding night,' Felicity replied acerbically.

'No, because such a shocking thing did not occur to me,' Ainsley replied, laughing. 'Though to be serious for a moment, it is becoming quite a challenge for Madame Hera to advise without entirely hiding her meaning behind the veil of polite euphemisms. The whole point of the column is to provide practical help.'

Felicity set the letter down. 'I've been pondering that very issue myself. You know how limited the space is for Madame's column each month, yet we are now receiving enough correspondence to fill the entire magazine.'

'Aren't you pleased? I know I am. It is proof that I was absolutely right about the need for such a thing, and you were absolutely right to take the chance to publish it.'

'Yes, the volume of mail is a true testament to the quality of Madame's advice but, Ainsley, the problem is we can't publish most of it, for our readers would consider the subjects far too warm. Even with your shipping metaphor, that reply to Anxious Miss is sailing close to the wind. Oh, good grief, you've got me at it now!' Felicity adjusted the long ink-stained cuffs that protected her blouse. 'I'm glad you stopped by, because I've got an idea I'd like to discuss. You know it will be exactly two years since we launched Madame Hera's column next month?'

'Of course I do.' It had been the first step away from self-pity towards self-sufficiency Ainsley had taken. She remembered it vividly—the thrill of dreaming up the idea after one particularly dispiriting evening with her husband. 'It's funny,' she said to Felicity, 'at first it was the secret of Madame's existence that I enjoyed most, knowing I had something all mine that John knew nothing about. But these days, it is the hope that some of Madame Hera's advice actually helps the women who write to her that I relish. Though of course, one can never really know if one has helped.'

'You do,' Felicity said firmly. 'You know you do, just by providing an ear. Now, as I said, there are a great deal more people asking for Madame's advice than we can cover in our column, which brings me to my idea. A more personal service.'

'What on earth do you mean by that?' Ainsley wondered, for a startled moment, if her friend had somehow heard of her remark about earning a living in the Cowgate the other day.

Felicity gave a gurgle of laughter. 'Your face! I do not mean anything immoral, never fear. I mean a personal *letter* service. For a price, of course, for matters of a more sensitive nature, we can offer a personal response from Madame. We'll split the fee between the journal and yourself, naturally. Depending on how many you can answer in a month I'd say your earnings from the journal could triple at least. What do you say?'

'I'm getting married,' Ainsley blurted out.

Felicity's dark brown eyes opened so wide as to appear quite round. 'You're doing what?'

'I know, it's a shock, but it's not what you think. I can explain,' Ainsley said, wondering now if she could. She'd hardly slept a wink these past few nights wondering if she had been an idiot, and coming here this morning had been a test she'd set herself, for if practical, outspoken, radical Felicity thought it was a good idea…

Half an hour and what seemed like a hundred questions later, her friend sat back at her desk, rummaging absent-mindedly for the pencil she had, as usual, lost in her heavy chignon of hair. 'And you're absolutely sure that this Mr Drummond has no ulterior motives?'

'As sure as I can be. He's started the process of paying all of John's debts.'

'At least you'd no longer be obliged to call yourself by that man's name. Does he include the mortgage on Wemyss Place in the debts?'

Ainsley shook her head. 'Innes wanted to pay it, but as far as I'm concerned, the creditors can have the house. It has nothing but unhappy memories for me. Besides, I have every intention of repaying it all when I inherit my trust fund, and that mortgage would take up nearly all of it.'

'So, you are going to be a Highland lady. The chatelaine of a real Scottish castle.' Felicity chuckled. 'How will you like that, I wonder? You've never been out of Edinburgh.'

'It's only a temporary thing, until Innes decides what he wants to do with the place.'

'And how long will that take?'

'I don't know. Weeks. Months? No more, though he must remain there for a year. I'm looking forward to the change of scenery. And to feeling useful.'

'It all sounds too good to be true. Sadly, in my experience, things that are too good to be true almost always are,' Felicity said drily.

'Do you think it's a mistake?'

'I don't know. I think you're half-mad, but you've had a raw deal of it these past few years, and I've not seen you this animated for a long time. Perhaps getting away from Edinburgh will be good for you.' Felicity finally located her pencil and pulled it out of her coiffure, along with a handful of bright copper hair. 'What is he like, this laird? Are you sure he'll not turn into some sort of savage Highlander who'll drag you off to his lair and have his wicked way with you the minute you arrive on his lands?'

'There is no question of him having his wicked way,' Ainsley said, trying to ignore the vision of Innes in a plaid. The same one she'd had the first day she'd met him. With a claymore. And no beard.

'You're blushing,' Felicity exclaimed. 'How very interesting. Ainsley McBrayne, I do believe you would not be averse to your Highlander being very wicked indeed.'

'Stop it! I haven't the first idea what you mean by wicked, but...'

Felicity laughed. 'I know you don't,' she said, 'and frankly, it's been the thing that's worried me most about this idea of mine for Madame Hera's personal letter service, but now I think you've solved the problem. I suppose you've already kissed him? Don't deny it, that guilty look is a complete giveaway. Did you like it?'

'Felicity!'

'Well?'

'Yes.' Ainsley laughed. 'Yes, I did.'

'Was it a good kiss? The kind of kiss to give you confidence that your Mr Drummond would know what he was doing? The kind of kiss that made you want him to do more than kiss you?'

Ainsley put her hands to her heated cheeks. 'Yes. If you must know, yes, it was! Goodness, the things you say. We did not— Our marriage is not— That sort of thing is not...'

'You're going to be out in the wilds. You've already

said that you're attracted to each other. It's bound to come up, if you'll forgive the dreadful *double entendre*. And when it does—provided you take care there are no consequences—then why not?' Felicity said. 'Do you want me to be blunt?'

'What, even more than you've been already?'

'Ainsley, from what you've told me—or not told me—about your marriage, it was not physically satisfying.'

'I can't talk about it.'

'No, and you know I won't push you, but you also know enough, surely, to realise that with the right man, lovemaking can be fun.'

'Fun?' Ainsley tried to imagine this, but her own experience, which was ultimately simply embarrassing, at times shameful, made this impossible.

'Fun,' Felicity repeated, 'and pleasurable, too. It should not be an ordeal.'

Which was exactly how it had been, latterly, Ainsley thought, flushing, realising that Felicity had perceived a great deal more than she had ever revealed. 'Is it fun and pleasurable for you, with your mystery man?'

'If it were not, I would not be his mistress.'

It was only because she knew her so well that Ainsley noticed the faint withdrawal, the very slight tightening of her lips that betrayed her. Felicity claimed that being a mistress gave her the satisfaction of a lover without curtailing her freedom, but there were times when Ainsley wondered. She suspected the man was married, and loved her friend too much to pain her by asking. They both had their shameful secrets.

Ainsley picked up the latest stack of letters from the desk and began to flick through them. What Felicity said was absolutely true. As Madame Hera's reputation spread, her post contained ever more intimate queries, and as things stood, Ainsley would be hard-pressed to answer some of them save in the vaguest of terms. She replaced the letters with a sigh. 'No. Even if Innes was interested...'

'You know perfectly well that he would be,' Felicity interjected drily. 'He's a man, and, despite the fact that John McBrayne stripped you of every ounce of self-esteem, you're an attractive woman. What else will you do to while away the dark nights in that godforsaken place?'

'Regardless,' Ainsley persisted, 'it would be quite wrong of me to use Innes merely to acquire the experience that would allow Madame Hera to dispense better advice.'

'Advice that would make such a difference to all these poor, tormented women,' Felicity said, patting the pile of letters. 'Wasn't that exactly what you set out to do?'

'Stop it. You cannot make me feel guilty enough to— Just stop it, Felicity. You know, sometimes I think you really are as ruthless an editor as you pretend.'

'Trust me, I have to be, since I, too, am a mere woman. But we were talking about you, Ainsley. I agree, it would be wrong if you were only lying back and thinking of Scotland for the sake of Madame Hera and her clients. Though I hope you've more in mind than lying back and thinking of Scotland.'

'Felicity!'

'Fun and pleasure, my dear, require participation,' her friend said with another of her mischievous smiles. 'You see, now you are intrigued, and now you can admit it would not only be for Madame Hera, but your-self. Confess, you want him.'

'Yes. No. I told you, it…'

'Has no part in your arrangement. I heard you. Me-thinks you protest just a little too much.'

'But do you approve?' Ainsley said anxiously.

Felicity picked up her pencil again and began to twist it into her hair. 'I approve of anything that will make you happy. When does the ceremony take place?'

'The banns are being called on Sunday for the first time. The ceremony will be immediately after the last calling, in three weeks. Will you come, Felicity? I'd like to have you by my side.'

'Will you promise me that if you change your mind before then, you will speak up? And if you are unhappy at this Strone Bridge place, you will come straight back here, regardless of whether you feel your obligations have been met?'

'I promise.'

Felicity got to her feet. 'Then I will be your atten-dant, if that's what you want.' She picked up the bundle of letters and held them out. 'Make a start on these. I will draw up the advertisement, we'll run it beside Madame's column for this month and I will send you a note of the terms once I have them agreed. Will you be disclosing your alter ego to the laird?'

'Absolutely not! Good grief, no, especially not if I am to— He will think…'

Felicity chuckled gleefully. 'I see I've given you food for thought, at the least. I look forward to reading the results—in the form of Madame's letters, I mean.' She hugged Ainsley tightly. 'I wish you luck. You will write to me, once you are there?'

Ainsley sniffed, kissing her friend on the cheek. 'You'll get sick of hearing from me.' She tucked the letters into the folder, which was already stuffed with the bills she was to hand over to Mr Ballard, Innes's lawyer.

'Just one thing,' Felicity called after her. 'I'll wager you five pounds that if your Highlander ever discovers that you are Madame Hera, he'll be far more interested in finding problems for the pair of you to resolve together than taking umbrage.'

'Since I shall take very good care that he never finds out, you will lose,' Ainsley said, laughing as she closed the door behind her.

Chapter Three

Dear Madame Hera,
I have been married for three months to a man
whose station in life is very superior to my own.
Having moved from a small house with only two
servants to a very large manor with a butler and a
housekeeper, I find myself in a perfect tizzy some
mornings, trying to understand who I should be
asking to do what. My husband has suggested
turning to his mother for advice, but she obviously thinks he has married beneath him and
would see my need for guidance as evidence of
this. As it is, I am sure the housekeeper is report-
ing my every failure in the domestic sphere to my
mother-in-law. Only last week, when I committed the cardinal sin of asking the second house-
maid to bring me a pot of tea, the woman actually
chastised me as if I were a child. Apparently, such
requests should be relayed through the footman,
and I should not desire to take tea outside the
usual hours, whatever these might be.

I love my husband, but I am being made to

feel like an upstart in my new home, and I dare not tell him for fear he will start to take on his mother's opinion of me. Is there some sort of school for new wives I can attend? Please advise me, for I am beginning to wonder if my house-keeper would have made a better wife to my husband than I can.

Timid Mouse

Argyll, July 1840

It was cold here on the west coast. Despite the watery sunshine, a stiff breeze had blown up in the bay at Rhubodach. Innes shivered inside his heavy greatcoat. He'd forgotten how much colder it was here, and it would be colder still in the boat. Sitting on a bandbox a few feet away, Ainsley was reading a letter, clutching the folds of her travelling cloak tightly around her and staring out over the Kyles of Bute. These past three weeks there had been so much business to attend to they'd barely had time to exchange more than a few words. Standing before the altar beside him just a few days ago, she had been almost as complete a stranger to him as the day he'd proposed. Yet in a very short while, they'd be on Strone Bridge, playing the part of a happily married couple.

The dread had been taking a slow hold of him. It had settled inside him with the news of his father's death. It had grown when he learned the terms of his inheritance, then became subdued when Ainsley agreed to marry him, and even suppressed as they made their arrangements and their vows. But on the coach from Edinburgh to Glasgow it had made itself known again.

Then on the paddle steamer *Rothesay Castle* as they sailed from the Broomilaw docks to the Isle of Bute it took root, and by this afternoon's journey from Rothesay town to the north part of the Isle of Bute where they now stood waiting, it had manifested itself in this horrible sick feeling, in this illogical but incredibly strong desire to turn tail and run, and to keep running, just as he had done fourteen years before.

He was Innes Drummond, self-made man of fortune and some fame in the business he called his own. He was a man who made his living building bridges, engineering solutions to problems, turning the impossible into reality. Yet standing here on the pebbled shores of Rhubodach bay, he felt as if none of this mattered. He was the second son, his father's runt, the upstart who had no right to be coming back to Strone Bridge to claim a dead man's property. The memories of his brother he had worked so long to suppress were lurking just across the water to claim him. On Strone Bridge, Malcolm's absence would make his death impossible to deny. Guilt was that sick feeling eating away at his stomach. Fear was the hard, cold lump growing inside of him. He had no right to be here. He was afraid that when he arrived, he'd be subsumed, that all he thought he was would be peeled ruthlessly back to expose the pretender beneath.

Innes swore under his breath, long and viciously. And in Gaelic. He noticed that too late, and then swore again in the harsher, more familiar language of his construction workers. Picking up a handful of pebbles, he began to launch them one after the other into the water, noting with faint satisfaction that they fell far out.

'Impressive.'

He hadn't heard her moving. How long had she been standing there, watching him? 'The boat is late.' Innes made a show of shading his eyes to squint out at the Kyles.

'You must be nervous,' Ainsley said. 'I know I would be, returning after such a long period of time. I expect you'll be wondering how much has changed.'

Her tone was light, almost indifferent. She was studiously avoiding his gaze, looking out at the water, but he was not fooled. She was an astute observer. One of those people who studied faces, who seemed to have the knack of reading the thoughts of complete strangers. 'Nothing will have changed,' Innes said with heavy certainty. 'My father prided himself on maintaining traditions that were hundreds of years old. You'll feel as if you've stepped back into the eighteenth century.'

Her brows lifted in surprise. He could see the wheels turning in her clever brain, but she chose merely to nod, and perversely, though he knew he would not like it, he wanted to know what she was thinking. 'Go on. Say it.'

'It is nothing. Only—you are very much a man of the nineteenth century.'

'You mean you're not surprised I left such a backward place.'

'Such a backward place must be crying out for a man like you.' Ainsley pushed her windswept hair out of her eyes. 'I meant that I am not surprised you and your father could not see eye to eye.'

She slipped her gloved hand into his, in the folds of his greatcoat. He twined his fingers around hers, glad of the contact. Ainsley Drummond, his wife. A stranger she might be, but he was glad of her presence, and when she smiled up at him like that, the dread contracted just a little. 'I think that's the boat,' she said, pointing.

It was, and he could see already that Eoin was at the helm. With a determined effort, Innes threw off his black mood. 'Are you ready?' he asked, sliding his arm around Ainsley to anchor her to his side.

'You sound like you're standing under the gallows, if you don't mind my saying.'

Innes managed a rigid smile. 'Judgement Day is what it feels like,' he said wryly, 'and I suspect it will be a harsh one.'

Looking out over the bay, Ainsley's nerves made themselves known in the form of a fluttering stomach as she watched the little boat approaching. Until now, she had lost herself in the bustle of arrangements, the thrill of the journey. Her first time on a paddle steamer, her first time on the west coast and now her first time in a sailing boat was looming. Then would be her arrival at Strone Bridge with the man who was her husband. She worried at the plain gold band on her finger, inside her glove. She still couldn't quite believe it. It did not feel at all real. She was now Mrs Drummond, wife of the laird of Strone Bridge, this stranger by her side whose dawning black mood had quite thrown her.

Innes didn't want to be here, though he was now doing a good job of covering it up. There was a lot going on below the surface of that handsome countenance. Secrets? Or was it merely that he had left his past behind and didn't want to be faced with it again? She could understand that. It was one of the reasons she'd been happy to leave Edinburgh for a while. Perhaps it was resentment, which was more than understandable, for unlike her, the life Innes was leaving behind was one he loved.

As he hefted their luggage down to the edge of the shoreline, Ainsley watched, distracted by the fluidity of his movements, the long stride over the pebbles, the smooth strength in the way he lifted even the heaviest pieces so effortlessly. She recalled Felicity's joke about him being a wild Highlander, and wondered if he would wear a plaid when he was back at Strone Bridge. He had the legs for it. A prickle of heat low in her belly made her shiver.

'Feasgar math.' The bump of the boat against the tiny jetty made her jump.

Ainsley stared blankly at the man. 'Good day to you, Mrs Drummond,' he repeated in a softly lilting accent, at odds with the curt nod he gave her before starting to heave the luggage Innes was handing him into the boat.

'Oh, good day,' Ainsley replied.

'This is Eoin Ferguson,' Innes told her, 'an old friend of mine. Eoin, this is my wife.'

'I'm afraid I don't speak any Gaelic,' Ainsley said to the boatman.

'Have the Gaelic,' he said to her. 'We don't say speak it, we say have it.'

'And there's no need to worry, almost everyone on Strone Bridge *speaks* English,' Innes said, frowning at the man he claimed for a friend, though Ainsley could see no trace of warmth between the two men.

'I have never been to the Highlands,' she said with a bright smile.

'Strone Bridge is not far north of Glasgow as the crow flies,' Eoin replied. 'If you're expecting us all to be wandering around in plaid and waving claymores, you'll be disappointed. Are you getting in or not?'

'Oh, right. Yes.' She could feel herself flushing, mortified as if he had read her earlier thoughts. He made no move to help her. Seeing Innes's frown deepen, Ainsley gave him a slight shake of the head, clambering awkwardly and with too much show of leg into the boat. Eoin watched impassively, indicating that she sit on the narrow bench at the front of the dinghy, making a point of folding his arms as she then proceeded to clamber over the luggage stacked mid-ship.

She tried not to feel either slighted or crushed, reminding herself she was a stranger, a Sassenach, a lowlander, who spoke—no, *had*—no Gaelic and knew nothing of their ways. Innes, his mouth drawn into a tight line, had leaped into the boat, and was deftly untying the rope from the jetty as Eoin tended the sail. She watched the pair of them working silently together as they set out into the water, the contrast between the harmony of their movements stark against the undercurrent of tension that ran between them. It spiked as Innes made to take the tiller.

'The tide is against us, and I know the currents,' Eoin said, keeping his hand on the polished wood.

'I know them every bit as well as you.'

'You used to.' Eoin made no attempt to hide his enmity, but glared at Innes, his eyes, the same deep blue as Innes's own, bright with challenge. 'It's been a long time.'

Innes's fists clenched and unclenched. 'I know exactly how long it's been.'

A gust of wind took Eoin's words away. When Innes spoke again, it was in a soft, menacing tone that made the hairs on the back of Ainsley's neck stand on end. And it was in Gaelic. Eoin flinched and made to hand over the tiller, but Innes shook his head, joining Ainsley in the prow, turning away from her to stare out at the white wake, his face unreadable.

The wind that filled the sail blew in her face, whipping her hair from under her bonnet, making her eyes stream. Innes had not worn a hat today, a wise move, for it would surely have blown into the sea. Though he was, as ever, conservatively dressed, his trousers and coat dark blue, his linen pristine white; compared to Eoin's rough tweed trews and heavy fisherman's jumper, Innes looked like a dandy. She had watched the other man noticing this when he docked, but couldn't decide whether the twitch of his mouth was contempt or envy.

The boat scudded along, the keel bumping over the waves of the outgoing tide. While the paddle steamer had felt—and smelled—rather like a train that ran on water instead of rails, in this dinghy, Ainsley was acutely conscious that only a few planks of wood and some tar separated her from the icy-cold strait. Spray made her lips salty. The sail snapped noisily. She began to feel nauseous, and looking up, catching a cold smile on Eoin's face as the boat lifted out of the water and then slapped down again, began to suspect that he was making their voyage deliberately rough.

'You're from the city, I hear. You'll not be used to the sea,' he shouted.

Ainsley gripped the wooden seat with both hands, determined to hold on to the contents of her breakfast. She wished she hadn't had the eggs. She mustn't think about the eggs. 'How did you know that?' she asked.

'Himself told Mhairi McIntosh, the housekeeper, in the letter he sent.'

Innes snapped his head round. 'Well, it wouldn't have done me any good to write to you.'

Eoin, to Ainsley's surprise, turned a dull shade of red, and looked away. Innes swallowed whatever else he had been about to say and resumed his staring out at the sea. The undercurrent of emotion that ran between the two men was as strong as the ebb of the tide that was making their entrance into the bay a battle.

The pier was old and crumbling, extending far out into the bay. The low tide forced them to berth right at the very end of the structure, where Innes threw the rope neatly over a post to make fast. It was only as he put one foot on the first rung of the ladder that Eoin spoke, putting a hand on his shoulder, making him freeze.

'You'll find the place much changed.'

'If you tell me once again that it's been fourteen years...' he said through gritted teeth.

'It's not that.' Eoin pulled his hand away, a bleak look in his eyes. 'You know Mhairi's got the Home Farm ready for you? The big house—ach, you'll see for yourself soon enough. Give Angus a shout; I can see he's there with the cart. I'll see to the luggage.'

Innes ascended the worn ladder quickly, then turned to help Ainsley. She was eyeing the gap between boat and pier with a trepidation she was trying—and failing—to disguise. Her cheeks were bright with the wind, her hair a tangle. She looked endearing. She was most likely wondering what the hell she'd let herself in for, with the enmity between himself and Eoin almost palpable. He swore under his breath. Whatever was going on in Eoin's head, there would be time enough to sort it out. Right now, he needed to get poor Ainsley, who might well be his only ally, out of that boat before she fell out of it. 'Put one foot on the bottom rung and give me your hand,' he said, leaning down over the end of the pier.

She looked at the seaweed-slimed lower struts of the ladder pier dubiously. 'I can't swim.'

Innes went down on his knees and leaned over. 'I can. If you fall, I promise I'll dive in right behind you.'

'And walk up the beach with me in your arms, dripping seawater and seaweed.'

'Just like a mermaid.'

Ainsley chuckled. 'More like a sea monster. Not the grand entrance that the laird and his lady are expected to make. It's as well we've no audience.'

'I told Mhairi—that's the housekeeper—that we did not want a formal welcome until we were settled. I must admit, I'm surprised she listened, though,' Innes said, looking about him. Save for Angus, making his lumbering way down the pier, there was not a soul in sight. Perhaps he'd maligned his friend after all. Eoin knew how much he hated the pomp and ceremony of the old ways that his father had gone to such pains to preserve. He looked over Ainsley's shoulder to thank him, but Eoin was busying himself with the ropes.

Shrugging inwardly, Innes held out his hand to Ainsley, pulling her up without a hitch and catching her in his arms. 'Welcome to Strone Bridge.'

She smiled weakly, clutching tight to him, her legs trembling on the wooden planking. 'I'm sorry, I think my legs have turned to jelly.'

'You don't mean your heart? I'm not sure what you've let yourself in for here, but I am pretty certain things are in a bad way. I'll understand if you want to go back to Edinburgh.'

'Your people are expecting you to arrive with a wife. A fine impression it would make if she turned tail before she'd even stepped off the pier—or more accurately, judging by the state of it, stepped through it. Besides, we made a bargain, and I plan to stick to my part of it.' Ainsley tilted her head up at him, her eyes narrowed, though she was smiling. 'Are you having cold feet?'

'Not about you.' He hadn't meant it to sound the way it did, like the words of a lover, but it was too late to retract. He pulled her roughly against him, and he kissed her, forgetting all about his resolution to do no such thing. Her lips were freezing. She tasted of salt. The thump of luggage being tossed with no regard for its contents from the boat to the pier made them spring apart.

Ainsley flushed. 'It is a shame we don't have more of an audience, for I feel sure that was quite convincing.'

Innes laughed. 'I won't pretend that had anything to do with acting the part of your husband. The truth is, you have a very kissable mouth, and I've been thinking about kissing you again since the first time all those weeks ago. And before you say it, it's got nothing to do with my needing an emotional safety valve either, and everything to do with the fact that I thoroughly enjoyed it, though I know perfectly well it's not part of our bargain.'

'Save that it can do no harm to put on a show, now and then,' Ainsley said with a teasing smile.

'Does that mean you'll only kiss me in public? I know there are men who like that sort of thing, but I confess I prefer to do my lovemaking in private.'

'Innes! I am sure we can persuade the people of Strone Bridge we are husband and wife without re-sorting to—to engaging in public marital relations.'

He gave a shout of laughter. 'Good grief, I hope not. That makes it sound like a meeting of foreign ministers.'

'It does? Really?' They began to make their way slowly to the head of the pier.

'Really,' Innes said.

'Oh. What is your opinion on *undergoing a husband's ministrations*?'

'That it sounds as if the husband is to carry out some sort of unsavoury medical procedure. You may as well talk about performing hymeneal duties, which is the sort of mealy-mouthed and utterly uninforma-tive phrase I imagine any number of poor girls hear from their mothers on the eve of their wedding. They probably think they're going to be sacrificed on the matrimonial altar. Whatever they imagine, you can be damned sure they won't be looking forward to it.'

'Oh, I couldn't agree more. The belief that inno-cence and ignorance must go hand in hand seems to me quite perverse. I wonder sometimes if there is a conspiracy by society to keep young girls uninformed in order to encourage them into marriages they would not otherwise make.'

The sparkle had returned to her hazel eyes, but it was no longer teasing. Rather, Innes thought, studying her in some surprise, it was martial. 'Are you speak-ing from experience?'

'My mother died when I was twelve, and I had no other female relative close enough to divulge the pertinent facts before my wedding night. It was a—a shock.'

He was appalled, but she was bristling like a porcupine. 'Perhaps there should be some sort of guidebook. An introduction to married life; or something of that sort.'

He meant it as a joke, but Ainsley seemed much struck. 'That is an excellent idea.'

'Though if what you say about the conspiracy is true, then mothers will surely forbid their daughters from reading it.'

'More likely fathers would.'

Most definitely martial. Intrigued, he could not resist pushing her. 'Since the shops that would sell such a thing are the kind frequented by men and not women, then your plan is defeated by the outset,' Innes said.

'That shows how little you know,' Ainsley said with a superior smile. 'Shops are not the only outlet for such information.'

Above them the white clouds had given way to iron-grey. The wind was picking up as the tide turned, making white crests on the water, which was turning the same colour as the sky. While they'd been talking, the luggage had been loaded onto the cart, where Angus was now waiting patiently. Of Eoin there was no sign. Reluctantly, Innes abandoned this intriguing conversation. 'Whatever else has changed,' he said, 'the weather is still as reliably fickle as ever. Come on, let's get out of this wind before you catch a cold.'

Ainsley woke with a start and sat up, staring around her at the unfamiliar surroundings. The room was panelled and sparsely furnished. It had the look of a place hastily put together, and it felt as if the fires had not been lit for some time. Shivering as she threw back the covers and stepped onto the bare floorboards, she could feel the cold begin to seep into her bones.

Though it was July, it felt more like April. She made haste with her ablutions. Without the help of a maid, she laced her corsets loosely and tied her hair into a simple knot before pulling a woollen dress from her trunk. The colours, broad stripes of cream and turquoise, made her think of a summer sky that bore no resemblance to the one she could see through the window. The narrow sleeves were long, the tight-fitting bodice made doubly warm with the overlapping kerchief-style collar that came to a point at her waist. Woollen stockings and boots completed her *toilette* in record time. Reluctantly, she abandoned the idea of wrapping her cloak around her, telling herself that a lesson in hardiness was in order.

The corridor outside was dark and windowless. The fading daylight darkened by the deluge that had erupted as she arrived yesterday had prevented her from gaining any perspective of her new residence. Exhaustion had set in once she had eaten, and Ainsley had retired almost immediately afterwards.

Start the way you mean to go on. Muttering Madame Hera's own advice like a charm, she stumbled her way towards the door where she had dined last night, cheered by the faint smell of coffee. The room looked much more attractive in the daylight, and the fire, which last evening had smouldered, today was burning brightly. 'Good morning,' she said.

Innes was seated at the table, staring moodily at

his empty plate, but he stood when she came into the room. His jaw looked raw. Most likely he'd shaved in water as cold as she'd used to wash. Perhaps he simply wasn't a morning person. Ainsley hovered at the door.

'Are you staying or going?' Innes asked, and she gave herself a little shake.

'Staying,' she said, seating herself opposite.

'I didn't know if you'd want tea or coffee, so I had Mhairi bring both.'

'Coffee, thank you.'

He sat down and poured her a cup. 'There's crowdie and oatcakes, but if you'd prefer a kipper, or some ham or porridge?'

'No, that will be fine—at least— What is crowdie?'

'Cheese.'

'Thank you.' She took the oatcakes and creamy cheese. 'This looks delicious.' Innes poured himself a cup of tea. 'Have you eaten?' she asked, cringing as she spoke, for she had already noticed his empty plate, and she sounded as if she was making polite conversation over the tinkling of teaspoons in an Edinburgh drawing room.

'Yes,' Innes said.

Ainsley bit into an oatcake. The crunch was embarrassingly loud. She took a sip of coffee. It sounded like a slurp. This was ridiculous. 'Innes, would you prefer...?'

'Ainsley, if you would prefer...?'

He stopped. She stopped. Then he laughed. 'I'm not used to having company at breakfast. I don't know whether you'd prefer to be left in peace, or— What?'

'I don't know. I'm not any more accustomed to it than you. It's silly, I know it's silly, but it feels strange.'

'Would you rather I went?'

'No. Unless you'd rather—' She broke off, laughing. 'For goodness' sake, I'd like you to stay, and I'd like to talk, but not if we're going to make polite chit-chat for the sake of it.'

Innes grinned. 'I am more than happy to promise never to make polite chit-chat, though I would like to know if your bedchamber was comfortable—and please, give me the real answer, and not the drawing-room one.'

Ainsley chuckled. 'One does not mention a lady's bedchamber in the drawing room.'

'Actually, that very much depends on the drawing room,' Innes said, smiling. 'Let me put it another way then—did you manage to sleep, or were you frozen to death?'

'I slept, but I confess I dressed very quickly.'

'I'm sorry about that. It seems that my father had the main part of the castle shut up and took to living in just two or three rooms. This place is sound and dry enough, but it's been empty awhile, and Mhairi had little notice of our arrival, as you know. She gave you that bedchamber because it was the best of a bad bunch.'

'She apologised for the fact it was several rooms away from your own,' Ainsley said, flushing. 'I got the impression she was worried the effort it would take to walk the distance would put you off. I confess, it did not do my ego much good to think my husband would be so easily deterred.'

'If I thought I would be welcomed into your bedchamber for a bout of debauchery, not even a chastity belt would deter me,' Innes said wickedly.

''Tis a shame I cannot lay my hands on such an item, else I would be tempted to test your resolve.'

'Don't be too sure, there are all sorts of things in the armoury,' Innes replied. 'Debauchery and chastity belts—who'd have thought that conversation over the breakfast cups could be so interesting?'

'*I* did not introduce the topic of debauchery,' Ainsley said, spluttering coffee.

'No, but you did say you didn't want to make polite chit-chat.'

'Innes Drummond, you should have considered entering the legal profession, for you can twist an argument better than any lawyer I've dealt with—and believe me, I've dealt with a few.'

He gave a theatrical sigh. 'Very well, we will change the topic, though it is your own fault, you know.'

She eyed him warily. 'I am very sure I should not ask what you mean by that.'

'Then do not.'

Ainsley took a sip of coffee. Innes folded his mouth primly. She took another sip, trying not to laugh, then finally cast her cup down in the saucer with a clatter. 'Oh, for goodness' sake, you win. Tell me what you meant.'

'No, for it is not true, it's not debauchery I think of when I look at that mouth of yours, it's kissing.'

'Just kissing.'

'Not *just* kissing.' Innes leaned forward over the table and took her hand. '*Kissing*. There's a difference.'

He was teasing. Or was it flirting? She wasn't sure. She didn't think she was the kind of woman that men flirted with. Did she amuse or arouse? Was it possible to combine the two? Ainsley had no idea, but she knew he was not laughing at her. There was complicity in the way he was looking at her, and something in those beguiling blue eyes of his that made her tingle. 'What difference?' she asked, knowing she ought not, sure that if she did not she would regret it.

Innes lifted her hand to his mouth, just barely brushing the back of it with his lips. 'That,' he said, 'was *just* a kiss.' He turned her hand over. *'This,'* he said softly, 'is the difference.'

His lips were warm on her palm. His tongue flicked over the pad of her thumb, giving her the most delicious little shiver. When he enveloped her thumb with his mouth and sucked, she inhaled sharply. 'You see,' he said, his voice husky. 'There is only one problem with those kinds of kisses.'

She knew exactly what he meant. She was experiencing that very problem. 'More?' Ainsley said, meaning it as an answer, though it sounded like a request.

'More,' Innes said, taking it as a request, pushing back his chair, leaning across the table, doing just as she asked.

He hadn't intended to kiss her, but he couldn't resist, and when she did not either, when she opened her mouth to him and twined her arms around his neck with the most delightful little sigh, his teasing kiss became something deeper. She kissed him back. The tip of her tongue touched his, triggering the rush of blood, the clenching of his muscles, the shiver of arousal. He slid his hand down to her breast under the shawl that formed part of her bodice, only to find himself frustrated by the bones of her corset, by the layers of clothes. A knife clattered to the ground, and they both jumped.

He was hard. He was very glad that the table lay between them. Ainsley's face was flushed, her lips soft, eyes dark with their kisses. The urge to pull her across the table and ravage that sinful mouth of hers was unbearably tempting. What the devil was wrong with him that he couldn't seem to keep his hands off her! Sitting carefully back down in his chair, Innes thought ruefully that it had been the same right from their first meeting. Why hadn't he realised it would be a problem? Was it a problem?

'Mhairi could have come into the room at any moment,' Ainsley said.

Innes ran his fingers through his hair. 'Is that why you kissed me?'

She picked up a teaspoon and began to trace a pattern on the table. 'Actually, you kissed me, though I cannot deny that I kissed you back,' she said, looking at him fleetingly from under her lashes. 'I don't know why, save that I wanted to, and I haven't wanted to for... And ever since I met you I have and—and so I did.'

'I can't tell you how relieved I am to hear that, because it's been exactly the same for me.' Innes swallowed a mouthful of cold coffee and grimaced. 'I never was one to toe the line, you know. Maybe it's because our bargain precludes it that I'm so tempted.'

'You mean you want to kiss me because it is illicit?'

'Oh, no, I want to kiss you because you have a mouth that makes me think of kissing. But perhaps it's so difficult not to because I know it's not permitted, even though we're married.' Innes shook his head and jumped to his feet. 'I don't know. Maybe we should check the armoury for a chastity belt.'

'Maybe we should stop worrying about it, and discussing it and analysing it,' Ainsley said. 'We are adults. We are neither of us interested in becoming attached. There is no harm in us having some—some fun.'

'Fun? You say that as if you are taking a dose of Mr Rush's patented pills for biliousness.'

'I am sure that they too are healthful.'

Innes burst out laughing. 'You say the strangest things. Healthful! It's the first time I've heard it referred to in that way.'

'You think it's an inaccurate term to use?'

She was frowning, looking genuinely puzzled, just as she had yesterday, now he thought about it, when she'd mentioned—what was it—marital relations? 'I think it's best if we think about something else entirely,' Innes said. 'Delightful as this breakfast has been, the day is getting away from us. First things first, we'll start with a tour of the castle. I warn you, it's a great barrack of a place and like to be as cold as an icehouse.'

Ainsley got to her feet. 'I'll go and fetch a shawl.'

The door closed behind her. Innes gazed out of the window, though the view was almost entirely obscured by an overgrown hedge. It looked as if it had not been cut for a good many years. Like everything he'd seen at Strone Bridge so far, from the jetty to the stables, it was neglected. Eoin had warned him that things had changed. He wondered, if the state of the house and grounds were anything to go by, what had happened to the lands. He was surprised, for though his father had been old-fashioned, archaic even in his practices, he had never been negligent. He was also angry, though guiltily aware he had little right to be so. These were Malcolm's lands. If Malcolm was here, he would be appalled at the state of them. Yet if Malcolm were here, Innes would not be. If Malcolm was here, he would not have allowed the place to fall into decline, and Innes...

He cursed. He could go round in circles for ever with that logic. He was not looking forward to this tour of the castle. It wasn't so much the state of disrepair he was now certain he'd find in the rooms, it was the history in those rooms, all *his* history. He didn't want anyone to see him coping—or not coping—with that history, and Ainsley was a very astute observer. It had been fourteen years. Surely that was long enough for him to at least put on a show of disaffection. Yet here he was, feeling distinctly edgy and wondering how to explain it away.

The castle was just a building. A heap of stones and wood of dubious aesthetic value. There was no ancient law that said he must live there if he chose to remain on Strone Bridge after a year, which was highly unlikely. No, he would have the Home Farm made more comfortable, because nothing would persuade him to play the laird in the castle, not even for a few weeks.

The vehemence of this thought took Innes so aback he did not notice Ainsley had returned until she spoke his name. 'Right,' Innes said, sounding appropriately businesslike. 'Let's get on with it.'

Chapter Four

The sun shone weakly from a pale blue sky dotted with puffy clouds, the kind a child would paint. Following in Innes's wake along the narrow path of damp paving slabs, Ainsley could see that the gloom inside the Home Farm's lower rooms was largely due to the height of the untended hedge. Emerging through an extremely overgrown arch, she came face-to-face with Strone Bridge Castle for the first time.

They were standing at the side of a long sweep of carriageway with what must have been a huge lawn on either side, though at present it was more like the remnants of a hayfield, part long yellowed grass falling over, part fresh green pushing through. The building loomed over them, such an imposing structure she could not imagine how she had missed its hulk yesterday, though the stone was indeed the grey colour the sky had been.

Ainsley walked backwards to gain some perspective. 'This is the rear of the house,' Innes said. 'The drive meets the main overland road, which cuts over to the other side of the peninsula and Loch Fyne, though to call it a road… It's far easier to travel by boat in this neck of the woods.'

'We did not come this way yesterday?'

He shook his head. 'The front of the house faces down to the shore. We came up that way. I'll show you, we'll go in by the main entrance, but I wanted you to see the scale of this damned monstrosity first.'

Strone Bridge Castle was indeed enormous, and though it was not precisely charming, Ainsley would not have called it a monstrosity. An imposing construction with a large tower at each corner, and another central turret projecting from the middle of the main building, it was like a castle from a Gothic novel. The sturdy turrets had unexpected ogee roofs, adding a hint of the east into the architectural mix, each roof topped with tall spires and embellished with slit windows. The turrets looked, with their rugged masonry walls and stolid, defensive air, quite at odds with the central part of the building, which was considerably more elegant, mostly Jacobean in style, with four storeys of tall French-style windows, a low Palladian roof ornamented with a stone balustrade and a huge portico that looked as if it had been added on as an afterthought. The overall effect was certainly not of beauty, but it was striking.

'It looks,' Ainsley said, studying it with bemusement, 'as if someone has jumbled up three or four different houses, or taken samples from a book of architectural styles through the ages.'

'You're not far off,' Innes said. 'The main house was built about 1700. The roof and that central tower were added about fifty or sixty years after that, and my own father put those corner towers up. There's no rhyme nor reason to it. As I said, it's a monstrosity.'

'That's not what I meant at all. It is like nothing I have ever seen.'

'One of a kind. That, thank heavens, is certainly true,' Innes said grimly.

'You are not fond of it, then?' Ainsley asked. 'Though there must be some interesting stories attached to a building so old. And perhaps even a few ghosts.'

He had taken her arm as they made their way over the untended lawn around the building, and now slanted her a curious look. 'Do you believe in such things?'

'Honestly, I've never considered the question before, but looking at this place, I could easily be persuaded.'

'There is a tale of one of the lairds who went off to fight in the 1715 Jacobite uprising. He was for the Old Pretender. There's a set of gates, right at the end of the carriageway, which he had locked, so they say, and made his wife promise never to unlock them until his return.'

'What happened?'

'He died in the Battle of Sheriffmuir. His wife had the gates unlocked for his corpse to pass through in its coffin, but—' Innes broke off, shaking his head. 'No, there's enough here already to give you nightmares without adding a walking, wailing, clanking ghost to the mix.'

Ainsley stopped in her tracks, looking up at him in horror. 'Walking and wailing and clanking?'

He bent down to whisper in her ear. 'He rattles the chain that should have been kept around the gates. He walks just over there, on the carriageway. He wails for the treachery of his lady wife, who married his enemy less than a year after he was slain.'

She shuddered, looked over to where he was pointing, then looked back at him. 'Have you actually seen him?' Innes made a noncommittal noise. Ainsley narrowed her eyes suspiciously. 'Has anyone ever seen him?'

'None who have lived to tell the tale,' he answered sorrowfully.

She punched him on the arm. 'Then how can the tale be told! You made that up.'

He laughed, rubbing his arm. 'Not all of it. The first part was true. The laird at the time did fight, he did die at Sheriffmuir and he did have the gates locked.'

'Are there any real ghosts?'

His laughter faded as he took her arm and urged her on. 'Plenty, believe me, though none that you will see, I hope.'

His expression was one she recognised. *Don't ask.* Not because she wouldn't like the answers, but because *he* would not. This was his home, this place that he was mocking and deriding, this place that he called a monstrosity. She wondered, then, if he really meant the bricks and mortar. Yesterday it was obvious that Innes had not wanted to come back to Strone Bridge. It was equally obvious from this morning that he'd not expected the place to be in such a state of disrepair, but now she wondered what else there was to disturb him here. What was at the heart of the quarrel that had so completely estranged him from his father?

How little of Innes she knew. His formative years had been spent here, yet he had left all of it behind without, it seemed, a backward glance, to make a new and very different life for himself. Why? It was all very well to tell herself it was none of her business, but—no, there was no *but*. It was absolutely none of her business, Ainsley told herself rather unconvincingly. Yet it was strange, and very distractingly intriguing, like the man himself.

'You were a million miles away. I was only teasing you about the ghosts. I didn't mean to give you the jitters,' Innes said, cutting in on her thoughts.

'You didn't.' Ainsley looked around her with slight surprise. They had reached the front of the house, and the prospect was stunning, for it sat on a hill directly above the bay where they had landed yesterday. 'My goodness, this is absolutely beautiful.'

'That's the Kyles of Bute over there, the stretch of water with all the small islands that you sailed yesterday,' Innes said. 'And over there, the crescent of sand you can see, that's Ettrick Bay on Bute, the other side of the island from which we set sail. And that bigger island you can just see in the distance, that's Arran.'

'I don't think I've ever seen such a wonderful prospect. It is exactly the sort of view that one conjures up, all misty-eyed, when one thinks of the Highlands. Like something from one of Mr Walter Scott's novels.'

'Aye, well, strictly speaking Eoin was right in what he said yesterday, though. We're only a wee bit farther north than Glasgow here, and Arran is south.'

'As the crow flies,' Ainsley said. 'It doesn't matter, it feels like another world, and it really is quite spectacular. There must be a magnificent view from the castle.' She looked back at the house, where a set of long French-style windows opened out on the first floor to what must have once been a beautiful terrace at the top of a flight of stairs.

'That's the drawing room,' Innes said, following her gaze.

'How lovely to take tea there on a summer's day. I can just imagine the ladies of old with their hoops and their wigs,' she said dreamily.

'The hoops and wigs are like as not still packed away up in the attics somewhere. My family never throws anything away. Do you really like this place?'

'It's entrancing. Do you really *not* like it?'

Innes shrugged. 'I can see it's a lovely view. I'd forgotten.'

Without waiting on her, he turned on his heel and began to walk quickly up the slope towards the central staircase. 'Like someone determined to swallow their medicine as quickly as they can and get it over with,' Ainsley muttered, stalking after him.

'What was that?'

'This may be a monstrosity to you, Innes, but to someone accustomed to a terraced house in Edinburgh, it's magical.'

Innes stopped abruptly. 'Ach, I'm like a beast with a sore head. I'm sorry. It's not your fault.'

No, it was most definitely this place. Curious as she was, and with a hundred questions to boot, Ainsley had no desire to see him suffer. 'We could leave it for today. Or I could look around myself.'

'No,' Innes said firmly, 'it has to be done.' He took her hand, forcing a smile. 'Besides, you came here thinking you'd be lady of the manor—you've a right to see over your domain. I'm only sorry that it's bound to be a disappointment.'

'I did not come here with any such expectations. Aside from the fact that I know absolutely nothing about the management of a place this size, I am perfectly well aware that your people will regard a destitute Edinburgh widow without a hint of anything close to blue in her blood as nothing more than an upstart.'

Innes gave a startled laugh. 'You're not seriously worried that people here will look down their noses at you, Ainsley?'

'A little,' she confessed, embarrassed. 'I hadn't really thought about it until I arrived here yesterday. Then your boatman...'

'Ach! Blasted Eoin. Listen to me. First, if there's an upstart here, then it's me. Second, for better or worse, I'll be the laird while I'm here, and while you're here, I will not tolerate anyone looking down their noses at you. Third, the state of your finances are nobody's business but our own.' He pulled her closer, pushing a strand of her hair out of her eyes. 'Finally, though I have no intention of playing the laird and therefore there's no need for you to play lady of the manor, if I did, and you did, then I think you'd play it very well. And on the off chance you couldn't quite follow me,' he added, 'that was me saying you've not a thing to worry about.'

She felt a stupid desire to cry. 'Thank you, I will try not to let you down.'

'Wheesht, now,' he said, kissing her cheek. 'You'll do your best, and that's all I ask. Anyway, it's not as if *you* are stepping into a dead person's shoes. My mother died when I was eight years old.'

'And your father never remarried?'

Innes gave a crack of laughter. 'What for, he'd already produced an heir and a spare.'

'What about your brother. Did he…?'

'No.'

Another of those 'do not dare ask' faces accompanied this stark denial. And Innes would not be married either, were it not for the terms of the old laird's will. Were the Drummond men all misogynists? Or perhaps there was some sort of dreadful hereditary disease? But Innes seemed perfectly healthy. A curse, then? Now she was being utterly fanciful. It was this place. Ainsley gave herself a little shake. 'Well, then, let us go and inspect this castle of yours, and see what needs to be done to make it habitable.'

Everything inside Strone Bridge Castle was done on a grand scale. The formal salons opened out one after the other around the central courtyard with the Great Hall forming the centrepiece, heavy with geometric panelling, topped with rich fretwork ceilings like icing on a cake, or one of those elaborate sugar constructions that decorates the table at a banquet. Massive fireplaces and overmantels rose to merge the two, and everywhere, it seemed to Ainsley, every opportunity had been taken to incorporate heraldic devices and crests. Dragons and lions poked and pawed from pilasters, banisters and pediments. Shields and swords augmented the cornicing, were carved into the marble fireplaces and fanned out above the windows. It was beautiful, in an oppressive and overwhelming way.

The turrets that marked each corner were dank places with treacherous-looking staircases winding their way steeply up, and which Ainsley decided she did not need to climb. 'They serve no real purpose,' Innes told her. 'A whim of my father's, nothing more.'

* * *

After two hours and only a fraction of the hundred and thirty rooms, she had seen enough for one day. Back in the courtyard, she gazed up at the central tower, which was square and not round, and faced directly out over the Kyles of Bute. Bigger than the others, it seemed to contain proper rooms, judging from the wide windows that took up most of the sea-facing wall on each of the four stories. Ainsley wrestled with the heavy latch, but it would not budge.

'It's locked.' Innes made no attempt to help her. 'Has been for years. Most likely the key is long gone, for it's not on here,' he said, waving the heavy bunch of keys he carried.

Ainsley frowned at the lock, which seemed surprisingly new, and showed no sign of rust, wondering how Innes would know such a thing when he himself had not been here for years. 'The view from up there must be spectacular,' she said, looking back up at the battlements.

Innes had already turned away. 'We'll take a look at the kitchens.'

'There must be a door from inside the castle,' Ainsley said, frowning at the tower in frustration, trying to recall the exact layout of rooms that lay behind it. 'Is that the dining room? I don't recall a door, but…'

'The door isn't in the dining room.' Innes was holding open another door. 'Do you want to see the kitchens? I was hoping to get out to some of the farms this afternoon.'

He sounded impatient. Though this was all new to her, for him it was different. 'I can come back myself another time,' Ainsley said, joining him.

'I don't want you going up there,' Innes said sharply. 'It's not safe.'

She cast a dubious look at the tower, thinking that it looked, like the rest of the castle, neglected though sound, but Innes was already heading down the narrow corridor, so she picked up her skirts and walked quickly after him.

A few moments later she forgot all about the locked tower, gazing in astonishment at the table that ran almost the full length of the servants' hall. It looked as if it would sit at least fifty. 'Good grief, how many staff does it take to keep this place running?'

Innes shook his head. 'I've no idea. Even in my youth, most of the rooms were closed up, save for formal occasions, and there were few of those. My father was not the most sociable of men.'

They exited the servants' hall and entered the main kitchen, which had two bread ovens, a row of charcoal braziers, a stove the size of a hay cart and the biggest fireplace Ainsley had ever seen. Out through another door, they wended their way through the warren of the basement, past linen rooms and still rooms, pantries and empty wine cellars, and then back up a steep flight of stairs to another door that took them out to the kitchen gardens.

Innes turned the lock and turned his back on the castle. 'As you can see, the place is uninhabitable,' he said.

He sounded relieved. She couldn't understand his reaction to it. 'Is the building itself in such a poor state of repair, is it the cost of restoring it you're worried about?'

'It's sound enough, I reckon. There's no smell of damp and no sign that the roof is anything but watertight, though I'd need to get one of my surveyors to take a look. But what would be the point?'

'I have no idea, but—you would surely not wish to let it simply fall into ruin?'

'I could knock it down and get it over with.' Innes tucked the weight of keys into his coat pocket with a despondent shrug. 'I don't know,' he said heavily, 'and I think I've more pressing matters to consider, to be honest. Maybe it was a mistake to start with the castle. For now, I think it would be best if you concentrated on the immediate issue of making the Home Farm a bit more comfortable. Speak to Mhairi, she'll help you. I'll need to spend some time out on the lands.'

Ainsley watched him walk away, feeling slightly put out. He was right, their living quarters left a lot to be desired, and it made sense for her to sort them out. 'Whatever that means,' she muttered. The idea of consulting the rather forbidding Mhairi McIntosh did not appeal to her. Madame Hera had suggested that Timid Mouse appeal to her housekeeper's softer side. Ainsley was not so sure that Mhairi McIntosh had one.

Besides, that wasn't the point. She had not come here to set up Innes's home for him, but to provide him with objective advice. How was she to do that if she was hanging curtains and making up beds while he was out inspecting his lands? Excluding her, in other words, and she had not protested. 'Same old Ainsley,' she said to herself in disgust. 'You should be ashamed of yourself!'

Dear Madame Hera,
My husband's mother gave me a household manual on my wedding day that she wrote herself.

It is extremely comprehensive, and at first I was pleased to know the foods my husband prefers, and how he likes them served. However, I must say that right from the start I was a bit worried when I read what his mother calls 'The Order of the Day'—and there is one for every day. I do try to follow it, but I confess I see no reason why I must do the washing on a Wednesday and polish the silver on a Saturday, any more than I see why we have to have shin of beef every single Tuesday, and kippers only on a Thursday. And as to her recipe for sheep's-head soup—I will not!

I tried to tell my husband that his mother's way is not the only way. I have many excellent recipes from my own mother that I am sure he would enjoy. I tried, with all my wifely wiles, to persuade him that I could run the household without following his mother's manual to the letter. He spurned my wifely wiles, Madame, and now he is threatening to have his mother, who has a perfectly good house of her own, to come and live with us. I love my husband, but I do not love his mother. What should I do?
Desperate Wife

Ainsley pulled a fresh sheet of paper on to the blotting pad. It was tempting to suggest that Desperate Wife invite her own mother to stay, and even more tempting to suggest that she simply swap abodes herself with her husband's mother, but she doubted Felicity would print either solution. Instead, she would advise Desperate Wife to put her foot down, throw away the manual and claim the hearth and home as her own domain. It was Madame Hera's standard response to this sort of letter, of which she received a great many. Mothers-in-law, if the readers of the *Scottish Ladies Companion* were to be believed, were an interfering lot, and their sons seemed to be singularly lacking in gumption.

Claiming this hearth and home as her own had turned out to be relatively easy. Yet looking around the room, which in the past ten days, like the rest of the Home Farm, had been made both warm and comfortable, Ainsley felt little satisfaction. Mhairi McIntosh had proved cooperative but reserved. She had not looked down her nose at Ainsley, nor had she mocked or derided a single one of her suggestions, which had made the task Innes had given her relatively easy, but it was not the challenge she had been looking forward to. She had, in essence, been relegated to the domestic sphere when he had promised her a different role.

Irked with herself, Ainsley tucked Madame Hera's correspondence into her leather folder and pushed it to one side of the desk, covering it with the latest copy of the *Scottish Ladies Companion*, which Felicity had sent to her. There could be no doubt that Innes needed help, but he had made no attempt to ask her for it. Though she rationalised that he most likely thought he'd fare better with his tenants alone, as the days passed, she felt more excluded and more uncomfortable with trying to address this fact. She was not unhappy, she was not regretting her decision to come here, but she felt overlooked and rather useless.

Standing on her tiptoes at the window, she could see the sky was an inviting bright blue above the monstrous hedge. Ainsley made her way outside, making for her favourite view out over the Kyles of Bute. Tiny puffs of clouds scudded overhead, like the steam from a train or a paddle steamer. It was a shame that the dilapidated jetty down in the bay was not big enough to allow a steamer to dock, for it would make it a great deal easier to get supplies.

She had to speak to Innes. She had a perfect right to demand that he allow her to do the task he had brought her here for. The fact that he was obviously floundering made it even more important. Yes, it also made him distant and unapproachable, but that was even more reason for her to tackle him. Besides, she couldn't in all conscience remain here without actually doing what she'd already been paid to do. She owed it to herself to speak to him. She had no option but to speak to him.

Mentally rehearsing various ways of introducing the subject, Ainsley wandered through the castle's neglected grounds, finding a path she had not taken before, which wended its way above the coastline before heading inwards to a small copse of trees. The chapel was built of the same grey granite as the castle, but it was warmed by the red sandstone that formed the arched windows, four on each side, and the heavy, worn door. It was a delightful church, simple and functional, with a small belfry on each gable end, a stark contrast to the castle it served.

The door was not locked. Inside, it was equally simple and charming, with wooden pews, the ones nearest the altar covered, the altar itself pink marble, a matching font beside it. It was clean swept. The tall candles were only half-burned. Sunlight, filtered through the leaves of the sheltering trees and the thick panes of glass in the arched windows, had warmed the air. Various Drummonds and their families were commemorated in plaques of brass and polished stone set into the walls. Presumably their bones were interred in the crypt under the altar, but Ainsley could find none more recent than nearly a hundred years ago.

Outside, she discovered the graveyard on the far side of the church. Servants, tenants, fishermen, infants. Some of the stones were so worn she could not read the inscription. The most recent of the lairds were segregated from the rest of the graveyard's inhabitants by a low iron railing.

Ainsley read the short list on the large Celtic cross.

Marjorie Mary Caldwell
1787-1813, spouse of
Malcolm Fraser Drummond

This must be Innes's mother. Below her, the last name, the lettering much brighter, his father:

Malcolm Fraser Drummond
Laird of Strone Bridge
1782-1840

The laird had married early. His wife must have been very young when she had Innes. Ainsley frowned, trying to work out the dates. Seventeen or eighteen? Even younger when she had her first son. Her frown deepened as she read the lettering on the cross again. Above Marjorie was the previous laird. Nothing between her and Innes's father. Innes's brother was not here, and she was certain he was not mentioned in the church. Perhaps he was buried elsewhere? What had Innes said? His brother's death had been the trigger for the split between Innes and his father, she remembered that.

She could ask him. Taking a seat on the stone bench by the main door, Ainsley knew she would not risk antagonising him. She began to pick at the thick rolls of moss, which were growing on the curved arm of the seat. Theirs was a marriage of convenience. Her role as Innes's wife was a public one—to appear on his arm at church on Sunday—and not a private one. She had no right to probe into his past, and she would not like it if he questioned her on hers.

Which did not alter the fact that he was preventing her from helping, and he quite patently needed help. She was bored, and she felt not only useless but rather like an outcast. What would Madame Hera say?

Wandering back along the path, with the sky, not surprisingly, now an ominous grey, Ainsley was thankful that Madame Hera had never been consulted on such a complex problem. There were a score of letters Madame Hera still had to answer, including the one to Desperate Wife. Was there an argument to defend the mother-in-law's precious household manual? Perhaps there were traditions, comforting customs, that Desperate Wife's husband valued or enjoyed, which he feared would be lost if the manual were ignored? Perhaps these very traditions were helping the husband adjust to his new life. Madame Hera rarely concerned herself with the men at the root of her correspondents' problems, but it must be supposed that some of them had feelings, too. Perhaps Desperate Wife might have better success with what she called her wifely wiles if she put them to a more positive use, to discover what parts of the dratted manual actually mattered to him? Though of course, there was always a chance it was simply the case that he simply did like to have kippers on a Thursday.

'I am glad one of us has something to smile about.' Innes was approaching the front door from the direction of the stables. His leather riding breeches and his long boots were spattered with mud, as were the skirts of his black coat. He had not worn a hat since he'd arrived at Strone Bridge, and his hair was windswept. 'What is so amusing, assuming it's not my appearance?' he asked, waiting for her on the path.

'Kippers,' Ainsley replied, smiling. He looked tired. There were shadows under his eyes. She had missed him at breakfast these past few days. 'You do look a bit as if you've been dragged through a hedge backwards. A very muddy hedge,' Ainsley said. 'I'll speak to Mhairi when we get in, I'll have her heat the water so you can have a bath. The chimney has been swept, so it shouldn't take long.'

Innes followed her down the hallway to the sitting room that doubled as their study. 'Thank you, that sounds good. Where have you been?'

'I came across the chapel. I saw your father's grave.'

He was sifting through the pile of mail that Mhairi had left on the desk and did not look up. 'Right.'

She wondered, surprised that it had not occurred to her until now, whether Innes himself had seen it. If so, he had made no mention of it. Another thing he would not talk about. 'I'll go and speak to Mhairi,' Ainsley said, irritated, knowing she had no right to be, and even more irritated by that fact.

* * *

When she returned, bearing a tea tray, Innes was sitting at the desk reading a letter, but he put it down as she entered and took the tray from her. 'I think half the population of Strone Bridge must now be in Canada or America,' he said. 'We've more empty farms than tenanted ones.'

She handed him a cup of tea. 'Why is it, do you think?'

'High rents. Poor maintenance—or more accurately, no maintenance. Better prospects elsewhere.' Innes sighed heavily.

'I know nothing about such matters, but even I can see from the weeds growing that some of the fields have not been tilled for years,' Ainsley said carefully. 'Is the land too poor?'

'It's sure as hell in bad heart now,' Innes said wretchedly, 'though whether that's through neglect or lack of innovation, new methods, whatever they might be. There are cotter families who have lived in the tied cottages for decades who have moved on. I'm sick of hearing the words, "I mentioned it to the laird but nothing happened". My father's factor apparently left Strone Bridge not long after I did, and he did not employ another, though no one will tell me why. In fact, no one will tell me anything. They treat me like a stranger.'

'What about Eoin?' Ainsley asked tentatively.

'What about him?'

'You said he was your friend. Couldn't you talk to him?'

'Eoin is as bad as the rest. It doesn't matter, it's not your problem.'

Innes picked up another letter. As far as he was

concerned, the conversation was over. *It's not your problem.* Ainsley sat perfectly still. The words were a horrible echo from the past. How many times had she been rebuffed by John with exactly that phrase, until she stopped asking any questions at all?

'Don't say that.'

Her tone made Innes look up in surprise. 'Don't say what?'

Ainsley stared down at her tea. 'It is my problem. At least it's supposed to be. It's what you brought me here for, to help you.'

'This place is beyond help. I can see that for myself.'

'So that's it? You've already decided—what? To sell? To walk away and let it continue to crumble? What?'

'I don't know.'

'So you haven't decided, but you're not going to ask me because my opinion counts for nothing.'

'No! Ainsley, what the devil is the matter with you?'

'What is the matter?' She jumped to her feet, unable to keep still. 'You brought me here to *help*! You have paid me a considerable sum of money, a sum I would not have dreamed of accepting if I thought all I was to do was sit about here and—and fluff cushions.'

'You've done a great deal more than that. I'm sorry if I have seemed unappreciative, but—'

'I have done nothing more than Mhairi McIntosh could have done. Oh, granted, I married you, and in doing so allowed you to claim this place, which seems to me to have been a completely pointless exercise, if all you're going to do is say that it's past help, and walk away.'

'I didn't say I was going to do that. Stop haranguing me like a fishwife.'

'Stop treating me like a child! I have a brain. I have opinions. I know I'm a Sassenach and a commoner to boot, but I'm not a parasite. I may know nothing about farming, but neither do you! Only you're so blooming well ashamed of the fact, though you've no reason to be, because why should you know anything about it when you told me yourself your father did not allow you to know anything, and—and...'

'Ainsley!' Innes wrested the teaspoon she was still clutching from her clenched hand and set it down on the tea tray. 'What on earth has come over you? You're shaking.'

'I'm not,' she said, doing just that. 'Now you've made me lose track of what I was saying.'

'You were saying that I'm an ignoramus not fit to own the lands.'

'No, that's what you think.' She sniffed loudly. 'If I could have got by without asking Mhairi for advice on this house, I would have, but I couldn't, Innes.'

'Why should you, you know nothing of the place.'

'Exactly.' She sniffed again, and drew him a meaningful look. Innes handed her a neatly folded handkerchief. 'I'm not crying,' Ainsley said.

'No.'

She blew her nose. 'I've never known a wetter July. I've likely got a cold.'

'It wouldn't surprise me.'

'I hate women who resort to tears to get their way.'

'I'm not sure it ever works. From what I've seen, what usually happens is that she cries, he runs away, and whatever it was gets swept under the carpet until the next time,' Innes said wryly.

'You know, for a man who has never been married before, you have an uncanny insight into the workings of matrimony.'

'I take it I've struck a chord?'

It was gently said, but she couldn't help prickling. 'Sometimes tears are not a weapon, but merely an expression of emotion,' Ainsley said, handing him his kerchief. 'Such as anger.'

'Stop glowering at me, and stop assuming that all men are tarred with the same brush as the man you married.'

The gentleness had gone from his voice. Ainsley sat, or rather slumped, feeling suddenly deflated. 'I don't.'

'You do, and I'm not like him.'

'I know. I wouldn't be here if I thought you were. But you are shutting me out, Innes, and it's making me feel as if I'm here under false pretences. If you won't talk to me, why not talk to Eoin? There's nothing shameful in asking for help.'

Her tea was cold, but she drank it anyway. The silence was uncomfortable, but she could think of no way of breaking it. She finished her tea.

'I'm not used to consulting anyone,' Innes said. 'You knew that.'

'But it was your idea to have me come along here. An objective eye.'

'I didn't realise things would be so bad. As I said, it's obvious that it's too late.'

'So you're giving up?'

'No! I'm saving you the effort of getting involved in something that is next to useless.'

'Giving up, in other words,' Ainsley said.

His face was quite white. The handle of his teacup snapped. He stared at it, then put it carefully down. 'I don't give up,' he said.

She bit her tongue.

'I'm not accustomed to— It's been difficult. Seeing it. Not having answers. That's been hard.'

Ainsley nodded.

'They are all judging me.'

She sighed in exasperation. 'Innes, you've been gone a long time. They don't know you.'

'I don't see how you can help.'

'I won't know if I can, if you don't talk to me.' Ainsley tried a tentative smile. 'At the very least, I would be on your side.'

'Aye, that would be something more than I have right now.' Innes smiled back. 'I'll think about it.'

'Please do. I have plenty of time on my hands.'

He tucked a strand of hair behind her ear, looking at her ruefully. 'You might want to use some of it to partition this place off into his and her domains. I'm like a bear with a sore head these days, though contrary to what you might think, I quite like having you around. And that's your cue, in case you missed it, to tell me you feel the same.'

Ainsley laughed. 'Would I have suggested helping you if I had wanted to avoid you?'

'True.'

'Perhaps you should consider having some sort of welcoming party.'

'Even though I'm not welcome.' He shook his head. 'No, I'm sorry, don't bite my head off.'

Ainsley frowned, thinking back to the letter she

had been reading that morning from Desperate Wife. 'Sometimes traditions can be a comfort. Sometimes they can even help heal wounds,' she said, making a mental note to include that phrase in Madame Hera's reply.

'Sometimes you sound like one of those self-help manuals, do you know that?'

'Do I?'

'"Engaging in marital relations,"' he quoted, smiling. '"Undergoing a husband's ministrations." No, don't get on your high horse, it's endearing.'

'It is?'

'It is. What were you suggesting?'

'Didn't you say that there ought to have been a ceremony when we arrived?' There was a smut of mud on his cheek. She reached up to brush it away.

'A ceremony. I'm not very keen on ceremonies.' Innes caught her hand between his and pressed a kiss on to her knuckles.

Was it just a kiss, or a *kiss*? It felt like more than just a kiss, for it made her heart do a silly little flip. But his mouth did not linger, and surely knuckles could not be—what was the word, *stimulating*? She wanted to ask him, but that would give too much away, and he might not have been at all stimulated. 'A celebration, then,' Ainsley said. 'Lots of food and drink. Something to mark the changes. You know, out with the old and in with the new.'

'Mmm.' He kissed her hand again. 'I like that,' he said, smiling at her.

'Do you?' She had no idea whether he meant her idea or the kiss.

'Mmm,' he said, pulling her towards him and wrapping his arms around her. 'I like that very much,' he said. And then he kissed her on the mouth.

It was definitely not *just* a kiss. He tasted of spring. Of outdoors. A little of sweat. And of something she could not name. Something sinful. Something that made her heat and tense and clench, and made her dig her fingers into the shoulders of his coat and tilt her body against his. And that made him groan, a guttural noise that seemed to vibrate inside her.

One hand roamed up her back, his fingers delving into her hair, the other roamed down to cup her bottom and pull her closer. She could feel the hard ridge of his arousal through his trousers, through her skirts. She touched her tongue to his and felt his shudder, and shuddered with him, pressing her thighs against his, wanting more, wanting to rid herself of the layers of cloth between them, wanting his flesh, and then thinking about her flesh, exposed, thinking about him looking at her. Or looking at her and then turning his head away. Then not wanting to look at her. Like John. And then...

'Ainsley?'

'Your bath,' she said, clutching at the first thing she could think of. 'Your bath will be ready.'

'Is something wrong?'

'No,' she said, managing a smile, forcing herself to meet his concerned gaze, hating herself for being the cause of that concern, frustrated at having started something she had not the nerve to finish, frustrated at how much she wished she could. 'No, I just don't want the water to get cold.'

'The state I'm in, I think cold is what I need. What happened? Did I do something wrong?'

She flushed. Men were not supposed to ask such questions. Men hated discussing anything intimate. She knew that it was not just John who had been like that, because Madame Hera's correspondence was full of women saying that their husbands were exactly the same. Why did Innes have to be different!

'Nothing. I changed my mind,' Ainsley said, mortified, not only for the lie, but for knowing she was relying on Innes being the kind of man who would always allow a woman to do so. And she was right.

'A lady's prerogative,' he said, making an ironic little bow. 'I'll see you at dinner.'

Chapter Five

'Come and sit by the fire.' Innes handed Ainsley a glass of sherry.

'I thought it was warm enough to wear this without shivering,' she answered him with a constrained smile, 'but now I'm not so sure.'

Her dress was cream patterned with dark blue, with a belt the same colour around her waist. Though it was long-sleeved, the little frill around the *décolleté* revealed her shoulders, the hollows at her collarbone, the most tantalising hint of the smooth slope of her breasts. She sat opposite him and began to twirl her glass about in her hand, a habit she had, Innes had noticed, when she was trying to work up to saying something uncomfortable.

Her face had that pinched look that leached the life from it. Earlier, he'd suspected that she had pulled away from him because of her memories connected to McBrayne. Lying in the cooling bath water in front of the feeble fire in his bedchamber, Innes had begun to wonder what, exactly, the man had done to her. It was more than the debts, or even the fact that they were incurred without her knowing. He couldn't understand how she could be kissing him with abandon one minute and then turning to ice the next, and he was fairly certain it wasn't anything he'd done—or not done. When she forgot herself, she was a different person from the one opposite him now, twisting away nervously at her glass and slanting him timid looks.

Innes threw another log on the fire. 'I think I've solved one problem, at least,' he said, picking up the magazine that he'd been flicking through while he waited on her. 'This thing, the *Scottish Ladies Companion*. There's a woman who doles out spurious advice to females in here, and she uses that very same phrase of yours.' He opened the periodical and ruffled through the pages. 'Aye, here it is. "Make a point of extinguishing the light before engaging in marital relations"—you see, your very phrase—"and your husband will likely not notice your having so unwittingly misled him. Better still, retain your modesty and your nightgown, and your little deceit will never have to be explained." This Madame Hera is either a virgin or a fool,' he said scathingly.

'What do you mean?'

'The lass has been stuffing her corsets with— What was it?'

'Stockings.'

'I see you have read it, then.' Innes shook his head.

'It was her mother's idea.'

'And a damned stupid one. Pitch dark or broad daylight, you can be certain the husband will know the difference. And as for the idea of keeping her nightgown on...'

'For modesty's sake. I am sure many women do.'

'Really? I've never come across a single one.'

'I doubt very much that the women you have—experienced—are—are— I mean— You know what I mean.'

'The women I've *experienced*, as you put it, have certainly not been married to another man at the time, but nor have they been harlots, if that is what you're implying.' She was blushing. She was unduly flustered, considering she was neither a virgin herself, nor as strait-laced as she now sounded. 'I'm finding you a puzzle,' Innes said, 'for the day I met you, I recall you were threatening to join the harlots on the Cowgate.'

'You know very well I was joking.' Ainsley set her glass of sherry down. 'Do you really think Madame Hera's advice misguided?'

'Does it matter?'

She bit her lip, then nodded.

Innes picked up the magazine and read the letter again. 'This woman, she's not exactly lied to the man she's betrothed to, but she's misled him, and it seems to me that Madame Hera is encouraging her to continue to mislead him. It's that I don't like. The lass is likely nervous enough about the wedding night without having to worry about subterfuge. Hardly a frame of mind conducive to her enjoying what you would call her husband's ministrations.'

'What would you call it?'

Innes grinned. 'Something that doesn't sound as if the pleasure is entirely one-sided. There's a dictionary worth of terms depending on what takes your fancy, but lovemaking will do.'

'You might think that innocuous enough, but I assure you, the *Scottish Ladies Companion* will not publish it,' Ainsley said.

'You are a subscriber to this magazine, then?'

She shrugged. 'But—this woman, Innes. Don't you think her husband will be angry if he discovers her deception? And anger is no more conducive to—to lovemaking than fraud.'

'In the grand scheme of things, I doubt it. Chances are he's not any more experienced than she, and like to be just as nervous. I'd say he's going to be more concerned about his own performance than anything else, something your Madame Hera doesn't seem to take any account of.'

'It is a column of advice for women.'

'And most of the letters in this issue seem to be about men. Anyway, Madame Hera is completely missing the main point.'

'Which is?'

'The lass thinks she's not well enough endowed, and Madame Hera is by implication agreeing by telling her to cover up. If she goes to her wedding night ashamed, thinking she's not got enough to offer, you can be sure that soon enough her husband will think the same.'

'So it's her fault?' Ainsley said.

'Don't be daft. If anyone's at fault it's that blasted Madame Hera—and the mother.' Innes threw the magazine down on the table. 'I don't know why we're wasting our time with this nonsense.'

Ainsley picked the magazine up, her face set. 'Because I wrote it,' she said. 'I'm Madame Hera.'

Innes laughed. Then, when she continued to look at him without joining in, his laughter stopped abruptly.

'I'll be damned. You mean it? You really do write this stuff?'

'It is not *stuff*. It is a very well-respected column. I'll have you know that in the past month, Madame Hera has received no less than fifty letters. In fact, such is the demand for Madame's advice that the magazine will from next month offer a personal reply service. Felicity has agreed a fee with the board, and I shall receive fifty per cent of it.'

'Felicity?'

'Blair. The editor, and my friend.'

'So all that correspondence you receive, they are letters to this Madame Hera.' Innes looked quite stunned. 'Why didn't you tell me?'

'Because it was none of your business.' Ainsley flushed. 'And because I knew you would most likely react exactly as you have. Though I am not ashamed, if that's what you're thinking. Madame Hera provides a much-needed service.'

'So why tell me now?'

Ainsley reached for her sherry and took a large gulp. She had not meant to tell him. She had been so caught up in worrying about how to explain away her earlier behaviour that Madame Hera had been far from her mind, though her advice would have been straightforward. *'Il faut me chercher'* was one of Madame's axioms. Men must hunt and women must avoid capture. Kissing, not even *just* kissing, without the benefit of a wedding band, was quite wrong. And though Ainsley did have the benefit of a wedding band, she was not really married, so it was still wrong. Kissing gave a man all sorts of immoral ideas. Such ideas were, in Madame Hera's world, the province only of men. That Ainsley herself had had *ideas*—her mind boggled, trying to imagine what Madame would say to that.

In fact, those very *ideas* cropped up in several of the letters Felicity had forwarded to her, variously referred to as 'unnatural desires', 'longing', 'carnal stirrings', 'fever of the blood', 'indecent thoughts' and even, memorably, 'an irrepressible need to scratch an itch'. On the one hand, it was consoling to know that she was not unusual, but on the other, she was utterly defeated when it came to even contemplating a reply. Felicity had been right—Ainsley knew very little of such matters. She'd been right, too, in suggesting that Ainsley would do well to learn. But Felicity had no idea of the hurdles Ainsley would have to overcome in order to do so.

She had concluded that her only option was to return the letters to Felicity until Innes had read out Madame Hera's letter, and she saw what she had suspected: that her advice wasn't only skewed but perhaps even hypocritical. Madame Hera existed to liberate women from ignorance, not to reflect Ainsley's own insecurities.

Her stomach had tied itself in knots in her bedroom earlier as she'd contemplated that kiss. Now she was aware of Innes studying her, waiting patiently for an explanation, and she had never felt more inarticulate in her life. Seeing with some surprise that her sherry glass was empty, Ainsley reached for the decanter and topped it up, taking another fortifying gulp. 'Felicity said that— Felicity suggested that— She said...' She took another sip of sherry. 'Felicity was concerned that I had not the experience to answer some of the more intimate queries made of Madame Hera. I agreed with her, but I thought—I was certain that in all other instances, my advice was sound.'

Ainsley took another sip of sherry. It was really rather good sherry. She took another sip. 'Then earlier today, when I was mulling over the contents of another letter, I began to wonder if perhaps I had been a little biased. Failing to take account the other side of the problem. A little. And then, when you read that letter out I realised that—that perhaps you were right. To a degree.'

Innes looked as confused by this rambling explanation as she felt. 'I'm sorry, but I still don't understand why this led you to confess your secret identity.'

Ainsley tried to sort out the tangle of threads in her head into some sort of logical order. 'These letters are written by real women with real problems. They are not printed in the journal to titillate, nor to provide some sort of vicarious enjoyment to readers who can congratulate themselves on their own superior, problem-free lives. The letters that are printed are chosen because the problems posed are sadly commonplace.' She swallowed the remainder of her sherry and topped her glass up once more, grimacing. 'I didn't mean Madame Hera to sound like a shrew.'

'Well, I didn't mean to sound like a pompous git when I criticised your advice,' Innes said ruefully. 'You've quite thrown me.'

His honesty disarmed her. That, and the sherry. And that smile of his, which was really just as warming as the sherry. Ainsley took another sip of her drink. 'Do you really want to know why I told you?'

'Yes.'

'Even if it is embarrassing?'

'Now I'm intrigued.'

'Really?' Ainsley eyed him warily. 'You're not angry?'

'I'm not sure what I am, but I'm definitely not angry.'

'I wonder if Felicity was right,' Ainsley said, raising her glass, her mood lightening considerably.

'Felicity again. I think I would like to meet her.'

'Then you must find an excuse to invite her here. A party. The welcoming thing. If you deign to listen to my advice. Oh, dear, now I sound like a shrew again.'

'Not a shrew, but you can be extremely prickly.'

'Like a hedgehog, you mean?'

'More like a porcupine. I am rather fond of porcupines.'

'That is downright perverse.' Ainsley helped herself to more sherry and topped up Innes's glass, even though it was virtually untouched. 'Do you really mean to invite Felicity? She is most keen to meet you.'

'No doubt she wishes to make sure I am being a good husband.'

'Well, you couldn't be worse than the last one, that is for sure,' Ainsley said. 'Sorry. Actually, I'm not really.' She sipped her sherry contemplatively. 'Anyway, she's not so much interested in your husbandly qualities, since she knows this is a business arrangement.' She wriggled back in her chair, because despite the thin calico of her gown, the heat from the fire was making her face flush. 'Now I suppose you want to know what she *is* interested in.'

Innes, who had been inspecting the sherry decanter, which seemed to have almost emptied itself, put it rather selfishly down on the table out of her reach. 'I do,' he said, 'but first I'd like to know why you confessed to being Madame Hera. You still haven't yet told me, in case you'd forgotten.'

'Aha! That's where you're wrong,' Ainsley exclaimed with a triumphant wave of her hand, 'because the two things are inexpressibly—no, inex—inextricably linked.' She picked up her glass, remembered it was empty and placed it very carefully back down again, because the side table had developed a wobble. Then, realising she had slumped unbecomingly back in her chair, she struggled upright, leaning forward confidentially. 'Those letters. The intimate ones to Madame Hera. They are all about marital—no, lovemaking. And—and the acquisition of womanly wiles. Felicity fears that I do not know enough about such things to be of any value, and I fear she is right. Are you perfectly well? Only your face has gone sort of fuzzy.'

Innes leaned forward. 'Better?'

Ainsley nodded. 'Do you know you have a charming smile?'

'Only because I am charmed by you.'

She giggled. 'Felicity said I should let you have your wicked way with me, and that you sounded like the kind of man who would not expect me to—to lie back and think of Scotland. And she said that we needed something to while away the long dark nights in this godforsaken place—though I don't think it is godforsaken, actually—and she said that I needed some lessons in—in fun. And pleasure. Do you have a kilt?'

'I do. Does Felicity's idea of fun and pleasure involve dressing up?'

Ainsley giggled. 'Not Felicity's idea—that was mine. I think you have a fine pair of legs, Innes Drummond. I would like to see you in Highland dress. But we are straying from the point, you know. Is there any more sherry?'

'No.'

Ainsley frowned over at the decanter. It seemed to her that it was not completely empty. Then she shrugged. 'Oh, well. What was I— Oh, yes, what Felicity said. She said that you would be well placed to teach me about womanly wiles and such—though I don't think she called it that, zactly—*ex*actly—and I don't know how she knew this, for she has not met you, and all I told her was that you kissed very nicely, which you know you do...'

'Only because you kiss me so very nicely back.'

'Really?' Ainsley smiled beatifically. 'What a lovely thing to say.'

'And true, into the bargain.' Innes took her hand. 'So this Felicity of yours believes that you need to be inducted into the palace of pleasure.'

'Palace of pleasure. I like that. Would you mind if Madame Hera borrowed it?'

'I would be honoured.'

'What would you say if I told you that Felicity also suggested I use you to assist me in finding answers to some of Madame Hera's problems?'

'You mean, provide you with practical experience of the solutions?'

Ainsley nodded sagely. 'You would be insulted, wouldn't you? That's what I told Felicity, that you would be insulted.'

'Would you be taking part in this experiment merely for the sake of obtaining better advice?'

'No.' She stared down at her hands. Despite the tingling, and the fuzziness and the warmth induced by the sherry, this was still proving surprisingly difficult, but she was determined to bring this embarrassing conversation to an end, one way or another. 'The reason I told you,' she said, 'about Madame Hera, I mean. It wasn't only that you were right about the advice I was dispensing, it was—it was—it was earlier. Me. When you kissed me. It was because I— Felicity says that he took away all my self-respect. John. My husband. Self-respect, that's what she called it. I don't know what to call it. I don't want to talk about it. But when you kissed me, it made me feel— I liked it. I liked it a lot. But then I remembered, you see. Him. What happened. Didn't happen. And it made me stop liking what you were doing and thinking about then, and him, and it wasn't that I think you're the same, you're so different, and he never, but— Well, that was it. That's what happened. Are you angry?'

She looked up. His eyes were stormy. 'No,' Innes said quickly. 'I'm not angry with you.'

She nodded several times.

'You don't have to say any more, Ainsley.'

'I want to finish telling you or I might not— I want to.' She clutched at his hand. 'I don't want to feel like this. I don't want to feel the way he made me feel. I want to feel what Felicity said, and what you made me feel before I thought about him. And that's why I told you about Madame Hera,' she finished in a rush. 'Because when you kiss me, I want to—and because you know, we're not really married and it can't ever mean anything, so it's sort of *safe*. You can help me, and then I can be better at helping other women. That's why I told you. Because I want you, and I really want to be able to— If you do? So now you know.'

'Now I know,' Innes said, looking rather stunned.

'You can say no.'

'I'm not going to say anything right now. You've given me a lot to think about.'

'And you're not angry about Madame Hera?'

Innes laughed. 'Absolutely not. I am more than happy to discuss these intimate problems that Madame Hera has to answer. In fact, if you ever run short of problems then I'm sure I will be able to think up a few for us to discuss.'

'No!' Ainsley exclaimed. 'That's what Felicity said you would say. Now I owe her five pounds.'

Innes laughed. 'I am looking forward to meeting Felicity.'

Ainsley yawned, frowning at the clock. 'It's past dinner time. I shall go and find Mhairi.'

She got to her feet, swaying, and Innes caught her. 'I think maybe you'd be better in your bed.'

Ainsley yawned again. 'I think maybe you're right.'

'Thank you for telling me what you did. I'm honoured,' Innes said. 'I mean it.'

'I didn't want you to think I was a cock tease.' Ainsley grinned. 'Proof that I am not always so mealy-mouthed.'

Innes kissed her cheek. 'What you are is…'

'A porcupine.'

'A wee darling.'

She smiled. 'I like that,' she murmured. Then she closed her eyes, sank gracefully back onto the chair and passed out.

'The laird said that you'd be hungry, seeing as you missed dinner, so I made you some eggs, and I've cut you a slice of ham.' Mhairi laid the plateful down in front of Ainsley.

'Thank you. It smells delicious,' Ainsley said, re-pressing a shudder.

'Himself had to go out, but he said to tell you he'd be back by mid-morn at the latest. Here, I'll do that.' Mhairi took the coffee pot from Ainsley's shaking hand and poured her a cup. 'Do you want me to put a hair of the dog in it?'

'Is it so obvious?' Lifting the cup in both hands, Ainsley took a grateful sip, shaking her head, flush-ing. 'I don't normally— I hope you don't think I usu-ally overindulge.'

'Oh, I'm not one to judge,' Mhairi said with a toss of her head. 'Unlike the rest of them.'

Sensing that the housekeeper was offering her an opening, and feeling that she had nothing much to lose, as she sat nursing her hangover, Ainsley smiled at her. 'Why don't you join me? It's about time we got to know each other a bit better. Please,' she added when the other woman demurred.

Mhairi studied her with pursed lips for a few sec-onds, then took a seat and poured herself a coffee, add-ing two lumps of sugar, though no cream. 'You're not at all what we expected when we heard Himself had wedded an Edinburgh widow woman,' she said.

'What were you expecting?'

'Someone fancier. You know, more up on her high horse, with more frills to her.'

'You mean not so plain?'

Mhairi shook her head. 'I mean not so nice,' she said with a wry smile. 'And you're not plain. Leastwise, you're not when you've some life in that face of yours. If you don't mind my saying.'

'I don't mind at all,' Ainsley said, buttering an oat-cake, and deciding to brave a forkful of eggs. 'Am I a disappointment, then?'

'No one knows enough about you to judge.'

'Yet you said that people do judge—or that is what you implied just a minute ago.'

Across from her, the housekeeper folded her arms. Ainsley ate another forkful of eggs and cut into the ham. Mhairi McIntosh was younger than she had thought at first, not much over forty, with a curvaceous figure hidden under her apron and heavy tweed skirt. Though she had a forbidding expression, her features were attractive, with high cheekbones and a mouth that curved sensually when it was not pulled into a grim line. Her eyes were grey and deep-set, and she had the kind of sallow skin that made the hollows beneath them look darkly shadowed. But she was what would be called a handsome woman, nevertheless. She wore no ring.

'No, I was never married,' Mhairi said, noticing the direction of Ainsley's gaze. 'I've worked here at the castle since I was ten years old, starting in the kitchens—the big kitchens—back in Mrs Drummond's day.'

'So you've known Innes since he was a boy?'

Mhairi nodded.

'And his brother?'

'Him, too.'

'Is it because of him that people judge Innes so harshly? Do they resent the fact that he is here and not Malcolm?'

Mhairi shook her head sadly. 'Himself should not have stayed away so long.'

'But surely people understand he had his own life to lead. And it's not as if— I mean, the state of the lands, the way things have been allowed to deteriorate… That was his father's fault, it was nothing to do with Innes.'

'He should not have stayed away,' Mhairi said implacably.

'Oh, for goodness' sake! It's not his fault.' Realising that recriminations were getting her nowhere, Ainsley reined in her temper. 'He's here now, and so am I, and what matters is the future of Strone Bridge.'

'It seems to many of us that Strone Bridge hasn't much of a future,' Mhairi said.

'What do you mean?'

'Himself has obviously decided that this place is not worth wasting his time on.'

'He hasn't decided anything. He's not even been here a month.'

'And not a single sign has there been that he's going to be remaining here another. He forbade the formal welcoming at the pier, and there's been no word of the Rescinding. Not that the castle is in any fit state to be used. And that's another thing. He's the laird, and he's living here at the Home Farm. It's obvious he has no plans to stay here. He'll be off as soon as he can decently go, back to building his bridges.'

There was no doubting the belligerence in the woman's voice now. 'Innes hasn't made any decisions about the castle. He's been spending his time looking at the land, because—'

'Because he plans to do what all the landlords are doing, break up the crofts and put sheep on them. Does he think we're daft? Sheep. That's what he'll do, that's what they all do. Get rid of the tenants. Bring in a bailiff. Out with the old, and in with the new. That's what Himself is doing, and then it will be back to Edinburgh or London or wherever he's been hiding these last fourteen years, and you with him, and he'll go back to pretending Strone Bridge doesn't exist because it's too hard for him to—' Mhairi broke off suddenly. 'Never mind.'

Ainsley stared at her in shock. 'He has made no mention of sheep, and he has no intentions of going anywhere for at least—for some time,' she amended, for she did not imagine that Innes would like the terms of his father's will made public.

A shrug greeted this remark. Ainsley risked pouring the pair of them another cup of coffee. 'What is this thing you mentioned? A restitution?'

'Rescinding.' Mhairi took a sip of her coffee. 'A forgiving and forgetting. After the burial of the old laird, a feast is held for all to welcome in the new laird. It is a wiping clean of the slate, of debts and grudges and disputes, a sign that they have been buried with the old. But since Himself was not here for the burial…'

'Can it not be held on another day?' Ainsley asked.

'To my knowledge it never has been.'

'Yes, but if it is held on another day would this Rescinding be invalid?'

Mhairi shook her head slowly. 'It's never been done. You'd have to consult the book. *The Customs and Ways of the Family Drummond of Strone Bridge,*' she said when Ainsley looked at her enquiringly. 'It's in the castle library.'

'Then I will do so, but do you think it's a good idea?' Ainsley persisted.

'It would mean using the Great Hall. I'd need a lot of help and good bit of supplies, and as to the food…'

'Yes, yes, we can see to that, but what do you think?'

The housekeeper smiled reluctantly. 'I think if you can persuade Himself, that it's an excellent idea.'

'A Rescinding?' Innes frowned. Ainsley had accosted him immediately when he had returned in the early afternoon. He had expected her to be sheepish, or reserved, or even defensive. He had not expected her to launch enthusiastically into some wild plan for a party. 'I'm not even sure that I know what's involved,' he said cautiously.

'It's a forgiving and forgetting, Mhairi says. She says that all debts and grudges are buried with the old laird to give the new one a clean start. She says that though it's customary to have it the day after the funeral, there is no reason why we cannot hold it on another day and combine it with a welcoming feast. She says that the chair that the laird uses for the ceremony is in the Great Hall. And there is a book in the library. *The Customs and Ways of the Family Drummond of Strone Bridge*, it's called.' Ainsley was looking at him anxiously. 'What do you think?'

'I think Mhairi has quite a lot to say all of a sudden. I wonder how she knows so much about it, for she cannot have seen one herself.'

'She has worked in the castle since she was ten years old. I suppose, these past few years while your father was alone here, he must have confided in her.'

'I can't imagine my father confiding in anyone,'

Innes said drily. 'To be honest, I can't imagine him forgiving or forgetting either, Rescinding or no. He was not a man who liked to be crossed, and he bore a long grudge.'

'Were you always at outs with him, even before—before your brother died?'

'Yes.'

Ainsley was watching him. Innes could feel her eyes on him, even though he was studiously looking down at a letter from his chief surveyor. He wondered what else Mhairi had said. She was as closed as a fist, and always had been. It surprised him that Ainsley had managed to have any sort of conversation with her. He pushed the letter to one side. 'The old ways were the only ways, as far as my father was concerned,' he said, 'and for my brother, too.'

'Sometimes the old ways can be a comfort.'

'You mean the Rescinding?'

Ainsley nodded.

'A—what did you call it—healing of wounds?' He smiled. 'There can be no denying the need for that.'

'So you agree, it's a good idea?'

'It sounds like a lot of work.'

'I will handle that. With Mhairi. I am not too proud to ask for help.'

'Is that a dig at me?'

Ainsley hesitated only fractionally. 'Yes.'

Innes sighed. 'If I speak to Eoin, will it make you happy?'

'It would be a start. A forgiving and forgetting, that's what the Rescinding is. Perhaps you could do some of that before the ceremony.'

Innes threw his hands up in surrender. 'Enough.

You've made your point. I will even write to your Miss Blair and invite her to attend. Unless you've changed your mind. Or perhaps forgotten that conversation entirely?'

'I was half-cut, not stotious!' Ainsley said stiffly.

'Ach, I didn't mean to bite your head off. At least I did, but don't take it personally. You make too good a case, and I don't want to hear it.' Innes got up from the desk and took her hand. He took her hand, pressing it between his own. 'Forgive me.'

Her fingers twined round his. 'It is I who should be begging your forgiveness. Last night, I propositioned you. In fact, I practically threw myself at you,' Ainsley said, flushing. 'You must not feel awkward at turning me down.'

'I have no intentions of turning you down, if you are not retracting your offer. I thought I'd made it clear, from almost the first moment I met you, that I find you very desirable.'

'You do?'

'I do.'

'I don't want to. Retract, I mean.'

'Are you sure? Yesterday, you turned to ice while I was kissing you.'

'It won't happen again.'

'I think maybe it will. I think, in fact, we should expect it. I wonder what Madame Hera would advise?'

'As you pointed out last night, Madame Hera would most likely provide quite unwise advice,' Ainsley said drily.

'I offended you. I'm sorry.'

'No,' she said, quite unconvincingly, and then she laughed. 'Yes, you did. I was upset.'

'If I had known that you and she were one and the same person...'

'I am glad you did not. It was a difficult lesson, but I hope that I have learned from it. I want Madame Hera to be helpful.' Ainsley opened the thick leather folder on the desk that contained her correspondence. 'These women are desperate enough to write to a complete stranger for help. They deserve honesty.' She replaced the folder and wandered over to her favourite chair by the fire, though she did not sit down. 'When John died, one of the things I promised myself was always to speak my mind, and that's what Madame Hera has done. I didn't realise, though, that my opinions were so coloured.'

'I think that you're being very hard on yourself, but if it would help, I'd be happy to provide you with a counterpoint when you're writing your replies.'

'Would you?'

'I think I might even enjoy it.'

'What if we disagree?'

Innes pulled her round to face him, sliding his arms around her waist. 'Madame Hera has the final say, naturally.'

'And as to the—the other thing?'

Innes smiled. 'Your introduction into the palace of pleasures? I was thinking that it would be best if we started first with some theory.'

Her eyes widened. 'You have textbooks?'

'Good lord, no. I meant Madame Hera's correspondence. We could discuss it. I could explain anything you are not sure of. That way, you will be able to start answering some of your letters, and at the same time, you can accustom yourself to—to—before you have to—if you do. You might decide not to.' Innes stopped, at a loss for words, wondering if what he was suggesting was idiotic, or even repugnant.

But Ainsley smiled at him. 'You mean that I become accustomed to what to expect?' she asked.

'And you can accustom me to what you want, too.'

'I don't know what I want.'

'Save that I must wear a kilt?'

Her cheeks flamed. 'I had forgotten that.'

'Do you dream of a wild Highlander?'

'No. Yes.'

'What does he do?'

'I don't know.' Ainsley's mouth trembled on the brink of a smile. 'He—he wants me.'

'You know I already do.'

'No, I mean he—he really wants me. He— No, it's silly.'

'He finds you irresistible,' Innes said, charmed and aroused. 'He wants you so much,' he whispered into her ear, 'that he carries you off, right in the middle of the day, and has his wicked way with you on the moor. Or would you prefer a cave?'

'A cave. In the firelight.'

He was hard. Innes cursed under his breath. He hadn't meant this to happen. He edged away from her carefully. 'You are a very apt pupil,' he said.

'Oh. I didn't realise— Is that what that was, a lesson?'

'It's all it was meant to be,' Innes said, 'but you are a little too good at this. Another minute and I'd be rushing off to find a kilt.'

'Oh.'

It was a different kind of 'oh' this time. She looked

at him with the most delightful, pleased little smile on her face, and Innes simply could not resist her. He kissed her, briefly but deeply. 'I am already looking forward to the next lesson,' he said.

Chapter Six

A week later, Innes stared down at the Celtic cross, at the bright lettering of the new inscription and the long empty space below that was left to fill. His own name would be next, but after that, it would be a distant cousin, if anyone. He dug his hands into the pockets of his leather breeches and hunched his shoulders against the squally breeze, steeling himself against the wall of emotions that threatened to engulf him. Until now, he'd been able to ignore what had happened, tell himself that this was a temporary thing, that he was not really the laird, that his life was not inextricably tangled up in Strone Bridge. He'd been able to contain and control whatever it was that was building inside him, fence it in with resentment and anger, let the waste and destruction he saw every day tack it down, the hurt and the suffering gnaw at his conscience and prevent him from thinking about the reason he was here at all.

He'd arranged to meet Eoin here, but had arrived early, wanting some time alone. He'd come here telling himself that fourteen years had bred indifference, but he was wrong. It was like one of those seventh waves, building from the swell, scooping up memories and guilt and remorse, hurtling them at him with an implacable force. Innes screwed his eyes so tightly shut he saw stars behind his lids.

'It was all done properly, if that's bothering you at all.' He opened his eyes to find Eoin standing a few feet away. 'Your father's funeral. It was all done as he would have wanted it,' he said. 'Mhairi made sure of that.'

His father's housekeeper had been the one to arrange his father's funeral. Innes refused to feel guilty.

'She had me play the chief mourner.' Eoin came a few steps closer. 'I didn't want to, but she said someone with Drummond blood had to bear the laird's standard, and bastard blood from two generations back was better than none.'

It had been a joke between them when they were boys, that bastard blood. Malcolm had traced the line once, working out that Eoin was their half cousin twice removed, or some such thing. Their father had a coat of arms made for Eoin, with the baton sinister prominently displayed. Malcolm had dreamed up a ceremony to hand it over, Innes remembered. The laird had given them all their first taste of whisky. They'd have been ten, maybe eleven. He had forgotten that there were days like those.

'I didn't get the letter in time to attend,' Innes said tersely.

'Would it have made any difference?' Eoin demanded, and when Innes said nothing, he shook his head impatiently and turned away. 'I meant it to be a comfort to you, knowing that all had been done as it ought. I wasn't casting it up.'

'Wait.' Innes covered the short distance between them, grabbing the thick fisherman's jumper Eoin wore. His friend shrugged him off, but made no further move to go. Blue eyes, the same colour as Innes's, the same colour as Malcolm's, the same colour as the dead laird's, glowered at him. 'I wrote to you,' Innes said. 'After—I wrote to you, and you did not reply.'

'I live here, Innes, and unlike you, I've never wanted to leave. It was not only that I owed a duty to your father as the laird, I respected him. When you left, the way you left, you forced me to choose. What else was I to do?'

'I was your friend.'

'You were his son,' Eoin said, nodding at the Celtic cross. 'When Malcolm died, it broke his heart.'

'What do you think it did to me?' Innes struggled, eyes smarting, the sick feeling that had been lurking inside him since he'd arrived here growing, acrid, clogging his throat. He turned away, fists clenched, taking painful breaths, fighting for control, forcing back the images, the guilt, waiting desperately for the sound of Eoin's footsteps disappearing, leaving him alone to deal with it, to make it go away.

Eoin didn't move. When he spoke, his voice was raw, grating. 'I could hardly look at you the other day. All these years, I've told myself it was the right thing to hold my peace. All these years, with the laird letting things go, letting the place wither, I've told myself that if that was what he wanted and— No, not just that. I've told myself you deserved it. If you did not care enough to look after your heritage…'

Innes had intended this as a reconciliation. It felt as though he was being tried, and found wanting, by the one person here on Strone Bridge he had thought might be on his side. The disappointment was crushing. 'It was never meant for me,' he roared. 'It was never mine.'

His words echoed around the enclosed space, but still Eoin stood his ground, his face grim, his own fists clenched. 'It is yours now. You've known for fourteen years that it would be yours.'

'And by the looks of it, for fourteen years my father has done his damnedest to run the place into the ground. Don't tell me I could have stopped him, Eoin. You of all people know he would never listen to me.'

There was silence. The two men glared at each other. Finally, as Innes was about to turn away, Eoin spoke. 'It's true,' he said grudgingly. 'I did blame you, and it was wrong of me. You've every bit as much right to choose your life as the next man, and it's obvious from the look of you that the life you've chosen suits you well. You're a rich man. A successful one.'

'Much good my successes will do me here. I know nothing about sheep, and certainly not enough to go clearing my lands to bring them in.'

'So you've heard that rumour, then?'

'And I'd be happy if you'd deny it for me.'

'I'll be delighted to, if it's the truth.' Eoin kicked at the ground. 'They do blame you, as I did. It's not fair, but that's how it is. Your father never got over Malcolm, and you're right, it was as if he was deliberately letting the place go to spite you. They think you should have put Strone Bridge first. They think if you'd have come back, you could have stopped him, so the longer you stayed away, and the worse it got, the more they blamed you.'

'Eoin, he wouldn't have listened to me. If I'd come back while he was alive I'd have ended up murdering him. Or more likely, he'd have murdered me.' Innes looked grimly at the cross. 'You know what he was like. I was the second son. He wanted me to study the law in Edinburgh, for goodness' sake! I was to be the family lackey.'

Eoin gave a bark of laughter. 'I'll admit, that was never on the cards.'

'No, but you know how hard I tried to do things his way—or more precisely, how hard I tried to make him see things my way. He couldn't care less about me. All he cared about was shaping my brother for the next laird in his own image, but he would not let me shape myself. I tried, but I was always going to leave. And when Malcolm— When it happened— How can you seriously think that would make me more likely to stay here?'

Eoin shook his head. 'But you could have come back, at least to visit,' he said stubbornly. 'You would have seen how things were going. Gradual it was. I didn't notice at first. And then— Well, like I said, I thought you deserved it. That was wrong of me. It's why I've been avoiding you. You're not the only one who feels guilty, Innes. I should have done something. I'm sorry. I should have done something, and now it's far too late. I truly am sorry.'

He held out his hand. Hesitating only a moment, Innes gripped it. 'I'm here now,' he said, 'and I need your help.'

Eoin nodded, returning the grip equally painfully. They sat together in silence on the stone bench. 'I did write,' Innes said eventually. 'Only once, but I did write to my father.'

'I didn't know that,' Eoin said. 'Mhairi would surely have told me, so she can't have known, either.'

'Why should she?'

Eoin looked surprised. 'She was his wife in all but name.' He laughed. 'You did not know?'

'No— I— No.' Innes shook his head in astonishment. 'He left no provision for her in his will.'

'Oh, he took care of that years ago. There's an annuity, you'll probably not have noticed it yet unless you've gone through the accounts, and she owns the farm over at Cairndow.'

'Then what the devil is she doing working for me when she does not have to?'

'Innes, for someone so far-sighted, you can be awfully blind. She's looking out for you. She's about the only one who is. She was ever on your side, you know, it's the one thing she and the laird had words about, but even she thinks you should have come back. I'm not saying it's right, I'm saying that's how it is.'

'I'm here now. Why can't they see that as a step in the right direction?'

'Maybe because they're wondering how long it will be before you go again.' Eoin got to his feet. 'Think about it from their point of view, Innes. The laird obviously believed he would be the last, else he would not have been so destructive.'

'He obviously thought I'd come back here simply to rid myself of the place. His will specifies I must remain here a year,' Innes conceded.

'The auld bugger obviously hoped being here would change your mind. Will you?'

Innes shook his head. 'I haven't a clue what I'm going to do,' he admitted ruefully, 'but I don't want to sell. I've spent every day, since I got off that boat of yours, going round the lands, making endless lists of things that need to be done.'

Eoin laughed. 'People think you've been sizing up the assets to sell.'

'For heaven's sake, why did no one tell me that?'

'Why didn't you say anything yourself, tell people your plans?'

Innes shook his head. 'Because I don't know what they are yet.'

'This is not one of your projects, where you have to have your blueprints and your costs and—I don't know—your list of materials all sorted out before you make your bid, Innes. Plans change, we all know that, but people would like to hear that they exist. They'd like to know you're not going to sell the roof over their heads.' Eoin got to his feet. 'I'm glad we talked. It's been eating away at me, the way we were when you arrived.'

This time it was Innes who held out his hand. 'It is good to see you, Eoin. I've not missed this place, but I've missed you. I would value your input to what needs done.'

'You know you have only to ask.'

'I wouldn't have, if it were not for Ainsley. She is the one who pushed me into this.'

Eoin smiled. 'Then I owe her. I look forward to meeting her properly.'

'You will do soon. She's planning a Rescinding.' Innes shook his head. 'Don't ask, because I'm not quite sure what it is myself, save that it will involve everyone.'

'Then I hope you will make sure not to let the water of life run dry. I must go, but we'll talk again.'

Innes watched his friend walk away. He felt as if his mind had been put through a washtub and then a mangle. Striding along the path that led round the front of the castle, he spotted the ramshackle pier and came to a sudden halt. Here was something he could do, and it was something, moreover, that Strone Bridge urgently needed, for it would allow paddle steamers to dock. He couldn't understand why he hadn't thought of it before. Vastly relieved to be able to focus on a project that was entirely within his control, Innes made his way down to the bay and began a survey of the jetty with the critical eye of the engineer it had cost him and, it seemed, the people of Strone Bridge, so much to become.

Dear Madame Hera,
I am a twenty-eight-year-old woman, married with two small children and absolutely bored stiff. My husband is a wealthy man and insists that our house is taken care of by servants and our children by a nanny, but this leaves me with nothing to do. I try to count my blessings, but even that occupation has become tedious. One of my friends suggested taking a lover would amply occupy my free afternoons, but lying convincingly is not one of my accomplishments. What shall I do?
Yours sincerely, Mrs A

Ainsley smiled to herself as she read this missive. Many of Madame Hera's correspondents complained of boredom, though none had suggested this novel answer. 'Take charge,' Ainsley wrote, 'of your children, of your housework, of your life!' She put the pen down, frowning. Mrs A's husband was doing exactly what was expected of him. More, in fact, than many could or would. Mrs A's friends might well even envy her. If Mrs A were to dismiss the nanny, or take over the housework, her husband would most likely be insulted. Or offended.

Ainsley looked at the clock. It was gone two. Innes had left before breakfast this morning, and she had not seen him since. Was he avoiding her? In the days since he had agreed to hold the Rescinding ceremony, he had continued with his visits to various farms and tenants, his poring over documents late into the night. True, she too had been very busy—too busy, in fact, to have any time to devote to anything else, but still, the niggling feeling that she was being pushed to one side would not go away.

With a sigh of frustration, Ainsley pushed Madame Hera's half-finished letter to one side and picked up the heavy bunch of castle keys from the desk, intending to consult the tome she had now christened the *Drummond Self-Help Manual* in the library once more, before taking another look at the Great Hall. Outside, as ever, it was blowy. There were several fishing boats in the bay. She paused to drink in her favourite view and spotted a figure down on the pier. Black coat with long skirts birling in the breeze. Long boots. All the Strone Bridge men wore trews and fishing jumpers or short tweed jackets. Tucking the keys into her pocket be-

side the notebook and pencil she had brought, Ainsley
began to pick her way carefully down the steep path.

The tide was far enough out for Innes to have clam-
bered down underneath the pier when she arrived.
'What on earth are you doing?' she asked, peering
through one of the planks down at him.

'I was inspecting the struts,' he said, looking up
at her, 'but now that you're here, there's a much nicer
view.'

'Innes!' Scandalised, laughing, she clutched her
skirts tightly around her.

Laughing, he appeared a few moments later on the
beach, climbing up the ancient wooden supports of
the pier fluidly. 'Do you always match your garters
to your gown?'

'What kind of question is that?'

'One you needn't answer if you don't want to, I'm
happy to imagine.' Innes picked a long strand of seaweed from the skirts of his coat and threw it on to the
beach. 'I'm going to have this thing rebuilt.'

'Of course you are! I wonder you didn't think of it
before.'

'Couldn't see the wood for the trees,' Innes said
wryly. 'I don't suppose you've got a pencil and a bit of
paper with you?'

Ainsley delved into her pocket and pulled out the
notebook and pencil. 'Here, I was on my way to the
castle when I saw you.'

'How are the arrangements progressing?'

She was about to launch into a stream of detail, but
stopped herself, giving Innes a dismissive shrug instead. 'Nothing for you to worry about,' she said.

He had been scribbling something in her notebook, but he looked up at the change in her tone. 'I thought you wanted to take this on—have you changed your mind?'

'No.'

'Is it too much? Do you need help?'

'No, I told you, there's nothing for you to worry about. It's not your problem.'

Frowning, Innes stuck her pencil behind his ear. 'Aye, that was it. *It's not your problem.* I remember now, that's what set you off before.'

'I don't know what you're implying, but...'

'Actually, it's what you're implying, Ainsley,' he exclaimed. 'I'm not shutting you out deliberately. I thought we were dividing and conquering, not just dividing, for heaven's sake. Once and for all, I'm not the man you married, so stop judging me as if I am.'

She wrapped her arms tightly around herself. 'I know you're not.'

'Then what are you accusing me of?'

'Nothing.' She bit her lip. 'You don't talk to me. You don't value my opinion.'

'Well, that's where you're wrong. Do you know what I was doing this morning? No, of course you don't, for I didn't tell you—and before you berate me for that, I didn't tell you because I wasn't sure he'd come.'

'Who?'

'Eoin.'

Her latent anger left her. Ainsley smiled. 'You've spoken to Eoin?'

'I have. I met him at the chapel.'

'And?'

Innes laughed nervously. 'And it was difficult.'

He was clearly uncomfortable. If she did not press him, he would leave it at that. She was pleased, no, more than pleased, that he had taken her advice, though it would most likely result in her further exclusion from matters of the lands. 'Has Eoin agreed to help you?' Ainsley asked carefully.

'He has.'

Innes was staring down at his notes, but she was not fooled. 'And you've made your peace?' Ainsley persisted.

'We've agreed to disagree.' Finally, Innes met her gaze. 'He thinks I should have come back sooner. Though he understands why I left, he doesn't understand why I stayed away. Though he knows fine that if I'd come back, my father and I would have done nothing but argue, and my father would have carried on down whatever path he'd chosen regardless, still Eoin thinks I should have tried.'

'That's ridiculous. Then you would have both been miserable. Besides, you had no cause to think that your father would choose this path of destruction,' Ainsley said fiercely. 'You told me yourself, he was a good laird.'

'Aye, well, it seems you're the only person to see it my way,' Innes said despondently.

She put her hand on his arm. 'You brought me here so you'd have someone on your side.'

'And I've done my damnedest to push you away since we arrived.' He smiled ruefully down at her. 'I'm sorry. I did warn you. You need to speak up more.'

She flinched. 'I know.'

Innes cursed under his breath. 'That was unfair of me.' He kissed her fingertips. 'This marriage business,

I'm not very good at it, I'm afraid. I'm too used to being on my own.'

'That's one thing you need to remember. You're not alone. May I see?' she asked, pointing at the notebook.

Innes had made several small sketches. He began to talk as he showed them to her, of tides, about the advantages of wood over stone, of angles and reinforcing. She nodded and listened, though she understood about a quarter of what he said, content to hear his voice full of enthusiasm, to watch the way he ran the pencil through his hair, reminded of the way Felicity did something very similar.

'That's quite enough,' he said eventually, closing the notebook. 'You're probably bored to death.'

'No. I didn't follow much of it, but it wasn't boring.'

Innes laughed, putting his arm around her.

'Do you think you'll be ready to announce the new pier after the Rescinding?' she asked. 'Perhaps you could show them a drawing. There's three weeks, would there be time?'

'I don't see why not. I could do the preliminary survey myself. It's what my trade is after all.'

Ainsley beamed up at him. 'If all the villagers and tenants see what a clever man you are, then perhaps they'll understand why you had to leave.'

'Atonement?'

'No, you've nothing to atone for. It is a gift. A symbol of the modern world brought to Strone Bridge by their modern laird.'

Innes laughed. 'I can just about hear my father turning in his grave from here.'

'Good.'

He pulled her closer. 'I saw it this morning at the

chapel. The grave I mean, and yes, it was for the first time. I could see you just about chewing your tongue off trying not to ask. Eoin told me about the funeral. It seems I have Mhairi to thank for doing things properly.'

'We have a lot to thank Mhairi for,' Ainsley agreed, enjoying the warmth of his body, the view, the salty tang of the air. 'She's at one with Eoin and everyone else in thinking that you should have come back here earlier, but now you're here, she's of the opinion that you should be given a chance.'

'That's big of her. Mhairi was my father's mistress,' Innes said.

Ainsley jerked her head up to look at him. 'Mhairi! Your father's mistress! Good grief. Are you sure?'

'Eoin told me.' Innes shook his head. 'I still can't believe it. He thought I knew. It seems everyone else does.'

'But—did he leave her anything in his will? You have not mentioned...'

'No. According to Eoin, he'd already made provision. A farm, an annuity. She did not need to stay on at the castle when he died.'

'But she did, so she must have wanted to. How very—surprising. It's funny, when I was talking to her over breakfast yesterday morning, I was thinking that she was an attractive woman and wondering why she had not married. There is something about her. Her mouth, I think. It's very sensual.'

'I believe I've said something similar to you.' Innes pulled her back towards him, tipping up her face. 'Infinitely kissable, that is what your mouth is, and if you don't mind...'

'I don't.'

'Good,' Innes said, and kissed her.

They took the path back up to the castle together. While the track used by the cart wound its serpentine way upwards, the footpath was a sheer climb. Out of breath at the top, Ainsley stood with her chest heaving. 'I don't suppose your engineering skills can come up with a solution for that,' she said.

'I will have my surveyor take a look,' Innes said. 'See if it can be widened, maybe change some of the angles so they're not so sharp. That way we can get bigger vehicles down to collect supplies.'

'And steamer passengers,' Ainsley said. 'Then you can build a tea pavilion up here on the terrace, where the view is best. Although there would be no need to build anything new if you set up a tearoom in that lovely drawing room. Then Mhairi could show the excursionists around the castle for a sixpence. She tells those ghost stories much better than you do, and she has lots more. There was one about a grey lady in the kitchens that gave me goosebumps.'

They began to walk together up to the castle. 'Mhairi's mother was the village fey wife when I was wee. A witch, though a good one, of course.'

'Better and better. She could make up some potions. You could sell them in the teashop. And some of the local tweed, too,' Ainsley said, handing Innes the keys to the main door, for they were going to inspect the Great Hall together. 'Before you know it, Strone Bridge will be so famous that the steamers will be fighting to berth at this new pier of yours.'

Innes paused in the act of unlocking the door. 'You're not being serious?'

She had forgotten, in her enthusiasm, how he felt about the place. Ainsley's smile faded. 'Don't you think it's a good idea?'

'I think it's a ridiculous idea. Besides the fact that I have no intentions of wasting my fortune having the place made habitable, it's a monstrosity—no one in their right mind would pay to see it.'

'Ridiculous.' She swallowed the lump that had appeared in her throat.

Innes looked immediately contrite. 'Don't take it like that, I didn't mean— It's not the idea. It's the place.'

'Why do you hate it so much? It's your home.'

'No. I could never live here.' He shuddered. 'There are more ghosts here than even Mhairi knows of.'

They were in the courtyard. Ainsley followed his gaze to the tower that stood at the centre. A huge bird of prey circled the parapet. She, too, shuddered, not because she thought it an omen, but at the look on Innes's face. She'd thought she was beginning to understand him, but now she was not so sure. That bleak expression could not merely be attributed to feelings of inadequacy or resentment. There was a reason beyond his quarrel with his father for Innes's absence from this place for fourteen long years. Ghosts. Who would have thought such a confident, practical man as Innes would believe in them, but he very obviously did. Something in his past haunted him. Something here, in this castle.

Above the tower, the sky was empty now. 'Come on,' Ainsley said, slipping her hand into Innes's arm. 'Let's go inside.'

She led him through to the Great Hall, their feet echoing on the stone flags. Innes seemed to have shaken off his black mood, and was now wandering around, sounding panelling, looking up with a worried frown at the high beams. 'I'll get Robert, my surveyor, to take a look at this while he's here. He'll be able to tell me if there are any structural problems.'

He said it hopefully, no doubt thinking that structural problems would give him the excuse to pull the place down. The castle seemed sound enough to her, no smell of damp, no sign of rot, but she was willing to admit she knew nothing about it.

Watching him out of the corner of her eye, Ainsley got on with her own measurements. 'I think we'll have to plan to feed about two hundred, including bairns,' she said. 'Mhairi is overseeing the work in the kitchens. I reckon we'll need to light the fires a few days in advance, once the chimneys are swept.' She scribbled in her notebook, which she had reclaimed from Innes, and began to tick items off from her list. Quickly absorbed in her task, she was struggling to pull the holland covers from what she assumed must be the laird's chair when Innes came to her aid.

'Let me,' he said.

A cloud of dust flew up, making them both choke. 'Good heavens, it's like a throne.'

Innes laughed. 'Now you can get some idea of the esteem in which the lairds of Strone Bridge have held themselves.'

Ainsley sat down on the chair. It was so high her feet didn't touch the ground. 'Mhairi would have a fit if she could see me. I'm probably bringing any amount of curses down on myself for daring to occupy the laird's seat.'

'I'm the laird now, and I'd be more than happy for you to occupy my seat.'

'Innes!' He was smiling down at her in a way that made her heart flutter. 'I don't know what you mean by that, but I am sure it is something utterly scurrilous.'

'Scandalous, not scurrilous.' He pulled her to her feet and into his arms. 'Want to find out?'

'Do you even know yourself?'

He laughed. 'No, but I am certain of one thing. It starts with a kiss,' he said, and suited action to words.

The second kiss of the day, and it picked up where the first had left off on the cold pier. Just a kiss at first, his hands on her shoulders, his mouth warm, soft. Then his hands slid down to cup her bottom, pulling her closer, and she twined hers around his neck, reaching up, and his tongue licked into her mouth, and heat flared.

He kissed her. She kissed him back, refusing to let herself think about what she was doing, concentrating her mind on the taste of him, and the smell of him, and the way he felt. The breadth of his shoulders. Her hands smoothing down his coat to the tautness of his buttocks, her fingers curling into him to tug him closer, wanting the shivery thrill of his arousal pressed into her belly.

Hard. Not just there, but all of him, hard muscle, tensed, powerful. She pressed into him, her eyes tight shut, her mouth open to him, her tongue touching his, surrendering to the galloping of her pulses, the flush of heat, the tingle in her breasts. Kissing. Her hands stroking, under the skirts of his coat now, on the leather of his breeches.

His hands were not moving. She wanted them to move. Took a moment to remember the last time, and opened her eyes to whisper to him, 'It's fine. I am— I won't.'

'Tell me,' he said then. 'What am I to do?'

She shook her head. 'Can't,' she mumbled, embarrassed.

He kissed her slowly, deeply. 'Tell me, Ainsley,' he said.

She was losing it, the heat, the shivery feeling, but not the desire. John had never asked what she wanted. Despite all the vague advice Madame Hera doled out about connubial bliss and mutual satisfaction, she had neither the experience nor knowledge of either. 'I don't know,' Ainsley said, sounding petulant, feeling frustrated. *You do it*, was what she wanted to say.

'You do know,' Innes insisted.

He kissed her again. He cupped her face, forcing her to meet his eyes. His own were not mocking, not cruel. Dark blue, slumberous. Colour on his cheeks. Passion, not anger or shame, though it was being held in check. She realised why, with a little shock, remembered how she had been the other night. 'I don't know what to say,' she said.

'Tell me where you feel it when I kiss you,' he said, putting his hand in hers, kissing her. 'Tell me where it makes you want me to touch you.'

'Here,' she said, putting his hand on her breast.

His hand covered the soft swell. Her nipple hardened. She caught her breath as he squeezed her lightly through the layers of her gown and her corsets. 'Like this?' he asked, and she nodded. He kissed her neck, her throat, still stoking, kneading, making her nipple ache for more, then turned his attention to the other breast, and she caught her breath again.

'You like that?' Innes said.

His thumb circled her taut nipple. 'Yes.'

'And that?'

Her other nipple. 'Yes.'

'What else?'

That smile of his. His hands teasing her. She wanted his hands on her skin. His mouth on her nipple. The thought shocked her and excited her and terrified her. Her breasts were so small. John had always said— But she was not going to think about John. And Innes had said— What had Innes said?

He was kissing her neck again, her throat again. And her mouth again. 'Ask me,' he whispered, nibbling on the lobe of her ear. 'Ask me to kiss you. Here,' he said, cupping her breast. 'Ask me to taste you. Tell me what you want, Ainsley. I want to please you. Tell me.'

'I want—I want you to kiss me. Here,' she said, putting her hand over his. 'I want you to— Innes, I want you not to be disappointed.'

'Ainsley, it is not possible. I absolutely assure you that I won't be disappointed,' Innes said, loosening her cloak and turning her around. Kissing the back of her neck, he began to loosen the buttons of her gown, just enough to slide the bodice down her arms. His hands covered her breasts, his body pressed into her back. She could feel his hard, rigid length against the swell of her bottom.

'You see,' he said, nuzzling the nape of her neck. 'You feel what you are doing to me?'

She wriggled, arching her back so that he pressed closer. Innes moaned, and she laughed, a soft, sensual sound deep in her throat, for it was potent, the effect she had on his potency, and it gave her a burst of confidence. 'Touch me,' she said, 'I want you to touch me. Your hands. Your mouth. On me.'

'It will be my pleasure.' He undid the knot of her stays, then turned her round. 'And yours, I hope.'

He dipped his head and kissed the swell of her breasts above her corset. His tongue licked into the valley between them, kissing, his lips soft on her skin. He loosened her stays and freed her breasts, cupping them, one in each hand. Her nipples were dark pink, tight. Innes's eyes were dark with excitement. 'I told you,' he said with a wicked smile. 'I told you.'

He dipped his head and took her nipple in his mouth and sucked. She jerked, the drag of sensation connecting directly with the growing tightness between her legs. He sucked again, slowly, and it was like the tightening of a cord. He kissed her. He traced the shape of her breast with his tongue and kissed his way over to the other one. Sucking. Dragging. She moaned. Sucking. Tension. She said his name in a voice she hardly recognised.

'What?' he asked, sounding just as ragged. 'Tell me what you want.'

'I can't.'

More sucking. Nipping. She clutched at his shoulders, for her knees had begun to shake. 'Tell me,' Innes insisted.

She felt as if her insides were coiling. She was so hot, and the heat was concentrated between her legs. There had been echoes of this before. She had forgotten that, but it had been further away, not like this, not so close. 'I don't know,' she said, frustration making her voice tense, her fingers digging deep into his shoulders. 'Innes, I really don't know.'

She thought he would stop. Or he would tell her what it was. That he would give her the words. That he would simply act. But he did none of those things. He smiled at her, his mouth curling in a way that made her insides tighten even more. 'Oh, I think you do,' he said.

His hand slid down, between her legs, and curled into her, through her gown. Instinctively she tilted up. 'Yes,' she said. 'Yes, I do.'

He caressed her, the flat of his palm against her skirts, her skirts and petticoats flattened, rubbing into the heat between her legs, and she realised that was what she wanted. 'More,' she said, helping him, arching her spine. 'More. No, less—no skirts.'

She pulled up her gown, her petticoats, shamelessly, not caring now, and put his hand underneath. Innes groaned. She pulled his face to hers and kissed him desperately. He groaned again. 'Innes,' she said, 'Innes I want— I think I want— Innes, for goodness' sake.'

He cupped her again, between her legs, only this time there was only the thin linen of her pantaloons between her and his hand. She was throbbing. There was a hard knot of her throbbing against his hand. And then he began to stroke her and the knot tightened, and throbbed, contracted and she thought she wouldn't be able to bear it, and for a few seconds she felt as if she were hovering, quivering, and then it broke, pulsing, the most delightful pulsing, making her cry out in pleasure, over and over, until it slowed, stopped, and she clung to him, her hair falling down her shoulders, panting, utterly abandoned, and for the first time in her life, utterly spent.

'I didn't know,' she said simply to Innes when she finally managed to let go her grip on him, surprised at her utter lack of embarrassment.

'Then I'm honoured.'

'Palpitations. That is how one woman described it to Madame Hera in a letter I read yesterday. "He does not give me the palpitations I can give myself."' Ainsley covered her mouth, her eyes wide. 'Good grief, does that mean that she...?'

'I reckon it does.'

She laughed. 'It is a whole new world. I thought the woman was talking about some sort of nervous condition. It's as well I've not replied yet.'

'I look forward to reading your reply.'

He was looking distinctly uncomfortable as he tried to arrange his coat around the very obvious swelling in his trousers. Catching Ainsley's eye, he blushed faintly. 'It's at times like this I can see the merit of a kilt.'

Were there rules that applied to this sort of situation? 'Should I do something to—to relieve you?' she blurted out, then flushed bright red. She sounded as if she was offering to bathe his wounds and not—not... She made a helpless gesture. 'I don't know the—the form.'

Innes burst out laughing. 'This is not a sport! Oh, don't go all prickly, I didn't mean— Ainsley, I would love you to *relieve* me, but there is no need. Well, there is, but I will— It will go away if we talk of something else.' He stroked her tangle of hair back from her face, his smile gentling. 'Your pleasure was very much mine, I assure you.'

Was he merely being nice? Polite? She eyed him dubiously. She had always suspected there was something missing even in the early days of her marriage before John began to find her body so repellent, but she had always been under the apprehension that the main event, so to speak, was a man's pleasure. Not that John had taken much pleasure latterly. A chore. Then a failure. Though he had not seemed to have any such problems alone. She shuddered, still mortified by that discovery.

'Ainsley, what is it?'

She was about to shake her head, but then she paused. 'Palpitations. The woman who wrote to Madame Hera, she gives them to herself because her husband does not—cannot. There is something wrong with her husband, then, is there not?'

'Ignorance, or perhaps he's just selfish. Is this another of Madame's problems?'

'It made me wonder,' Ainsley said, ignoring this question. 'Would a man—a husband— If he cannot, with his wife, I mean, but he can—you know, do that…' She swallowed. She did know the words for this, they had been thrown in her face. 'Bring pleasure to himself. If he can do that for himself, but he can't with his wife, then there is something wrong with his wife, isn't there?'

Innes looked at her strangely. 'I thought only women wrote to you?'

Ainsley managed a noncommittal shrug.

'Do you mean can't or won't?'

Were they the same thing? She forced herself to

think back. No. John had tried, and it had shamed him. 'Can't,' Ainsley said sadly.

He touched her cheek gently. 'Poor wife. And poor husband. Though I'd say the problem was most definitely his.'

Chapter Seven

August 1840, three weeks later

Felicity threw herself down on the bed, careless of the creases it would put in the emerald-green gown she wore for the Rescinding ceremony. 'So tell me, since this looks like the only opportunity I'll have to get you to myself, how are you enjoying married life?'

Ainsley, still in the woollen wrapper she had donned after her bath, was perched on a stool in front of the dressing table. Her hair ought to be curled, but it would take for ever, and in the breeze that would no doubt be blowing outside, it would probably be straight again by the time they reached the church. 'We're not really married. I like it a lot better than my real marriage was.'

'I'm sorry I couldn't get here until yesterday. I've been so busy. I've barely had a chance to talk to your Mr Drummond.'

'I've barely had a chance myself lately, there's been so much to do to get this ceremony organised, and when Innes has not been closeted with Eoin talking agriculture, he's been with his surveyor, Robert Alexander, talking engineering. They're finalising the plans for a new pier and road. Mr Alexander has made a model of the pier and the road out of paper and paste. It is quite realistic. Innes will unveil it today, after the Rescinding.' Ainsley picked up her brush but made no attempt to apply it. 'So I suppose it's no surprise that we've been like ships that pass in the night.'

'I'd have thought you'd be happy about that, not having to live in his pocket.'

'I am. I don't want to. You're right.' Ainsley put the brush down and picked up a comb.

'You don't sound very convincing. Please don't tell me you're falling in love with the man.'

'That is one mistake I won't make twice,' Ainsley said scornfully, 'and even if I did—which I assure you I won't—Innes has made it very clear that he will not.'

Felicity raised her brows. 'Has he, now? Why not?'

'He likes his independence too much.'

'Marriage makes no difference to independence for a man, they carry on just as they please, regardless of the little woman waiting at home. It is only a wife who is shackled by matrimony.'

'You sound so bitter, Felicity.'

'Now, that is definitely a case of the pot calling the kettle black.'

Ainsley nodded. 'Yes, but I have reason to be bitter. My marriage—you know what it was like.'

'I know what it did to you, even though you refused to confide the particulars.' Felicity's smile was twisted. 'And as you must have guessed, I know enough, from being the other woman, not to want to be the wife. But that is over now.'

'You mean your—your…'

'*Affaire*, why not call it what it was.'

'Why did you not say?'

'Because I'm ashamed, and because it has taken up quite enough of my life for me to wish to grant it any more,' Felicity said bracingly. 'I read Madame Hera's latest batch of correspondence last night, by the light of a candle that threatened to blow out in the gale that was howling through my bedchamber.'

Ainsley and Mhairi had been forced to put all their visitors up in the west wing of the castle, which had latterly been the old laird's quarters. 'I'm so sorry,' she said. 'Were you freezing?'

'I certainly don't fancy being here in the winter. Though Madame's correspondence heated me up,' Felicity said with a saucy smile. 'I assume that you and Mr Drummond have not been ships that passed each other every night.'

Ainsley flushed. 'Well, I know now that palpitations are not necessarily the prelude to a fainting attack,' she said. 'The rest you can deduce from Madame Hera's letters.'

'Does he know that you're writing them?'

'Yes. And before you ask, you were right. I owe you five pounds. He thought it was fun.' Ainsley's laughter faded. 'He made me realise that some of my advice has been— Well, frankly, not the best, Felicity. I don't mean because I've been forced to modify my language to avoid offence—'

'I did notice a tendency to use rather less euphemisms and rather more—shall we say colloquial terms, in those personal replies,' Felicity interjected. 'I take it those were Mr Drummond's phrases?'

'Do you think they are too much?'

'I think they make it impossible for the recipients to misunderstand. We shall see. I have found in this business that while people rarely praise, they are very quick to let you know when they're not happy. But I interrupted you. You were saying, about your advice…'

Ainsley finished combing her hair and began to pin it up in what she hoped would be a wind-resistant knot. 'Looking back over my replies since Madame Hera came into being, I realised my advice has often been—defensive? No, sometimes rather combative. I assumed, you see, that the women who write are in need of— That they need to stand up for themselves. Madame Hera is very belligerent. She sees marriage as a battlefield.'

'In many cases she's right.'

'Yes.' Ainsley turned away from the mirror to face her friend, her hair half-pinned. 'Madame Hera was born of war. She ought to have been called Madame Mars, or whatever the female equivalent is.'

'Athena. No, she is Greek.' Felicity shook her head impatiently. 'It doesn't matter. Go on.'

'I've been thinking about John a lot these past few weeks. I blamed him for everything. I hated him, in the end, for what he did to me, for the constant undermining and the—the other things. I was furious about the debts, and about the mess he left me in. Much of it was his fault, of course. He was weak and he was a spendthrift and he was completely gullible when it came to moneymaking schemes, but I wonder how different things would have been if, instead of blaming him and shutting him out, and setting off on my own vengeful path, I had shown him a little understanding.'

'None at all!' Felicity said scornfully. 'The man was

a useless profligate and you are better off by far without him.'

'Perhaps he would have been better off without me.'

'What do you mean?'

'When things started to go wrong, I didn't try very hard to make them right. Oh, I challenged him about the money—but not really with the conviction I thought I had at the time. I think—this is awful—but I think I *wanted* him to be in the wrong, more than I wanted to make things right between us.'

'Ainsley, he *was* in the wrong.'

'Yes, but so, too, was I. I would do things differently if I got the chance again.'

'But you are getting the chance again. Don't tell me it doesn't count because you're not really married, Ainsley, you know what I mean. I hope you're not letting Drummond walk all over you?'

'Not exactly. I don't think he deliberately excludes me, but he's not in the habit of including anyone in his life. I told you, he is very attached to his independence.'

'Blasted men,' Felicity said feelingly. Looking down at the little gold watch she always wore on a fob on her gown, she clapped her hand over her mouth in dismay. 'Ainsley, we've to be at the chapel for the start of proceedings in an hour and you haven't even done your hair. Turn round. Let me.' Jumping to her feet, she gathered up a handful of pins. 'You could come back to Edinburgh with me after this, you know.'

'Thank you, but no.' Ainsley met her friend's eyes in the mirror and smiled. 'It's good for me, being here at the moment. It's helped me think.'

'Don't think too hard, else you'll be turning that

John McBrayne into a saint, and that he was not,' Felicity said, pinning frantically.

'No, but I had turned him into a devil, and he wasn't that, either.'

'Hmm.' Felicity carried on pinning. 'I'm sorry I can't stay longer. You know how it is, being a female in a man's world. If I'm not back, they'll replace me.'

'It's fine. I know how important your job is to you. And to me. Madame Hera depends on you.'

'Madame Hera is becoming so popular that she doesn't need my support. There.' Felicity threw down the remainder of the pins. 'Let's get you into your gown.' She pulled the dress from its hanger and gave it a shake.

'I'm getting nervous,' Ainsley said as she stepped into it. 'I haven't thought about it until now. I've been too busy planning it, but it's a big thing, Felicity. It's really important for Innes that it goes well. I thought about asking Mhairi for a good luck spell, but asking her is probably bad luck. You've no idea how superstitious she can be.'

'The housekeeper?' Felicity was busy hooking the buttons on Ainsley's gown. 'Is she the witch?'

'Her mother was.'

'And she was the old laird's mistress, too, you tell me. You should ask her for a potion. You know, just to make sure that there are no consequences from the palpitations your husband is giving you.'

Ainsley's face fell. 'I don't think that will be necessary.'

'Oh, Ainsley, I'm so sorry. I didn't think.'

'It doesn't matter.' Ainsley managed to smile. 'Really. Are you done? May I look?' Ainsley turned towards the mirror and shook out her skirts.

'I do hope your Mr Drummond is making sure he takes appropriate measures.' Felicity gave her a grave look. 'You cannot take the risk.'

'There is no risk, and even if there were, I am very sure that the last thing Innes would risk is such a complication.' Seeing that her friend was about to question her further, Ainsley picked up her shawl. 'We should go.'

'Wait. I brought you something.' Felicity handed her a velvet-covered box. 'A belated wedding present. It's not much, but it's pretty.'

It was a gold pendant set with a tiny cluster of diamonds around an amethyst. Ainsley hugged her tightly. 'It's lovely. Thank you.' She hugged Felicity again, then handed her the necklace to fasten. She stared down at her left hand, with the simple gold band Innes had given her more than two months ago. 'Do you think I'll pass muster. As the laird's wife, I mean?' she asked anxiously. 'I don't want to let Innes down.'

'That is exactly the kind of talk I don't want to hear. You will do your best, and that's all you can do. The rest is up to him. He's lucky to have you, Ainsley. Am I permitted to wish you good luck, or is that bad luck?'

'I don't know, probably.'

'Then I will say what the actors say. Break a leg. But make sure that you do not break your heart.' Felicity cast a quick glance at the mirror. 'My hair. As usual. Give me just a minute, for that rather gorgeous man who brought me over in his rather rustic fishing boat yesterday is to be one of your escorts, and I'd like to look a little less ravaged than I did the last time he saw me.'

'You mean Eoin?'

'That's the one. I am to be one of your Mr Drummond's escorts in the walk to the chapel. He asked me last night.' Felicity grimaced. 'Two virgins, it's supposed to be. I hope my lack of maidenhead will not bring you bad luck.'

Ainsley choked. 'I think what matters is that you are unmarried. Shall we go?'

'Are you ready?'

Ainsley kissed her cheek. 'As I'll ever be,' she said.

Innes hadn't thought about the ceremony until he was walking to the church between his escorts, with what felt like the entire population of Strone Bridge behind him. He was putting on a show, that was all. It was just a daft tradition; it meant something to the people who would be attending, but nothing to him. Except he felt nervous, and it did matter, and realising that made him feel slightly sick, because that meant Strone Bridge had come to matter, and that complicated everything.

It was not raining, which Eoin had assured him was a good sign. From somewhere behind him came the skirl of the bagpipes. On one side of him Felicity, Ainsley's eccentric friend, picked her way along the path, sliding him what he could only describe as assessing glances every now and then. He wondered what Ainsley had told her. He doubted very much that this very self-assured and rather sultrily attractive woman fulfilled the criteria expected of his escort. Of Mhairi's niece Flora's qualifications, he had no doubt at all.

They arrived at the door of the church, and the crowd behind him filtered in to become the congregation. Begging a moment of privacy, Innes made his way alone to the Drummond Celtic cross, not to commune with the dead man so recently interred there, but the one whose corpse lay elsewhere. In a few moments, he was going to have to stand at that altar, in front of those people, and be blessed as the new laird. It should have been Malcolm standing there. If things had gone as they had been planned, as his brother had so desperately wanted them to, Malcolm would have been standing at that altar fourteen years ago beside Blanche, taking part in another ritual.

Blanche. He never allowed her name into his head. Until he'd come back to Strone Bridge, he rarely even allowed himself to think of Malcolm. Now, standing in front of the cross where Malcolm should have been buried, Innes felt overwhelmed with grief and regrets. If he could turn back time, make it all as it should be—Malcolm leading the Rescinding, Blanche at his side, and perhaps three or four bairns, too. Strone Bridge would be flourishing. The congregation would be celebrating.

'And you,' he hissed at the cross, 'you would have gone to your grave a damn sight happier, that's for sure. You never thought you'd see this day, any more than I did.'

Innes leaned his forehead on the cold stone and closed his eyes. If Malcolm could see what had happened to his precious lands, he'd be appalled. He could not bring his brother back, but he could do his damnedest to restore the lands to what they had been. 'No, I can do better,' Innes said to the stone. 'I will make them flourish, better than they have ever, and what's more, I'll do it my way.'

For better or for worse, he thought to himself, turning his back on the cross. The same words he'd said in front of another altar not so very long ago, with Ainsley by his side. For better or for worse, it looked as if he'd made up his mind to stay here, for the time being. He'd rather have Ainsley by his side than any other woman. 'For the time being, any road,' he muttered, squaring his shoulders and making his way towards the chapel.

She was waiting at the porch, with Eoin and Robert by her side. She looked so nervous as she made her way towards him, Innes was worried for a moment that she might actually faint. Her gown was of pale silk, embroidered with pink and blue flowers. The long puffed sleeves gave it a demure look, at odds with the ruffled neckline. She wore a pretty pendant he had not seen before.

Her hand, when he took it, was icy cold. Muttering an apology, Innes squeezed it reassuringly. Was she thinking as he was, how like a wedding this whole thing was turning out to be? Was she thinking back to the other time, when she had stood beside another man, in another church? It shouldn't bother him. He hadn't thought about it before, and wished he had not now. It shouldn't bother him, any more than the idea, which had only just occurred to him, that she would leave here soon. He might have committed to the place, but it had always been a temporary location for her. There would come a time when he'd be here alone. When things were clearer. They were very far from clear now. No need to think of that just yet.

Ainsley winced, and Innes immediately loosened

his grip. 'Ready?' he asked. She nodded. She put her arm in his and prepared to walk down the aisle with him, and Innes closed his mind to everything save playing his part.

Standing in the church porch, offering her cheek to be kissed by yet another well-wisher, Ainsley felt as if her smile was frozen to her face. The Drummond ring that Innes had placed on the middle finger of her right hand felt strange. It was apparently worn by every laird's wife. A rose-tinted diamond coincidentally almost the same colour as the pendant Felicity had given her, surrounded by a cluster of smaller stones, it was obviously an heirloom. She felt quite ambivalent about it, for there was bound to be some sort of curse attached to anyone who wore it under false pretences. She would ask Innes. No, she decided almost immediately, she would rather not know.

The last of the men kissed her cheek. The church door closed and the minister shook Innes's hand before heading along the path to join the rest of the guests at the castle. 'They can wait for us a bit,' Innes said when she made to follow him. 'I haven't even had the chance to tell you that you look lovely.'

'Don't be daft. There's no one watching.'

'I know. Why do you think I kept you here?' he asked, smiling down at her. 'I believe the laird has the right to kiss his lady.'

'You already have, at the end of the blessing.'

He laughed, that low, growling laugh that did things to her insides. 'That wasn't what I had in mind,' he said, and pulled her into his arms.

His kiss was gentle, reassuring. He held her tightly,

as if he, too, needed reassurance. Her poke bonnet bumped against his forehead, and they broke apart. 'I didn't think it would matter,' Innes said, running a hand through his carefully combed hair.

'Do you feel like a real laird now?'

She meant it lightly, but Innes took the question seriously. 'I feel as though I've made a promise to the place,' he said. 'I think— I don't know how I will manage it, but I owe it to Strone Bridge to restore it. Somehow.' He pulled her back into his arms. 'I know I was sceptical about the Rescinding, but I think it was a good idea, and it was your idea. So thank you.'

She was touched as well as gratified. Unwilling to show it, she looked down at the ring. 'Was this your mother's?'

'And my grandmother's and so on. Do you like it? Don't tell me you're worried that there's some sort of curse attached to it.'

She laughed. 'I don't appreciate having my mind read. I was worried that it would be bad luck to wear it, since I'm not really the laird's lady.'

'There's no need to worry, I promise you. Generations of Drummond men have married for the good of Strone Bridge before all else, and that's exactly what I've done,' Innes said. 'In our own way, we're carrying on a tradition. Drummonds don't marry for love.' His expression darkened. 'It's when they try to, that's when they become cursed.'

She wanted to ask him what he meant, but she was afraid, looking at his face. He could only be thinking of himself. It was so obvious; she couldn't believe she hadn't thought of it before. That was why he was so insistent he'd never fall in love. Because he already had, and it had come to nothing.

She felt slightly sick. She oughtn't to. The pair of them were even better matched than she had realised, both of them burned by that most revered of emotions. She should be relieved to finally understand. Actually, there was no cause for her to feel anything at all. Innes's heart was no concern of hers.

'We should go,' Innes said, dragging his mind back from whatever dark place he had gone to. 'I want to get the formal Rescinding out of the way before too much whisky had been taken. What is it? You look as if you've seen a ghost.'

Ainsley managed to smile. 'Just my husband, in his full Highland regalia, looking every bit the part of the laird. I have not told you how very handsome you look.'

He tucked her hand in his, smiling down at her wickedly, his black mood seemingly vanished. 'Do I live up to your expectations of a wild Highlander?'

Her own mood lightened. 'I don't know.' Ainsley gave him a teasing smile. 'It's a shame we have a party to attend, else I would say I was looking forward to finding out.'

A fire had been burning constantly in the huge hearth of the Great Hall for the past few days. The mantel was of carved oak set on two huge marble pillars, and the hearth itself was big enough to hold a massive log cut from a very old tree in one whole piece. The Great Hall was a long, narrow room done in the Elizabethan style, though it had been created less than a hundred years before. The walls were panelled to head height, then timbered and rendered, giving the impression of great age, as did the vaulted oak ceiling. Ainsley stood at the far end of the room, where a balconied recess had been formed with yet more oak, this time in the form of three arches rather like a rood screen.

The hall was full of people, very few of whom she recognised. Innes had not wanted anyone from his old life here. When Ainsley had enquired about inviting other local gentry, having heard the name Caldwell mentioned as the owners of the next estate, she thought he had flinched, though she could not be sure. 'We've enough to do, to win the hearts and minds of our own,' he'd said quickly. 'Let's keep it a Strone Bridge celebration.' Everyone present, save herself, Felicity and Robert Alexander had been born here, or had married someone who had been born here. Which for now included her, though she did not really count.

Innes was standing a few feet away, holding one of those intense conversations with his surveyor that seemed to require Robert Alexander to flap his arms about a lot. The model of the pier and the new road was to be revealed after the Rescinding. Mr Alexander was nervous. She could see that Innes was reassuring him.

The laird. Her husband, in his Highland dress, which he claimed to have worn just for her, though she knew he was only teasing. He had opted for the short jacket, and not the long, cloak-like plaid, of a dark wool that was fitted tight across his shoulders, the front cut in a curve, finishing at his neat waist. Under it, he wore a waistcoat and a white shirt. And below it, the kilt, a long length of wool folded into narrow pleats and held in place by a thick leather belt with a large silver buckle. When he turned, as he did now, granting her a delightful view of his rear, the pleats swung out. As she suspected, he had very shapely legs, not at all scrawny, but muscled. His long, knit hose covered what Mhairi called a fine calf, and Ainsley had to agree. There was a small jewelled dagger tucked into one of his hose, and another, longer dagger attached to his belt. The kilt stopped at his knee. He could not possibly be wearing undergarments.

He caught her looking at him and came to join her. 'I would very much like to ask you what you're think-ing,' he said softly into her ear, 'but if you told me, I reckon I'd have to carry you off and have my wicked Highland way with you, and we've a lot of ceremony to get through, unfortunately.'

'And a party to attend afterwards.'

'Actually, Eoin was just telling me that it's custom-ary for the laird and his lady to celebrate their new life alone.'

'I read nothing of that in the book.'

'It's known as the—the Bonding,' Innes said.

She bit her lip, trying not to laugh. 'You made that up.'

'It's one of the new traditions I'm thinking of es-tablishing.' Innes smiled one of his sinful smiles that made her feel as if she were blushing inside. 'What do you say?'

'I would certainly not wish to break with tradition on a night like this. And I would not wish all that effort you've made with your Highland dress to go to waste.'

His eyes darkened. She felt the flush inside her spreading. 'If it were not for the Rescinding, I would carry you off right now.'

'I have gone to an enormous effort to get this Rescinding organised, Laird. You are not going to spoil it for me.'

'No. I would not dream of it. I'm truly grateful, Ainsley.' He kissed her cheek. 'But just as soon as it's over, my lady...'

'I know. A Bonding! Whatever that entails.'

'Haven't you imagined it? I know I have. Lots of times.'

'Innes! Let us concentrate on one ceremony before we start discussing another.'

He laughed. 'Very well. I see your Miss Blair conferring with Eoin. Again. Is she spoken for?' Innes asked.

'She's wedded to her career,' Ainsley replied.

'Do you know, you have a way of pursing up your mouth just at one corner when you fib, as if you're trying to swallow whatever it is you're determined not to say.'

'I was not fibbing.'

'You weren't telling the truth, either.' Innes smiled down at her. 'I suspect your Felicity is a woman of many secrets.' Innes put his arm around her waist, pulling her into his side. 'I'm not really interested in Miss Blair's private life, nor indeed Eoin's. I'm more interested in our own. But first, it's time for the Rescinding. Are you ready?'

'What if I forget something?' Ainsley asked, suddenly panicked.

'You've made the whole thing go like a dream so far. Now all you have to do is to remember all the promises I make, lest I forget any. And I must forgive and forget.' Innes rolled his eyes. 'I cannot believe my father did this and meant it.'

* * *

The chair, like most of the Great Hall, was carved in oak and had been polished to a soft gleam. The canopy that covered it was of the same faded green velvet as the cushion. After handing Ainsley into the much simpler chair by his side, Innes sat down. He felt part foolish, part—good grief, surely not proud? No, but it was something close. The ghosts of his ancestors had got into his blood. Or having all those eyes on him had gone to his head. Or maybe it was this chair, and the hall, which was only ever used for formal occasions. His father's birthday had always been celebrated here. The annual party for the tenants and cotters. His and Malcolm's coming of age.

No. This was a time to look forward, not back. Innes jumped up. The room fell silent. He picked up the sword that lay at his feet, the wicked blade glittering. The sheath lay beside it. Carefully, he placed the sword inside the sheath, a signal of peace, and handed it to Eoin, who was once again playing the part of the nearest living blood relative. All of this was prescribed in the book that Ainsley had shown him. *The Customs and Ways of the Family Drummond of Strone Bridge*, it pompously declared itself in faded gold script. Mhairi had been insulted when he'd laughed. Ainsley had apologised on his behalf. Later, she'd teased him, calling it the *Drummond Self-Help Manual*. Now he was simply glad Ainsley had read it so carefully for him.

'Friends,' Innes said, 'I bid you welcome. Before we begin the ceremony, it is traditional to toast the departed.' He lifted the glass of whisky that lay ready, nodding to Ainsley to do the same, and waiting to make sure everyone watching had a glass. *'Slàinte!'* he said.

'To the old laird, my father. *Cha bhithidh a leithid ami riamh.* We'll never see his like again.' He drank, surprised to discover that the toast had not stuck in his craw quite as much as he'd thought it would. Perhaps it was because it was true, he thought to himself wryly. He was making sure of it.

Innes put his glass down. 'The laird has met his maker. With him must be buried all grudges, all debts, all quarrels. A forgiving and forgetting. A Rescinding. A new beginning. And I promise you,' he said, departing from his script, 'that it is not the case of sweeping the dirt out of one door and blowing it into the other. That is one change. The first, I hope of many. This Rescinding is an old tradition, but today it will be done in quite a new way. No recriminations. No half measures. No payback. That is my vow to you. Let us begin.'

He sat down heavily. Sweat trickled down his back. He never made speeches. The words, his words, had not been planned, but they were *his*, and he'd meant them. Scanning the room anxiously, he waited for the reaction. They were an inscrutable lot, the people of Strone Bridge. The lightest of touches on his hand, which was resting by the side of his chair, made him look over at Ainsley. 'Perfect,' she mouthed, and smiled at him. When she made to take her hand away, he captured it, twining his fingers in hers. He felt good.

Ainsley waited anxiously. Innes had been nervous making his speech. His palm was damp. He'd been treating the Rescinding almost as a joke, at the very least a mere formality, but when he spoke it was clear that he meant every word he said. Such a confident man, and such a successful one, she had assumed

speech-making came easily to him. It was oddly reassuring to discover it did not. She couldn't decide
whether she wanted there to be lots of petitioners or
few, but she was vastly relieved when the first came
forward, for none at all would have been a disaster.

The man was a tenant, and by the looks of him, one
of long standing. 'Mr Stewart,' Innes said, 'of Auchenlochan farm. What is it you wish from me?'

The old man, who had been gazing anxiously down
at his booted feet, straightened and looked Innes firmly
in the eye. 'I petition the laird to forgive two wrongs,'
he said. 'For my son, John Angus Stewart, who left
two quarters rent unpaid on Auchenlochan Beag farm
when he sailed for Canada. And for myself, for failing
to inform the laird that the rent was unpaid.' Mr Stewart looked over his shoulder at the rest of the room,
before turning back to Innes. 'The laird did raise the
rents far beyond the value of the farms, it is true, and
many of us here felt the injustice of that, but...' He
waved his hand, to silence the rumbles of agreement
emanating from behind him. 'But it was his right, and
those of us who took advantage of his failing to collect were wrong, and they should be saying so now,'
he finished pointedly.

Innes got to his feet, and said the words as specified in the Drummond manual. 'Angus Stewart of
Auchenlochan, and John Angus Stewart, who was of
Auchenlochan Beag, your petitions are granted, the
debt is Rescinded.'

Mr Stewart nodded, his lips pursed. Before he had
reached his wife, another man had come forward to
proclaim another unpaid rent, and after him another,
and another. Some went reluctantly, some resignedly,

some went in response to Crofter Stewart's beady-eyed stare, but they all went. The debts Innes was waiving amounted to a large sum of money. Ainsley couldn't understand the old laird—the man was something of a conundrum—putting rents sky-high on one hand, then failing to collect them on the other. Since Mhairi assured her the laird's mind had not wandered, she could only assume that it must have been severely warped. *Twisted.* That was a better word.

As Innes continued to forgive and forget, the Rescinding began to take on a lighter note. A woman admitted to burying a dog along with her husband in the graveyard of the Strone Bridge chapel. 'Though I know it is forbidden, but he always preferred that beast's company to mine, and the pair of them were that crabbit, I thought they would be happy together,' she declared, arms akimbo. Laughter greeted this confession, and Innes earned himself a fat kiss when he promised the dog and the master's mortal remains would not be torn asunder.

Whisky flowed, and wine, too, along with the strong local heather ale. Innes was preparing to end the ceremony when a man came forward whom Ainsley recognised as Mhairi's taciturn brother, the father of Flora, the pretty lass who had been one half of Innes's escort.

'Donald McIntosh of High Strone farm.' Expecting another case of rent arrears, Ainsley's mind was on the banquet, which would be needed to sop up some of the drink that had been taken. She was trying to catch Mhairi's eye, and was surprised to see the housekeeper stiffen, her gaze fixed on her brother.

'Your father did wrong by my sister for many years,' Donald McIntosh said.

'Dodds!' Mhairi protested, but her brother ignored her.

'The laird took my sister's innocence and spoilt her for any other man. He shamed my sister. He shamed my family.'

'Dodds!' Mhairi grabbed her brother by the arm, her face set. 'I loved the man, will you not understand that? He did not take anything from me.'

'Love! That cold-hearted, thrawn old bastard didn't love you. You were fit to warm his bed, but not fit to bear his name. You were his hoor, Mhairi.'

Hoor? Shocked, Ainsley realised he meant *whore*.

Mhairi paled, taking a staggering step back. 'It's true, he didn't love me, but I loved him. I don't care if that makes me his hoor, and I don't know what you think you're doing, standing here in front of the man's son. This is a celebration.'

'It's a Rescinding.' Donald McIntosh turned back towards Innes. 'I beg forgiveness for the curse I put upon your family.'

Along with almost everyone else in the room, Ainsley gasped. Almost everyone else. Felicity, she noticed, was looking fascinated rather than shocked. What Innes thought, she could not tell. 'What particular curse?' he asked.

'That the bloodline would fail.' Donald spoke not to Innes, but to his sister. 'I had the spell from our mother, though she made me swear not to use it.'

'No. *Màthair* would never have told *you* her magic, Dodds McIntosh. No fey wife worth her salt would have trusted a mere man.'

'You're wrong, Mhairi. Like me, she felt the shame that man brought on our family.'

Mhairi's mouth fell open. 'And now she is dead it cannot be retracted. What have you done?'

Donald stiffened. 'I am entitled to be forgiven.'

'And forgiven you shall be,' Innes said, breaking the tense silence. 'The potency of the Drummond men is legendary. I refuse to believe that any curse could interfere with it.'

The mood eased. Laughter once more echoed around the hall, and another supplicant shuffled forward. Stricken, Ainsley barely heard his petition. Until she came to Strone Bridge, she had not considered herself superstitious, but Mhairi's tireless efforts to appease the wee people and to keep the changelings at bay seemed to have infected her. By some terrible quirk of fate, Dodds McIntosh's curse had come true. Ainsley felt doubly cursed.

Faintly, she was aware of Innes bringing proceedings to a close. Mechanically, she got to her feet while he said the final words. It didn't matter, she told herself. It would matter if she and Innes were truly married, but they were not. Innes did not want a child. He'd told her so on that very first day, hadn't he? She tried to remember his precise words. No, he'd said he didn't want a wife. *One must necessarily precede the other*, that was what he had said. But she was his wife. And she could not— But she wasn't really his wife. She could not let him down in this most basic of things, because he did not require it of her. She clung to this, and told herself it was a comfort.

'I declare the Rescinding complete, the door closed on the old and open on the new,' Innes was saying. 'It's time to celebrate. Mr Alexander here will fill you all in on the details of our plans for a new pier and a new road, too. There is food and drink aplenty to be had, but first, and most important, one last toast.' Innes lifted his glass and turned towards Ainsley. 'To my lady wife, who made this day possible. I thank you. I could not have done this without you.'

He kissed her full on the lips; the guests roared their approval and Ainsley's heart swelled with pride. She had done this. She had proved something by doing this. For the moment, at least, nothing else mattered.

Chapter Eight

It was dark, but the party was only just hotting up, thanks to the fiddlers. A bundle of bairns slept snuggled together like a litter of puppies, some of them still clutching their sugar candy. In the recess at the far end of the room, in front of Robert Alexander's model of the pier, Mhairi was holding court with a group of local wives. Miss Blair was dancing a wild reel with Eoin. This, Innes decided, was as good a time as any for them to make their getaway unobserved.

The night air was cool. He wrapped a soft shawl around Ainsley's shoulders and led her down to her favourite spot, overlooking the Kyles. Above them, the stars formed a carpet of twinkling lights in the unusually clear sky. 'It went well, didn't it?' she asked. 'Save for that curse Mhairi's brother made.'

'Stupid man. If he really was so ashamed, he should have done something about it when my father was alive.'

'From what you've told me about your father, Mr McIntosh would then have found himself homeless.'

Innes considered this for a few moments. 'No. More

likely my father despised Dodds McIntosh for not challenging him. His sense of honour was twisted, but he did have one.'

'Perhaps he did love Mhairi, in his own way.'

'My father never loved anyone, save himself.'

'Not even your brother?'

Ainsley spoke so tentatively, Innes could not but realise she knew perfectly well how sensitive was the subject. He hesitated on the brink of a dismissive shrug, but she had done so much for him today, he felt he wanted to give her something back. 'You're thinking that my father's wilful neglect of Strone Bridge is evidence of his grief for my brother, is that it?'

'Yes.'

'I'm not so sure. My brother loved this place. If my father really cared, why would he destroy the thing Malcolm loved the most? Besides, Eoin said it was a gradual thing, the neglect.'

'A slow realisation of what he'd lost?'

Innes shook his head. 'A slow realisation that I was not coming back, more like. He destroyed it so that I would be left with nothing.'

'And you are determined to prove him wrong?'

'I'd prefer to say that I'm determined to put things right.'

'How will you do that?'

'I have no idea, and at the moment I have better things to think about.'

He kissed her in the moonlight, underneath the stars, to the accompaniment of the scrape of fiddles and the stomping of feet in the distance. She was not really his wife, but she understood him in a way that no one else did. He kissed her, telling her with his lips and his tongue and his hands not only of his desire, but that he wanted her here, like this.

'Are you sure someone won't come chasing after us to come back to the party?' Ainsley whispered.

'If they do, I'll tell them they're in danger of incurring a year of bad luck for interfering with the ancient and revered tradition of the Bonding,' Innes replied.

He felt the soft tremor of her laughter. 'Will you run up a special flag to declare it over, in the morning?'

'I haven't thought that far ahead. You know that you can change your mind if you don't want to do this, don't you? You must be tired.'

'I'm not the least bit tired, and I don't want to change my mind,' she answered. 'I think we've waited long enough.'

He kissed her again. She tasted so sweet. Her skin was luminous in the moonlight, her eyes dark. He kissed her, and she wrapped herself around him and kissed him back, and their kisses moved from sweet to urgent. Panting, Innes tore his mouth from hers. 'I meant it,' he said. 'I am not expecting you to— We don't have to...'

'But you want to?' she asked, with that smile of hers that seemed to connect straight to his groin.

'I don't think there can be any mistaking that.'

And she laughed, that other sound that connected up to his groin. 'Good,' she said, 'because I want you, too.'

It was the way she said it, with confidence, unprompted, that delighted him most. He grabbed her hand, not trusting himself to kiss her again, and began to walk, as quickly as he could, towards the Home Farm. Ten minutes. It felt like an hour.

'Does this Bonding take place in the laird's bed or his lady's?' Ainsley asked as Innes opened the front door.

He kicked it shut, locking it securely, before he swept her up into his arms. 'Right now, I'm not even sure we'll make it to the bed.'

They did at least make it to her bedchamber. A fire burned in the cast-iron grate. Mhairi must have sent someone down from the castle to tend it. The curtains were drawn. A lamp stood on the hearth, another one on the nightstand, lending the room a pleasant glow. Ainsley stood, clasping her hands and wondering what she ought to do now. The excitement that had bubbled inside her dissipated as she eyed the bed, and memories of that other first night tried to poke their way into this one. She shivered, though it was not at all cold.

'You can still change your mind,' Innes said gently.

He meant it, too. A few days ago, Ainsley would have assumed that what he meant was that *he* had changed *his* mind. Even now, despite the fact that she knew how much he wanted her, she had to work to believe it. 'No,' she said. 'I don't want to change my mind. I don't.' She looked at the lamps, wondering.

'Do you want me to put them out?'

Like the last time. Like all of the last times. She shook her head. She would not have it like any other time.

'Do you want me to leave you to undress?' Innes asked.

'I want...' She studied him, focusing on him, drinking him in so that he was the only one there in the room with her. 'I want you inside me,' she said, meaning in her head, not meaning it how it sounded, though when she saw the results, the leap of desire in his eyes, the way he looked at her, with such passion, she meant that, too. 'I want *you*,' she said, closing the space between them, 'and I want you to show me just how much you want me. That's what I want.'

Innes pulled her tight up against him, lifting her off her feet. 'I think I can manage that,' he said, and kissed her, and she realised that he already had.

He picked her up, but instead of laying her down on the bed, he pulled the quilt onto the floor and laid her down by the fire. Quickly divesting himself of his jacket, his waistcoat, his boots and stockings, he stood over her wearing just his plaid and his shirt. The firelight flickered over the naked flesh of his legs. She caught a glimpse of muscled thighs as he knelt down beside her, pulling her into his arms again to kiss her. There was heat inside her. There was heat on her skin from the fire. There were little trails of heat where he touched her. Her face. Her neck. His mouth on her throat. Kissing his way along the curve of her décolletage, his tongue licking the swell of her breasts, his hands splayed on her back, feathering over the exposed skin of her nape, the knot at the top of her spine, then down to pick open the buttons of her gown.

He kissed the tender spot behind her ears. He slid her gown over her arms, kissing her shoulders, the crook of her elbow, her wrists, tilting her gently back to work her gown down, over her legs. When he took off her shoes, he kissed her ankles through the silk of her stockings. And her calves. The backs of her knees. His mouth, thin silk, her skin. She watched him, her eyes wide open, not wanting to miss a moment, enthralled, astonished that simply watching could be so stimulating. His cheeks were flushed. His blue-black hair, grown longer since he came to Strone Bridge, was ruffled. She ran her fingers through it. Soft as silk. She pulled him down towards her, wanting the weight of him on her, and claimed his mouth. Hot, his mouth was. 'Sinful,' she murmured, lips against lips. 'I want to be sinful.'

Innes laughed, rolling to his knees again, pulling her with him to work at the ties of her stays. His eyes were dark in this light, midnight blue, his pupils dilated. His shirt was open at the neck. The firelight danced over it, showing her shadows of muscle, making her ache to touch him. While he worked on her corsets, cursing under his breath at the time it was taking, she tugged at the shirt, pulling it free from the leather belt, sighing as her palms found his flesh, sighing again when he flexed and his muscles tensed. Flesh. Heated flesh. She pressed her mouth to his throat and licked his skin, feeling the vibration of his response. Then his triumphant growl as he finally cast her corsets aside and tore at her shift, leaving her in just her pantaloons and her stockings, the bright pink of her garters, which perfectly matched the flowers on her gown.

A fleeting urge to cover up her breasts faded as Innes devoured her with his eyes and then feasted on her with his mouth. Sucking. Nipping. Stroking. Setting up paths of heat, making her blood pulse and the muscles inside her contract. She fell back onto the quilt, tensing, heating, watching him kiss her, touch her, watching his hands on her skin, tanned, rough hands, covering her breasts, flattened over her belly, then pulling at the drawstring of her last undergarment. She looked so pale in the firelight. Her skin milky. The curls between her thighs seemed tinged with autumn colours.

Innes smiled at her. She smiled back. Sinful. Sure. He pulled his shirt over his head, and she watched, clenching inside, the revelation of flesh and muscle, the smattering of dark hair on his chest, the thinner line from his navel to the belt of his kilt. The plaid tickled her thighs and her belly as he knelt over to kiss her. She could feel the tip of his shaft nudging between her legs. She tilted towards him, her fingers gripping into the muscles of his shoulders, and it touched her, the tensest part of her. 'Yes,' she said, not meaning to, not quite sure what she meant.

He sat up, still straddling her, and reached under his kilt, which was spread over the two of them. She could not see what he did, but she could see the intent in his eyes. Stroking, up and down, slick sliding, unmistakably not his hand, sliding. He was watching her. 'Yes,' she said, quite deliberately, 'again.'

Stroking. Sliding. She must be wet. She was tight. She was getting tighter. Stroking and sliding. And then more stroking. And more sliding. And she came. Suddenly. What she now knew was a climax, though it felt like an explosion. He lifted her, his hands under her, cupping the bare flesh of her bottom as she cried out, and the pulsing took her over, and he pushed his way inside her, thick, hard, pushing her apart, finding his way higher as her muscles pulsed around him, pulling him in, tighter, and higher and tighter.

He paused, his face tense, his breathing heavy. 'Ainsley?'

'Yes. Oh, yes.' She dug her fingers into his shoulder, remembering just in time Felicity's caution. 'But, Innes, be careful.'

'Of course. I promise. Always.' It pained her that he believed there was a need, then he tilted her farther, his hands cupping her bottom, and she forgot about it. She wrapped her legs around him, anxious, feeling anxious, not nervous, but like a runner, wanting to run, wanting to be off, wanting.

And then she was. Not running but better. He thrust inside her, and she met him, held him, thrust back. He thrust again, and she met him again. Not a race. But like a race. Inside her, tensing again, pooling, holding him tight. His chest was slick with sweat. The firelight danced over the planes of his chest. His eyes, midnight-dark eyes, were on her, watching her. She did not look away. She looked down at their bodies. At the dark, hard peaks of her nipples, at the shudder of her breasts as he thrust, and the entity that they were beneath his kilt, joined, flesh melding into flesh, heat and sweat. And then it happened, different but the same, a climax pulsing, and she heard him cry out, and pull away from her, chest heaving, as his climax took him, too.

Afterwards, she wanted to laugh with the sheer delight of it. Fun and pleasure, Felicity had said, and she had been right. 'Astonishing,' she said to Innes, and he laughed. 'I had no idea,' she said, and he laughed again, only it was a different kind of laugh. There was pride in it, and something proprietary. She would have minded that, under any other circumstances. Tonight, on what Madame Hera would no doubt call a voyage of discovery, Ainsley found that there was something rather exciting about a man in a kilt who looked as if he would like to mark every bit of her body as his own. She wanted to do the same to him herself.

She kissed him, tangling her tongue with his, pressing her breasts into the still-damp skin of his chest, relishing the *frisson* that the contact made, the roughness of his hair on the sensitive skin of her nipples. She straddled him in the firelight, as he had straddled her, and felt the stirrings of his member against her. Deciding that this time she wanted to see for herself, she undid the ornate buckle of his belt. The kilt fell open. She watched, fascinated, as he thickened and hardened before her eyes. She wanted to touch him, but this was quite new territory for her. Even the wanting was new.

Innes was leaning up on his elbows. She could see the ripple of his belly muscles as he breathed. His eyes on her. Waiting for her. 'Tell me what you want,' she said, an echo of what he had said, wanting to know, sure that what he wanted so too would she.

'Touch me.' She reached for him, running a tentative finger down the sleek length of him. He shuddered. She did it again. A finger, from the thick base of him, to the tip.

Innes's chest rose and fell. 'More,' he said.

She could guess what he wanted now, but she would not. 'Tell me,' she said.

He knew she was playing. She could see he liked it. 'Stroke me,' he said.

She did, feathering her fingers up and down the length of him. 'Like that?'

'No. You know what I want.'

She leaned forward again, brushing her breasts against his chest. Her nipples ached. 'Then tell me,

Innes,' she said, nipping his earlobe. 'Tell me exactly what you want.'

'Put your hands around me, Ainsley.'

She was shocked, not by what he asked, but by the effect it had on her. She sat up, sliding against him so that the soft folds of her sex touched his body, enjoying the separate *frisson* of pleasure this sent through her. Then she did what he asked. She wrapped her hand around his girth, and stroked. 'Like that?'

He groaned.

She did it again. 'Like that, Innes?'

'Yes. Oh, Ainsley, yes.'

'Not like this,' she said, squeezing him lightly.

He swore.

'Or like this?' She slid herself against him. Her skin on his, her hand, her sex. Different textures. Same heat. She stroked. 'Do you mean like this, Innes?' she persisted.

'You are a witch.'

'A white witch, or a black witch?' she asked, her fingers tightening and releasing, tightening and releasing.

He put his hands around her waist and lifted her, pulling her swiftly back down on top of him, entering her in one long, hard thrust. 'A very, very bad witch,' he said, pulling her down towards him and kissing her hard.

His kisses matched his thrusts. She matched his kisses first, and then dragged her mouth away to push back, to force him to match his thrusts to hers as she rode him, harder, faster and harder again, until they were both shouting, crying out. Hearing him, the change of note, feeling him, the thickening, feeling herself topple over the edge, she heaved herself free of him just in time to lie panting by his side on the quilt, by the fireside, utterly abandoned, utterly wanton, utterly satisfied.

'So did you enjoy your wild Highlander?' Innes asked her a few moments later.

'I did not know it was expected that a lady should compliment a laird on his performance.'

'Contrary to what you seem to think, we men like to know that we've pleased.'

Ainsley chuckled. 'You definitely pleased, as you very well know.'

'I'm glad you think so,' Innes said with a teasing smile, 'for I most certainly agree. In fact, it was so delightful I think we might even try it again in a wee while.'

'I'm extremely sorry to intrude, but I could wait no longer, and your housekeeper told me she would not be the one to interrupt you, so—so here I am.'

Innes, clad only in his hastily donned plaid, sketched Felicity a bow. 'I'll leave you to it.'

Felicity handed the breakfast tray to Ainsley, flushing. 'Never fear, I will not keep her long. I came only to bid you good morning and goodbye.' As the door closed behind him, she turned towards Ainsley. 'Not quite true, of course. I came to make sure you made it through the night unscathed. Did you?'

Ainsley, who had scrambled into the nightgown she had not worn last night, now pushed back the covers, blushing wildly, picking up her woollen wrapper from where it had fallen on the floor. 'You can see I did.'

Felicity put her hands on her hips. 'Well? Come on, I guessed after what you told me yesterday that it was your first time together.'

'You were right. *Again.* It was both fun and pleasurable. And that's all you're getting,' Ainsley said, sticking her nose in the air and trying to look smug. 'Is that coffee? Would you like some?'

'Yes, it is and no, I won't, thank you. That scary housekeeper of yours produced breakfast for everyone who was left up at the Great Hall hours ago. Eoin said it's true, her mother really was a witch.'

'Do you mean you were there all night?'

'Lots of people stayed. There's not been a ceilidh at the castle for years. Did you know that the old laird stopped holding the Hogmanay celebrations when—'

'The old laird! You've gone native, Felicity Blair. Was it Eoin who told you this, by chance?'

Felicity, to Ainsley's amazement, blushed. 'People used to look forward to the Hogmanay party for months,' she said. 'They're already wondering, after yesterday, whether Innes will be holding one.'

'And I'm wondering why you're avoiding answering my question.'

'Because I'm going back to Edinburgh today, and my life is complicated enough without adding a farmer who lives in the middle of nowhere into the mix,' Felicity said tartly. 'Sorry, Ains. Sorry.'

'What's wrong, Fliss?'

Her friend shook her head, blinking rapidly. 'Nothing. I am tired from all that dancing and too much whisky, probably, and I have to go and pack, for the steamer leaves Rothesay this afternoon and I can't afford to miss it.'

'But...'

'No. I'm fine.' Felicity spoke brusquely. 'Much more important, I can see that you are fine, so I can leave

you without worrying too much. I've some more letters for Madame Hera. They're on the dressing table
in my room at the castle. And I've got the ones you've
written to take with me. I think that Madame Hera's
latest venture is going to prove very popular. You are
going to carry on with her, aren't you?'

'Of course I am,' Ainsley said. 'Why wouldn't I?
This— You know I'm only here temporarily. I'll be
back in Edinburgh soon enough.'

'Or sooner, if you are unhappy. You promised, you
remember?'

'Yes, but...' Ainsley stopped, on the verge of saying that she could not imagine being unhappy. She'd
thought that before. 'I remember,' she said.

Felicity hugged her. 'I'd better go. Just be careful,
Ainsley, your Mr Drummond is a charmer. Don't let
him charm you too much. Take care of yourself, dearest. I'll write.'

A kiss on the cheek, a flutter of her hands, the fainter
sound of her bidding farewell to Innes and she was
gone.

'It's bad luck to frown on the morning after the
Bonding,' Innes said, closing the bedroom door behind
him. 'What has Miss Blair said to upset you?'

'Nothing.' Ainsley poured the coffee. 'I don't know
where we're going to sit for breakfast. There are no
chairs.'

'We'll take it in bed.' Innes placed the tray in the
centre of the mattress, patting the place beside him.

'I wonder what possessed Mhairi to send up a tray?
She never has before.'

'Second sight,' Innes said flippantly, handing her an
oatcake. 'She knew today was a holiday.'

'I suppose that's part of the tradition, is it?'

Innes grinned. 'It is now.'

Ainsley looked down at the oatcake, which was spread with a generous layer of crowdie, just exactly as she liked it. She wondered if Innes would return to his own room tonight. She took a sip of coffee. It had always been John who decided whether or not to visit her. She had never once been in his bed. He had never once slept in hers. She took another sip of coffee. Not even in the earliest days of her marriage had John made love to her twice in one night. He'd never asked her what she wanted. Never seemed to imagine that she could want something more. It had never been fun, and there had been very little pleasure. This was different in every way.

'What are you smiling at?'

Ainsley's smile widened. 'You'd think, after last night, that we'd want to spend the day in bed. Sleeping,' she clarified hastily.

Innes refilled their coffee cups, and cut into a slice of ham. 'Tempting as it sounds, I have other plans.'

'You've tired of my charms already,' Ainsley said, through a mouthful of oatcake.

'I said I didn't want to spend the day in bed, I did not say that I didn't want to experience more of your charms.'

'The palace of pleasures. There's more, then?'

'Keep looking at me like that and I'll show you more right now.'

'No, thank you, I'm much more interested in my breakfast,' Ainsley said primly.

Innes leaned across the tray to lick a smear of crowdie from the corner of her mouth. 'Fibber,' he said.

She touched the tip of her tongue to his, then pushed him away. 'You are not irresistible, Innes Drummond.'

'No, I'm not.' He pulled the oatcake from her hand and put it back down on the tray. 'But you are,' he said.

Ainsley leaned back, tilting her face to the sky. It was a guileless blue today, with not even a trace of puffy cloud as yet, and the sun was high enough to have some real warmth in it. The boat scudded along, bumping over the white-crested waves. The breeze was just sufficient to fill the red sail, to flick spray on to her face, but not enough to chill her. 'It's perfect,' she said.

Innes took her hand and placed it on the tiller on top of his. 'You're supposed to be helping,' he said.

'I am.' She smiled at him lazily. 'By not interfering. Besides, I want to look at the view, it's so lovely.'

They had sailed south down the Kyles of Bute towards the Isle of Arran, whose craggy peaks were such a contrast to the gentle, greener Isle of Bute, before veering east, round the very tip of the peninsula on which Strone Bridge was built, to follow the coastline north. 'It's only about fifteen miles overland from the castle,' Innes told her, 'but there's just the drover's roads and sheep tracks to follow.'

'This is much nicer.' Innes was wearing a thick fisherman's jumper in navy blue that made his eyes seem the colour of the sea. With his tweed trews and heavy boots, his hair wildly tumbled and his jaw blue-black, for he had not shaved that morning, he looked very different from the man she had met all those weeks, months ago, at the lawyer's office in Edinburgh. 'Your London friends would not recognise you,' she said. 'You look like a native.'

'A wild Highlander.'

She smoothed her palm over the roughness of his stubble. 'Is this for me, then? Is this the day you drag me off to your lair and have your wicked way with me?'

'Wasn't last night enough?'

'Didn't you say this morning that there was more?'

Innes caught her hand and kissed it. His lips cold on her palm, then his mouth warm on each of her fingers. 'Are you going to prove insatiable?'

'Will that be a problem?'

Innes gave a shout of laughter. 'It's every man's dream. There's plenty more,' he said, releasing her and hauling at the tiller to straighten the dinghy, 'but unless you want us to end up on the rocks, maybe not just yet.'

Ainsley shuffled over on the narrow bench. 'Where are we going?'

'Wait and see. This is Ardlamont Bay. We are headed to the next one round. You can see now that we've not really come that far. If you look straight across, you'll get a glimpse of the castle's turrets.'

The breeze began to die down as they headed into St Ostell Bay. Directly across, the Isle of Arran lay like a sleeping lion, a bank of low, pinkish cloud that looked more like mist sitting behind it and giving it a mysterious air. In front of them stretched a crescent of beach, the sand turning from golden at the water's edge to silver where high dunes covered in rough grass formed the border. Behind, a dark forest made the bay feel completely secluded.

The waters were very shallow. Innes pulled off his boots and stockings and rolled his trews up before jumping in and hauling the boat by the prow. Seeing that the water lapped only as high as his knees, Ainsley, who was wearing a skirt made from the local tweed, pulled off her stockings and shoes and followed suit. The little boat rocked precariously as she jumped over the side, and she gasped with the cold, stumbling as her feet sank into the soft sand.

The tide was on the ebb. Leaving the boat at the water's edge, they made their way up the beach, Innes carrying the basket that he'd had Mhairi pack. There was not a trace of a breeze. The sun blazed down on them, giving the illusion of summer. The air was heady with salt and the scent of the pine trees. Shaking out her dripping skirts, Ainsley stopped to breathe it in, gazing around her with wonder. 'It's just beautiful.'

'I'm glad you like it.'

They deposited the hamper and their shoes in the shelter of a high dune before picking their way along the stretch of the sands. 'I like your Highland outfit,' Innes said. 'I'm not the only one who would be unrecognisable to their friends.'

Ainsley's skirt was cut short, the hem finishing at her calf, in the local style, which gave her considerably more freedom of movement. She wore only a thin petticoat beneath, not the layers that were required to give fullness to her usual gowns, and a simple blouse on top, with a plaid. 'It took me hours of practice to get this right,' she said. 'You see how it is folded to form these pockets? The local women have their knitting tucked into them. They can knit without even looking, have you noticed?'

'Are you planning on making me a jersey?'

'Good grief, no. I'll wager Mhairi knitted that one.'

'She did.' Innes caught her as she stumbled, and tucked her hand into his. They headed down to the

shoreline where the sand was harder packed and easier to walk on, but he did not release her. The wavelets
were icy on her toes. In the shallows, flounders rippled
under the sand. Spoots, the long, thin razor clams, blew
up giveaway bubbles. At the western tip of the beach,
a river burbled into the sea. 'The Allt Osda,' Innes
said. 'There's often otters here. I don't see any today.'

It was only then that she realised he must have come
here as a boy. He talked about his childhood so rarely,
it was easy to forget that he must have a host of memories attached to all these beautiful places, must have
sailed around that coastline countless times. It was obvious, when she thought about it. The way he handled
the boat. The fact that he'd navigated almost without
looking. As they followed the river upstream on banks
where the sand became dotted with shale, Ainsley puzzled over this. She still had no idea what haunted him,
but she was certain something did.

The river narrowed before twisting onto higher
ground. They crossed it, Innes holding her close as
her feet slid on the weed-covered rocks, his own grip
sure. It was odd, knowing him so well in some ways
yet knowing so little of his past. Strange, for they had
shared so much last night, yet she had no idea whatsoever right now of what he might be thinking, no idea
of the memories he associated with this place, save
they could not be bad. No, definitely not bad. He was
distant but not defensive, simply lost in his thoughts.

It was a different ache, she felt. Not the sharp pang
of feeling excluded, but something akin to nostalgia.
Like pressing her nose against a toyshop as a child and
seeing all the things she could not have. Silly. Fanciful. Wrong. It was not as if Innes had any more idea of

what she was thinking after all. Nor cared. She caught herself short on that thought. Last night had been a revelation, but it was fun and pleasure, nothing more. Surprising as it was, this discovery that she could be so uninhibited, that the body she had been so ashamed of could be the source of such delight, she would do well not to read anything more into it. She and Innes were, as luck would have it, extremely well matched physically. No, it was not luck. That connection had been evident right from the start. And that was all it was. She'd better remember that.

Innes left her to unpack the basket while he went into the forest in search of wood. The sun was so warm, and the dune in which they sat so sheltered, that Ainsley could see no need for a fire, but when she said so, he told her she would be glad of it when she had had her swim.

'You were teasing me,' she said later, watching him as he made a small pit in the sand and lined it with stones. 'The water is freezing.'

Innes began to kindle the sticks. 'That's why we need the fire.'

'I can't swim.'

'Do you want to learn?'

Ainsley looked at the sea. Turquoise-blue, and, she had to admit, extremely alluring, with the sun sparkling on the shallows, the little wavelets making a shushing noise. Then she remembered the shock of cold on her feet when they had first landed. 'No,' she said decisively. 'Perhaps another day, when it's warmer.'

Innes, feeding bigger sticks to the small flame, shook his head. 'It's nearly September, the end of the summer—it doesn't get much warmer, nor much colder, either.' He settled a larger piece of wood on the fire, before joining her on the blanket. 'We used to…'

The fire sparked. Innes put his arms around his knees, staring out at the sea. She waited for him to change the subject, as he always did when he stumbled on a memory, but he surprised her. 'Malcolm and I,' he said. 'We used to come here the first day of the New Year to swim. It was our own personal ritual, after the Hogmanay celebrations.'

'A cleansing?' Ainsley joked. 'Another form of a fresh start?'

'Aye, the Drummonds are fond of those, aren't they?' Innes said ruefully. 'Funnily enough, that's how my brother always put it. He was an awful one for dressing things up, but the truth is, a dip in water that cold is the best cure for a whisky head that I know.'

'Did you and your brother often have whisky heads, then?'

'Only on special occasions, and in truth, it was mostly me. My father believed that the laird should be able to drink everyone under the table. When he gave Malcolm his first dram, he made him drink the whole lot in one swallow. Malcolm was sick. He never could hold his drink, but he became very good at pouring it down his sleeve or over his shoulder, or on one occasion into a suit of armour.' Innes picked up a handful of soft sand, and watched as the grains trickled through his fingers. 'Since I was not obliged to prove myself, I could drink until I was stotious.'

'Like I was, on the sherry?' Ainsley said, blushing faintly.

'You were endearing. I fear that I was simply obnoxious, which is why I take good care not to drink too much these days.' Innes wiped the last few grains of sand from his palm and pulled his jumper over his head. 'Right, it's now or never.'

'You're not really going to swim?'

'I am.' Innes pulled off his shirt and got to his feet. 'I take it you'll not be coming with me?'

'I think this is one ritual you had better perform on your own,' Ainsley said.

Innes paused in the act of unbuckling his belt. 'I think I've told you before that you see a deal too much,' he said. Before she could answer, he grinned and began to unfasten his trews. 'Now, if you don't turn your back, you're going to see a great deal more.'

Ainsley looked up, deliberately running the tip of her tongue over her lower lip. 'I think the view from here is going to prove even more attractive than the one out there,' she said, waving vaguely in the direction of Arran without taking her eyes from Innes.

'If you keep looking at me like that, the view will be considerably more defined than it is right now.'

She got to her feet, unable to resist flattening her palms over the hard breadth of his shoulders, down over his chest, grazing the hard nubs of his nipples. Innes's eyes were beginning to glaze. Her own breathing was becoming rapid. He did not move. She slid her hands lower, to cup him through his trews. She trailed her fingers up his satisfyingly hard shaft. 'I do believe you are my idea of perfect Highland scenery.'

Innes pulled her to him roughly. 'Did I tell you that you're a witch?'

She wanted him. He was more than ready. His mouth was inches away from hers. All she had to do was tilt her head. Ainsley laughed, that soft, guttural sound she knew he found arousing. 'I think I'll be perfectly satisfied just taking in the view,' she said, freeing herself.

She turned away, but Innes caught her and hauled her back. His smile looked like hers felt. Teasing. Aroused. 'I'll be cold when I come out of the water.'

'And wet,' she said.

'And wet,' he said softly.

His hand covered her breast. Even through her corset, she felt her nipple harden in response. She shuddered. 'I'll keep the fire going.'

Innes nipped her ear lobe. 'I hope so, though I suspect that I'll need a little help with my blood flow.'

Her own blood was positively pulsing. 'What did you have in mind?' Ainsley whispered.

'I am sure you'll think of something.' His lips found hers in the briefest of kisses. 'Unless you've changed your mind and decided to swim with me?'

It was tempting, but she forced herself to wriggle free. 'The best things come to those who wait, isn't that what they say?'

'I just hope it's worth it,' Innes said, laughing, pulling off the rest of his clothes.

He stood before her quite naked, and completely aroused. Ainsley watched him making his way down the beach, long legs, tight, muscled buttocks, and thought she had never seen such a wickedly tempting sight in her life. 'Innes,' she called, waiting for him to turn around. 'It already is.'

Innes began to run down the beach, forcing himself to continue as he hit the shallows, knowing that if he stopped, if he turned around, he would immediately turn back. The water was freezing. He'd forgotten. With the tide out, the shallows went on for ever. He'd forgotten that, too. It had been a joke between them, he and Malcolm, that you would reach Arran before it was deep enough to swim.

It was over his knees now, and up to his thighs. He slowed, took to wading, his feet sinking into the soft sand, the flounder scooting out from under him the merest ripple of sand. When a wave hit his groin, he gasped and looked ruefully down. It wasn't just a whisky head the water cured. He dipped his hands into the water, and splashed water over his arms, his shoulders, then caught himself as he dipped his head down to throw more over his face. Malcolm, who always dived straight under, used to laugh at him when he did this. Innes stood up, closing his eyes and lifting his face up to the sun. It didn't hurt here. It didn't hurt to think of him. The memories here were all good. Looking over his shoulder, he saw that Ainsley had followed him down the beach and was standing in the shadows, clutching the blanket. He gave her a mocking salute and dived in.

When he emerged, fifteen minutes later, she was still there, holding the blanket open. Innes was shivering, and embarrassed at the effect the icy water had had on him. Instinctively, his hand moved to cover himself, but she was watching him, and her watching him was far better for his condition than the cold skin of his own hand. He waded out slowly, pushing his hair out of his eyes, relishing the rays of the sun on his back, his skin tingling from the salt. He liked to look at women naked, and he liked them to look at him, but it had always been in the privacy of a bedchamber, and it had never been like this. Ainsley found the idea of him as some sort of savage Highlander arousing, and he found that he liked playing the part. He'd never done that before.

By the time he reached her, the effect of the cold was definitely wearing off. Ainsley handed him the blanket, which he wrapped around his shoulders. 'Well?' he asked.

'The scenery was most elevating,' she said, then blushed. 'I did not mean…'

Innes laughed. 'Not quite, but it will be.'

'I don't know how it is, but when I am with you I say the most shocking things.'

'Delightful is what I'd call them. Why is it, do you think?'

'I will not pander to your ego by telling you.'

They had reached the dune. Innes put some wood on the fire. 'That's a shame, because I rather like the idea of you pandering to me.'

'What particular kind of pandering do you have in mind?'

'You could heat me up.'

'It's only fair, I suppose, since you got so cold at my request.'

'I did.' He made a point of shivering, and tried to look soulful. 'You could rub me down with the blanket.'

She eyed him speculatively. 'I could certainly rub you down,' she said, pulling the blanket from his shoulders and shaking it out onto the sand, 'but I don't think we need the blanket. Lie down.'

He did as she asked, his body already stirring in anticipation. Ainsley slipped off her undergarments, then sat on top of him. She was warm and wet. His shaft thickened, eager to be inside her, but she slid away from him, spreading her skirts around them, just as he had spread his kilt over the pair of them last night. Then she touched him, her hands forming a cocoon around him, and slowly, gently, delightfully, began to stroke.

He bucked under her. She gripped him with her thighs. He closed his eyes, praying for control. It was agonising, her touch feathery, the slightest of friction, not enough but almost too much. He dug his hands into the sand. He dug his heels in, but it was unbearable. With a guttural cry and a surge of desire he would have thought impossible after the night's exertions, Innes rolled her over onto her back, imprisoning her wrists above her head. 'Please,' he said, in a voice he barely recognised, 'say that you are ready, because I don't want to wait.'

'Then don't,' she said.

He kissed her, plunging his tongue into her mouth and entering her at the same time in one long, deep thrust. She met him, pushing up underneath him, clenching hard around him. He thrust again. Her mouth was hot on his, her kisses wild. She struggled to release her arms. When he held her, she dug her heels into his behind. He thrust again, and she met him with equal force, and he felt her tense, the sudden stillness before the crash that made him contract and sent the blood rushing, and he thrust again, hard, and again, deeper, with her crying out and holding him and digging her heels in and urging him on, to pound deep, deep inside her, so that when she came, pulsing around him, it took every ounce of his resolution to pull away, spilling onto the sand, then falling down onto the blanket, gasping, slick with sweat, panting, pulling her on top of him, the frantic beat of her heart clashing with his.

Chapter Nine

Dear Madame Hera,
I have been married for eighteen months. I love my husband very much, and relations between us have always been most satisfactory, him being a perfect gentleman, if you understand my meaning. Indeed, I had no cause at all to complain, until that fateful tea party with my three closest friends several weeks ago. It was my birthday, and I must confess that along with tea, we did partake of some strong drink. Conversation turned to intimate matters. I was shocked to discover that my husband's method of ministering to my needs was considered by my friends to be downright old-fashioned. Imagine my astonishment when they revealed the variety of other ways—well, I will draw a veil over that.

But the problem was that I could not. Draw a veil, that is. For my curiosity was aroused. Alas! Would that I had been content with what I had. When my husband came to my arms as usual on the following Saturday night, I tried to instruct him in one of these variations. It is true, I did fortify myself with a glass or two of his special port beforehand, but I rather think it was my inadequate instructions that were to blame. With hindsight, it is clear that his failure was not a cause for merriment, and that perhaps it was a mistake, after he had expended so much energy, to expect him to renew his efforts in the traditional way.

Now no amount of reassurance will convince my husband to repeat the attempt, despite the fact that I have obtained more complete instructions from my friends. Worse still, my husband assumes my desire to introduce an element of diversity into the bedchamber is actually implied criticism of his previous efforts, and has accused me of having simulated satisfaction in the past. As a result, my Saturday evenings are utterly bereft of marital comfort. What should I do?

Mrs J-A

September, 1840

Ainsley finished reading the letter aloud and looked enquiringly at Innes, seated at his desk and frowning as usual over the account books. 'There, I told you I'd find something to distract you. What do you think she means when she said that her husband is a "perfect gentleman"? I'm assuming it is not that he gets to his feet when she enters a room.'

Innes pushed his papers away and came to join her on the large, overstuffed sofa that sat in front of the hearth. 'She means that he ensures she is satisfied before he allows himself to complete his own pleasure.'

'Oh.' Ainsley grimaced, scanning the letter again. 'I had no idea. I hate to think how many times Madame Hera has quite missed the point of some of her letters.'

'What proportion of her correspondence do these sorts of problems form?'

'That's a good point.' Ainsley brightened. 'It is only since Felicity launched our personal answering service that they have grown. What do you think Madame Hera should advise Mrs J-A? Her poor husband is most likely imagining himself wholly inadequate. She will have to do something to reassure him.'

'Not so long ago, Madame Hera would have been pretty certain that the problem lay with that poor husband.'

'Not so long ago, Madame Hera wouldn't have had an inkling as to what Mrs J-A meant by variety,' Ainsley said drily, 'and she would most certainly never have believed that it was acceptable for a woman to make actual requests. Though perhaps it is not, in general, acceptable at all. I have no idea how other men feel about it. Are you an exception?'

She looked expectantly at Innes, who laughed. 'I have no idea, but I doubt it.'

'I do feel it's a shame that so many women know so little about the variations, as Mrs J-A calls them.'

'Because variety really is the spice of life?'

He was teasing her. She felt the now-familiar tingle make itself known, but refused to be drawn. 'Because it seems wrong that only men do,' Ainsley said.

'Not *only* men, else...'

'You know what I mean, Innes. Lots of women think it is wrong to enjoy what is perfectly natural, and downright sinful to want to enjoy it any way other than what this woman calls traditional.'

'So we are conspiring to keep our wives ignorant, is that what you're saying? Because I'd like to point out to you that you're my wife, and I've been doing my very best, to the point of exhaustion, to enlighten you. In fact, if you would care to set that letter aside, I'd be happy to oblige you right now with a—what was it—variation?'

'Really?' Ainsley bit her lip, trying not to respond to that wicked smile of his. 'I thought you were exhausted?'

He pulled her stocking-clad foot onto his lap and began to caress her leg from ankle to knee. 'I'm also dedicated to providing Madame Hera with the raw material she needs to write the fullest of replies.'

'You have provided Madame Hera with enough material to fill a book.'

'Well, why don't you?'

She was somehow lying back on the sofa with both of her feet on his lap. Innes had found his way to the top of her stockings and the absurdly sensitive skin there. Stroking. How did he know that she liked that? 'Why don't I what?' Ainsley asked, distracted.

'Write a book.'

His fingers traced a smooth line from her knee to her thigh, stroking her through the linen of her pantaloons. Down, then up. Down. Then up. Then higher. Finding the opening in her undergarments. Her flesh. More stroking. 'What kind of book?'

Sliding inside her. Stroking. 'An instruction book.'

Sliding. 'A guide to health and matrimonial well-being, or something along those lines,' Innes said. 'Didn't you mention to me once that you thought it would be a good idea? Madame could offer copies to her private correspondents. I'm sure your Miss Blair would be more than happy to advertise something of that sort discreetly in her magazine.'

'I'd quite forgotten that conversation. Do you really think such a book would sell?'

'You're the expert, what do you think?'

She seemed to have stopped thinking. He was still stroking her. And thrusting now, with his fingers. And she was already tensing around him. Was it faster, her response, because of the experience of these past few weeks? Or was she making up for years of deprivation? Perhaps she was a wanton? Could one be a wanton and not realise it? The stroking stopped. Innes slid onto the floor. She opened her eyes. 'What are you doing?'

'Making sure your instruction manual covers every eventuality,' he said, disappearing under her skirts.

When he licked her she cried out in surprise. Then his mouth possessed her in the most devastating way, and she moaned. Heat twisted inside her, and she began to tense, already teetering on the edge, as he licked and thrust and stroked. She gathered handfuls of her skirts between her fingers, clutching at her gown in an effort to hold on, but it was impossible. Such delight, such unbearable delight as he teased from her, that she tumbled over into her climax, shuddering, and shuddering again as he licked her into another wave, and another, until she cried out for him to stop because she really thought that the next wave would send her into oblivion.

'What is it in those account books that is causing you to sigh so much?' Several hours later, Ainsley was pouring their after-dinner coffee. The maid who helped out in the house had left, along with Mhairi, once dinner had been served, for the housekeeper preferred to sleep where she had always slept, in her quarters at the castle.

Innes stretched his feet out towards the fire and shook his head wearily. 'It doesn't matter.'

'It obviously does, else you would not have been sighing.'

'When it comes to sighing, I seem to recall there was someone else in this room doing their fair share earlier this evening. You didn't say whether you approved of that particular variation, now I come to think of it.'

'I thought it was obvious.'

'A man likes to know he's appreciated.'

'You are.'

'I'm looking forward to reading that particular chapter of your guidebook. I reckon it will tax even Madame Hera's newfound vocabulary to describe it.'

'So you were serious when you suggested that I write it?' Her smile was perfunctory.

Innes frowned. 'Why not? It makes perfect sense.'

'And it will give me something to do.'

Innes put his coffee cup down. 'Have you something on your mind?'

'It's been more than three weeks since the Rescinding. I don't have anything to do, yet every time I ask you how things are going with the lands, you find something else to distract me. I'm wondering if tonight's *variation*, as you call it, was simply a better tactic than telling me it was late, and that you were tired.'

'What's that supposed to mean?'

'Nothing.' She set down her cup. 'They are your lands,' she said, getting to her feet. 'You are the one who has set himself the task of making Strone Bridge better than it ever has been. You did not consult me before you made that decision. Why should I possibly imagine that you would think my opinion worthwhile now, when you obviously have no idea how to go about it?'

'Where on earth did that come from?'

'From being ignored! I have tried. I have tried several times now to remind you of the terms on which I agreed to come here, and you've ignored me.'

'But you have helped. The Home Farm. The Rescinding…'

'And I've entertained you, too, when you've found the real problems of this place overwhelming.'

'You're joking.'

He looked at her aghast, but she was too angry to care, and had bottled up her feelings for too long to hold them in. 'I don't know why I'm still here,' Ainsley said. 'I'm not serving any purpose, and I'm a long way from earning back that money you lent me.'

'Gave you.'

'It was supposed to be a fee. A professional fee. Unless you're thinking that it was the other sort of profession after all.'

'Ainsley, that's enough.' Innes caught her arm as she tried to brush past him. 'What has got into you?

You can't honestly believe that I deliberately—what was it you said?—distract you by making love to you?'

Ainsley stared at him stonily.

'What?'

She shook her head. 'It doesn't matter.'

'Which means that it does,' Innes said wryly. 'You should put that in your book, you know, if you're including a section for husbands. Whenever your wife says it doesn't matter, you can be sure it's of dire importance.'

'I could write the same advice for wives.'

'I suppose I asked for that.' Innes held out his hand. 'Don't go, Ainsley.'

She hesitated, but she did not really want to run away, so she allowed him to pull her down on to the arm of his chair. 'I don't think it's deliberate,' she said, 'but when you don't want to talk about something, you—you distract yourself. With me, I mean.' She made a wry face. 'I am not complaining. I did not even notice it until tonight.'

'And you immediately decided that I was pulling the wool over your eyes. You should know me better.'

She flinched at the roughness in his voice. 'I do. That was not deliberate, either.'

Innes rested his head against the back of the chair, closing his eyes with a heavy sigh. 'You do know me, better than I know myself, it seems.'

He looked unutterably weary. Ainsley slid off the chair to stand behind him, put her hand on his temples. 'Do you have a headache?'

'I do, but I'm not going to risk another excuse,' he said with a shadow of a smile.

'Why won't you talk to me, Innes?'

'Because despite my resolve to be the saviour of Strone Bridge, I can't see how it's to be done. There's nothing to discuss, Ainsley, and I'm gutted. That's why I've not wanted to talk to you.'

She pushed him gently forward and began to knead the knots in his shoulders. 'If the situation truly is irredeemable, you should turn your mind to something else more constructive, such as that pier of yours.'

'Now that Robert has started work on the foundations and we have most of the supplies in hand, that pier of mine needs little of my time.' Innes sighed. 'That's nice.'

Ainsley said nothing but continued to ease the tension in his shoulders, her fingers working deep into his muscles.

'It's different,' Innes said after a little while. 'The pier, the new road. I know what I'm doing with those. When things go wrong—as they no doubt will—I know how to put them right. You can't just pluck new tenant farmers out of thin air. You can't put heart back into the soil overnight. You can't make a soil fit only for oats and barley yield wheat or hops, and even if you could, you can't do anything about the rain or the cold. There's so much wrong, and every solution I think of causes another problem somewhere else. There isn't a solution, Ainsley. If the lands here were ever profitable, then it was a long time ago, and I will not clear the land just to turn a profit. I go round in circles with it all.'

'If it's any consolation, I do know how that feels,' Ainsley said drily. 'I also know from experience that bemoaning one's ignorance and endlessly reassuring oneself that it is both impossible and futile to act is not only fruitless but a self-fulfilling prophecy.'

'You are talking of your marriage.'

She gave his shoulders a final rub, then came round by the side of his chair to stand by the fire. 'Yes, I am. I was afraid to speak up because I thought it would make things worse. I was afraid to act because I thought it would make the situation irretrievable. So I said nothing and I did nothing and—and if John had not died, who knows what would have happened, but one thing is for certain, matters would not have miraculously cured themselves.'

'You're telling me that I'm dithering, and I'm making things worse.'

'I'd have put it a little more tactfully, but yes.'

'You're right,' he said with a sigh, 'I know you are.'

She settled in the chair opposite him. He was staring into the fire, avoiding her gaze. 'It is the not knowing,' he admitted. 'The ignorance. That's the hardest bit. I'm so accustomed to knowing every aspect of my own business, to being the man people turn to when there's a problem. As I said, if something went wrong with the pier, or the new road, I'd know what to do. Or I'd be certain of finding a solution. But here, when it comes to the essence of Strone Bridge, I'm—I'm ashamed. People ask me questions. They look to me for solutions. And I don't have answers. It's—it's— Dammit, Ainsley, I feel like a wee laddie sometimes and I hate it.'

'Did you imagine I would think less of you for admitting to all this?'

Innes rubbed his eyes. 'I think less of myself, truth be told. I don't know what to do, and I don't see how you can possibly help, for you don't know any more of the matter than I do. What's more, though the Rescinding bought me a deal of goodwill, in some ways it's made matters worse, for not only have I raised all sorts of expectations, I've had to write off a load of debt, and the poor, honest souls who have been paying their rent without fail are now resentful of the fact that defaulters have been let off the hook.'

'Oh. I hadn't thought of that.'

'Nor I. How could we have?'

Ainsley wrinkled her brow. 'I don't suppose you could simply balance the books somehow by writing the other rents off in advance. But no, that wouldn't really balance the books, would it? It would simply mean that you were in more debt.'

'It's not the money that's the problem, but...' Innes sat forward. 'You mean I could give the tenants who are up to date a rent holiday to even matters up?'

'Do you think it would work?'

'It's worth a try. Have you any other genius ideas in that clever wee head of yours?'

Ainsley tried not to feel too pleased. 'It was hardly genius. In fact it was pretty obvious.'

'So obvious it didn't occur to me. Does that mean that you're a genius or that I'm an idiot? And be careful how you answer that, mind,' Innes said, grinning.

'Thank you,' Ainsley said with a prim smile. 'I will opt for genius.'

Waking with a start to the distinctive sound of the heavy front door closing, Ainsley found herself alone. Innes's pillow was cold. She lay for a while going over their conversation this evening. She wished she hadn't lost her temper, but on the other hand, if she had not, she doubted she'd have found the courage to say some of those things to him. She had hurt him, but she had forced him to listen. Then when he had, she had been lucid. She had been articulate. She had not backed down.

She sat up to shake out her pillow, which seemed to be most uncomfortable tonight. And her nightgown, too, seemed to be determined to wrap itself around her legs. She had put it on because it had been laid out at the bottom of the bed, as it was every night. Almost every morning, it ended up on the floor. Some nights, she never even got so far as to wear it.

She pummelled at her pillow again, turning it over to find a cool spot. Where was Innes? Was he angry with her? He hadn't seemed angry. He'd seemed defeated. He was a proud man. Self-made. Independent. All the things she admired about him were also the things that made him the kind of man who found failure impossible to take, and talking about failure even worse. And she had forced him into doing just that. Was he regretting it?

She padded over to the bedroom window, but it looked inland, and there was no sign of Innes, who had most likely headed down to the bay and the workings that would become the pier. Hoping he had more sense than to take a boat out, telling herself he was a grown man who could look after himself and was entitled to his privacy, Ainsley crawled back into bed and screwed her eyes tight.

But it was no good. In overcoming her own reticence, she couldn't help thinking she had forced him to confront a very harsh reality without having any real solutions to offer. Maybe there simply weren't any. She sat up, staring wide-eyed into the gloom of the bed-chamber, thinking hard. They were neither of them very good at discussions. She was too busy looking for signs that she was being excluded to listen properly, and Innes was too determined not to discuss at all.

Pushing back the covers, Ainsley knelt upon the window seat, peering forlornly and pointlessly out at the empty landscape. Innes was so determined to solve every problem himself, and it wasn't just because that was what he was used to. He'd admitted it himself, this very night, how small this place made him feel. 'Like a wee laddie,' he'd said. He was ashamed, that was what lay at the root of his inability to ask for help, yet he had not a thing to be ashamed of. There had to be a way to save this place without causing further hard-ship. There had to be.

Ainsley grabbed what she thought were a pair of stockings. Only as she pulled them on, she saw that they were in fact a pair of the thick woollen ones, which Innes had started to wear with his trews. Though he dressed more formally for dinner, he almost always wore trews and a jumper for his forays out on to the estate these days. Tying her boots around the stockings, she decided that one of those heavy jumpers would pro-vide her with much better insulation against the night air than her own cloak, and pulled it over her head. It smelled of fresh air, and somehow distinctively of Innes. The sleeves were far too long, but they'd keep her hands warm, and the garment came almost to her knees. Smiling fleetingly as she pictured Felicity's face should she ever see her in such an outfit, Ainsley quit the bedchamber and made her way outside.

* * *

She found Innes sitting down in the bay, watching the ebbing tide swirl and eddy around the huge timbers that were the beginnings of the new pier. 'I couldn't sleep,' Ainsley said, sitting down beside him on one of the thick planks that lay ready for use, and which had been brought on to the peninsula on an enormous barge that had caused a storm of interest in the village.

He put his arm around her and pulled her close. 'I'm sorry.'

'No, I am.' Tempting as it was to simply leave it at that and give herself over to the simple comfort of his arm on her shoulders, her cheek on his chest, Ainsley sat up. 'I do judge you, Innes. I am too much on the lookout for reasons to judge you to listen to what you're telling me sometimes. I'm sorry.'

'I forget,' he said softly. 'You seem so strong-willed, I forget that there was a time when you did not dare voice your opinions.' He pushed her hair back from her face. 'I know it's not my business. I know you want only to forget, but—did he hurt you, Ainsley?'

'No.' She shook her head vehemently. 'No. Not physically, if that's what you mean.'

'It's what I mean.'

'Then, no.'

'Thank heavens. Not that I mean to belittle...'

'It's fine. At least it was not, but it will be.' Ainsley gave a shaky laugh. The breeze caught the full skirts of her nightgown, lifting them up to expose her legs.

'Are those my stockings you're wearing?'

'I thought they were mine, and then when I put them on they were so warm, I didn't want to take them off.'

'I'm glad you didn't. I had no idea they could look so well. Nor my jumper, for that matter.'

'I must look a sight.'

'For sore eyes.' He leaned over to kiss her softly. 'I'm glad you're here. I know we didn't really quarrel, but it felt as though we were at odds, and I didn't like it.'

The sky was grey-blue, covered by a thin layer of cloud. The distant stars played peekaboo through the gaps, glinting rather than twinkling. The sea shushed quietly, the waves growing smaller as the tide receded. Ainsley leaned closer to Innes, shoulder to shoulder, thigh to thigh, staring out at the water. 'It wasn't that he lifted a hand to me, not once, but I was afraid of him. Partly it was his fault, but partly it was my own. I told you that it was the debts,' she said, 'but it wasn't just that. When you feel worthless, it's difficult to have a say in other things, even when they concern you.'

'Why would you feel worthless?'

She hadn't planned this at all but it seemed right, somehow, to match Innes's vulnerability by exposing her own. 'The obvious reason,' Ainsley whispered. 'I could not give him what he married me for.'

'You mean a child?'

She nodded, forgetting he could not see her. 'Yes.' She was glad of the dark. Such an old story, such an old pain, she had thought it long healed, but it seemed it was not. She could blame her tears on the wind, so she let them fall silently, biting her lip.

His arm hovered at her back. She could feel him, trying to decide whether to pull her closer or let her alone. She was relieved when he let it fall, let her wrap her own arms around herself, hug his jumper to her.

'Ainsley, forgive me, but I know from how you were with me at first. I know that things between you and— and him— They could not have been conducive to your conceiving.'

He did not ever say John's name, she noticed. He did not call him her husband. He was being absurdly delicate. If they had been discussing one of Madame Hera's letters, he would have been much more forthright. If she had been one of Madame Hera's correspondents, how much more of the truth would she have told? Ainsley shuddered. 'When we were first married,' she said, 'things were—were normal between us.' As normal as they were for many of the women who wrote to her, though she was not as fortunate as Mrs J-A, for John's idea of traditional ministering took no account of her pleasure. For some reason, it was important that Innes know this. 'Not as it is between us. He was not a—a *gentleman* in the sense you explained.'

'No,' Innes said gently.

So he had guessed that much, too. Ainsley tried to work out what it was she wanted to tell him. Not all. The memory of Donald McIntosh's curse made it impossible to say it all, for though he had not actually cursed *her*, she felt as though he had. And though she knew it did not really diminish her, her flawed state, still she felt as though it did, and she couldn't bear to reveal herself in that way to Innes.

Ainsley felt for his hand, seeking comfort and strength. 'He was not a cruel man, not really, though some of the things he said and did felt cruel,' she said. 'It was when I first discovered the debts. That's when he accused me of failing him. Until then, I had thought—told myself—hoped—that it was just a mat-

ter of time. Then, later, when our relationship deterio-
rated, he could not— He could not perform.'

It was not easy, but she had the words now; she understood so much more about herself now, and about
men, since meeting Innes. 'He blamed me. The worse
things got between us— He said I unmanned him, you
see. But I knew I had not because I saw him. Alone. I
saw he could be aroused, only not by me.'

'I remember now. You asked me about it, whether
it was the wife's fault.'

'Yes. Don't be angry. He's dead. If he was not dead
I wouldn't be here.'

She felt his reluctant laugh. 'Then I won't be angry,
for I'm very glad you're here,' Innes said.

'Are you?'

She turned, trying to read his face in the darkness.
It was impossible, but there was no need. He kissed
her softly on the mouth. 'I thought it was obvious,' he
said, borrowing her own words from earlier.

'We're neither of us very good at seeing that, are
we?'

'Not very.' Innes touched her cheek, his fingers tracing a curve to her ear, her jaw, her throat. 'It's true,
what you said earlier. There are times when I want to
lose myself in you, to forget all the things I can't resolve, but it's you I want.'

'Truly?'

'You must not doubt it. You're thinking that it's another way of doing the same thing, my wanting you, his
not. That the end result is you're left out in the cold?'

'Yes. I hadn't— Not until tonight.'

Innes kissed her again. 'Never, ever doubt that I
want you for one reason, and one only. Whatever it is

between us has been there from the start. I have never
met a woman who brings me more pleasure than you.'

'If you carry on kissing me, this thing, as you call
it, will be between us again, and I'm trying to be serious.' Ainsley sat up reluctantly, pushing her tangle
of hair from her eyes. 'I did not love John. I thought I
did, but I did not. I thought he gave me no option but
to ignore his—our—problems, but the truth is, I was
relieved to be told they were none of my business, and
when our marital relations broke down, I was relieved
about that, too. What's more, what I've learned from
being with you, Innes, has made me realise it wasn't
just John who could not perform. I'm afraid my performance was pretty appalling, too. Partly it was because I didn't know any better. Partly it was because
I didn't want to know. It was a mess I couldn't fix because there was simply no solution.'

'You can't possibly be sorry that he died.'

'That's what Felicity said. I would never have
wished him dead, but I don't wish I was still married
to him. You see what I mean?'

'I'm not sure.'

Ainsley laughed drily. 'I know, I've told this in
a very convoluted way. I couldn't give John a child,
Innes.'

'You don't know that. It may not have been your
fault. The chances are…'

Nil, was the answer. 'Slim,' Ainsley said, because
she could not say it. 'It's not my fault, but it feels as if
it is. Do you see now?'

'You mean my lands.'

'You could not help the fact that you were raised
without any knowledge of them. You did not know

what your father was doing—or not doing—in your absence.'

'My elected absence. Regardless of who is to blame, they are in a mess.'

'No, you blame yourself for the problem and for failing to fix it.'

'I'm not accustomed to failing.'

Ainsley laughed. 'Then we must make sure that you do not, but I don't think the solution lies with making your lands more fertile. What we need to do is think differently.'

'We?'

'Yes, we,' she said confidently. 'Between your stubbornness and my as-yet-untested objectivity, we shall come up with something. We have to. But right now it's very late, and it's getting very cold. We'll catch a chill if we sit here much longer, and you need to try to get a wee bit of sleep at least.'

Ainsley got resolutely to her feet, but Innes stood in front of her, blocking her path. 'I'm not stubborn.'

'You could have taken one look at the mess of this place and turned around back to your own life, but you have not. You've invested a lot more than money in the future of this place. What would you call that, if not stubborn?'

'Determined? Pig ignorant?' He pulled her into his arms, laughing. 'Have it your way. How do you fancy taking a stubborn man to your bed? Because fetching as you look in that rig-out, what I really want is to take it off you, to lie naked in bed with you.' He kissed her. 'Beside me.' He kissed her again. 'Under me.' And again. 'Or on top of me.' And again, this time more deeply, his hands on her bottom through the thin

layer of her nightgown, pulling her up against the un-
mistakable ridge of his erection. 'You see, this is me
consulting you. Over, under, beside—the choice,' he
said, 'is yours.'

Chapter Ten

Dear Adventurous Wife,
I must tell you, and other readers of this column, how very refreshing it is to hear of a marriage that is still so happy and so fulfilled after
twenty-two years. Instead of being ashamed of
your continuing physical desires, you should celebrate them. I applaud your wish to explore new
territory, as you call it. No matter how enthralling
a favourite, well-thumbed book might be, no matter how satisfying the conclusion, it is human nature to wish to read other volumes, provided that
you are prepared to find some of them less—shall
we say enthralling? Their conclusions perhaps
even less satisfying. What matters, Adventurous
Wife, is the journey rather than the destination.

Ainsley laid down her pen, smiling to herself as she
remembered some of the journeys she and Innes had
taken in the past few weeks. The destination had never
been anything other than satisfying, but Madame Hera
was a cautious soul, and Ainsley was inclined to think

Innes rather more talented than most husbands. Not that she would dream of boasting, though she had indeed, during one particular *adventure* involving a feather and the silk sash from his dressing gown, informed him that he had the cleverest mouth of any man in the world. But that had been under extreme circumstances, and he had returned the compliment when she had employed the same combination of mouth, feather and silken tie on him. She picked up her pen again.

> Certain everyday items can, with a little imagination, be employed as secondary aids. Think of these articles as theatrical props. Provided that proper consideration is given as to texture and, it goes without saying, hygiene, and provided, naturally, that both adventurers are content with the selection, then I think you will find that your journey will be much enhanced.
>
> I wish you *bon voyage*!

Ainsley signed Madame Hera's name with a flourish just as Mhairi entered the room. 'Excellent timing,' she said to the housekeeper. 'I've been wanting to have a word with you while Innes is out. He's with Eoin, so he's bound to be away most of the morning. Do you have a moment for a cup of tea?'

Mhairi smiled. 'I was just about to ask you the same thing. I've the tray ready. It's a lovely day, and we won't get many of those come October, so I thought you might fancy taking it outside.'

'Perfect.' Ainsley tucked Madame Hera's correspondence into the leather portfolio and followed Mhairi on to the terrace that looked out over the bay. The view was not nearly so spectacular as that from the castle terrace, but it was still lovely.

'I could never tire of this,' Ainsley said, taking a seat at the little wooden table.

'It's been a fair summer,' Mhairi said, 'better than the past few.'

'I hope a good omen for Innes's first summer as laird,' Ainsley said, pouring the tea and helping herself to one of Mhairi's scones, still hot from the griddle.

'Better still if the weather holds for the tattie howking in a few weeks, and better yet if there's more than tatties to bring in, for the land is not the only thing being ploughed, if you take my meaning.' Mhairi smiled primly. 'It would be nice if that husband of yours could see some fruits from all his labours.'

'Oh.' Flushing, Ainsley put down the scone, which suddenly tasted of sawdust. 'I see.' She tried for a smile, but her mouth merely wobbled.

Mhairi leaned across the table and patted her hand consolingly. 'It's early days, but it's well-known that the Drummond men carry potent seed.'

Ainsley took a sip of her tea, pleased to see that her hand was perfectly steady, studying the housekeeper over the rim of the cup. Mhairi spoke so matter-of-factly, though her words were shockingly blunt. 'But the old laird had only the two children,' she said.

'Two boys was considered more than enough. 'Tis easy enough to limit your litter if you don't service the sow.' Mhairi buttered herself a scone. 'I've shocked you.'

Unable to think of a polite lie, Ainsley opted for the truth. 'You have.'

'You must not be thinking I hold a grudge against

Marjorie Caldwell. Poor soul, she was affianced to the laird when she was in her cradle. She can't have been more than seventeen when she married him and, knowing him as I did, I doubt he made any pretence of affection, not even in the early days. It was all about the getting of sons, that marriage, and once he'd got them—well, she'd served her purpose.'

'Innes said as much,' Ainsley said, frowning over the memory, 'but I thought his views highly coloured.'

'No, Himself has always seen the way things are here clearly enough. The laird thought the sun shone out of Malcolm's behind, as they say. Innes was only ever the spare, just as I was. The difference between us being that I stuck to the role he gave me and your husband went his own road.'

Mhairi stared off into the distance, her scone untouched on her plate. The insistent pounding of mallets on wood told them that the tide was low. The skeleton of the pier emerging beside the old one made the bay look as if it was growing a mouth of new teeth.

Mhairi stirred another cube of sugar into her tea, seemingly forgetting that she'd already put two in, and took a long drink. 'I loved that man, but that does not mean I was blind to his faults, and he had a good many. What my brother, Dodds, said at the Rescinding was true. I was fit to warm the laird's bed, but that was all. He never pretended more, I'll give him that. That annuity, the farm he made over to me, it was his way of making it right. Payment for services rendered,' she concluded grimly.

'But you loved him all the same.'

Mhairi nodded sadly. 'I'd have done anything for him, and he knew it. Until the Rescinding, I thought myself at peace with the one sacrifice I made, but now the laird is dead and buried, and I am too old and it's far too late, I resent it.'

Her fingers were clenched so tightly around the empty china cup that Ainsley feared it might break. Gently, she disentangled them and poured them both fresh tea. Though the late-September sun beat down, hot enough to have chased all the chickens into the cool of the henhouse, she shivered. 'A child,' she said gently, for it was the only explanation. 'That was what you sacrificed.'

Mhairi nodded. 'He would not have stood me bearing his bairn. Of course, the laird being the laird, it did not occur to him to have a care where he planted his seed. If it took root, that was my problem. He made that clear enough, so I made sure it never took root. I do not practise as my mother did, but I knew enough to do that.'

'The fey wife?' Ainsley's head was reeling. 'Do you mean your mother really could cast spells?'

Mhairi shrugged, but her face was anxious. 'She was a natural healer. Her potions were mostly herbs, but she did have other powers. The curse that Dodds made— Mrs Drummond, I have to tell you it's been on my mind.'

'That the bloodline would fail,' Ainsley said faintly.

'I made sure to bear no child. The old laird's only other child died fourteen years ago. There is only Innes, Mrs Drummond. You will think me daft to believe in such things, but I know how powerful my mother's gift was. You must forgive me for talking about such personal matters, but I can't tell you the good it does me, knowing that the pair of you are so—so enthusiastic about your vows, shall we say. And I was hoping—as I said, I know you'll think it's daft, worrying about a silly curse—but still, I was hoping you could maybe reassure me that we'll be hearing some good news soon. About the harvest I was talking about?'

Ainsley slopped her tea, and felt her face burn dull red. Mhairi was looking at her with an odd mixture of anticipation and concern. She believed in that curse, and as things stood she would be right to. Making a fuss of wiping up her tea with a napkin, Ainsley tried to compose herself. 'Silly me,' she said. 'I'm not usually so clumsy.'

'I've upset you.'

'No.' She smiled brightly. 'Not at all. Why would you— I was merely— Well, it is a rather embarrassing topic of conversation. Though I suppose it is perfectly natural that people are wondering…' She placed the soiled napkin on top of her half-eaten scone. 'Are people wondering? Is an heir really so important?'

Mhairi looked as if she had asked if the land needed rain. 'The estate has been passed from father to son directly for as long as anyone can remember.'

Innes had told her so, back in Edinburgh when they first met. He hadn't cared then, but he had not been to Strone Bridge then, and he had no notion of truly claiming his inheritance. It was different now. She thought back to the pain in his voice a few nights ago, when he had finally admitted how much it meant to him, and how desperately he wanted to make his mark on the place. It would not be long before he realised an heir was a vital element of his restitution.

Ainsley smiled brightly at Mhairi. 'As you said, it is early days.'

Mhairi was not fooled. 'Is there a problem?' she asked sharply. 'Because if there is a problem, I can help.'

Ainsley's poor attempt at a smile faded. 'What do you mean?'

'Just as there are ways to prevent, so there are ways to encourage.'

'Magic?'

'Helping nature, my mother always called it.'

A gust of longing filled her before she could catch it. It was like a punch in the guts, so strong she all but doubled over from it. Impossible not to wonder what difference such a spell would have made all those years ago. A spell! She gave herself a mental shake. She had the word of medical science, and no spell would counteract that. 'If nature needs assistance, it is not natural,' Ainsley said, pleased at how firm she sounded. Magic, white or black, real or imagined, formed no part of her life. She got to her feet and began to stack the tea things on the tray.

The next day Innes left early with Eoin for Rothesay, and then on to Glasgow where they had various meetings with paddle-steamer companies. Though she started missing him the moment he set out, Ainsley was relieved to have some time to spend alone.

She headed out of the Home Farm in the direction of the castle. Sunshine dappled down through the leaves of rowan and oak that bordered the path here. The bracken was high, almost to her waist and already beginning to turn brown, exuding that distinctive smell, a mixture of damp earth and old leather. Autumn was settling in. The sense of time ticking too fast was making her anxious. Though Innes had said nothing of her returning to Edinburgh, Ainsley had a horrible feeling that very soon she would have no option.

Peering down to the bay from her favourite spot on the castle's terrace, she could see Robert Alexander standing with a cluster of men, consulting their plans. The new road would be cut into the cliff. Innes was investigating the possibility of using a steam engine to help with the work. Since that night in the bay, they had spent a great deal of time together poring over maps and account books. She now fully understood his despair.

Crofting was still the tradition here, with each farmer producing enough to meet his own small needs, keeping a few cattle and sheep on the common grounds, and fishing to supplement his family's diet. The crofts were simply too small to grow more, and far too small to meet the huge demands from the growing metropolis of Glasgow, it seemed. The new road, the new pier, the paddle steamers that could berth there, would solve the transport problems, but the crofters of Strone Bridge simply could not produce enough to benefit from these markets. Eoin was encouraging Innes to merge some of the farms, but while many of them had been lying fallow, their former tenants having fled to Canada and America, hardly any of those lands lay together. Innes's farms were dotted about the landscape like patchwork, each a different size and shape. Innes was determined not to take the route that so many of the Highland landlords had done, which was to oust his tenants by fair means of foul, and to turn the lands over to sheep.

Despite the melancholy subject matter, Ainsley had revelled in these hours spent together. It wasn't only that she felt useful, that her opinion was valued, that Innes truly listened to what she said. She had felt included. And there was the problem. She was not part of this place, and never could be, but with every day that passed, that was exactly what she wanted. To belong here. To remain here. With Innes. She was close to letting Strone Bridge into her heart, and even closer, frighteningly close, to allowing her husband in, too.

She could love him. She could very easily love him, but it would be disastrous to allow herself to do so. Gazing out over the Kyles of Bute, watching the dark-grey clouds gather over the Isle of Arran, cloaking it from view, Ainsley forced herself to list all the reasons why it was impossible.

For a start, she was not the stuff that a laird's wife was made of. Not a trace of blue blood. Neither money nor property—quite the contrary. No connections. The Drummonds married for the name and the lands, and Ainsley contributed no good to either. She could not weave or spin or even knit. She knew nothing of animal husbandry, or keeping a house larger than the Home Farm. What she knew of the Drummond traditions Mhairi had taught her. In fact, Mhairi was far better qualified than she was for the role. No one could tell a tale of the castle's history and ghosts the way Mhairi did.

Then there was the fact that Innes didn't actually want a wife. It would be easy to persuade herself he'd changed his mind. He'd managed to overcome his precious need to be the one and only person in control of his life in so many ways. He even confided in her without prompting sometimes, and he made her feel that Madame Hera was every bit as important a venture as Strone Bridge. He had changed, and he had changed her. She was more confident. She was more ambitious. She no longer doubted her femininity, and she knew the satisfaction of pleasure and pleasing. She was cured of John for ever, but the role that had cured her was temporary. She was not a wife. A business partner. A lover. But not a wife. Innes did not want a wife, and Innes would never love her as a wife. She did not think that the mystery woman who had stolen his heart kept it still, but she was fairly certain he would not let it go again. But he would take a real wife because he would realise, very soon, that his commitment to Strone Bridge required him to produce an heir.

Which brought her to the biggest stumbling block of all. The one thing she could not give him. Swallowing the lump that rose in her throat, Ainsley decided to follow the path round to the chapel. It was cool here, in the little copse of trees and rhododendrons. She sat on the moss-covered bench in the lee of the chapel, idly watching a small brown bird wrestling with a large brown worm. She smiled to herself, remembering the woman at the Rescinding who had begged forgiveness for having her husband's dog buried beside him. His grave must be hereabouts. What was the name? Emerson, that was it. But as she crossed the path to start peering at the gravestones, Ainsley was distracted by the Drummond Celtic cross.

She read the old laird's name thoughtfully, and then his lady's inscription, too. Marjorie Mary Caldwell had been only twenty-six when she died, and if what Mhairi had said was true, she couldn't have had a very happy life. Caldwell. She remembered now—that was the name of the family who owned the lands that bordered Strone Bridge, somewhere north of here. Innes's nearest gentry neighbours. The ones he'd not wanted invited to the Rescinding, though they must be some sort of relation of his.

The atmosphere in the graveyard was only adding to her melancholy. It was very clear that she had no future here, but she did want to leave a legacy. Furrowing her brow, Ainsley made her way back to the castle. The Great Hall still smelled faintly of whisky fumes and ash. Though it was not yet October, Mhairi was already asking if the traditional Hogmanay party would be held here. It was a room made for great occasions. Parties. Banquets. Ceilidhs. Wedding feasts.

Would their marriage be annulled? Would Innes divorce her? She was fairly certain that the law, which was written by men and for men, would perceive her infertility as ample reason for either. Then some other woman with property and the right pedigree would benefit from the changes in Innes that had cost Ainsley so much. He would not love her, his real wife, but he would respect her, and he would confide in her, make love to her, rely on her to play the role of the laird's lady. And she would give him the son he didn't yet know he needed.

Ainsley dug her knuckles deep into her eyes. No point in crying. In the long drawing room, she gazed out of the French windows at her view. It was a pity more people could not share it, and fall in love with it. Excursionists from the paddle steamers that would be able to dock here within months. They could take tea here in the drawing room. Smiling, she remembered joking about that very thing the day Innes had decided to build the pier. Excursionists who would pay for Mhairi to show them round the castle and tell her ghost stories. Who would buy the local tweed, or the local heather ale.

She stood stock-still. Would they pay to spend the night here? Pay extra to spend the night in one of the haunted bedchambers? Her heart began to race. Innes had told her that the railway between Glasgow and Greenock was due to open next year. He had shares. The journey would be much easier than it was now, a quicker, cheaper escape from the smoke of the city to the delights of the country. There would be more excursionists able to afford the trip, perhaps wanting to take a holiday rather than merely come for the day. And there would be richer people, too, who would be willing to pay a premium to hire the castle for a family occasion. To marry in the chapel and hold their wedding feast in the Great Hall.

She hesitated, remembering the scorn Innes had poured on the idea when she had first, jokingly, suggested it. Ridiculous, he had called it. But that had been weeks ago, before he had decided to stay here. Before the success of the Rescinding, here in this very hall. He must have changed his mind about the castle by now. Certainly he had not suggested knocking it down again. And there would be jobs. The lands would provide enough produce to feed the visitors.

It could work. She just might have been right after all, when she'd said to Innes that they would have to think differently. Strone Bridge Castle Hotel. Ainsley's stomach fluttered with excitement. This would be her legacy.

* * *

Innes was gone ten days, during which Ainsley worked on her plan for the castle, determined to surprise him and equally determined not to dwell on the growing sense she had that her time on Strone Bridge was ticking inexorably to a close. He arrived with the morning tide, tired but immensely pleased to see her. Watching his tall, achingly familiar figure stride along the old pier towards her, she forgot all her resolutions and threw herself into his arms.

He held her tightly, burying his face in her hair, exchanging barely a word with Robert Alexander, telling the surveyor brusquely that he had business to attend to before rushing Ainsley back to the Home Farm, leaving old Angus and Eoin to take the cart and deal with the luggage.

They arrived breathless, and headed straight for their bedchamber. 'I feel like I've been gone an age,' Innes said, locking the door firmly behind him. 'I missed you.'

'Did you?' She felt as if she couldn't get enough of looking at him, and stood in the middle of the room, simply drinking him in.

'I missed having breakfast with you,' Innes said, putting his arm around her, steering her towards the bed.

Her heart was beating from the effort of climbing the hill, from the effort of trying not to let him see how very much she had missed him, and from anticipation, too. 'I'm sure you and Eoin had plenty to talk about,' Ainsley said.

Innes smiled. 'We did, but when Eoin smiles at me over his porridge, it doesn't make me want to kiss him.'

'I expect the feeling is entirely mutual,' Ainsley teased.

'Did you miss me?' Innes kissed each corner of her mouth.

'A little.' She kissed him back, her words a whisper on his ear.

'Just a little?' He kissed her again, more fully this time, running his fingers down her body, brushing the side of her breast, her waist, to rest his hand on her thigh.

She shivered. 'Maybe a wee bit more than a little,' she said, imitating his action, her hand stroking down his shoulder, under his coat to his chest, his waist, his thigh. He was hard already, his arousal jutting up through his trousers. She slid her hand up his thigh to curl lightly around him. 'I can see you missed me a good bit more than a little,' she said.

Innes reached under her skirts to cup her sex. 'Do you want to know how much more?' he asked.

He had a finger inside her. She contracted around him. 'Yes,' she said. He started to stroke her. 'Oh, Innes, yes.'

They lost control then. She pulled him roughly to her, her mouth claiming his. He kissed her urgently. Their passion spiralled, focused on the overwhelming, desperate need to be joined. She had to have him inside her. He had to be inside her. There was no finesse to it. Speed, necessity, drove them. Innes struggled out of his trousers enough to free himself. He rolled onto the bed, taking her with him, lifting her to straddle him, her knees on either side of him. She sank onto him, taking him in so high, so quickly, that they both cried out.

Their kisses grew wild. She clung to his shoulders,

then braced herself using the headboard, arching back as she drew him in, as he thrust higher, harder, furiously, until the deep-rooted shiver that preceded her climax took her, and he came, too, pulsing, shaking them both to the core, making them forget, in the utter satisfaction of it, that he was still inside her, clinging to her, holding her there, with his arms, with his mouth, though she needed no holding, clinging, too, her harsh breath mingling with is, his heart beating against hers.

She had not planned it, but the connection, having him deep inside her as he came, had been momentous.

A true joining.

A true mistake.

Her body had betrayed her. Ainsley felt as if her world was shattering. She loved him. And even as she felt the truth of it settle itself inside her, she saw his face. Innes looked appalled.

'I'm sorry. Ainsley, I'm sorry. I don't know what— I didn't mean— I'm sorry.'

She shook her head, not quite meeting his eyes as she lifted herself free of him. 'It doesn't matter.' Though it did. It had changed everything.

Innes could not have made his feelings any clearer, but he seemed to want to try. 'It does matter,' he said, hurriedly adjusting his clothing. 'You asked me— I promised I would always be careful. I don't know why I...'

'It wasn't your fault. It was mine.' She would not cry in front of him, but she needed him gone. She gave him what she hoped was a reassuring smile. 'I told you, there is almost certainly nothing to worry about.' He was staring at her, horrified. 'It was simply— We were incautious because we had grown accustomed to more regular release,' Ainsley said, cringing at the words even as she spoke them.

She rolled off the bed. She couldn't look at him now. 'There are a hundred letters waiting for you, and Robert will be wishing to talk to you. Go on downstairs, I will rejoin you shortly.'

Ainsley held open the door, giving him no option but to leave her. Dazed, Innes did as she bade him and made his way downstairs to the sitting room. He sat at the desk, staring at the neat piles of correspondence, feeling as if he'd been punched in the gut.

He cursed long and hard, then poured himself a glass of malt. What had happened? He swallowed the dram in one. It burned fire down his throat and hit his belly too fast. He coughed, then poured himself another. *I'm sorry*, he'd said, but he had not been. That was the worst thing. It had felt so good, spilling himself inside her. He hadn't thought of the consequences. He hadn't been thinking of anything at all, save for his need to be with her. In all honesty, he couldn't have cared less about the consequences. But Ainsley had. Her face. *Stricken*, that was the word. She'd tried to cover it up, but he was not fooled.

Innes finished his second glass of whisky, feeling as if he'd just been given a death sentence. All he'd been able to think about these past few days was coming home to Strone Bridge and to Ainsley.

Home. Ainsley. The two words had somehow become connected, and as if determined to make sure his mind made the connection, too, his body had made it impossible for him to ignore. Which left him where, exactly?

He swore again, bitterly. Terrified and confused as hell, was where it left him. He could no longer trust himself, and Ainsley would no longer trust him. Things had changed fundamentally, yet some things would never change. He still carried the burden of the past with him. Whatever he felt for Ainsley, he had no right to let it flourish.

This was a warning, a very timely one. The truth would see to the outcome. He felt sick at the thought of it, but he didn't doubt it was the right thing to do. The only thing. He cared enough to want her to understand, which was a lot more than he'd ever cared for any woman since that first one. He cared too much. Far too much.

Checking the clock on the mantel, Innes saw that half an hour had elapsed. With a heavy heart but with his mind resolute, he set out to find her.

Ainsley was seated in front of the mirror, staring at her reflection as if it was another person entirely. She loved him. Did she really love him? How could she be so foolish as to have allowed herself to fall in love with him? Had she forgotten how miserable she'd been, married to John?

No. She had not loved John. Innes was not John. This marriage was not at all like her first. 'Because it is not real,' she hissed at her reflection. 'Not real, Ainsley, and you have to remember that. This is not your life, it's a part you're playing, and that is all, so there is no point in hoping or wishing or dreaming that it will continue.'

Yet for a blissful few moments, that was exactly what she allowed herself to do. She was in love, and for those few moments, that was all that mattered. For those few moments, she allowed herself to believe that love would conquer all the barriers she had so painstakingly examined and deemed immovable. She was so overwhelmed with love, surely anything was possible. She loved Innes so much, he could not fail to love her back. They could not fail to have a future together, because the idea of a future without him was incomprehensible.

The knock on the door made her jump. Innes looked as if he was carrying the weight of the world on his shoulders. 'We need to talk,' he said, and not even her newly discovered love could persuade Ainsley that the words were anything other than ominous.

Fleetingly, she considered pretending that nothing momentous had happened, but looking at the expression on Innes's face, she just as quickly dismissed the notion. Feeling quite as sick now as he looked, Ainsley got to her feet and followed him out of the door.

To her surprise, he led them outside, along the path towards the castle. At the terrace they paused automatically to drink in the view. 'I went through to Edinburgh when I was away,' Innes told her. 'There were matters to tie up with the lawyers. I was going to call on Miss Blair. I know you'd have wanted me to let her know that you were well, but—you'll never believe this.'

'What?'

'Eoin,' Innes said, shaking his head. 'I wondered why he insisted on coming through to Edinburgh with me when the man never wants to leave Strone Bridge. It turns out that he and your Miss Blair have been corresponding, if you please. He went off to take tea with her and made it very clear I was not wanted. He was away most of the day, what's more, and not a word could I get out of him after, save that he was to pass her love on to you. What do you make of that?'

'I don't know what to make of it at all. I had no idea—she certainly has not mentioned this correspondence to me.'

'Do you think they'll make a match of it?'

'Oh, no.' Ainsley shook her head adamantly. 'That will never happen.'

'You seem very sure. I thought you'd be pleased. You would have been neighbours.'

'Innes, I will not be...'

'No, don't say it,' he said hurriedly.

'You don't know what I was about to say.'

'I do. I do, Ainsley.' His smile was tinged with sadness. 'Poor Eoin. But I didn't bring you here to talk about Eoin. I can see you're bursting to talk, but let me speak first. Then perhaps I will have spared you the need.'

Chapter Eleven

Ainsley had assumed they were going to the chapel, but when they got there Innes left the well-trodden path to push through a gap in the high rhododendron bushes in the nook forming the elbow of the grave-yard, which she had not noticed before. The grass here was high, the path narrow, forcing them to walk single file. It led through the tunnel of the overgrown shrubs, emerging on a remote part of the cliff top looking not over the bay where the pier was being constructed, but over the far end of the Kyles, and the northern tip of the Isle of Bute.

'That's Loch Riddon you can see,' Innes said, putting his arm around her shoulder, 'and over there in the distance is Loch Striven.'

'It's lovely.'

'It was Malcolm's favourite view.' Innes took her hand, leading her to the farthest edge of the path. Here, the grass was fresh mown around a small mound, on top of which was a cross. A Celtic cross, a miniature of the Drummond one. And on it, one name. 'My brother,' Innes said.

Ainsley stared at the birthdate recorded on the stone in consternation. 'He was your twin! Oh, Innes, I had no idea.'

He was frowning deeply. She could see his throat working, his fingers clenching and unclenching as he stared down at the stone. She was not sure if he was going to punch the stone or break down in front of it. She was afraid to touch him, and aching to. 'It's a very beautiful spot,' Ainsley said rather desperately.

'Aye. And it was his favourite view, but all the same he would not have chosen to spend eternity here. Malcolm...' Innes swallowed compulsively. 'I've said before, Malcolm— It wasn't just that he was raised to be the heir, Ainsley, he lived and breathed this place. The traditions meant as much to him as they did to my father. He would have wanted to be buried with the rest of them. Except they would not let that happen. No matter how much I tried to persuade them, they would not allow it.'

'Why not?' Ainsley asked, though she had a horrible premonition as to the answer.

'Consecrated ground,' Innes said. 'My brother killed himself.'

Shock kept her silent for long moments. Then came a wrenching pain as she tried to imagine the agonies Innes must have suffered. Must still be suffering. 'No wonder you left,' she said, the first coherent thought she had. Tears came then, though she tried to stop them, feeling she had no right, but his face, so pale, so stiff, the tension in the muscles of his throat, working and working for control were too much for her. 'Oh, Innes, I am so, so sorry.'

Seeking only to comfort, wordless, distraught, she

wrapped her arms around his waist. He stood rigid for a moment, then his arms enfolded her. 'I'm sorry,' Ainsley said, over and over, rocking her body against him, and he held her, saying nothing, but holding on to her, his chest heaving, his hands clasping tighter and tighter around her waist, as if he was trying to hold himself together.

Gradually, his breathing calmed. Her tears dried. His hand relaxed its hold on her shoulder. 'I had no idea,' Ainsley said, scrubbing at her tear-stained cheeks.

'Why should you?' Innes replied gruffly. 'I made sure not to tell you anything. While I was away from here, I could pretend it had not happened.'

'That's why you never came back?'

'One of the reasons.' He heaved a deep sigh, tracing the inscription on the cross, before turning away. 'Come, there's a rock over there that makes a fairly comfortable seat. It's time you knew the whole of it.' He touched her cheek, then dipped his head to kiss her. A fleeting kiss, tinged with sadness. 'After this morning, we both know we can't carry on as we have been.'

She knew, but only when he said it did she realise that she still had not accepted it. She'd hoped. Despite all, she had hoped. Sitting down beside him on the huge chair-shaped boulder, her heart sank. Whatever Innes was about to tell her would destroy that hope for ever.

Innes was staring out at the sea, where the turning tide was making ripples on the summer blue of the surface. 'You know how things were with me here, when I was growing up,' he said. 'I can't remember a time when I didn't want to leave, but to leave without my father's permission would undoubtedly have caused a breach between myself and my twin. It would be an exile for me, unless I returned under the whip, and one that Malcolm would feel obliged to uphold. You must remember, in those days, my father was not so old. An enforced separation from my twin for years, maybe even decades, was not something I wanted to have to deal with.'

'And yet you left,' Ainsley said.

'I had planned to wait until after I came into an inheritance from my mother. I had persuaded myself that it would make a difference, my having independent means, that my father would not see it as a flaunting of his authority. As it turned out, I didn't have to put it to the test. Events—events took over.'

Ainsley's hand sought his. She braced herself.

'There was a woman,' Innes said.

He was still staring out to sea, his eyes almost the exact colour of the waters below. She loved him so much. A sigh escaped her, and he turned that beloved face towards her.

'You guessed?' he asked.

She stared at him blankly, her mind still trying to come to terms with what her heart had been trying to tell her for days now. Weeks? How long had she loved him?

'I suppose it was obvious,' Innes said. 'My being so dead-set against marriage—I always wondered what you made of that.'

'I thought...' What? What! She gazed at him, such longing in her heart, letting it flood her for just a moment. Just a moment. She loved him so much.

'Ainsley? You thought...' Innes prompted.

He must not guess she loved him, that was what

she thought. Because if he guessed, he would send her away immediately, and she needed a few more weeks. Just a few more. 'I thought there must have been,' she said. 'A woman. I thought that's what it must have been.'

'Well, you were right.'

She waited, trying not to show what she was feeling. Was she looking at him differently? Innes was staring out to sea again, his throat working. Whatever was coming next, he was struggling with it. She didn't want to hear him talking about another woman, but he obviously needed to tell her. Ainsley ruthlessly thrust her own storm of feelings to one side. 'Go on,' she said. 'There was a woman. And of course she was lovely.'

'She was. She was very lovely.'

She hadn't meant him to agree with her. Now, perversely, she wanted to twist the knife, as if knowing how very different she was from his one true love would stop her loving him. 'No doubt she was graced with a fortune, too,' Ainsley said.

'She was rich. An orphan and an only child, she was brought to live at Glen Vadie when she was just a bairn.'

'Glen Vadie. That is the Caldwell estate?'

Innes nodded. 'Aye, she was a distant relative of my mother's. We grew up together.'

It was beginning to sound horribly like a fairy story, though without the happy ending, Ainsley thought. She already hated this rich, charming, well-born, beautiful woman.

Innes heaved a sigh. 'I'm sorry, I'm not being very articulate. The truth is, I can hardly bear to think of it, for even after all this time I'm ashamed, and I don't know what you'll think of me.'

'Innes, I could never think ill of you.'

He shifted uncomfortably on the stone and then got to his feet. 'Ainsley, you will.' His expression was deeply troubled, his eyes stormy. 'I could let you go without telling you. I considered it, but I did not want this all to end on a lie.'

'End?' He had said it. She had known he was going to say it, but she wished he had not.

'It was always going to end, Ainsley. We both knew that. It was what we agreed. You made it very clear you did not want anything else.'

Felled. Could a person be felled? She was felled. 'And you?'

She hadn't meant it to sound like a question. She couldn't bear the way he answered her with such finality. 'And me, too,' Innes said gently. 'Your being here, it was only meant to be for a wee while, to help me decide what to do with the place.'

'But you haven't decided,' Ainsley said, unable to disguise the desperation in her voice. She was clutching at straws, she knew that, and knew, too, that it was pointless, but she couldn't help herself.

'I've decided that I'm going to stay,' Innes said. 'Besides, you know that's not the point.' He was flushed, but his mouth set firm, and when he spoke, though the words were said softly enough, the tone was resolute. 'This morning I realised how much I have come to care for you, Ainsley. It's not only that it breaks the terms of our agreement that makes my feelings for you wrong, nor that I know you don't *want* the complication of any feelings at all, it's that I can't. It has to stop before either of us gets in too deep, for I will not allow myself to love you, Ainsley. I won't.'

It hurt even more than she'd expected. She bit her lip hard, dug her nails into her palms, telling herself that she was glad he had not guessed her own feelings.

'You'll think me arrogant,' he said, 'telling you I won't love you when you have no thought in your head of loving me.' He sat down beside her again and took her hand, which she quickly unfurled from its fist. 'This morning, we both got carried away. I could see from the look on your face afterwards that it—it shocked you as much as me. I don't know what it is between us, maybe it's spending so much time together that's…I don't know, intensified it, made it seem more than it is?' He shrugged. 'I do know that we neither of us want it, though. I do know that if I wasn't telling you that it's over, you'd be saying it to me, wouldn't you?'

She ached to tell him just how far off the mark he had been in his interpretation of her reaction, but she was not so foolish. It was not pride that stopped her telling him how wrong he was, but love. Heartsick, she could only nod.

'Aye.' Innes nodded slowly. 'I thought about letting you go without telling you, but I couldn't. I want you to know, you see, not only because I owe it to you but because I—I can't afford to allow myself to hope. This morning was like a glimpse of heaven and glimpse of hell at the same time.' He stopped, running a shaky hand through his hair, and drew her a very ragged smile. 'That's why I brought you here. To remind me why it can't go any further, and by showing you the worst of me, I'll be making sure that even if I kept on wanting what I am not entitled to, I could never have it.'

As he looked over his shoulder at the cross, beneath which lay his brother's mortal remains, goose-bumps made Ainsley shudder. Her heart was clinging to Innes's confession of how much he had come to care for her, wanting to believe it would be enough to turn the situation around, to persuade him that he could care more. Hope, that treacherous thing she could not seem to extinguish, blew this tiny flame to determined life. All she had to do was tell him that she loved him. That was all it would take.

But her head was having none of this. Innes did not want her love. Innes *would not* love. Innes did not feel entitled to love. It was a strange word to use, but as he turned back to her, his face bleak, the question died on her lips.

'Her name was Blanche,' he said.

It was, as Ainsley anticipated, horribly like a fairy tale. Blanche, Malcolm and Innes, like brothers and sister at first, until Blanche changed, seemingly over-night, blossoming into a beauty. The brothers no longer felt at all filial towards her. Desire, lust, and with it competition, had entered into their Garden of Eden.

'But Blanche preferred you?' Ainsley said, because of course she would, and who would not?

Innes looked genuinely puzzled. 'How did you guess?' Fortunately, he did not wait for an answer. 'We tried to ignore it,' he said. 'How pathetic that sounds.'

'You were very young.'

'Old enough to know better.'

'But if you were old enough—and you and she— If you were in love, then why— I don't understand what the problem was.'

'The problem,' Innes said grimly, 'was that Blanche was betrothed to my brother.'

Ainsley put her hand to her mouth, caught Innes watching and made a conscious effort to wipe the shock from her face. 'But you were twins. Surely if Malcolm knew how you felt…'

'He did not. We made sure he did not. At least, I thought we did,' Innes told her, his mouth curled with disgust. 'Besides, you're forgetting that this is Strone Bridge. My father and Caldwell of Glen Vadie had signed the betrothal papers. A younger son would be no substitute for the heir.'

'But if Blanche was in love with you…'

'But Malcolm was in love with Blanche. And since Malcolm was my twin, I persuaded myself that I would be doing the honourable thing in giving her up, then I set about persuading Blanche that marrying Malcolm would not be so very different to marrying me. She and I enacted a most touching little scene, worthy of Shakespeare.' Innes's voice dripped sarcasm. 'The lovers renouncing each other. There were tears and kisses aplenty, though needless to say, there were more kisses than tears.'

He couldn't look at her. His hands were dug deep in his pockets as he stood before her, gazing over her shoulder at the cross on the grassy mound. 'Blanche refused to go along with it at first, but I was determined. Carried away with my own sense of honour, I thought I was,' Innes continued in a voice that poured scorn on his own youthful self. 'I pushed her. I was determined, and Blanche was in the end a pliant and a dutiful wee thing, so she agreed, and the betrothal was formalised at a party in the Great Hall. I thought myself heartbroken, needless to say, but I told myself that I'd done the right thing by my brother and I told myself that what she felt— Well, I told myself that I knew best and she'd come to realise it. I told myself a lot of things, all of them utter drivel. I was that sure I was right, it didn't even occur to me to ask what anyone else thought. What a fool I was.'

Ainsley made a sound of protest. Innes shook his head. 'No, I really was, and arrogant with it. If you give me a minute, I'm nearly done. I just need a minute.'

He took a deep breath, then another, obviously steeling himself. Ainsley had no option but to wait, feeling quite sick at what he told her, and at what the telling of it was doing to him.

With a little nod, as if in answer to some internal dialogue, Innes continued brusquely, 'Blanche wrote to Malcolm. It hadn't occurred to me that she'd do that, that she'd want to try to explain herself—and me, too, in the process. She had the letter delivered after she'd fled. She had relatives in London. They were happy to take her and her fortune, I assume. I don't know. She ran, and Malcolm got her letter, and when he showed it to me, I am ashamed to say what I felt was anger. I'd done my best to make all right, and she'd thwarted me. I didn't think of her feelings or even his at first, only mine.'

Innes was speaking quickly now, the words tumbling out, as if they'd been packed deep inside him all these years. 'So I was angry with her. I think I even went so far as to tell Malcolm I'd get her back for him, persuade her to marry him. The arrogance of me! It was that word I used, *persuade*, that betrayed me. Malcolm had suspected of course, but he had not been sure. "What do you mean, persuade her?" he asked me, and you should have seen the look on his face. Even now

I can picture it. "How could you persuade her? Why should you?" I felt sick. Then, when the accusations finally came, I tried to lie to him, but we could never lie to each other, Malcolm and I, I should have remembered that from the first. So finally I told him, trying to sound as noble as I thought I'd been, only in the face of it, seeing his face, seeing his hopes, his dreams, crushed—for he had loved her truly, you see. Unlike me. He really had loved Blanche. "I'd have given her up," he told me. "I only ever wanted her to be happy. How could you think I would marry her, knowing that she wanted you?"'

Ainsley sat as still as stone, her attention riveted on Innes, but he kept his eyes on the cross. His voice was cold now, as stripped of emotion, as his face was stripped of colour. Listening to him, she felt chilled.

'I told him it all,' he was saying, 'and Malcolm—Malcolm got quieter and quieter. When I asked him if he forgave me, he said there was nothing to forgive, but that he wanted to be left alone, and I was so racked with guilt that I wanted nothing more than to leave him. Then he said that I should go after her. That I should make her happy. He said again that all he ever wanted was for us to be happy, and then he closed the door on me, and—and those were the last words he ever spoke to me.'

Ainsley was lost for words, but Innes was not finished tearing himself apart. 'So you see,' he said, with a painful crack in his voice, finally meeting her eyes, 'my brother took his own life, but it was me who killed him. And now I have his lands, too,' he said with a bitter laugh. 'I have all of it, and I deserve none of it.'

'You do not have Blanche,' Ainsley whispered. 'You

gave her up, though you loved her.' It was dreadful, but that was the thing that hurt the most.

'Don't go thinking there was anything noble about that,' Innes said with a sneer, 'because there was not. I didn't love her. That's why it was so easy to try to hand her back to Malcolm like an unwanted parcel, only I was so carried away with my own lofty gesture that I didn't notice that until later.' He rubbed his knuckles into his eyes, looking deeply weary. 'When it came down to it, what I really wanted was to give my brother a reason to side with me against our father. If Malcolm was beholden to me for the love of his life, then he'd take my part, he'd help force my father to let me leave Strone Bridge on my terms. Do you see, Ainsley?' Innes said earnestly, clasping her hands in his. 'I was selfish at every step of the way. It cost my brother his life. I owe it to Malcolm to restore the heritage I deprived him of. I can atone here for what I've done, but I don't deserve to be happy. This morning, I caught a glimpse of what that might be like. A timely reminder of what I deprived my brother of. I don't deserve it, but you do. Do you understand now, why I told you?'

Sadly, Ainsley understood only too well. He thought to drive her away. He thought to disgust her. She felt only unutterably sad, for his tragic confession changed everything and nothing. 'I understand that I can't make you happy,' she said, 'but if what you intended was to make me despise you, then you have failed. You were all so very young.'

'That is no excuse.'

His tone made it clear he would not be swayed. Only a few months ago, Ainsley would have accepted this. 'It is,' she said. 'We all make mistakes through lack of experience. If I had loved John as much as I thought I did, perhaps he would not have died.'

'That's ridiculous. You know—'

'I know *now* how much my own lack of confidence contributed to the—the deterioration of our marriage, but I did not know then,' Ainsley said heatedly. 'I know *now*, thanks to your encouragement, that I'm neither useless nor unattractive.'

'Ainsley, he did that to you—'

'No,' she interrupted him determinedly. 'I am not saying John was without fault, but nor was he entirely to blame. We were a—a fatal combination, but, Innes, how were we to know that?' She clutched tightly at his fingers, pulling him towards her. 'I have learned so much since I came here. I still feel guilty, and I still have regrets, but I am no longer eaten up with them. John is dead, and there's nothing I can do about it, save make sure I don't make the same mistakes again. You can do the same. Would not Malcolm want you to be happy?'

He held her gaze for a long moment, then flung her away, getting to his feet. 'That's not the point. I understand that you're trying to make me feel better, but you can't. You don't understand.'

'I do.' She got slowly to her feet, feeling quite leaden. 'You have made up your mind that I must go, and that is the one thing upon which we agree. I ask only that you allow me to remain here until I can— There are some things that I…'

'Of course. Obviously we must wait to ensure that there were no consequences from this morning.'

It took her a moment to understand his meaning, and when she did, another moment to control the tears that welled suddenly into her eyes. Ainsley turned towards the sea, hoping to blame the breeze. 'A few weeks,' she said, thinking that would suffice to both torture her and accustom her.

'The end of the year,' Innes said. 'An ending and a beginning.'

She whirled round, thinking for an awful moment that he was making fun of her, but his expression was as bleak as she felt. The thought that he was finding this almost as difficult as she was, however, was no comfort at all. 'Until the end of the year,' she agreed.

They made their way back past the chapel in silence, each wrapped up in their own tortuous thoughts. It was not until they reached the terrace again, and both stopped of their own accord, that Ainsley remembered her plans for the castle, but immediately abandoned any notion of sharing them with Innes right now. Instead, she asked one of the two unanswered questions. 'What about Blanche? What happened to her?'

Innes stared at her blankly. 'I have no idea.' Did he care too little or too much? It seemed impossible that he should not know, for the Glen Vadie estate was less than twenty miles from here. 'She never returned to Scotland,' he added, presumably in response to her sceptical look.

'Don't you want to know if she's happy?'

Innes shrugged dismissively. 'I never sought her out, and she has never, to my knowledge, tried to get in touch with me for the same reason. Guilt,' he clarified. 'She will not wish to be reminded of those times any more than I do, and I have done enough damage, without dragging it all up for her. I know you think that's hard, Ainsley, but it's best left alone.'

'You are very sure of that,' she said.

'Yes. That's not arrogance. I've had fourteen years to make sure.' He pushed his hair back from his face and smiled very wearily. 'You do understand, Ainsley, this is how it has to be? I won't—I won't— I will sleep in my own bedchamber from now on.'

'Yes,' she whispered.

He took a step towards her, then stopped. 'I must go and speak to Robert. Don't wait dinner for me.'

He turned away, but she caught his arm. 'Innes, I— Thank you for telling me. I won't— I promise I won't make it difficult for you.'

He enveloped her in a fierce hug. 'I never thought you would. I only want— I'm sorry.'

She watched him go, hurtling down the scar in the cliff that would be the new road, allowing the tears to run down her cheeks now that he could no longer see her. She stood for a long time, staring out at the Kyles of Bute, her mind numb, her heart aching. Then she scrubbed at her eyes with her sleeve and drew a shaky breath. Innes had done so much to help free her from the burden of her past. She had until the end of the year to do what she could to return the favour. Which meant she had better make haste if she was going to track down Blanche Caldwell.

Chapter Twelve

Dear 'Anna',

Your letter touched my heart. The love you feel for this man shines like a beacon from the page. I do not doubt that, as you say, you have in him found your soul mate. It therefore pains me all the more to tell you that I can see no way for you to have a future with him that could be anything other than troubled. Were you a woman of fewer principles, if you loved this man less, then I would gladly tell you what you so desperately want to hear, that love can triumph over all. But, my dear, this can only happen when that love is equally given and received, and sadly, in your case, it is not. This widower, you have made clear, loves his three children before all else, and these children have made their unequivocal opposition to his proposed marriage to you abundantly clear over a prolonged period. You have done all you can to win them round. Their opposition has increased rather than decreased over time, and now encompasses their dead mother's family, too. Frankly, if this man loved you as much as you love him, he would have made a stand by now. He will never put you first. The rights and wrongs of this make no difference, 'Anna', because you love him too much to endanger his happiness, and if you truly believed that this was with you at the potential cost of his relationship with his children, you would have acted accordingly. That you have turned to me for advice tells its own story, don't you think?

It is therefore with profound regret that I am forced to advise you this: you must leave him, for he will never let you go, but nor will he marry you while the situation remains as it is. I hope you will take strength from doing what is right for you. I pray, as I am sure all our readers will, too, that you will find the future happiness that you deserve.

With my very best wishes,
Madame Hera

Ainsley put down her pen and dabbed at her cheeks with her handkerchief. This was one letter that she would not show to Innes. It was now the beginning of December. Having bared his soul, he had retreated like a wounded animal, making it clear that he wanted neither comfort nor further discussion on the subject of Blanche and Malcolm. Or the date of Ainsley's departure from Strone Bridge, set for the first week in January.

She had been through the wringer of emotions, from shock to horror, from pity to compassion, sorrow and sadness, jealousy, anger, dejection, but she had not once doubted, since that day at Malcolm's graveside, that she must leave. Reading over Madame Hera's advice to 'Anna', Ainsley was confronted with how fundamentally her own feelings had changed in the face of Innes's determination not to allow himself to be reconciled to his past. She had not given up hope of contacting Blanche to help with this, but having had no response to her letter, and with only a few weeks left till the end of the year when she must leave Strone Bridge, Ainsley was not optimistic.

In one sense, it made no difference. Like 'Anna', she had found her soul mate, but unlike 'Anna', Ainsley could now see very clearly that her soul mate was not free to love her as she deserved to be loved, and also unlike 'Anna', Ainsley had grown to believe that she would settle for nothing less. It was strange and surprising, too, how much less important her inability to bear children had become. It grieved her deeply, but in a sense, she had been forced to acknowledge, she had been hiding behind it, pretending to herself that it was this that prevented her from declaring her love, telling herself that she was making a noble sacrifice in removing herself from Innes's life when in fact she must have known that it would have made no difference. He would not love her. He would not allow himself to love her. And Ainsley, having experienced second best, was not about to accept it again.

Lying wide awake and aching with longing at night, she could not decide which was worse: knowing that Innes wanted her so much, or knowing that he did not want her enough. She loved him, but in her time here she had come to love the person she had become, too.

She knew he still wanted her, she no longer questioned her own desirability, but she would not use it to push them both into temporarily satisfying a passion that would ultimately make it harder for her to leave.

She longed more than anything to force Innes to see his past more clearly, but she could not, and the woman who could do so remained incommunicado. So Ainsley concentrated on the one thing she could do to help, her plans for the castle, which today she had decided were finally in an advanced enough state for her to share with Innes. Putting Madame Hera's correspondence to one side, she hurried to her room to check her *toilette*. Her dress was of taffeta, printed in autumn colours. The bodice was fitted tightly to her waist, and came to a deep point. The fashionable oval neckline was trimmed with shirring of the same material, and the long sleeves, like the bodice, ended in a sharp point.

Though it was early December, the sun had a hint of unseasonable warmth as she made her way to the pier in search of Innes. He was in his shirtsleeves. He had lost weight since coming to Strone Bridge. Days spent in the fields and out here in the bay had sculpted his muscles. He would smell of sweat and the sea and the peaty air, and of himself. There was a spot, just where his ribs met, where she liked to rest her cheek and listen to his heartbeat and where she always imagined she could breathe in the essence of him.

'Ainsley? Did you want me?'

'Yes.' Too late, she heard the longing in her voice. It was no consolation to see it reflected momentarily in his eyes, too. 'I mean, I was hoping to speak to you,' she amended hastily. 'I have something I'd like to discuss with you.' Innes nodded, pulling his heavy fisherman's jumper over his shirt. 'I thought we could go up to the castle,' she said when he looked at her expectantly. 'That way we won't be interrupted.'

The climb back up helped calm her flutter of nerves. She had worked so hard on her plans, but though she had been sure that it would be a pleasant surprise for Innes, it occurred to her belatedly that she had, by keeping her work a secret, contradicted her own hard-won wish to be consulted.

She opened the heavy front door with her keys and led the way through to the Great Hall. 'Do you remember,' she asked nervously, 'that I said the solution to Strone Bridge's economy would prove to be something other than modernising the crofts? In fact, you came up with the idea yourself, that first day you showed me round this place.'

Innes shook his head, frowning in puzzlement. 'I'm not sure I'm following you.'

'Napier did it a few years ago—the Loch Eck tour,' Ainsley said. 'I've been reading about it. He built the pier for the steamer and arranged the onward connections to places of interest. Do you not remember joking about it—a tea room, a gift shop for the tweed?'

'Vaguely, but I'm not sure...'

'And you told me yourself that the railway will run all the way from Glasgow to Greenock soon, so that there will be any number of people able to make the trip.'

'Excursionists. Is that what you're talking about?'

'More than that.' Ainsley smiled, excitement taking over from her nerves as she led him over to the table where she had laid everything out so carefully. 'Welcome to Strone Bridge Castle Hotel,' she said with a flourish.

Innes stared down at the plans, the drawings she and Mr Alexander had pulled together, the sketch she herself had made of the railway poster. He picked up the draft of the guidebook, leafing through it, and then the pages of costings she had so painstakingly worked on. 'You did all this?' he asked.

'I should have told you,' she said. 'I know I ought to have consulted you, but I wanted to surprise you.'

'You have.' He wandered round the table, picking up papers and putting them down again, the frown deepening on his face. 'Do you really believe people will pay to stay here?'

'Innes, I can't imagine anyone *not* wanting to spend the night here. I know you hate the place, but it's a real castle, for goodness' sake, with real turrets, and all these huge big rooms, and lots of pomp and splendour, and the views and— Yes, I really do think there would be any number of people willing to spend the night here. Or several. As you can see, I've even considered the possibility of leasing it out for weddings and the like. You can charge different prices, depending on which of the bedchambers people occupy, and more for the ones with ghosts in them.'

He was staring down at the railway poster. She had no idea what he was thinking. 'I thought that Mhairi would be the perfect candidate to run the place,' Ainsley continued. 'I thought it was the sort of restitution that would appeal to you, to have her installed as a chatelaine here.'

Now he did smile, albeit fleetingly. 'You were right about that. My father would be furious.'

'More important, there isn't anyone who could do a better job,' Ainsley rushed on. 'And there will be employment for any number of people here. Staff for the hotel, groundsmen. There's room for about forty or fifty guests at least, I'd say. And then there will be the food that can be provided direct from the crofts, and the tweed to sell, and—and it will mean that people don't have to emigrate to find a new life, Innes.' She laced her hands together tightly. 'What do you think?'

'I don't know.' He ran his hand through his hair. 'I can't believe you've done all this yourself.'

'Not myself. Robert has been helping, though I've sworn him to secrecy, for I did not want anyone else to know before you.' Still, Innes gave her no clue as to what he was thinking. 'You're worried it still won't be enough,' Ainsley rushed on. 'I wondered that myself, and also I was thinking that even fifty well-paying guests would not turn enough profit to justify the renovations for several years—you can see the rough figures—very rough, I'm no expert. So I thought— Well, actually it would be better if I showed you.'

'Showed me what?'

She led them through the Great Hall out into the atrium and produced the key that opened the hidden door. 'Wait till you see. I've got it all thought out, I...'

'Where are you going?' Innes stopped dead in front of the doorway.

'The tower. The view is magnificent, and it is easier to show you what I'm proposing from there.'

'You've been up there?' He had his hands dug deep into his pockets. 'I told you not to go up there.'

He looked angry. 'It's perfectly safe, if that's what you're worried about,' Ainsley said. 'I had Mr Alexander look at it, and he said that it was structurally sound. I had him look over all of the castle, and in fact he said…'

'I'm not interested in Robert's opinion. I thought I'd made it very clear that this tower was off limits.'

'No, you didn't. You said the key was lost, and that it was unsafe, and since neither have proved to be the case—' She broke off, at a loss to understand his reaction. 'It's the cottages,' she said. 'The tied cottages that have been empty for several years. I was thinking we could renovate them and let them out to families who cannot afford to holiday in the hotel, and who—'

'Enough!'

Ainsley flinched at the fury in his voice. 'What is wrong?'

'I told you,' Innes roared. 'I said to you not to go up there.'

'You didn't. You're being quite unreasonable. You said…'

'Did you not ask yourself why the place was locked? For God's sake, did not Mhairi say anything?'

'Mhairi doesn't know anything of what I'm doing. No one does, save Mr Alexander. I— It was meant to be a surprise. Is it because I didn't tell you, Innes? Is that what's wrong?'

He gazed at her for a long moment, his eyes dark, his lips thinned. 'My brother died by throwing himself from that tower, that's what's wrong, and that's why all your plans must come to nothing.'

Innes turned the key in the lock of the hidden door, then detached it from the rest of the bunch and pocketed it. 'I'm sorry for all the hard work you've put into this, but you've wasted your time,' he said curtly before turning on his heel and walking away without a backward glance.

Chapter Thirteen

Innes did not return to the Home Farm until late that night, and he was gone for the rest of the next day. It was late and Ainsley had been lying wide awake for several hours, torn between fretting and anger, when she heard his footsteps in the corridor. They did not stop outside his room, but carried on to hers. She scrambled up in bed as the door was flung open. 'You couldn't leave it, could you?'

'I don't know what you mean.'

'This!' He strode over to the bed, waving a piece of paper at her. 'Don't pretend it wasn't your doing, for she mentions you herself, and even if she had not, I recognise some of your handiwork—or should I say Madame Hera's! "Take the opportunity to put the past to rest." That's one of yours,' Innes quoted, his voice heavy with sarcasm, 'and then there's "free to make a fresh start." One thing hasn't changed. Blanche's letters leave no room for misinterpretation.'

'Blanche?' Ainsley repeated. 'You mean Blanche wrote to you?'

'At your behest.'

'Yes, but— No, I thought she would write to me, but—Innes, what does she say?'

'That fourteen years is enough time to realise that love should conquer all and it's time we surrendered to the happiness Malcolm sacrificed himself to give us,' he said mockingly. 'Wouldn't your Madame Hera just love it if she did? Isn't that exactly what you hoped for when you interfered?'

His words were like whiplashes, deliberately and painfully cruel. The old Ainsley would have been intimidated, frightened, silent. The new Ainsley was hurt, but also furious. 'I hoped that you'd take the opportunity to at least listen to whatever she had to say,' she said through clenched teeth. 'What you call interfering was actually done through a genuine concern for your happiness, which, contrary to what you believe, I think you deserve. I hoped that you would credit me with actually caring about you, Innes, enough to risk meddling. Obviously I was wrong, and you are for reasons known only to yourself absolutely set on making the rest of your life as miserable as you can, though why you think that will make any sort of restitution when… Och, what the hell does it matter now what I thought! If you won't listen to Blanche, why would I think you'd listen to me?'

Innes crunched the letter into a ball and threw it at the grate. 'Dammit, Ainsley, it's you who won't listen! Why must you— I told you, I don't want you to care for me. I told you…'

She had had enough. Pushing back the blankets, Ainsley got out of bed and stood before him, hands on her hips. 'Do you think I could forget for a moment what you told me when it almost broke my heart!' she exclaimed. 'For goodness' sake, Innes, just because you want something to be so doesn't make it so! There are some things you can't control, and how I feel is one of them.'

'You think you're so damn clever! Can you not see, you annoying, interfering woman, that how I feel is another?' he said, yanking her into his arms.

He gave her no chance to respond, but covered her mouth with his. His kiss was passionate, dark and desperate. Exactly how she felt. Ainsley kissed him back with an abandon that left no room for thought. They staggered together, kissing, tearing at each other's clothes, kissing. Her back was pressed against the wall. His hands were on her breasts, her waist, her bottom. She wrapped one leg around him to steady herself. He pulled his jumper over his head and tore at the opening of her nightgown, groaning as he took her nipple into his mouth and sucked hard, making her moan, arch against him, thrust herself shamelessly against the thick bulge of his arousal.

She clutched at his behind, her fingers digging into the taut muscles of his buttocks. His mouth enveloped her other breast now, tugging at her nipple, making her ache and thrust and moan. Her fingers fumbled with the opening of his breeches. Her hands slid in, wrapping around the satin-soft length of him, sliding up to the hot, wet tip, and back down. 'Innes,' she said, the strain in her voice making her sound as if she'd run a mile.

'Ainsley,' he said raggedly, 'I need to be inside you.'

'Yes.' There was no hesitation in her agreement. She knew without a doubt that this was no beginning but an end, but she wanted him, needed to be part of him, this one last time. 'Yes,' she said, and when he hesitated, she arched against him. 'Yes, Innes, now.'

His face was dark, colour slashing his cheeks, his eyes deep pools. He lifted her onto the edge of the bed, pulling up the skirts of her nightgown. She wrapped her legs around his flanks, bracing herself on the mattress. He kissed her. He lifted her. He entered her. She started to come as he slid inside her. Tension, unstoppable, winding tighter and tighter as she thrust, pulsing around him as he thrust for the second time, her cries harsh, loud, demanding more and harder and more. Not enough, she didn't want it to stop, but she wanted him to have what she had. 'Come now,' she said. 'Innes, come with me.'

He did just as she asked, though he did not spend himself inside her, and panting, spiralling out of control, clinging, she did not regret that, because she knew he would, and this had to be it, the last time, the perfect time. She kissed him deeply, her lips clinging to his, her tongue touching his, touching, clinging, kissing, telling him with her mouth what she could not speak. There were tears lurking, but she would not shed those. Only she kissed him again. His mouth. His jaw. His neck. Nuzzling her face into the hollow of his shoulder, closing her eyes and trying to etch it all in her mind, as his heart thundered under her and his chest heaved, and his hands held her so tight, as if he would not let her go, though she knew he would.

Ainsley knew, even as they lay there, breathing heavily in the aftermath of their union, that it was completely and irrevocably over. Innes cared for her, but it tormented him. He had lost himself in her to stop that torment, and she had lost herself in him because she could not resist him. But she could not carry on this way, and she would not allow herself to be the means by which he escaped his past.

'I'm sorry.'

She dragged her eyes open as Innes rolled away from her, his expression troubled. 'What for?' she asked.

'Not this, but the way it happened. You meant well—the idea for the hotel, writing to—to her. You meant well, I know that. I shouldn't have lost my temper.'

But he wasn't going to change his mind. Ainsley got to her feet and pulled on her wrapper. 'I should have consulted you,' she said, turning her back to him to tend the fire.

'It would certainly have saved you a lot of effort.'

The final confirmation, as if she needed it. He was standing behind her now. 'You must be tired,' she said. 'You should get some sleep.'

'Ainsley, I really am sorry.'

He looked quite wretched. She surrendered to the temptation to comfort him one last time and went to him, wrapping her arms around his waist, resting her cheek on his chest. He pulled her tight, almost crushing the breath from her. 'You do understand,' he said.

'I do, Innes.' She looked up, brushing his hair from his eyes, and kissed him gently on the lips. 'I understand perfectly,' she said. 'Now go and get some sleep.'

He went. He would have stayed if she had asked him, but she did not. Instead, she set about making her preparations to leave, packing a few necessities in a bandbox, leaving the rest to be sent on. She found Blanche's balled-up letter lying under the nightstand and smoothed it out. Her own words, quoted in the other woman's elegant hand, leaped out of the page at her, and at the end, a plaintive request from Blanche for a meeting. Nothing more. It was signed with a flourish, the first name only.

Innes had been joking when he suggested marrying Blanche would make all right, but there was still a chance it would. Blanche was his first love. His only one? How easy would it be for him to fall in love with her again if he could be persuaded his dead brother sanctioned the match? Blanche had always been intended to be the wife of the laird of Strone Bridge. She had been groomed for it. She had birth and money and beauty. She would be a laird's wife worth her salt. A woman who belonged here. A woman blessed by the last laird. No usurper. A woman who was perfect in just about every way, including, no doubt, her ability to pop out any number of the requisite heirs.

Feeling slightly sick, Ainsley folded the letter carefully. Pulling Innes's discarded jumper on over her nightclothes, she made her way softly down the stairs. Outside, the air was sharp with the first hint of frost. The stars were mere pinpricks, the moon a waning crescent, but she knew her way now, without looking. Up to the castle, along the path, to the terrace and her view. That was how she thought of it, though it would not be hers after today. Gazing out at the black shape that was the Isle of Bute, longing gripped her, tinged with anger. All her hard work had come to naught. When she was gone from here, there would be nothing of her left. Perhaps that was what Innes wanted, to forget all about her, and to immolate himself on the altar of the past. Tragic as it was, Ainsley was becoming impatient with his determination to earn a martyrdom. She loved him with all her heart, and more than anything, she wanted him to be happy, even if he did decide to marry Blanche. He had lived with guilt and regret for so long, she would not add to that with tears, with long goodbyes, with dragging out her time here.

Eyes straining into the inky blackness, she sought to capture the view in her mind for all time. Then she turned away and headed back to the Home Farm to complete her preparations. Before dawn broke she was tapping on the front door of Eoin's croft, her luggage already left waiting down in the bay.

Dearest Innes,

I am writing this as myself, and not Madame Hera, though the truth is, in my time at Strone Bridge, I believe we have become more or less one and the same thing. No doubt reading this as Madame's advice will make it easier for you to ignore. I expect you will. I wish with all my heart that you will not.

As you can see, I have rescued Blanche's letter. I hope you forgive me when I confess to having read it. Innes, please do as she asks and meet her. If you cannot put your own demons of guilt to bed, then perhaps you can help her. The poor woman was but a child when these tragic events that have shaped both your lives took place—as indeed were you, though I know you do not agree with me on that score. You are in the unique position of being able to help each other. I beg you to try to do so.

As to the rest. Robert Alexander can answer any questions about my proposal for Strone Bridge's future, which my documentation leaves unanswered. It is not pride—well, only a little!—that leads me to ask you to consider this, but a genuine belief that it will help save your estates and the people who live there. I'd like to think I've left something of value behind. I hope it's obvious how much I have come to love the place and the people.

I leave it to you to manage the termination of our agreement in whatever way you think best. I leave Strone Bridge a much stronger person than the poor wee soul you met at the lawyer's office all those months ago. I leave it ready to do battle with whatever the future holds, and confident that I can. You have helped me in too many ways to list. I do not regret a second spent with you. With all my heart I wish you happiness, because you're wrong, Innes, it is something you well and truly deserve.

A.

Innes finished reading the letter, then started all over again, as if a second reading would change the content. He looked up from the breakfast table to discover Mhairi was still there, watching him with such an expression of compassion on her face that he knew there was no point in pretending.

'Do you know when—or how—she left?' Innes asked.

'Eoin took her at first light. She left me a note asking to have the rest of her things sent on.'

'Where to?'

'It is a carrier's address in Edinburgh.'

Innes looked at the housekeeper helplessly. 'I don't even know if she's got any money. She has her allowance, but—I'll need to— I'll have to arrange to— She'll need a place to stay. I…'

'I think Mrs Drummond's more than capable of sorting that out for herself, if you don't mind my saying,' Mhairi interrupted drily. 'It seems to me that you'd better concentrate on sorting yourself out.'

'What do you mean?'

'Blanche Caldwell is back at Glen Vadie, did you know?'

Innes tore his eyes away from a third, fruitless reading of Ainsley's missive. 'At Glen Vadie? No, I didn't know. She wrote me a letter, though.'

'Does Mrs Drummond know?'

'About the letter?'

'About Blanche, Innes,' Mhairi spoke sharply. 'If that good woman has gone haring back to Edinburgh to leave the way clear for you to pick up where you never should have started with that Caldwell woman…'

'Dear God, do you think that's it?' For a moment, his heart leaped. If that was all it was, he could fetch her back. But for what purpose, and for how long? Innes slumped back miserably in his chair. 'What are you waiting for?' he demanded, seeing Mhairi, arms akimbo, was still there. 'She's gone, and she's made it very clear she won't be coming back, so go and pack her things and leave me in peace.'

* * *

But peace was not something Innes could find over the next few days. On the one hand, he was tracking Ainsley's journey in his mind, wondering where she was, who she was with, whether she was thinking of him, whether she was missing him as he ached for her. On the other, he was determinedly trying to put her firmly out of his mind and refusing to allow himself to think about what was staring him in the face—or, more accurately, fighting to be heard from his heart.

He did love her. He had, despite all his best efforts, fallen completely in love with her. He loved her in a way he had never loved Blanche, as if she were part of himself. Without her, he felt as if that part was missing. It did not help that every corner of Strone Bridge reminded him of her. It did not help, lying in her bed, the scent of her on the pillow. It did not help, avoiding her favourite view, any more than it helped forcing himself to stare at it. Mhairi's tight-lipped disapproval didn't help any more than her misguided attempts to comfort him, or Eoin's insistence that when he left her on the Isle of Bute, Ainsley had been 'very well', whatever that meant. Innes hoped she was very well. It was wrong of him to hope that she was as miserable as he, wrong of him to hope that she missed him as much, ached for him as much, loved him as much.

She had never said the words, but he was standing on the castle terrace looking out at the Kyles of Bute when he realised that she did love him, and it hit him then, how much he was wilfully throwing away. What was wrong with him? Looking up at the tower, he remembered exactly what was wrong with him. Standing in front of Malcolm's grave a while later confirmed it. Guilt. The demons of the past. Ainsley was right.

Something glinted in the browning grass by the stone. Stooping to pick it up, Innes found a brooch. A simple thing of silver, with a name etched into it. He recognised it, for she had always worn it. So she had been here. He wondered how she'd managed it without his knowing, but it wasn't much of a puzzle. Mhairi or Eoin, or both.

Finally, Innes allowed himself to consider the advice Ainsley had left him in her letter. Heading back to the Home Farm, he read it again. And again. He found the keys on the desk where Ainsley had left them. The tower key, he still had in his coat pocket. In the Great Hall, all Ainsley's plans were still there as she had laid them out for him. So much work. He couldn't believe how stupid he'd been not to see the love that had gone into it. He felt sick to the back teeth thinking of how ungrateful he'd sounded, how much it must have hurt her to have it all thrown back in her face.

He lit a lamp and picked it up. At the doorway, goosebumps prickled on his arms. Mhairi always said there was no mistaking what she called a presence. It grew cold, she said, as if you'd walked into an ice-house, and you got a sense of it, like a breath of wind over your shoulder. Innes whirled round, but there was nothing there.

The lock turned easily. He climbed the stairs slowly, his feet remembering the twists and turns as if it had been yesterday, and not fourteen years since last he was there. Past the first-floor landing and then the second. The door at the top was closed. Heart pounding, he took a deep breath, pushed it open and stepped inside.

Nothing. Standing on the threshold, lamp held high, he felt absolutely nothing of his brother's presence. Mouth dry, he made his way over to the window. The view, in the gloaming, was as Ainsley had always said: spectacular. He opened the casement and forced himself to look down. The ground rose up to meet him, dizzying. Innes drew back hurriedly, looking over his shoulder, feeling like an idiot but unable to stop himself.

No Malcolm. Instead, he saw the table, so carefully set out. The scale model that Robert must have made of the castle and its grounds, the tied cottages, the newly landscaped gardens. Setting the lamp down, Innes pulled up a chair, picked up the sheaf of papers covered in Ainsley's distinctive scrawl and began to read.

Edinburgh, two weeks later

Ainsley put down the book she thought she'd been reading when she realised she'd been turning pages for the past half hour and could remember not a single word. Getting up from the nest of cushions and blankets she'd made for herself on Felicity's worn but comfortable sofa, she wandered over to the window. Outside, the streets of Edinburgh's New Town were quiet, for it was the Sunday after Christmas, and the church bells of St Andrew's and St George's were silent, the morning services well underway.

Felicity was spending the week with her family, so Ainsley had the flat to herself. While Felicity had been here, she'd forced herself to pin a smile onto her face and get on. With Felicity absent, Ainsley had allowed herself a few days to mope. Not that she was regretting what she had done, but she needed time to make sure it had sunk in. Innes hadn't been in touch. Though her luggage had arrived at the carrier, it had contained no note from him. Not that she'd been expecting it. She certainly hadn't been expecting him to rush after her, and even if he had it wouldn't have changed anything, so there was no point in wishing for such a stupid waste of effort.

Sighing, bored with the circles her mind was running round, she pressed her forehead to the windowpane. Next week, the first of the New Year, she would start to look for a room. Even if she'd remained at Strone Bridge as agreed, that time would now be over. She wondered how Innes would see in the New Year. Ainsley—or Madame Hera—had been invited to a party hosted by the *Scottish Ladies Companion*. She knew she ought to go.

Outside, a post chaise pulled up on the cobbled street. Her heart did a daft wee flip, then sank as the door opened and a maidservant descended, followed by a young woman. Ainsley watched listlessly as the baggage was unloaded. Farther along the crescent, a man had appeared. Tall, dressed in black, he was making his way slowly along, checking the numbers on each of the doors.

It wasn't him. Why should it be him? All the same, Ainsley gazed down in dismay at her crumpled gown, put a hand to her hair, which was falling down from the loose knot she'd put it up in this morning. She dare not leave the window to consult the mirror over the fireplace. Not that it could possibly be Innes. Even though he did walk like Innes.

It *was* him. Her heart stopped and then began to race

as she looked down into his face. Such blue eyes. He raised his hand in recognition. She couldn't move. He disappeared up the steps. The bell clanged. Still partly inclined to believe he was a figment of her imagination, Ainsley went down to open the door.

'It is you.' He looked tired. He looked—nervous? Afraid? 'Has something happened?' Ainsley asked, panicking. 'Is someone— Is everyone…?'

'Fine. They're all fine.'

'And you?'

Innes shrugged. He smiled, or he seemed to be trying to smile. 'I don't know. I'm hoping to find out. Can I come in?'

'How did you know I'd be here?'

'Eoin finally gave me Miss Blair's address.'

'She's not here. She's gone to her parents for New Year.'

'Ainsley, can I come in?'

She opened the door wider and Innes stepped through, following her up the stairs to the living room. She closed this door behind her, then simply leaned against it, unsure what to say, refusing to allow herself to think about what this might mean. It had been hard enough to leave him the first time. 'What is it?' she asked, and her voice sounded sharper than she meant, but it couldn't be helped.

Innes took off his greatcoat and put it over one of the chairs. His hat went on the table, and his gloves. He stood in front of the fire, hands clasped behind his back. Then he went over to the window, where she had been standing a few moments ago. Then he joined her at the door. 'I don't know where to start,' he said. 'I had a speech, but I can't remember it now.'

He waited, but she could think of nothing to say. 'I've seen Blanche,' he said.

Ainsley's heart plummeted, even as she told herself firmly that this was good news. 'Good,' she said, as if saying out loud would make it so.

Innes nodded. 'Yes, yes, it was.' He took another turn round the room, to the fireplace, to the window, back to her. 'You were right. Or Madame Hera was,' he said with another of those lopsided smiles.

'Good,' Ainsley said again, this time with a firm nod. 'I'm glad.' She didn't sound glad. She sounded as if she were being strangled. 'Did it help?'

Innes ran his hand through his hair. He had had it cut. Suddenly she couldn't bear that he'd had it cut and she hadn't been there. She blinked furiously, but a tear escaped and ran down her cheek. She brushed it away quickly, but another fell.

'Ainsley...'

'It's nothing. I'm fine.' She pushed him away and went to sit on the sofa, pulling the comforting woollen blanket over her, not caring how she looked or what he thought. 'Just tell me, Innes, and get it over with.'

'I thought you'd be pleased.'

'I am! I will be,' she said through gritted teeth. 'Would you just tell me?'

He stared at her in astonishment, and then he laughed. 'Don't tell me Mhairi was right.'

When she had nothing to say to this strange remark, Innes came to sit beside her. He was smiling, this time in a way that made her heart, which had become as wayward as her voice, start to do what felt peculiarly like a dance. 'Ainsley, you can't possibly be thinking that I would want Blanche?'

She shrugged, though the gesture was somewhat obscured by the blanket covering her. 'You did before,' she said, and though she sounded like a petulant child now, she couldn't help adding, 'You told me yourself that she is beautiful, rich, well born.'

'But I'm married to you.'

'Not really. I told you in my letter that I would co-operate with however you saw fit to end it.'

'And in the meantime, you don't mind if I'm bedding my first love, is that it?'

'No!' Though he had not raised his voice, he sounded angry. Ainsley pushed back the blanket and got to her feet. 'You should not use a word like that in reference to your— To someone— To Blanche,' she said, picking up the poker and applying it furiously to the coals.

'Ainsley, I'm not bedding Blanche. I've no intentions of bedding her or even of making love to her. I can't believe you would think that. I'm married to you.'

'Not for much longer.'

The poker was wrested from her fingers. She was yanked to her feet, and held very tightly in an embrace. 'I came here in the hope of persuading you to make it for life. Please tell me I'm not wasting my time, Ainsley.'

Now her heart felt as though it was about to jump out of her mouth. The way he was looking at her, as if his life depended on her. But it did not. Surely it did not. She shook her head. 'I don't know what you're doing here.'

'I'm trying, in a very, very roundabout and long-winded way, to tell you that I love you. My only excuse for doing it so badly is that I've not said it before. Not like this. I've never meant it like this, and if you mention Blanche one more time...'

'It was you who mentioned her.'

He laughed. 'I was trying to show you that I'd understood. That I'd done what you advised. That I'd taken the opportunity to "put the past to rest", to quote Madame Hera.'

'That was me, actually.'

'But, as you pointed out to *me*, they are become one and the same person.' Innes pushed her hair back from her face. 'I thought I had to prove myself worthy before I told you, but I think I did it the wrong way round. I love you, Ainsley. I love you with all my heart, and though I can live without you, I can get by with my guilt and my demons persuading myself that it's all I deserve, I don't want to. I want to be happy, and the only thing that will make me truly happy is you.'

She had never believed there was such a thing, but she could have sworn what she saw in his face was the light of love. She had so many questions, but right now all that mattered was that. 'I love you,' Ainsley said, 'I love you every bit as much, and I could do as you said, too, I could live without you, but, Innes, I really don't want to.'

'You don't have to. Dearest, darling Ainsley, you don't have to.'

He kissed her in a way he'd never kissed her before. Gently. Tenderly. Tentatively. He kissed her as if he was afraid she would not kiss him back. He kissed her as if he was begging that she would. 'Ainsley, I know it's all back to front, but I love you so much,' he said. And then he kissed her again, and she told him, with her hands and her lips, how very, very much his love was returned.

Later, Innes thought, kissing her. There would be all the time in the world for explanations later. What mattered now was that he loved her, and she loved him, and she was in his arms and he could finally admit just how much he had missed her and how close he had come to losing her. He kissed her, whispering her name over, whispering the words over, kissing her, touching her, pulling her so close there was no space between them. He never wanted to let her go. He wanted to make love to her right now. Make real love. Make love that he'd never made before. 'I love you,' he said. 'I can't believe how much I love you. I can't believe how daft I've been not to realise.'

He kissed her again. She laughed. She kissed him. She laughed. She kissed him. They fell, kissing, laughing with happiness, on to the sofa. And there, they made love. Laughter giving way to sighs, and then seamlessly to bliss. Love. Who would have thought it? Love.

'I meant to do this the other way round,' Innes said afterwards, lying splayed on the couch, with Ainsley draped languorously on top of him.

She giggled. 'Is this a new variation in the palace of pleasures you haven't told me about?'

'Hussy!' He grinned. 'I meant that I planned to tell you what's been happening since I read your parting letter before declaring myself, but if it's variations you're interested in, my wanton wife, then I am sure I can come up with something.'

'Really? Already?' Ainsley wriggled against him,

her smile teasing. 'Are you trying to live up to the Drummond reputation for potency?'

Her face fell at her own silly words. Though she tried to hide it, he saw the flash of pain there as she moved away from him. 'Listen to me a moment,' Innes said urgently, pulling her right back to where she had been, lying over him. 'I love you exactly as you are. You need to believe me.' He touched her face gently. 'Strone Bridge is our legacy. It's all the legacy we need, and your love is all I need. I don't need you to prove it any other way than by being by my side, for better or for worse. I don't need a bairn, and I don't want you to go down the track of thinking that, or of thinking that you've somehow failed me if it doesn't happen. I need you to promise me that you believe me.'

A tear rolled down her cheek. 'Innes, you need to understand, I've been told by a doctor it's simply not possible.'

'And you need to understand that I mean what I say. I want you. That's all that matters to me. If it turned out I could not have a child, would you walk away?'

'Of course not!'

'Well, then, is this not a case of what's good for the goose being good for the gander?'

'Shouldn't it be the other way round?'

'Ainsley, I'm serious. I want you to be my wife. My real wife. My forever wife. My only love. I won't have this become an issue between us. I want us to have a fresh start in everything. I want us to be married. Will you marry me, my darling?'

'Again?'

'If that's what it takes.'

'Love me, that's all that it takes, and I promise, I won't let anything come between us.'

She kissed him softly on the mouth. Then she smiled at him, and Innes thought that maybe it was true what they said, that hearts could melt. He hugged her tightly, then he sat up, pulling her into the crook of his arm, wrapping the blanket around them. 'Now,' he said, 'I think I owe you a story. It's a long one, but I'll give you the gist of it now.'

He frowned, thinking back on all that had happened over the past two weeks. 'It wasn't finding the brooch that made me get in touch with her, or even her letter, but yours,' he concluded some time later, smiling fleetingly down at Ainsley. 'Your leaving like that brought to me my senses about how I felt for you. I'd always thought Strone Bridge was haunted by the ghosts of the past, but that was nothing compared to how it felt without you there. I kept expecting to see you at every turn. Especially at that view of the Kyles. Then there was Mhairi. And Eoin. And Robert—my goodness, that man went on and on about you. Everyone, asking me where you'd gone, when you'd be back.'

'Really?'

He laughed. 'You've no idea how much people have taken you to their hearts. It's not just me. You're part of the place, Ainsley.'

She kissed his hand, her eyes shining. 'It's part of me, too. I missed it nearly as much as I missed you.'

'Who'd have thought it?' He kissed the top of her head. 'It was when I was away the last time with Eoin I realised I'd come to think of it as home, and to think of you there, too. It scared the living daylights out of me.'

'That's when you told me about Malcolm?'

'Aye, there are no flies on you.' Innes kissed her again. 'That letter you left me—you said I deserved to be happy. That was the biggest problem, for I just couldn't see that I did. But then I was standing there in the tower looking at all the hard work you'd put into those plans, and I realised it wasn't just about me, but you, too. And Blanche—that point in your letter hit home, too. Was I actually glorying in my guilt, or so used to it that I couldn't see a way of escaping it? That turret room, I thought it held the bogeyman, but it was just a room with a view. You were right about that. It was there I began to think maybe you could have been right about other things. So I went to see her at Glen Vadie.'

Ainsley scrambled upright. 'And?'

'And it turns out things were not quite as I'd imagined,' Innes said wryly. 'Blanche ran away because she couldn't bring herself to marry Malcolm, as I told you. She wrote the letter to him, thinking that it was the right thing to do, to tell him, though she could not find the courage to do so to his face. She didn't think what it would do to him, because she didn't really think about what she'd said. That she didn't love him. That she couldn't marry him. She didn't say that she wanted to marry me, because she didn't.'

'What?'

'I know. It's farcical. Or it would be if it weren't so tragic. I'm not the only one who's been tying themselves in knots of guilt for the past fourteen years, nor am I the only one who swore off love, either.' Innes shook his head. 'I still can't believe it. She's been living in London unmarried all these years, until she met her man Murchison and fell head over heels at the age of thirty-two. So when your letter found her, out of the blue, she was delighted at the chance to finally come clean.'

Ainsley's jaw dropped. 'Blanche never wanted to marry you?'

'I know, love, it's unbelievable,' Innes said, grinning.

She slapped him playfully. 'You know what I mean.'

'I do.' He sobered. 'She said the same thing as you about Malcolm—that he'd have wanted us both to be happy. He thought, in his tragic, misguided way, that was what he was doing, clearing the way to make us so. It finally clicked with me, after you'd gone, that paying him back by making myself miserable was a stupid thing to do.'

'And Blanche?'

'Realised the same thing, not so very long ago, but all she did was confirm what you'd been telling me, Ainsley.'

'So she's as lovely on the inside as she is on the outside.'

He laughed. 'I expect she is, but there is no one as lovely as you for me. I thought I'd just proved that.'

'I hope you'll prove it again very soon.'

'Now, if you like.'

She smiled at him, the smile that sent the blood rushing to his groin, the smile he'd thought he would never see again. He kissed her on those delicious lips that were made for kissing. 'Now, and always,' he said, 'and for ever, too.'

Epilogue

Strone Bridge, New Year's Eve, 1840

Ainsley's gown for the first Hogmanay party to be held at Strone Bridge by the new laird and his lady, was of ivory silk. Cut very plainly, both the *décolleté* and the bodice were her favourite V-shape, showing her waist and her modest cleavage to advantage. The sleeves were short, puffed and trimmed with the same black lace that bordered the hem, and was formed into little flowers at the end of the ruched silk that ran in vertical stripes down the skirt, like waves on the sand.

The party was to be held in the Great Hall. She and Innes had arrived from Edinburgh only the day before, but it seemed Innes had left matters in Mhairi's capable hands beforehand. 'What if you had not found me? What if I had refused to come back?' Ainsley had asked him on the paddle steamer. Failure, he'd told her, was not an option. The look he'd given her then, aglow with love, made her want to kiss him then and there, on the blustery and freezing-cold deck of the *Rothesay Castle*.

It had begun snowing when they'd arrived at Strone Bridge, and it was snowing still. The last day of the year was spent making sure that the Home Farm was spotless, hanging rowan in the doorways for luck, and hazel to stop the bad spirits who'd been swept out getting back in again. Mhairi's advice, of course, but Ainsley had become so accustomed to pandering to good faeries and warding off bad that she'd almost started to believe in them.

She was making a final check in the mirror when the door opened and Innes entered the bedchamber. He was in the full Highland regalia he'd worn for the Rescinding. Her pulses leaped when he smiled at her. His hair was black as night. His eyes were the blue of the sea. She loved him so much.

'May I tell you, wife, that you look absolutely ravishing?'

'You may.' She dropped him a curtsy. 'May I tell you, husband, that you look absolutely ravishable?'

He laughed. 'I'm not sure that's a word, but I like it.'

'I think it's an excellent word, and I intend that Madame Hera makes it a popular one.'

'To keep a happy marriage, make sure your husband is ravishable at all times.'

'You see, it's perfect.' She put her arms around him and stood on her tiptoes to kiss him.

'Shall I prove how perfect?' he whispered.

She chuckled. 'Maybe next year. We have a ceilidh to attend.'

'A whole six hours, you're making me wait!'

'I'll make it worth your while, I promise,' Ainsley said with a meaningful look.

'I shall hold you to that,' Innes said with one of his devilish smiles. 'Did I tell you about the tradition of Reaffirming?'

'Is this another one of your invented customs?'

'It is.' He reached under the pillow and pulled out a leather box. 'I had this done in Edinburgh. Open it.'

Her fingers shaking, she did as she was bid. The rose-tinted diamond was the same, perfectly cut stone as before, but the setting was completely different. The diamond sat flat inside a very modern-looking circlet of gold, and the white diamonds that had encircled it were now also sunk inside the gold band. 'I've never seen anything like it,' Ainsley said. 'It's breathtaking.'

Innes slid the ring onto her finger, not where she had worn it for the Rescinding, on the middle finger of her right hand, but on her left hand, above her wedding band. 'A symbol of the passing of the old and the birth of the new,' he said. 'A reaffirming of what we promised, and a promise of so much more. I love you, Ainsley. I plan on loving you a little bit more every day.'

'A Reaffirming.' Her eyes were wet with tears, but she had never felt so happy. 'I think that might be my favourite custom yet.'

She had not thought she could be any happier, but as she stood by her husband's side in the Great Hall awaiting the bells that would herald the New Year, Ainsley thought she might burst with it. Looking around her at the faces, bright with the exertions of the reels and jigs, she couldn't help but compare it with the last time she had been here in this hall, a virtual stranger among them. Now she knew every person here by name. She knew which of the huddle of bairns at the far end of the hall belonged to which family and which croft.

But tonight, it was not only the people of Strone Bridge who were here to celebrate the New Year. There were new faces, too, from as far afield as Arran and Bute. The laird of Glen Vadie was here, and so, too, was his ward. Blanche Murchison, née Caldwell, was every bit as beautiful as Ainsley had imagined. Her hair was golden blonde. Her eyes were cornflower blue. Her brows were perfect arches. Her lips were a perfect Cupid's bow. The gown she wore was of silk the same colour as those big eyes of hers, and the diamonds on her necklace were obviously not paste. She was slight, several inches smaller than Ainsley, and she was most infuriatingly curvaceous. She had a smile to melt a man's heart, and she had one of those bell-like voices into the bargain. Were she not so obviously besotted by the man whose name she bore, Ainsley might have been worried. Then she turned to her own husband, who had made the introductions, and saw the way Innes smiled at her, felt the pressure of his hand on hers and looked down at the diamond glinting on her hand, and she decided that she had no need to be worried about a single thing.

The bells rang for midnight. On cue at the last chime came a thumping at the door, and the first foot arrived, chosen for his coal-black hair, sheepishly bearing a bottle of whisky and a black bun cake. Glasses were filled, and the call for a toast went up.

Innes put his arm around Ainsley's waist and called for silence. 'I'll keep this short and sweet,' he said, 'for you've better things to do than to listen to me. At the

Rescinding, we put the past to bed. Tonight, this first day of 1841, I want to talk about the future. The future my wife and I have planned here at Strone Bridge. The future I hope you will all share with us. Robert?'

He nodded over at the surveyor, who, with the help of several men, brought a long table into the centre of the room. 'This, I am proud to tell you, is all my lovely wife's idea,' Innes said. 'This is our promise to you. A Reaffirming,' he said, giving Ainsley a glowing look. 'A symbol of the passing of the old, and the birth of the new. Ladies and gentlemen, lads and lassies, I'd like you to raise your glasses to Strone Bridge Castle Hotel. *Sláinte*.'

* * * * *

HISTORICAL NOTE

Paddle steamers and the railways brought tourism to the west coast of Scotland at around the time when Ainsley and Innes decided to set up their hotel. Though the original and most popular destinations 'doon the watter' on the Clyde were Rothesay, Largs and Dunoon, Tighnabruaich (aka Strone Bridge) had its share of excursionists. The engineer David Napier, whose Loch Eck tours inspired Ainsley, built a pier on the Holy Loch in the 1830s, not far from my own home.

Numerous versions of the *Rothesay Castle* paddle steamer made the journey from Glasgow, Gourock and eventually Wemyss Bay railway terminals to the Isle of Bute. Today, the last sea-going paddle steamer, the *Waverley*, makes the same journey from Glasgow to Bute and down the beautiful Kyles all the way to Tighnabruaich.

Strone Bridge Castle is actually based on Panmure House, the seat of the Maules near Dundee, which was demolished in 1955. The story which Innes tells Ainsley of the locked gates following the 1715 Jacobite rebellion belongs to Panmure, details and pictures of which are in Ian Gow's beautiful book *Scotland's Lost Houses*. The chapel attached to Strone Bridge Castle, though, is based on the one belonging to Mount Stuart in Rothesay.

Agony Aunts existed, astonishingly, as far back as the seventeenth century, though they reached their peak in the mid-Victorian era—a little after Madame Hera was writing. There are some fantastic examples of their letters in Tanith Carey's book *Never Kiss a Man in a Canoe*.

As to the traditions and customs in this book—well, I must admit that I've let my imagination loose a wee bit. All the Hogmanay customs are traditional, but the Rescinding ceremony is not. I actually invented it for an earlier book set in Argyll, THE HIGHLANDER'S REDEMPTION, and I liked it so much I thought I'd start a tradition of my own and re-use it.

THE WARRIOR'S WINTER BRIDE

DENISE LYNN

For Mom, with love

Award-winning author **Denise Lynn** lives in the USA with her husband, son and numerous 4-legged "kids". Between the pages of romance novels she has travelled to lands and times filled with brave knights, courageous ladies and never-ending love. Now she can share with others her dream of telling tales of adventure and romance. You can write to her at PO Box 17, Monclova, OH 43542, USA, or visit her website, www.denise-lynn.com

Chapter One

Warehaven Keep—autumn 1145

Men were no better than toads, hopping mindlessly one way and then the next without warning. Before, she'd only wondered about it, but now she knew for certain it was true.

The cool night air did little to soothe her raging anger. Isabella of Warehaven shouldered her way through the throng of people crowded in her father's bailey. She needed some time alone before returning to the celebration about to take place inside the keep.

Her betrothal and upcoming marriage to Wade of Glenforde had been painstakingly planned for months. Each detail had been overseen with the utmost of care. Every line of the agreement had been scrutinised with an eye to the future—her future.

And in a few moments' time she would toss all of her father's planning into the fire. Her parents would be so upset with her and she hated the idea of disappointing them, but she just couldn't, she wouldn't marry Glenforde. He could wed the whore she'd seen him kissing while he pulled the giggling strumpet into a private alcove.

Thankfully, her mother and father had given her, and her younger sister, Beatrice, the rare blessing of choice. And while she'd dragged her feet until her father, out of impatience, took it upon himself to find her a husband, Isabella was certain he would not force her to go through with this betrothal or marriage. Especially when she shed light on Glenforde's unseemly behaviour.

Isabella picked up her pace as the recent memory renewed her rage. It was one thing for him to have a whore, but it was another entirely for him to so openly flaunt the relationship inside her father's keep. And to do so on the evening of their betrothal was beyond acceptable.

Adding this indiscretion to the way he'd pushed her to the ground in anger earlier this afternoon when discussing her sister was more than Isabella was willing to accept.

If he acted in such reprehensible ways now, what would he do once they were wed?

She had no intention of discovering the answer to that question. She was certain that once she explained all to her parents, they would understand her misgivings about this arrangement and she'd never have to worry about the answer. They would more than likely be upset that they'd been so duped into believing he was a suitable choice by her aunt. Her father's half-sister, the Empress Matilda, had insisted Wade of Glenforde was not just suitable, but the perfect choice all round: he was young, wealthy, available and, more importantly, supported her claim to the crown over King Stephen's. To sweeten the pot, the empress had promised to supply Wade with a keep, demesne lands and a title worthy of Isabella. How could her parents turn down such an offer?

Fisting her hands, she lengthened her stride in an effort to get clear of the guests milling their way to the keep. Isabella nearly choked on the urge to scream.

The sound of a splash and the ice-cold wetness seeping into her embroidered slippers made the scream impossible to resist. 'My God, what more ills will this cursed day from hell bring me?'

She slapped one hand over her mouth, lifted the long skirt of her gown with the other and then ran at an unladylike pace towards the stables at the other end of the bailey. No one would hear her curses there.

Quickly gaining the privacy offered by the stables, she ducked to the far side of the building. With her chest heaving from the effort and speed of her escape, she lowered her hand from her mouth. This far away from the keep no one would hear, or see, what was about to be one of her finest bouts of temper since she'd gained adulthood.

Isabella closed her eyes and took a deep breath before parting her lips. Only to have a large work-worn hand slapped firmly over her mouth.

She opened her eyes wide in shock as she swallowed the scream she'd been so eager to let fly.

'My, my, what have we here?' the man standing behind her asked softly over her shoulder.

He ignored her struggles to free herself to ask, 'Why, I wonder, would Warehaven's whelp travel this far from safety in the dark?'

He leaned closer, his chest hard against her back, his breath hot across her ear. 'Unescorted and unprotected.'

The deepening timbre of his voice acted like a bucket of ice-cold water sluicing down her body, making her tremble as she suddenly realised the danger in which she'd placed herself.

She'd been a fool to have flown the keep so rashly. Alone, without protection, she had foolishly risked her life. Her family had repeatedly warned her about her rashness. They'd gone to great lengths to frighten her with terror-filled tales of what happened to headstrong maidens who cavorted about in such a thoughtless manner.

Was she now about to be killed—or worse—for paying no heed to their dire warnings?

His deadly soft chuckle served to increase her tremors. 'Do you smell that?' He inhaled deeply. 'It's the scent of fear.' Pulling her closer against him, he stroked the flat edge of a blade against her cheek adding, 'Are you afraid, Isabella of Warehaven?'

Of course she was afraid. It was a time of anarchy and unrest, when no one could truly be safe. With the great number of people who'd been invited to Warehaven for this betrothal ceremony, countless criminals—men who had no sense of honour or decency—would surely follow.

Cut-throats and pickpockets alike would flock to Warehaven simply to take advantage of the opportunity to line their pouches with gold, jewels and any other item that might garner them a goodly sum.

Her breath caught in her throat. Would not the lord's daughter gain such a man much wealth?

The ground beneath her feet seemed to sway. She desperately tried to gasp for breath, but his hand over her mouth and nose prevented her from drawing in the air she needed. And his arm, now wrapped so tightly around her waist, made even normal breathing nearly impossible.

Isabella kicked back, frantic to free herself from his hold, and more frantic not to swoon. She had to escape. There was no telling what this unchivalrous knave intended.

Richard of Dunstan did his best to ignore the misplaced bit of guilt pricking at him as he held tight to Glenforde's betrothed. He tamped it down, squashing it as one would a bothersome gnat. Useless things like morals and guilt were best left to those who still cared about the niceties of life.

Guilt had provided him with nothing more than a way to avoid doing what needed to be done. And morals had only held him back from exacting vengeance for what had been done to his family.

The only thing Richard cared about any more was satisfying his need for revenge—Wade of Glenforde had seen to that by his murderous actions on Dunstan.

With that solitary end focused sharply in his mind, Richard and one of his men had slipped into Warehaven's bailey with the throng of arriving guests, intent on discovering a way to kidnap Glenforde's bride-to-be after their betrothal ceremony.

He and his man Matthew had quickly stepped away from the throng to take a position alongside the wall and survey the lay of the bailey. That was where Richard had overheard two of the guards, on the wooden walkway above them, talking to each other about the bride-to-be. It appeared that the lady in question was currently alone in the bailey and the two men were debating if they should be overly concerned for her safety or not.

To Richard's relief the older-sounding guard had set the other man's worries at ease by asking what could possibly happen with so many of Warehaven's armed guards on duty. Who, he had asked, would be daft enough, with so much manpower in evidence, to harm Lady Isabella?

Who indeed?

However, he'd never seen either of Warehaven's daughters, so he'd paid close attention to the guards' discussion, hoping they'd supply the information he needed. It was imperative he seize the right daughter. Thankfully, it didn't take long for them to provide enough detail for him to realise the richly dressed young woman rushing towards the stables was the woman he sought.

This had been an opportunity he couldn't afford to ignore. And once the guards broke apart to go their separate ways, he'd put his hastily revised plan into action. With his prey so near at hand that very moment, it had made no sense to wait until after the ceremony. Certainly not when it had seemed to be divine intervention. It was as if God himself had blessed his quest for vengeance by placing this woman neatly in Richard's hands.

Eventually, Glenforde would get the death he so deserved, but first he would suffer. He would be outraged that his bride-to-be had been taken. If he cared for the woman at all, he would suffer torment as he thought of the horrors his beloved might face.

And if Glenforde didn't hold any feelings for her, he would still be in agony at the lost riches Warehaven's daughter would have brought with her into their marriage.

Lord Warehaven possessed land and gold aplenty. He was aligned through blood with the royals on both sides of this never-ending war. There was little doubt that his daughter would bring not just wealth, but also political advantage to a marriage—the combination would be too much for Glenforde to willingly set aside.

Yes, Glenforde's pride and greed would draw him to Dunstan. He would come intent on rescuing the woman and retaining a secure hold on his future. But success would be far from his reach. He would arrive on Dunstan to find his beloved already wed and instead would be greeted only by the sharp blade of Richard's sword.

By luring Glenforde back to the scene of his heinous crime, the spirits of his innocent victims would have the opportunity to lead the blackguard's worthless soul to the gaping mouth of hell.

The woman in his arms struggled yet again, drawing Richard's attention back to his captive. Her apparent youth almost made him regret the future she was about to begin, but a fleeting memory wove through his mind. The vision of a perfect blonde curl resting against a lifeless, blood-streaked cheek chased away any regret.

Warehaven's daughter would accept what fate decreed for her—or she would perish. That choice would be up to her.

He hadn't come this far, or taken such a risk, to turn back now. For months he had set aside duty and responsibility, existing solely for vengeance.

Now that the key to his revenge was securely in his arms, he wasn't about to let go. At this moment she likely thought him nothing more than a knave seeking to take advantage of her. Little did she know exactly what type of advantage he would take.

Against her ear, he warned softly, 'We are leaving the keep and if you scream, if you so much as think to draw attention to us, I will slit your throat.' He paused, allowing his threat to settle into her mind, then asked, 'Do you understand me?'

Richard waited until she nodded before moving them slowly back towards the shadows behind the stable where his man waited.

A hand touched his back, bringing him to an instant halt. Light from a torch fell across them. Richard tensed, prepared to defend himself and somehow still retain his unsuspecting captive.

'Lord Richard, all is ready.'

He relaxed his defences at the sound of Matthew's voice. However, the woman in his arms stiffened. Richard tightened his hand over her mouth and placed the edge of his dagger against her throat. 'Your betrothed thought nothing of killing an innocent, defenceless six-year-old girl. Rest assured, I can easily even the score if you so much as sneeze.'

He loosened his grasp over her face slightly, relieved that she kept her lips together. 'You will live as long as you remain silent.' He waited a moment to let his threat take hold, then ordered, 'Nod if you understand me.'

She nodded. But something in the stiffness of her spine warned him that she wasn't going to be as compliant as he'd hoped. He would deal with that later—for now he only required her silence.

Matthew held up a hooded cloak. 'For the lady.'

As Warehaven's daughter, she would be too easily identified. The long, dark woollen garment would conceal her form and features. Richard uncovered her mouth, grasped her shoulder and pulled her further into the shadows, away from the glare of Matthew's torch, before releasing her. 'Stand still.'

He draped the cloak around her shoulders, secured it in front and pulled up the hood. After tucking her hair inside the fabric, he checked to make sure there was nothing visible to mark her as Warehaven's daughter.

Richard held his blade up, pointed towards her face and explained, 'You are feeling unwell and as your concerned brothers, we are escorting you home. If you give warning of any kind, you will forfeit your life before the guards can take mine.'

To his relief, she nodded her understanding without being told to do so again. With one arm across her shoulders, he motioned Matthew to her other side. Richard pressed down on her shoulder. 'Slump over as if you are ill.'

He could only hope she feared him enough to follow

his orders. But when they took their first step, she tripped over the excess fabric of the cloak.

With a soft curse, he slid the dagger back into his boot and then swung her up into his arms.

She gasped, jerking away from him.

He held her tight against his chest. 'I won't warn you again. Rest your head against me and be silent.' With a nod towards Matthew, he ordered, 'Lead on.'

Isabella wasn't sure who deserved her curses more. While she knew that Wade of Glenforde was far from a gallant knight, she didn't think he'd stoop low enough to harm innocent children. But for whatever reason this man thought he had. So, Glenforde also deserved a portion of her curses.

And she was most certainly deserving of them—it was her own rashness that had got her into this situation. Or did the unkempt lout holding her deserve the curses more?

His man had called him *Lord Richard*. So, he was not a lowly cur as she'd first feared. He didn't lack status, nor did he lack the ingenuity to be armed.

Most of the revellers—invited or not—had left their weapons in the tents they'd erected outside the walls of the keep. Since it was easier to control an overlarge crowd when they were unarmed, those who hadn't stowed their weapons were relieved of the items upon entering Warehaven.

From the dagger in this man's possession, at least one guard had lacked thoroughness with his given task. A serious lapse in duty of which her father should be made aware.

The man holding her tightened his grasp as they neared the gate. She understood the silent warning and hoped they wouldn't be stopped. Not for a single heartbeat did she think the man wouldn't carry through with his threat to kill her.

Isabella took a deep breath to keep her fear at bay. She knew this warrior—this knave—would interpret any tremors on her part as a weakness he could use to his advantage. She could only pray that he released her before she could no longer suppress the need to quake with dread.

To her relief no one paid them the least bit of attention. Yet, as they passed beyond the gates and towards the open field now littered with tents and larger pavilions, the man didn't release his hold.

She thought he would hold her captive in one of those tents until Glenforde, or her father, came to claim her. But he kept walking and seemed to gather her even closer—impossibly close. His heart beat strong beneath her cheek. She felt the steady rise and fall of his chest with each breath he took.

His fingers pressing into the side of her breast drew an unrestrained gasp from her lips. Even through the layers of her clothing and the cloak, the heat of his touch seemed to scorch her skin before it skittered along her nerves, escalating her need to escape.

She twisted away and shoved at his shoulder, trying to lunge from his hold. 'Where are you taking me? Put me down.'

Richard stopped at the head of the trail leading down to the beach. If she screamed now, they would be close enough to board his ship before anyone from the keep could come to her rescue.

And that was the whole point of this unorthodox kidnapping—he wanted Warehaven to know who had taken his daughter, but he did not want to get caught. More importantly, he needed Glenforde to know who had possession of his betrothed. Otherwise, if they didn't know where to find the lady, this entire task could prove a waste in more ways than one.

He relaxed his hold on her legs and let her slide down the length of his body until she stood on her feet. But he had no intention of releasing her. 'Where am I taking you? You are going to be my guest for a time.'

She frowned, rightfully confused by his statement. 'Your guest?'

Anxious to be away, he ignored her to motion Matthew ahead with the torch. Then Richard turned the woman around so her back was against his chest and, with his arms wrapped about her waist, bodily forced her down the path.

Only then did he answer, 'Yes. You are going to Dunstan.'

He wasn't surprised at her cry of dismay or at the way she dug her heels into the ground in a feeble attempt to halt their progress. He'd expected some type of struggle from her, especially after he'd divulged the first part of his intentions.

'Dunstan is no friend of Warehaven.' She explained what he already knew. 'Why would you deliver me to him?' Her tone rose with each word. He heard her inhale sharply before asking, 'Who are you?'

He tightened his hold round her, lifted her feet from the ground and resumed their trek towards the beach. He was certain from the tightness of her voice that she'd already guessed the answer. Dipping his head, so he could whisper into her ear, he responded, 'Who am I?' He brushed his lips along the delicate curve of her ear. 'Why, fair maiden of Warehaven, I am Richard of Dunstan.'

She trembled against him. 'Why are you doing this?'

'Glenforde must pay for his crimes.' Richard hardened his voice. 'And you, as his intended bride, will ensure he does.'

She jerked her head back, most likely to slam it against his nose. He was quicker and easily dodged her attempt to injure him. 'Come now, you can do better than that.'

However, her heels drumming sharply into his shins and kneecaps was a distraction he feared would send them both crashing to the ground. Unwilling to take a chance of either of them being injured, he lowered her to the path, with the intention of taking her hand to lead her to the beach.

Her scream, loud and piercing, changed his mind. By her glare of mutinous rage and fear, he quickly realised there would be no leading her anywhere. Instead, Richard hauled her over his shoulder and ran down the narrow path. He shouted at Matthew just ahead, 'Move faster, before Warehaven's men catch up to us.'

He was fairly certain they were far enough away from the keep that while her screams would be heard, just as he had planned, her plea for rescue would go unanswered long enough for him to reach his ship. But it was a risk he didn't want to take.

'Lord Richard, here. This way.' Bruce's voice tore through the darkness ahead. A younger man from Dunstan stepped out from the cover of the overgrown vegetation. After lighting his torch from Matthew's, he held it aloft, illuminating a winding, narrow path down the face of the jagged cliffs.

'It's steeper than the path we climbed up.' He glanced at the burden slung over Richard's shoulder, adding, 'But quicker, if—'

Richard waved off his man's unspoken concern of him falling with his wildly fighting bundle and ordered, 'Go.'

Just before they reached the beach, Richard paused at a sound behind them. Apparently the woman's desperate screams *had* been heard. However, Warehaven's men were closer than he'd expected.

He swallowed a curse, then barked an order at the men in front of him. 'Move. Faster.'

'There they are!'

At the shout from Warehaven's guards, Matthew and Bruce dropped their torches and scrambled over the final sets of boulders. Richard none too gently lowered the still struggling woman over the last boulder.

Just as her bottom hit the wet sand, he flung himself over the rock to land beside her.

But when he reached down to haul her back over his shoulder she quickly rolled away, shouting, 'No! Help!'

Determined to get away safely, without losing his captive, he tried to grab her again.

Slapping at his reaching arms, she shrieked, 'Warehaven, to me!'

Richard could now hear the jangle of mail and weapons from the men racing to their lady's aid.

Out of time and out of patience, he stomped on the length of cloak he'd wrapped around her, effectively holding her still long enough for him to reach down to grab her.

Still screaming, the lady had enough sense to curl her fingers tightly and ram her fist upward towards his nose. Richard turned his head to avoid the contact and the force of her punch caught him in the eye.

He cursed, chagrined that he'd let this slip of a woman plant him such a stinging blow. Without pausing to wipe the watery blur from his sight, he pulled her up and once again slung her across his shoulder.

His captive somewhat secured, Richard shouted to his men in the small rowing boat that would take them out to his ship anchored further offshore, 'Shove off!'

Bruce and Matthew nearly dived into the boat as it bobbed in the water. Bruce manned an oar, while Matthew notched an arrow in his bow and let it sail.

Richard splashed through the knee-deep water, dodged the sweeping oars and unceremoniously flung the woman into the boat before scrambling in behind her, ordering, 'Put some muscle in it, men.'

When she tried to sit up, he pushed her back down. 'Stay put, lest you want one of Warehaven's arrows to accidently end your life.'

He grabbed his own waiting bow, then turned towards the beach. Another curse escaped him at the sight of her father amongst the men shooting at them. Warehaven's death might delay—or prevent—Glenforde from coming to Dunstan.

An arrow whooshed past his ear. Richard ducked. His own life and the lives of his men were at stake, he would do what had to be done. He notched an arrow and let it sail towards the beach along with another volley of arrows from his men.

'No! Oh, dear Lord, no!' the lady cried from where she knelt on the bottom of the tiny boat as one of the arrows found its way to her sire's chest, dropping the man on to the wet sand.

She screamed again and wrapped a hand around Richard's leg. Before he could free himself, an arrow from one of Warehaven's archers pierced his shoulder. Richard jerked back in pain, only to trip over the woman still clinging to his leg.

Chapter Two

'Hold him down!'

Isabella stared at Dunstan's rough-looking soldier as if through a heavy, thick fog. They had killed her father. The tightness building in her throat and stomach intensified. She could barely imagine the pain and agony her mother must now be suffering. What would she do?

'Help me!'

Help him?

He wanted her help with his commander? Isabella shook her head, brokenly whispering, 'No.'

She couldn't—she wouldn't help any of them. They'd stolen her from Warehaven, killed her father before her eyes and had forcibly dragged her from the rowing boat into this ship as if she'd been nothing more than a sack of grain.

And then, when she'd tried to climb back over the high side of the vessel, intent on reaching the beach to help her father, this man—this filthy, ragged-haired, scar-faced knave—had bodily carried her into Dunstan's small cabin beneath the aft castle.

'Damn you, woman, help me.'

'No. Get one of your men to help.' Dunstan's well-being would be better trusted to one of his own men than to her.

'They are all needed on deck.'

She knew that. Of course the men were all needed on deck—to man the oars in the hopes that rowing would lend the ship enough speed to get away before her father's men unleashed flaming arrows.

Isabella hoped a few of those arrows found their mark and set this flat-bottomed oak ship blazing. The single square-rigged sail alone wouldn't be enough power to get this cog away fast enough.

Maybe, if she were lucky and God saw fit, she along with these men would find themselves back on Warehaven's beach in a very short time.

'Get over here and help me or I will send you to your maker.'

'Then do it and be done with me!' She would rather die than make landfall at Dunstan.

The dagger in his hand wavered briefly before he tightened his grip on the weapon. As quick as a darting snake, he reached out with his free hand and grabbed her arm. 'You are far too eager. I'll not grant you such an escape from what Lord Dunstan has planned.'

'He murdered my father!' She tore her arm free. 'Do what you will.'

'Murdered? We were defending ourselves. Besides, you don't know if your sire is dead or not. He could simply be injured the same as Lord Dunstan.' He tipped his blade towards the man on the pallet. 'However, if his lordship dies you will belong to me instead.' He narrowed his eyes to mere slits. 'And rest assured, I will make every remaining moment of your life a living hell.'

Could her father still be alive? A tiny flicker of hope sprang to life. A flicker she quickly doused in fear that her relief would be short-lived. No. She'd seen the arrow pierce his chest. Had seen him sink lifeless on to the beach. Since he'd not been protected by chain mail—he'd been dressed for a celebration, not battle—he couldn't have survived. Isabella choked on a sob.

'Is that what you want?' The man leaned closer to her, crowding her in the already small confines of this cabin. 'Do you value your life so little?'

When she didn't answer, he warned, 'If the thought of becoming mine doesn't frighten you as it should, don't forget that there are over a dozen more men on this ship who would gladly make you suffer unimaginable horrors should Lord Dunstan die.'

The deadly earnest tone of his voice made her realise that his threat was not an idle warning. But it was the cheers from the men on the deck and the sound of oars scraping across wood as they were pulled into the ship that dashed her hopes of freedom. The sounds of a sail being hoisted and unfurled as it caught the wind to take her far from her home made his threat even more deadly.

Self-preservation overrode her desire to give in to uncontrollable tears and wailing, prompting her to join him near the bed built into the side of the ship.

Dunstan's man had used the dagger to remove his commander's clothing. She stared at the blood covering Dunstan's chest and bedclothes. Like her father, Dunstan hadn't worn armour either, making his body an easy target for the arrow to pierce. If they did nothing, the man would likely die from loss of blood.

The thought of his death did not bother her overmuch, since he deserved nothing less, but if he died while aboard this ship…what would happen to her?

No. She would not worry about that. Instead, she would assist Dunstan's man in caring for his overlord. The knave would heal. She would ensure that he'd soon be hale and hearty. Otherwise, how would she gain her own measure of revenge?

Swallowing the grief threatening to choke her, and willing her resolve to stand firm, she asked, 'What do you wish me to do?'

'I have already given him a sleeping potion.' The man wrapped his hand around the shaft of the arrow still lodged below Dunstan's shoulder. 'Now, I need you to hold him up.'

Isabella shivered. No matter how many times she'd watched her mother employ an arrow spoon to remove the tip, shove the arrow the rest of the way through one of Warehaven's men, or break the shaft leaving the arrow tip in place, the operation had never failed to make her ill.

Even though she knew the answer, Isabella asked, 'Can you not simply pull it free?'

The brief grunted response required no explanation. The arrow was nearly all the way through Dunstan's body. Without an implement to dig the tip out, they could try working the shaft free of the tip and leave the tip inside for now. The other option was to shove the arrow the rest of the way through his body, while hoping everything stayed intact, then either snap off the shaft or the tip at the tang and remove the weapon.

Either option meant someone was going to have to hold him up and try to keep him from thrashing about if the pain seeped through the fog of his drugged sleep, while someone else worked the arrow free.

She doubted if she was strong enough to hold him, but she preferred that task over the other more gruesome one. Besides, there was no one to protect her and God only knew what the crew would do to her if she bungled the procedure enough that Dunstan died.

Isabella shivered and set aside the dark images forming

in her mind. She took a deep breath and then knelt on the bed to support Dunstan's body. Between the two of them, they rolled Dunstan on to his side, his stomach and lower chest propped against her bent legs.

The man poured more liquid from a small bottle into Dunstan's mouth. If he was using the juice of poppies, he could very well send his master into a deep, permanent sleep. And the blame for his death would be placed on her.

'Are you ready?'

She nodded, then leaned over Dunstan's body to hold him in place and answered, 'Be quick about it.'

To her relief Dunstan jerked only once when his man took a firmer hold on the arrow's shaft. He immediately relaxed, as if he knew it would help make his man's task easier.

Isabella, however, couldn't relax. She tensed, fully expecting Dunstan to thrash about at any moment, fighting the pain he surely must suffer.

She hoped the pain was unbearable—hoped he suffered as much agony as she did. It would be so much less than what he deserved. After killing her father, nothing short of Dunstan's death would even the score.

But somehow, he managed to withstand the pain as his man shoved the arrow tip through, broke the shaft and pulled both parts of the weapon from his body. While she could feel his muscles tense and go lax beneath her, and could hear his ragged, uneven breaths, he offered no resistance. She was unable to determine if he slept, if the medicine was working this fast or if his self-control was stronger than most.

The procedure was over quickly, but as Isabella shifted to get off the bed, Dunstan's man stopped her. 'Stay there. I still have to sew the wound.'

She snatched the needle from his hand. 'Are you seeking to kill him?'

'He will bleed to death.'

Isabella studied Dunstan. She had originally thought the same thing, but the arrow had hit him high—just beneath his shoulder, closer to his arm than his chest or neck. Using the skirt of her undergown, she wiped at the blood covering him and then shook her head. 'The bleeding has slowed, so I doubt he will perish from loss of blood.' Pinning his man with a stare, she added, 'But if you close the wound now, it could fester and that very likely *will* bring about his death.'

'Then what do you suggest?'

She had a few suggestions—all of them uncharitable, so she kept those to herself. 'Do you have any wax?'

At the shake of his head, she stated, 'Surely you have some wine and yarrow or woundwort available. Some cloth would help, too.'

These were fighting men. Hopefully, more than one of them would carry yarrow or the wort in their pouch. Both were common ways to staunch the flow of blood from a wound and promote healing.

He left her side to rummage through a satchel in the corner of the cabin and returned with a skin of wine and a clean shirt.

Isabella hesitated. 'No herbs?'

He shrugged.

'You could go ask the others.'

Her comment provoked only a raised eyebrow from him. Isabella frowned a moment before the reason for his hesitation dawned on her.

'As much as I'd like to…' she nodded towards Dunstan '…I am not going to harm him.'

When the man didn't budge, she added, 'Besides, I

would prefer he be whole and completely alert when I cut out his blackened heart with an old crooked spoon.'

Even though her words were true—to a point. When the time came, she would use his own sword, not a spoon—she'd been seeking to lighten the mood.

Her ploy wasn't very successful. While his lips did twitch, he only shook his head.

Now what would she do?

Isabella knew that her mother would use the wine to wash the blood from the wound and then make a wax tent to hold it open, allowing any further drainage to run free. Once there was no more seepage, she would remove the tent and then sew, or cauterise, the wound closed.

However, from the smell of the tallow burning in the lamp she should have realised that there wasn't any wax at hand. And she didn't know what else to use.

'What are you going to do?' Dunstan's man drew her back to the task at hand.

'The only thing I can do is bind his wound after I clean it. For that I need some water, please.' When the man reached for a pitcher on the small table, she amended her request. 'From over the side of the ship.'

She didn't know how they did things on Dunstan, but her mother preferred seawater when cleansing an injury, claiming it helped to heal and dry out the wound.

The man studied her carefully for a long moment, then left the cabin.

While he was gone, Isabella poured the wine over Dunstan's shoulder and used the clean shirt to wipe away the rest of the blood and the wine.

'Here.' A bucket hit the floor beside her. Ice-cold water sloshed over the sides, soaking through her already sodden shoes and making her shiver.

Once the skin around Dunstan's wounds were as clean

as she could get them, she blew on her near-freezing fingers, asking, 'Is there another shirt or anything?'

'No.'

She glanced at the weapon now strapped to the man's side. 'Then I need your dagger.'

His eyes widened briefly before narrowing to mere slits. 'For what?'

She'd already told him of her plans to wait until Dunstan was healthy before killing him. Did he not believe her? Isabella sighed, then explained, 'I need to bind his wounds. To do that I need strips of cloth.' She plucked at the hem of her undergown. 'From this.'

Frowning, he hesitated, but finally, with obvious reluctance, slowly extended the weapon towards her.

Isabella rose and lifted her skirts, only to drop them at the man's gasp. She glared at him and ordered, 'Turn around.'

Satisfied that he did as she'd ordered, she paused. With his back to her, it would be an easy thing to run him through. Isabella sighed, knowing that the other men would hear the commotion and rush to his aid.

She gave up her brief dream, pulled the hem up and cut through the thin fabric. Wincing at what she was about to do to her finest chemise, Isabella took a deep breath, then tore a good length of cloth from the hem.

'Now, you hold him up for me.'

Once his man had him upright, Isabella cross-wrapped the cloth around Dunstan's chest and back. 'I'm finished. All we can do now is wait.'

After placing him back on the bed, the man suggested, 'You might want to add prayer to the waiting.'

She shrugged. While it was true, for her own selfish reasons, she did want him hale and whole, praying for this man's health would seem more blasphemous than holy.

Isabella straightened, preparing to get off the pallet, but Dunstan wrapped a hand around her wrist and pulled her down next to him. She gasped at his unexpected strength. Nose to nose, she stared into the blue of his now open eyes. His pupils were huge, his eyes shimmering from the effect of the medicine he'd been given.

It was doubtful he knew what he was doing, or was even aware of doing anything, but when she tried to pull free, he only tightened his hold, trapping her hand between them, against his chest.

Behind her, she heard his man gathering up the discarded cloths and the bucket. 'I'll return shortly to check the wound.'

'Wait! You cannot leave me here alone with him like this.'

'It is not as if he can harm you. But if any further harm comes to him, you will be the one to suffer the consequence.' On his way towards the door, he paused to douse the lamp before leaving her alone on Dunstan's pallet in the dark.

The warmth of his breath brushed against her face. Even in the utter darkness of the room she could feel his stare.

'I cannot harm you.' His deep voice was low, his words slightly slurred.

His heart beat steady against her palm. The heat of his body against hers nearly took her breath away. She couldn't remain on this pallet with him. 'Please, let me go.'

'Too late.' Dunstan rested his forehead against hers. 'You had better be worth all this.'

Worth all what? Being wounded? Isabella opened her mouth to ask, but the steadiness of his light breathing let her know her questions would go unanswered.

She rolled as far on to her back as his hold would allow, stared up into the darkness of the cabin and tried to ignore the man so close to her side. Before she could stop it, a tear rolled down her cheek, followed by another and yet another. The need to cry, to sob aloud her grief at losing her father and being taken forcibly from her home was overwhelming.

No matter how hard she fought, her wayward mind always came back to worries and questions—each more heartrending than the last.

Who would assist her mother in the lonely, sad tasks that must now be completed to lay her father to rest? Who would stand by her side at the service, or lend a hand with those attending the wake? Who would be there in the middle of the night to soothe away the tears and the fears for the future?

Her sister? No. By now Beatrice would have locked herself into her chamber to give way to her own grief. It would be days before she'd think of their mother.

Jared? No, her brother would be too busy amassing a force to come after her—and the man who'd torn their family asunder.

While Jared's wife, Lea, would no doubt try her best, she was too new to the family to know that if she tried to do too much, in the mistaken belief that her mother-by-marriage would welcome the respite from duty, she would be unwittingly angering the Lady of Warehaven.

The first time Lea instructed a servant not to disturb the lady, or if she greeted a guest as the stand-in for the lady of the keep, she'd find her help met with near uncontrollable anger. Isabella knew how closely her mother oversaw every aspect of running Warehaven. It was her keep, her home, her domain and she'd not brook any interference, not even if it was offered in the most well-meaning of manners, lightly.

And what would now happen to Beatrice and her?

Beatrice was also of marriageable age. While she had her mind set on Charles of Wardham, Isabella knew her parents disliked him and would never permit Beatrice to wed the lout.

But would Jared let Beatrice have her way?

What about her? She hadn't had the opportunity to tell her parents about her decision not to wed Glenforde. Would her brother, who would now be the Lord of Warehaven, take it upon himself to sign the documents and force her into an unwanted marriage?

Under normal circumstances the answer to that question would be a resounding no. Her brother would never force her into anything.

However, these weren't normal circumstances. If he wasn't thinking clearly, there was no way for her to know exactly what he'd do.

Which meant Jared might either see her wed to Glenforde or someone else of his choosing.

His choosing. Another shudder racked her. Why had she not listened to her parents?

None of this would have happened had she not been so determined to always have her own way.

When her parents had first given her the rare gift of choice they'd done so only because they'd known full well that it would be easier than trying to force her into a betrothal she would fight no matter how perfect the man was for her.

An odd arrangement to be sure, but one her father had chosen because of his own marriage. As one of old King Henry's bastards, her father had been forced to wed the daughter of a keep he'd conquered. And while, yes, her parents had learned to deeply care for and love one another over time, he wanted his children to at least know of love before they pledged their future to another. Even though it went against everything considered normal, he wanted them to have the choice.

She knew that—his wishes for his children had never been a secret. Just as she knew that had she simply gone to him about Glenforde the betrothal would have been called off.

Instead, she'd let anger at Glenforde's behaviour with the strumpet get the best of her and she had stormed from the keep.

And now…

Isabella clenched her jaw until it hurt, in an effort to keep a sob from escaping.

Now her father was dead and her mother alone.

Her chest and throat burned with the need to cry, but she'd not let the murdering lout next to her know the level of suffering and grief he'd caused her.

She'd sooner throw herself from this ship and drown in the depths of the black icy waters than give him the satisfaction of witnessing her pain.

If anyone was going to suffer it would be him. Richard of Dunstan thought he'd steal her away from her home, kill her father and get away with it?

No. Not while she had breath in her body.

Oh, yes, she would ensure he recovered from his wound—and then he would learn the meaning of pain.

Chapter Three

The creaking of wood, the swaying beneath her and the sound of waves crashing nearby dragged Isabella from her fitful dreams. *Where was she? Why was her bed moving? What was that sound...?*

Consciousness swept over her like a racing storm, bringing her fully awake with a heart-pounding jolt. She was still aboard Dunstan's ship, heading towards his island stronghold. A keep that would become her future prison.

They'd been at sea for nearly three days now. She struggled to draw in enough breath to fill her chest. Three days—three of the longest days of her entire life. She'd done penances that hadn't seemed as arduous as this forced journey.

Sleep had been her only escape from the fears and worries chasing her, threatening to tear reason from her mind and send her screaming with misery and anger. She'd sought its comforting embrace as often as she could.

Isabella knew what caused her heart to race, her breathing to become laboured and her palms to perspire. She was well aware what brought about the darkness tormenting her.

It was more than just having been captured and witnessing her father's death. And it was more than the over-warm body next to her on the bed. She stared into the pitch blackness of the cabin. Even without the benefit of sight, she felt the walls closing around her, suffocating her, stealing her ability to think, to employ any rational measure of common sense.

This airless cabin was far too small, too confining and more of a cell than a cabin. It was a constant reminder of what she had to look forward to on Dunstan.

And the unconscious man next to her on the narrow bed didn't help lessen the feeling of being trapped in an ever-shrinking cage.

Isabella closed her eyes and conjured the image of her airy, open bedchamber at Warehaven. She concentrated, bringing the vision into sharper focus. When the memories of fresh-strewn herbs floated to her nose and the softness of her pillow cushioning her head, along with the warmth of her bedcovers surrounding her, she willed her pulse to slow.

She drew in a long, deep breath, filling her lungs near to bursting before letting it out ever so slowly, over and over until the trick her father had taught her so many years ago when she was a frightened child cleared her mind and calmed her spirit.

Once certain she could function with some semblance of reason, she sat up.

The door to the cabin opened, letting in a glimmer of evening light and air—icy-cold blasts of frigid air, along with Dunstan's man... Matthew, Sir Matthew as she'd discovered yesterday when she'd overheard the other men aboard the ship talking just outside the cabin.

'Are you hungry?' Without waiting for her answer, he handed her a hunk of dry, coarse bread and a skin filled with what she knew was wine so sour that it rivalled any verjuice she'd ever encountered.

Shivering, she frowned. It had been so hot beneath the covers that she'd been unprepared for such a cold, bracing wind.

No. Her heart nearly leapt from her chest.

Setting the offered meal on the floor, she turned towards Dunstan and jerked the covers from his chest.

'What is wrong?' Sir Matthew was at her side in an instant, crowding her, hovering like a mother fretting over her sick child.

'I'm not sure.' She placed her palm against Dunstan's forehead and then his cheek. Biting back an oath at the unnatural warmth of his skin, she ordered, 'Bring the lamp over here.'

To her surprise he did as she'd requested and held the lamp over the pallet, allowing the light to fall on a flushed, sweat-soaked Dunstan.

Sir Matthew cursed, before asking, 'How long has he been like this?'

'He was fine when last I checked.'

'What are you going to do?' Tight concern tinged his question.

Isabella raised a hand. 'Give me a moment to think.'

'His wound is most likely infected.'

What she didn't require were statements of the obvious. The need to get Sir Matthew out of the cabin prompted her to make him useful. 'Get me a knife and have someone heat some water. Find something I can use for new bindings. And if no one aboard this ship has any healing herbs, then you must make port immediately.'

'We will be at Dunstan in another two or three days.'

She turned her head to glare at him. 'He could be dead by then.'

The man tossed her his dagger, placed the lamp on a

stool near the pallet and then thankfully left without another word.

Isabella turned to the task at hand—making sure Dunstan lived so he could die by her hand at a time she deemed appropriate and in a manner that suited her. Kneeling over him, she slipped the dagger beneath the bandages, prepared to strip them from his body, then hesitated, fearful of what she might see. What if...?

'Can you not decide?'

Startled by hearing him speak for the first time in three days, she jumped, nicking the tip of the dagger against his chest.

Fingers closed around her wrist. 'I would prefer death by infection, thank you.'

Isabella lifted her gaze to Dunstan's face. 'You are awake.'

He stared at her with bloodshot eyes that never once wavered. And for a moment—the very briefest of moments—Isabella wished they might have met under different circumstances.

With his squared jawline, slightly crooked nose, even teeth and full lower lip, the man needed only a bath, a change of clothes and a razor to be what her sister, Beatrice, would call a very fine figure of a man. A description that would have drawn a soft, agreeing laugh from her.

Neither the fading bruise from the black eye she'd given him, nor the small gash running across his cheek from when he fell, lessened the more-than-pleasing appearance.

And his voice... Oh, how that deeply rugged voice brushed so easy across her ears before flowing deeper to touch her soul. Even the most pious of women would throw all thought of morals and chastity into the breeze just to hear another word fall from his mouth.

Dunstan's eyebrows arched as if he somehow sensed

the direction of her thoughts and Isabella felt her cheeks
flame with embarrassment, shame and not a small measure of self-loathing.

Sweet heavens, where had her mind flown?

The man was nothing more than a savage beast. He'd
captured her, taken her from her home, from safety and
caused her father's death. And here she sat like some besotted girl mooning over this murderer's looks and the
sound of his voice?

'You are still here.'

Isabella blinked at his statement. 'Since Sir Matthew
stopped me from jumping overboard, where else would
I be?'

Instead of answering her, Dunstan tugged slightly at
her arm. 'What is this?'

*It was her arm. Was he seeing things? What did he
think...oh...he meant the knife.* 'I need to remove your
bandages.'

He released her wrist, then nodded.

'Does that mean I should continue?'

'If you want.'

'Well, no. I don't *want* to do anything for you.' A quick
glance towards the still-open door assured her Sir Matthew
was not standing there. 'I wasn't given a choice.'

'No, of course you...'

His words trailed off and Isabella realised he'd once
again fallen prey to the beckoning spell of the sleeping
drug. It was to be expected since very few people could
resist the siren's call of poppy juice.

She cut away at the bandages, peeling them back as
she did so. Holding her breath, she focused on the wound
left by the arrow.

To her relief, while it was an angry red and puffy, there
weren't any telltale dark lines of advanced infection.

She'd need only to reopen the wounds front and back, let them drain and after cleaning them out, pack them with some herbs—if Sir Matthew found any. And if not, perhaps that verjuice they called wine would be strong enough to burn away any evil humours.

The bigger concern was his fever.

'What worries you so?'

And once again Dunstan was awake. As much as she'd like to rail at him for killing her father and kidnapping her, she knew that within moments he'd only fall asleep again and not hear a word she uttered.

In hopes that he might be alert enough to assist in his own recovery, she said, 'You have a fever and it seems there is nothing aboard this ship to help banish it.'

'Beneath my chainmail.'

She looked around the cabin. Not locating his mail, Isabella asked, 'And where is your armour?'

'Why would you want my lord's armour?' Sir Matthew asked, walking into the cabin carrying a bucket of steaming water, a length of linen and another skin of wine.

'He claims there are some herbs beneath it.'

Without voicing anything more than undecipherable grumbles to himself, Matthew put down the items he carried and headed out of the cabin once more.

In his absence, Isabella went to work on Dunstan's injuries. By the unevenness of his breathing, she assumed he was floating in that twilight region between sleep and wakefulness.

Hoping her assumption was correct, she pushed at his shoulder, asking, 'Can you roll on to your side?'

Thankfully, even though he groaned while doing so, he complied. By the time Sir Matthew returned, she was nearly finished.

He tossed a pouch on the pallet. 'Here. This is what I found.'

Isabella shook off a thin coating of sand before opening the small leather bag. She didn't need to ask about the sand since her father and brother stored their armour in barrels of sand when out to sea. Although, the herb pouch would have been in their cabin. The all-heal herbs inside were wrapped in waxed leather to keep them dry.

She tossed a pinch into a cup, then extended it to Dunstan's man. 'Could you pour a bit of the wine in here?'

While he did that, she put a larger pinch into a second cup and used the pommel of his dagger to grind the herb into a powder. Adding some of the still-warm seawater, she made a poultice, then applied it to his wounds, holding it in place with the bindings she'd made from the linen.

When they had Dunstan situated once again on his back, with the covers over him, she tipped his head up to give him some of the herb-and-wine decoction.

'No more.' He tried to push the cup away, but was too weak to do much more than try. However, he was strong enough to tightly clamp his lips together.

Sir Matthew stayed Dunstan's hand. 'My lord, you need to drink this.'

'No more.'

She'd seen other scars, ones more gruesome than Warehaven's arrow would leave behind, on his body. So it wasn't as if he'd never been injured before. However, Isabella wondered if maybe this was the first time he'd been given poppy juice.

After her brother's first time, he'd refused to take the brew. He'd rather pass out from the pain than ever swallow the liquid again. Perhaps Dunstan had come to the same decision.

'It's not the sleeping draught,' Isabella explained. 'This is for your fever.'

He turned his head way. 'Stinks.'

'You will either take it like a man, or we will force it on you like a child, the choice is yours.'

He shook his head at her threat. 'No.'

'Listen to me, Dunstan.' She tightened her grasp on his head. 'You *will* take this medicine. You are not going to die until I decide it's time, do you hear me? And it's not yet time.'

'Very poor wife.'

His words might have been slightly slurred, but she clearly understood what he'd said. 'I am *not* your wife.'

'Will be soon.'

Isabella froze.

Cursing, Matthew grabbed Dunstan's face, forcing his lips apart, and poured the liquid into his mouth.

Will be soon? She released her hold on the back of his head as if he were suddenly made of fire and scrambled from the bed. Isabella staggered backwards until she hit the side of the ship.

Shaking with fear, dismay and anger, she clasped her hands to her chest, as if that would offer some measure of protection, and asked Sir Matthew, 'What does he mean?'

He remained silent, seemingly intent on settling his commander more firmly under the covers.

'Answer me!' Isabella shouted. 'After all that has been done to me, I have still helped save his miserable, worthless life. I deserve an answer. What did that miscreant scoundrel mean?'

Sir Matthew lowered his head, his chin nearly resting on his chest, he turned away from the bed and said, 'Dunstan's priest awaits his lordship's return—with his bride-to-be.'

Isabella's choked gasp nearly stuck in her throat. 'His

bride-to-be?' She feared she knew the answer, but hoping she was wrong, asked, 'And who would that unlucky lady be?'

As he quickly headed for the door, Matthew answered, 'You.'

Chapter Four

Richard groaned as the surface beneath him heaved to and fro as if being pitched by a windswept wave. The motion let him know that he was aboard a ship. Hopefully, his own.

Outside of a strange dream about Warehaven's daughter leaning over him with a knife to his chest, the last thing he clearly remembered was vaulting into the small rowboat, grabbing a bow and turning to face Warehaven's men just as a hand grasped his leg. Distracted, he'd glanced down and fire had sliced through him, sending him head first against a cross-brace.

He raised his arm and half-swallowed a gasp at the pain lacing across his shoulder.

'Warehaven's archers rarely miss. You took an arrow.'

He opened his eyes, squinting against the flicker of a lit lamp and stared up with relief at the crudely drawn map he'd nailed to the ceiling of his cabin.

'What a shame they hadn't taken aim at your heart.'

Richard raised a brow at the barely suppressed rage in her voice. If anyone should be angry, he should be. 'Then perhaps, instead of being vexed, I should be grateful for your timely distraction.'

'Distraction? I was kneeling on the hull.'

'Which didn't prevent you from grabbing my leg.'

'Should I have done nothing while you took aim at my father and his men?'

'They were aiming at me and my men.'

'I owe no loyalty to the men of Dunstan and had little concern about the arrows aimed at them.'

Valid as it was, he wasn't about to concede her point. 'You should be grateful the men of Dunstan didn't toss you overboard.' She didn't need to know that his men would never treat his bride-to-be so harshly.

She'd been pacing at the other side of the cabin, but changed direction and approached his bed. 'They would have, but you fell atop me.' With a toss of her head she turned to take a seat on a nearby stool, adding, 'So I've nothing to be thankful for.'

'I would think you might be thankful for your life.'

'As should you.'

Richard knew that she would find a contrary response to anything he said. At another time, under different circumstances, this verbal sparring might provide an entertaining moment or two. Right now, however, she was his captive, not his guest, and her contrariness did nothing but make his head throb even more.

Unmindful of his shoulder, he sat upright, shouting, 'Matthew!'

The man entered the quarters immediately. 'You are awake.'

'Could you find no other place for—?' Try as he might, he couldn't push through the fog still swirling about his mind to remember her given name. Richard settled his gaze on her long enough to say, 'I can refer to you as she, or her, or that woman, but a name would be easier.'

'Isabella.' She ground out the answer between clenched teeth. 'Isabella of Warehaven.'

Richard turned back to Matthew and asked, 'Could you find no other place for *her*?' Her hiss of displeasure whipped through the small cabin.

Matthew shrugged. 'Since she was caring for your injury, I thought it better she stayed in here, rather than on the deck with the men.'

'*She* cared for my injury?'

Her gasp and wide-eyed stare spoke of her surprise at his lack of memory. 'You remember nothing?' She looked at him, questioning, 'Who do you think cared for you?'

He ignored her to ask his man, 'What did you threaten her with?'

Matthew flashed him a crooked smile. 'My tender loving care, with the men's assistance, should you die.'

That she hadn't thrown herself overboard at such a threat was interesting. Most women would have done so or fallen dead of fright when confronted in such a manner by any of his men. They were an imposing lot who hadn't been selected for their good manners or refinement. Warehaven's daughter was either braver than most, or possessed not one ounce of common sense.

He did owe her his gratitude. 'I do thank you—'

'No need,' she interrupted him, but then frowned as if debating what to say next. Finally, after pursing and then unpursing her lips a time or two, announced, 'I am not going to marry you.'

Richard swung his gaze back to his man. Why had that information been divulged? Matthew tripped while making a hasty exit. Over his shoulder, he said, 'We'll be home within a day or so.'

A day or so? Depending on the winds, it was a five or six days journey back to Dunstan. That meant—

'Did you hear me?'

He shook his head, trying to clear his thoughts. If they were docking at the island in a day or two, that meant he'd been unconscious—

'You'll get my hand in marriage only if you remove it from my dead body first.'

Obviously she wasn't going to give him a moment of peace. Her acceptance—or lack of—hadn't been a consideration in his plans. He wasn't about to let her thwart his quest for vengeance.

'It is truly simple, Isabella of Warehaven, you'll do as you're told.'

'I…I will do what?' she sputtered, staring at him as if he'd gone mad. 'Killing my father does not grant you his place in my life.'

Richard paused at the bitterness of her voice. He frowned, thinking back to the day he'd taken Warehaven's whelp from her home. Scattered scenes rushed in swiftly filling in some of the holes of his faulty memory. Her father had taken an arrow on the beach. Since he'd also taken an arrow, why would she assume her sire had died?

'You don't know if he died or not. Like me, he might only have been injured.'

'I saw him fall to the beach with an arrow piercing his chest. He wore no armour for protection, so I…I can only believe he was killed.'

The catch in her voice warned him that she was already emotional, as was to be expected, but the last thing he wanted was for her to become hysterical over some imagined happening.

'Is believing the worst your attempt at logic?'

Her eyes widened briefly before narrowing into a fierce glare. Obviously his insincere question had the intended effect—she'd set aside the need to grieve a father who might or might not be dead for anger directed towards him.

'I guess we'll find out how valid my logic is when he or my brother come to pay you a visit.'

'That was the whole point of being seen. Otherwise they wouldn't know where to find you.'

She waved off his answer, to order, 'Turn this ship around.' Her eyes blazing, she informed him, 'They'll have no reason to find me as I am *not* marrying you, nor am I spending the winter on Dunstan.'

Since he had no intention of turning this ship about and every intention of marrying her within a matter of days, she would be spending much longer than just the winter on his island.

The crash of another wave sent the ship pitching dangerously. Without thinking, he quickly reached out and grasped Isabella's shoulders to keep her from being tossed from her seat on a stool to the floor.

She shrugged off his touch and leaned away. 'I can see to myself.'

He didn't get a chance to respond before the ship danced wildly once again, sending Isabella flying from the stool. The thin metal band confining her hair slipped from her head to spin like a top before it then clattered to the floor. On her hands and knees she glared at him as if daring him to give voice to the comments teasing his tongue.

To his relief, instead of trying to scramble back on to the stool, Isabella snatched her hair band from the floor, then crawled to a corner and wedged herself securely between the timbers.

From the ire evident on her face, she would be grateful if he took it upon himself to fall overboard. How high would her anger flame when she realised the depth of her predicament?

Isabella leaned forward and warned, 'You had better hope my family comes for me soon. Because I swear I will not be forced to marry you.'

'What makes you think you have a choice in this matter?'

'My family—'

'Is not here. The deed will be done long before they arrive.'

The blood appeared to drain from her face, leaving her pale and, from her trembling, more than a little shaken.

When she finally found her voice, she asked, 'Why would you wish to wed me?'

'*Wish* to wed you?' Richard shook his head. 'You misunderstand. I have no *wish* to wed anyone. You are merely a means to an end. One that our marriage will help ensure.'

One finely arched eyebrow winged higher. 'It matters not what petty grievance you seek to avenge. With my family's wealth, they will assume marriage was the reason for this madness of yours.'

Petty grievance? The murder of a small, defenceless child was far more than a simple grievance. Richard studied her carefully. The hazel eyes staring back at him appeared clear. Still, to be certain, he asked, 'Did you hit your head?'

'Are you asking if I have my wits about me?'

'Do you?'

'Of course I do.'

'That is up for debate if you think murder is nothing more than a petty grievance. I couldn't care less what your family thinks. They can rant and demand all they want, it will avail them not at all. My concerns are with Glenforde. I long for the day he comes to your rescue.'

Isabella frowned. 'You kidnapped me for some crime Glenforde committed?'

'What better way to get him to come to me on Dunstan than to kidnap and wed his bride-to-be on nearly the eve of his marriage?'

'You assume much since you can't be certain he will come.'

Richard slowly trailed his gaze from her wildly disordered, burnished gold hair, across the purely feminine features of her heart-shaped face, over the gentle swell of her breasts, past her bent legs, to the toes of her mud-stained shoes.

He dragged his gaze up to stare into her speckled hazel eyes. She quickly turned her head away, but not before he caught a glimpse of her flushed cheeks. 'Oh, rest assured, Isabella of Warehaven, he *will* come.' And when he did, Richard would be waiting.

'Brides are easily bought.' She leaned forward to wrap her arms round her knees. 'I am certain Wade of Glenforde will find another with little difficulty.'

Her pensive tone and response surprised him. Richard wondered what Glenforde had done, or said, to cause Isabella such doubt of her worth as a bride, or as a woman.

'Perhaps, but you forget what else he stands to gain in this union. Glenforde is greedy. He will not throw away the opportunity to secure his relationship with royal blood.'

Isabella shook her head. 'Now *you* forget, my father was never recognised. King Henry might have been his sire, but his mother was little more than a whore.'

'That's a fine way to speak of a blood relative.'

'Relative? She was a servant who sold herself for nothing more than a warm bed and a meal. Once my father was weaned she was never seen or heard from again. What would you call her if not a whore?'

She stared at his naked chest and then turned her flushed face away.

Richard retrieved a shirt from the clothes peg near his bed. 'A woman who sells herself for a warm bed and food isn't necessarily a whore.' He knew exactly what a whore was—a bed-hopping liar with not a trace of honour.

Something in the bitter tone of his voice caught her attention. What reason had he to sound so…resentful or cynical? Isabella turned to look at him. His shirt hung around his neck and he frowned down at it. He was no doubt trying to determine how to get dressed without using his injured shoulder.

As far as she was concerned she'd already helped him enough—more than enough. The obvious fact that he didn't seem to remember clearly was just as well. It was better for her if he had no reason to see her as anything but the enemy.

She didn't want Dunstan to think that she cared for his welfare—she didn't, not in the least.

It was imperative that he not misconstrue her actions. Because if he went through with this farce of a marriage, she would make his life miserable.

Not only would this marriage never be consummated— doing so would tie her to this knave for ever and she was not about to spend the rest of her life wed to a man she despised—but he would soon learn just how little his wife cared for him.

By the time her family came to rescue her, Dunstan would be glad to let her go.

Her family rarely used their connection to either royal— Stephen or Matilda—but in this matter she would use every advantage at her disposal to gain an annulment. However, freedom from this marriage would never be granted were she to let this man have his way with her.

No, she fully recognised the need to keep him at arm's length and to repel him at every turn.

Dunstan glanced in her direction and she held her breath, certain he was going to ask for help. Instead, he clenched his jaw and managed to get the shirt on by himself.

A sheen of sweat beaded his forehead, but she refused to acknowledge his pain and weakness—not when his actions thus far would cause her much more than a moment or two of discomfort.

Her whole world would now be turned upside down. Her mother would be distraught with worry and fear. Her brother's rage would know no boundaries, his anger at her kidnapping and their father's death would surely make Dunstan's world tremble. But Glenforde was another story... Would her betrothed set aside their differences to come to find her, or would he think himself better off without her?

After all, there was another heiress still living at Warehaven—her sister, Beatrice. If Isabella's newly forming suspicions were right, Glenforde had formed no tender feelings for her. He was concerned more with the land, gold and regardless of what she'd told Dunstan, yes, Glenforde would also be concerned with the connections that would come with marrying a daughter of Warehaven. Once he learned that the daughters shared equally in Warehaven's wealth it was possible that either daughter would suffice.

The knowledge that she alone would pay the consequences for his actions with the whore that night at Warehaven made her head spin. How would she find the strength to do what she must to survive? And even when she did gain an annulment, would she be able to salvage anything of her dignity, her future or of her worth?

To take her mind off of the dark thoughts gathering in her mind, she asked, 'So, you think it is appropriate for a woman to sell herself for the necessities of life?'

Isabella truly didn't care what he thought. She just needed something to distract her.

He leaned forward, his elbows on his knees, his hard stare making her far more than uncomfortable. Her belly tightened at his single-minded focus.

It wasn't that he frightened her, even though a part of her mind whispered that she should be afraid. After all, her well-being was completely in his hands.

But had he wanted to cause her harm, would he not have already done so? There'd been nothing to stop him—except for the simple fact that he'd been drugged, unconscious and unable to cause anyone harm.

She swallowed. Perhaps questioning him on his thoughts about women of loose morals had been unwise. Especially considering the assessing look he'd given her when trying to convince her that Wade would come to her rescue for her features alone.

His smouldering stare had left little doubt in her mind that he found her physical form...pleasing. His perusal then had sent a heated flush from her cheeks to her toes. Much like it did now.

Isabella shook off the unwanted warmth and mentally chastised herself. The narrowing of his eyes warned her that she'd held his stare far too long. He knew full well what his pointed gaze did to her and she'd just unintentionally made him more aware of her response.

'Appropriate?'

She pressed her back more firmly into the corner, but it did little to stop the tremor lacing down her spine. She should be afraid—needed to be very afraid of what the deep timbre of his one-word question did to her senses.

He had kidnapped her—stolen her away from her family and home, taken her from everything she knew and brought death to her father. It made no sense for her to note the blueness of his eyes, or the way his overlong ebony hair fell across his face.

It was wrong, near shameful to let the mere sound of his voice set heat racing along her spine and loosen tiny wings to flutter low in her belly.

The walls closed in around her, making her nearness to this man more acute, bringing their privacy more into focus. She raised a shaking hand to her chest, pressing it over her wildly pounding heart and struggled to draw in breath.

Oh, yes, she should be very afraid of him, but more so of herself.

One dark eyebrow hitched over a shimmering sapphire-hued eye, giving her the distinct impression that he some-how knew where her thoughts had flown. Horrified of what that might mean for her continued well-being, Isa-bella forced herself to look away.

'I cannot judge whether her actions were appropriate or not. People do what they must to stay alive.'

He rose and she felt his stare as he loomed over her. The very air around them crackled with tension. When she fi-nally met his gaze, he suggested, 'That is something you might want to remember.'

It was on the tip of her tongue to ask if he was threat-ening her, but she held her words inside. She wasn't com-pletely witless, of course he was threatening her, warning her that some day she, too, might need to do something dire to save herself. So she kept her thoughts and questions to herself, fearful of forcing his hand this soon.

'I need to see to my ship and men. You stay here.'

When she didn't respond, he nudged the toe of her ru-ined slipper with the side of his foot. 'Did you hear me?'

'I am not deaf, you lack-witted oaf. I heard you.' The moment the words were out, she winced. There was a time for mockery or name-calling, but this wasn't the time to give her tongue free rein.

He bent over. Then, unmindful of his shoulder, grasped her beneath her arms and hauled her up from the floor. When they were nose to nose, her feet dangling in the air, he asked, 'Do you think it wise to bait an enemy when you are the prey?'

'No.' Thinking quickly, she reminded him of his obligation as her captor. 'But as your hostage you need to keep me safe.'

'I will soon be your husband and while I may be honour bound to keep you alive, your tender feelings concern me not at all.' He dumped her on to his bed and came over her, resting most of his weight on his forearms. 'Keep your wits about you, Isabella of Warehaven. Not all injuries can be seen.'

While it was easy to ignore the beads of sweat on his brow attesting to the strain he'd placed on his body, it wasn't as easy to ignore the evident strength in the hard muscled thighs trapping her securely on the bed.

And even harder to ignore the implication of his threat.

'Honour? You killed my father, that proves you have little honour, Dunstan.' She turned her head away from the heat glimmering in his eyes.

He drew her head back so she faced him and Isabella fought the dread overtaking her shaking limbs.

His breath was hot against her cheek, his lips trailed flames across her skin. He paused, his mouth a hairsbreadth above her own, pinned her with his stare and asked, 'Why should I show you more honour than Glenforde did when last he visited Dunstan?'

Her chest tightened even more until her breaths were ragged gasps for air. His nearness, the physical contact of their bodies made thinking almost as impossible.

'I am not Glenforde.' It was the only answer that could find its way through the confusion and fear casting a fog over her thoughts.

He rose to stand over her. 'No you are not Glenforde. But you were to become his wife and you are here. Forget not your place, Isabella.'

Silently, she watched him exit the cabin. Relief washed through her, making her limp with near exhaustion.

Even though he'd told her that Glenforde had murdered someone on Dunstan—someone young, a child—she had no way of knowing if the crime was real or imagined. She couldn't help but wonder what had held Dunstan's temper in place. Had it been her reminder that she wasn't Glenforde? Or had he somehow sensed her confused fear and relented?

This was not a man to take for granted. He was more of a threat than she'd first thought. This man, above all others, seemed to have the power to reduce her to a mindless muddle with little more than a look.

She couldn't begin to imagine how she would have reacted had he carried through with his threat. Would she have fought him with every fibre of her being?

Or would she have followed the whispered longings of her traitorous body?

The only thing she knew for certain was that she needed to take charge of her wayward emotions before *she* became the greater threat to her well-being. Otherwise, she would bring about her own downfall.

Chapter Five

Richard leaned against a timber beam long enough to catch his breath before climbing the ladder to the open aft deck above. The hardest part of this venture was to have been the actual kidnapping and making a hasty retreat towards Dunstan unscathed.

His throbbing shoulder reminded him that he hadn't escaped unscathed. But at this moment, his injury was the least of his concerns. What bothered him was the uneasy feeling that there was more to his fragmented dreams than he could fathom.

He knew from the unquenchable dryness of his mouth that Matthew had drugged him. The lingering bitter taste meant the man had probably broken into their limited stores of opium. While the concoction was a pain reliever of miraculous proportion, it left the patient's mind foggy for days afterwards.

Still, the memory of a soft, warm body next to him on the pallet was too vivid to have been only a dream. Why would his mind have conjured gentle hands and a hushed soothing whisper to ease him when the pain grew close to unbearable?

His past experience with women hadn't led him to believe they were gentle or soothing with any except their offspring. Not for one heartbeat could he imagine Agnes easing anyone's pain but her own.

Yet in his dreams it had been a woman. There was only one woman aboard this ship—Isabella of Warehaven. Had she soothed him, gentled his need to rage against the agony chasing him?

Impossible.

None of it made any sense. And it was that unexplained senselessness that had him worried that marrying this woman would prove more difficult than the act of capturing her.

Why couldn't she be a few years younger or a great many years older? Either one would have made her less attractive in his mind, drugged or not.

Unfortunately, she was a woman full grown and too obviously aware of the untried desires teasing her body. Going into a battle without armour and weapons would be less dangerous than being in her company overlong.

When he'd loomed over her, threatening her, he'd hoped to see a glimmer of fear. Even though that had been his intent, it wasn't fear shimmering in her wary gaze—it had been an awareness of him, followed by curiosity and then confusion about what she felt.

Once he'd recognised her emotions, his body had threatened to betray him. The vision of their naked limbs entwined as he brought her across the threshold into womanhood had nearly been his undoing.

Nobody would have stopped him. They were soon to be wed. Had he been physically able, he could easily have taken her, shown her the pleasures of the flesh and then called it revenge for what her betrothed had done to his family. And no one would have faulted him.

But Isabella of Warehaven was not the object of his revenge. She was only the means to an end. He needed to remember that.

This desire, this unbidden lust for her was nothing more than a drug-induced torment that could and would fade with time. He would simply need to keep a tight rein on his desires until that time came.

Richard sighed and leaned on the rail for support. If he was this breathless and shaken from what little physical exertion he'd performed since rising from his bed, reining in his desires should prove an easy task.

Boisterous laughter from the men on the deck drew his attention. By the nods in his direction it was apparent that he was the focus of their conversation.

Richard straightened, squared his shoulders and then stepped away from the railing. Regardless of his injury he was not about to appear weak, or incapable of command, in front of his men.

He pinned a hard stare on Theodore, the largest in the group. When the guffaws ceased abruptly, he asked, 'What amuses you?'

Theodore shuffled his feet, batted at one of the other men, then answered, 'Nothing, my lord.'

At Richard's raised eyebrow, he added, 'We are simply glad to see you up and about.'

While they might be relieved to see him up, he resisted the urge to roll his eyes at the obvious attempt to garner his good graces. Richard doubted if his health had been the sole topic of their amusement.

If he knew anything about his men, it was that they enjoyed a good gossip almost as much as they enjoyed fighting. At times they were as bad—if not worse—than the women of Dunstan's village. There was little doubt in his mind they'd been making assumptions about him and Isabella.

Assumptions that might have been on target had he not been unconscious.

He bore her no ill will, but neither did he care over-much about her feelings. For the most part she was un-known to him, he knew very little about her, something he needed to resolve since she would become his wife in a matter of days.

Richard frowned and gingerly moved his shoulder about. The men aboard this ship knew little about mixing potions or salves, meaning the woman had probably saved his life. Regardless of his hatred for her betrothed, he did owe her something.

His gaze settled south, towards the Continent for a mo-ment, and then with a heavy sigh he climbed down the lad-der to speak to his men before heading back into his cabin.

Isabella flicked her thumbnail at the dried mud on her slippers. They were ruined beyond repair, but she hoped the pearls could be salvaged.

Her father had given her and her sister a bag to share. Every night for a week she and Beatrice had painstakingly attached the small pearls to their slippers. She'd formed hers into the shape of a flower, while her sister had spi-ralled hers around the edges.

The stool beneath her shifted slightly, just enough to make her reach out to keep from falling on to the floor. The thin slivers of light came into the cabin from the port side of the ship. The sun had been behind them, mean-ing the ship had changed direction. A glimmer of hope sprang to her heart.

The cabin door banged against the wall, making her jump as Dunstan pushed through. He spared her a brief glance before dropping on to his bed to stare at the ceiling.

Eager to know if perhaps he'd changed his mind, she asked, 'Are we turning about?'

'No.'

Her newly borne spark of hope flickered out as quickly as it had formed. 'But the ship has changed direction.' She paused to get her bearings straight in her mind. Warehaven was off the south-east coast of England. Her little knowledge of Dunstan Isle was that it lay north-east towards Denmark. 'We are now headed south instead of further east.'

His soft chuckle grated on her patience. 'Don't think for a moment you are going anywhere but to Dunstan. I simply had the men adjust the course for home.'

She'd been aboard her father's and brother's ships enough to know how often the currents and the winds set them off course. 'Oh.'

'Tell me about yourself.'

Isabella blinked at the sudden request. 'What?'

Still staring at the ceiling, Dunstan repeated. 'Tell me about yourself.'

'Why?'

He turned his head and gave her a pleading look. 'Because I am injured, I don't feel well, I want a distraction.'

Dear heavens above, he was using the same tactic her father and brother had when they were unwell. That sad two-year-old's *feel sorry for me* gaze that always had her mother giving in to their whining with no more than a sigh. Well, she wasn't about to feel for sorry for him, not when he'd brought all of his misery on himself.

'Please.'

She crumpled the slipper in her hand and sighed. 'What do you wish to know?'

He stared back up at the ceiling. 'I should know something about you since you will soon be my wife.'

If he did anything that foolish, he would soon learn to rue the day he forced her into a marriage. However, between the lingering effect of the opium and the paleness of his face, arguing with him now would be pointless. If she read his features correctly, the drooping eyelids and down-turned mouth signalled he would soon fall back to sleep.

To humour him in the meantime, she said, 'I have an older brother, a younger sister, a mother and no father.'

'And again you assume he is dead. Do you dislike your father so much that you secretly hope the worst?'

Isabella gasped at his insinuation that she would wish such foulness for her father. 'I love my parents dearly.'

'Love?' He shook his head. 'Of what use is love? I would think they'd rather have your respect and obedience.'

At this moment, he was most likely correct. Had she paid heed to her parents' warnings, she wouldn't be on this ship heading to Dunstan.

Although she found it interesting that he had such a lowly opinion of love. 'Did you not care for your parents?'

'I did not know my mother, she died when I was a babe. And my father did his duty by me.'

'Did his duty?'

'A roof over my head. Food in my belly and a suitable place to foster once I was old enough to hold a weapon.'

'Oh.' She felt no pity for the man, but found herself aching for the small boy. Had he had no one to offer him any gentleness? No welcoming arms to chase away the childish nightmares and hurts? She could not fathom such a life. She'd had both a mother and father who'd cared for their children dearly.

'You sound surprised. Did your brother not foster elsewhere?'

'Of course he did.' But he'd done so with their mother's

family until he gained squire status and then he'd joined Matilda's court.

'What about you and your sister?'

'No.' Isabella wrinkled her nose, waiting for what would be disbelief on his part.

'No?' Dunstan turned his head to look at her. 'Surely you spent time at Glenforde's keep?'

She smoothed out her crushed slipper, brushing the caked mud on to the floor—busy work to keep from returning his gaze. 'No.'

'You expect me to believe that King Henry's granddaughter, Empress Matilda's niece, did not learn how to be a lady at the knee of her future mother-by-marriage?'

'My mother taught me how to be a lady. Regardless of acceptable convention, she would not surrender such a task to a stranger. Besides, I was betrothed to no one, so there was no future mother-by-marriage.'

He sat up on the bed and swung his legs over the side. 'Is there something wrong with you?'

Isabella paused. Since it would be normal for her and Beatrice to have been betrothed at a very young age, of course he would wonder at the reason for such a lack. She should lie and tell him that there was something drastically wrong with her.

It had to be something that would make him think twice about forcing a marriage between them. Something— gruesome. Some terrible thing that would make him shiver with dread. Perhaps something that would convince him to turn the ship about and return her to her family.

But what?

'Too late.' Dunstan leaned forward. 'It has taken far too long for you to answer.'

She narrowed her eyes and lifted her chin a notch. 'Perhaps my…condition is so severe I've no desire to sicken you with the details.'

'Other than a smart tongue and lack of common sense, there is nothing wrong with you.'

His smug certainty nipped at her temper. 'You can't be sure of that.'

'Actually—' he rose from the bed and stepped towards her '—I can.'

She held her slipper out like a shield, as if the scrap of fabric and pearls would protect her from his advance. 'What are you going to do?'

Dunstan snatched the slipper from her hands, tossed it across the cabin, then slowly circled her. He passed by her side, touching her ear as he kept walking. 'I know your ears are fine.'

He brushed a fingertip across her lips as he crossed before her, making her lips tingle. 'It is obvious you are capable of speech. And I know you can see, so nothing is wrong with your eyes.'

Isabella silently cursed her own stupidity. He'd accepted her statement as a dare—as a way to intentionally trap her in her own lie.

He stopped behind her and placed his hands on her shoulders. Isabella fought the urge to shiver beneath his touch.

Patting her shoulders, he lowered his hands, running them down to her wrists. Leaning over her, he commented softly, 'And if I am not mistaken, these two arms seem to be normal.'

He trailed his hands up to caress the back of her neck, asking, 'I wonder what else needs to be investigated?'

She tried unsuccessfully to pull away from him. 'Nothing.'

'No? Then how can I be certain you are whole?'

Isabella ground her teeth before answering, 'I am fine. There is nothing wrong with me.'

'Ah.' With his thumbs still on the back of her neck, he snaked his fingers to encircle her throat and with his fingertips beneath her chin tipped her head back, forcing her to look up at him.

While the placid expression on his face warned her of no ill-conceived plans to choke the life from her, the gentle, deadly warmth of his hold silently threatened her in a way no brandished sword ever could.

This hold was more personal than the tip of cold metal against flesh. The heat of his fingers belied the damage he could cause.

'So, you were seeking to lie to me?'

She stared up at him. He knew full well she'd lied. He had only been mocking her, baiting her, and she'd stepped into his trap with little thought.

If she kept up this ruse, she knew he would follow through with his examination until she cried off. Unwilling to be humiliated any more than she already was, she whispered, 'Yes.'

'What?' He stroked the ridge of her throat. 'I didn't hear you.'

'Yes.' Isabella reached up and grasped his wrist. 'Yes, I lied.'

He slid his fingers lower to circle the base of her neck, but did not remove his hands. The less-threatening hold did nothing to ease the trembling of her limbs.

'You are being forced into a marriage you do not want. There is nothing you can do to prevent it.'

His hands, gently rubbing the tension from her neck, might be welcome another time, another place. Now, however, his caressing touch was an unwelcome reminder of what was to come. If they wed, and unless she could convince the priest on Dunstan to not perform the rites, it was becoming a certainty that they would, he would own her body and soul.

'Rest assured, Isabella, that I expect little from you as a wife.'

Her breath caught in her chest. Did that mean they would not share a bed? Once his business with Glenforde was complete, would she be able to petition for an annulment?

'We will wed. You will share my bedchamber.'

Isabella's heart sank. Sharing his bed would dash her hopes for an annulment. What would she do, how could…? She bit her lower lip to keep from crying out in surprise at the sudden clarity of the devious vision springing to life in her mind. If all else failed, her family could make her a widow.

'As long as you do not seek to lie to me, I will treat you well. Deal with me honestly and you will want for little.'

His statements gave her pause. He would not say such things unless someone, at some point in time, had deceived him. A woman most likely—a wife, or love interest, perhaps?

The irony of this moment was not lost on her. Now, as she plotted his imminent demise, he swore to treat her well if she did not lie to him.

A tiny pang of guilt grew deep in her belly, twisting its way towards her heart. Isabella swallowed a groan, refusing to let misgivings rule her future.

Dunstan stepped back. With his hands no longer on her, she was able to tamp down the guilt.

'I am weary and need rest.' He headed to the bed. 'Come.'

She stared at him in shocked dismay. 'I will not join you in that bed.'

'You have done so these past nights.'

'When you were incapable of doing anything more than sleep.'

'That is all I intend to do now.'

His intentions didn't matter, he was more than capable of doing whatever he wanted, should she agree or not. She shook her head. 'No.'

Dunstan sat on the edge of the bed. 'My bandages need to be changed.'

Isabella narrowed her eyes at his subterfuge. He was giving her that sad *oh, woe is me* look again. The same one her father had used on her mother when he wanted something he knew full well he didn't need.

She wasn't yet Dunstan's wife and she didn't care for him, his wants or his well-being in the least. 'Your man Matthew is quite capable of changing the bindings.'

'His touch isn't as gentle as yours.'

She shrugged. 'Then perhaps you need to speak nicer to him.'

'I rest easier with you at my side.'

Again, she shook her head. 'We are not wed yet. Until that day comes…' Because she held tightly to a slim thread of hope that Dunstan's priest would see reason, she silently added, *if it comes*. 'I will not share a bed with you.'

'Then where do you think you will sleep?'

She didn't know. But she was certain of one thing—she was not sharing his bed.

He'd been correct—she had done so these last few nights, but she hadn't felt threatened or in any danger. However, the situation had changed. Dunstan had already proven he was more than capable of forcing her to do his will.

Feeling his hard stare, she answered, 'Since I am not tired, it doesn't matter where I sleep.' At his frown, Isabella rose from the stool and plopped down into the corner of the cabin, wedging herself tightly against the hull's timbers. 'This will do fine.'

Dunstan shook his head and rose from the bed. 'It is cold. Permitting you to develop the chills and a fever will not suit my plans.'

His plans? What about the plans she'd had? 'What do I care about your plans?'

He ignored her question and motioned towards the bed. 'Join me of your own free will, like an adult, or I'll carry you like a child. The choice is yours.'

She clenched her jaw at having a version of her own words tossed back at her, but refused to move.

He rubbed his forehead as if seeking to ease the throbbing of an aching head. Then he shouted, 'Matthew!' When his man hastened into the cabin, he held out his hand. 'Give me your dagger.'

Matthew did so without question and, when waved away, left the cabin without a word.

Isabella gasped. He would kill her for not sharing his bed? She turned her face into the timber beam to avoid witnessing her own death.

'Oh, for the love of—' He broke off on a harshly snarled curse and grasped her wrist. 'If my intent had been to kill you, I would have done so at Warehaven. Open your hand.'

She did as he ordered, but kept her face averted.

'What is wrong with you? I thought a Warehaven would be braver than this.' When she turned her head to stare up at him, he slapped the dagger's handle on to her palm and tightly closed her fingers around it. 'Now, get in the bed.'

Chapter Six

Finally. After endless weeks of searching for Glenforde's whereabouts and these last six days at sea, this journey was nearly at an end.

A cold wind raced across Richard's face, bringing a chill to his cheeks and reminding him of the narrow margin in which they'd beaten the turn of the season. With the onset of winter at hand, this venture home had been a race against time. Another week at sea would have found them in dire straits. Strong winds, enormous waves and deathly cold water could have spelt doom for any foolish enough to set sail.

Yet he'd intentionally detoured this journey home by a day—long enough to set one of his trusted men ashore on the Continent with orders to return with the information he sought. The man would return to Dunstan on the last of his ships that would hopefully soon leave Domburg. Once that ship and this one reached Dunstan's harbour his entire fleet would be safely careened during the long winter for repairs and general maintenance.

Richard directed his attention towards the fast-approaching coastline. The quickly setting sun behind them cast shadows on the rock face of the cliffs. Soon, night would fall and they would be unable to safely enter the harbour until daylight.

A quick glance assured him that Matthew had the men and ship well under control. The sail slid down the mast as oars splashed into the water.

It was imperative that the ship be manually steered through the narrow inlet into Dunstan's harbour lest she be smashed to pieces against the jagged boulders hiding beneath the surface of the water on either side of the inlet.

Once again he looked shoreward, relieved to see the torches flare to life in the towers flanking the entrance to the harbour. It was necessary to have those lights as guideposts.

Richard positioned himself at the centre of the aft deck, noting that the bow of the ship was just off-centre of the torchlights.

'Hard to port!' he shouted down to the men on the rudder. When the bow pointed dead centre between the lights, he yelled, 'Hold!'

While steering the ship past the boulders, then between the cliffs wasn't as easy as it might appear with a crew not as well trained as this one, he was grateful for the natural protection Dunstan's unwelcoming coastline provided.

Most of the island rose up from the sea like a rock-faced mountain and needed little protection from unlikely intruders. Those who were brave enough to try either gave up in frustration, or drowned after their ship broke apart against the boulders.

The short, narrow strip of beach on the other side of the island existed only at the whims of the tide and wind. If a ship anchored there, it risked being either blown against the cliff face, or left high and dry on the exposed sandbar.

The other danger, as he'd learned, was anchoring just off the beach, only to later watch his ship sail away without him when the tide unexpectedly turned and the anchor failed to hold against the rapidly rising water. Chasing the unmanned ship down had proven far easier than bearing his father's wrath.

Even with the dangers of anchoring at the beach, his grandfather had determined it the weakest point on the island. Which is why a stone-fortified keep had been built at the highest point above the beach.

If a force did manage to make landfall there, they would be unable to gain entrance to the keep without suffering the loss of many lives.

And still, even with all of this protection—natural and manmade—Glenforde had broken through Dunstan's defences. Richard knew the man had not done so unaided. Someone on the island had to have offered assistance.

Who? And why?

A sharp gasp caught his attention. He turned to see Isabella's head appear over the edge of the forecastle deck. 'Go back inside.'

But instead of doing as she was told, she scrambled the rest of the way up the ladder to stand beside him. After planting her feet for balance, she tipped her head back to look up at the sheer rock cliffs flanking them.

Richard swallowed his groan. When his wife had first witnessed this sight, she'd been terrified, claiming that he'd brought her to the entrance of hell. Agnes had hidden her face in her hands and cried with fear.

Since he'd expected the same reaction from Isabella of Warehaven he'd ordered her to stay below. Following orders was obviously not one of her strengths—a lack he would see remedied quickly.

From the way she easily fell into the rhythm of the slightly rolling deck, it was apparent that the Lord of Warehaven hadn't cosseted his daughters inside the keep on dry land. This one at least had been aboard a ship or two in her life.

Without looking at him, she said, 'The rocks are close enough to touch.'

'No. It only appears that way.' Although they were close enough that men were stationed along both sides of the ship with long, sturdy poles in hand just in case they did get too close to the cliffs.

'Has this always been here?'

Richard frowned. Did she think he built it? He could hardly imagine the feat. 'Yes. Of course.'

'Does it cut all the way across the island?'

'No. The cliffs will become lower and level out. After the curve ahead this inlet will open into the harbour. Beyond that is a small inland river that leads to the shipyard.'

'Oh.' So fascinated by the towering walls of rock, she barely glanced to the curve ahead. 'Is this the only way into the harbour?'

'Why?'

'I just wondered.'

He knew exactly what she wondered. Half-tempted to let her worry, he left her to stew a few moments before he finally relented. 'Your father and brother have both been here before. They know how to gain safe entrance to the inlet.'

'I thought perhaps…'

When her words trailed off, Richard laughed. 'You thought what? That I would lure your family here only to watch their ship crash against the rocks?' He shook his head, adding, 'Since their death is not what I am seeking, doing so would not serve my purpose.'

She closed her eyes, shivering a moment at the memory of watching an arrow find its mark in her father's chest, before asking, 'Then it is only Glenforde's death you seek?'

'As I said before—I am not interested in your family.'

He hadn't answered her question. 'I know you think Glenforde will come for me.' She shrugged her shoulders. 'I am still not certain.'

'And I say you are wrong.' He leaned closer to warn, 'You might want to pray that he does come.'

Isabella understood the unspoken warning—if Glenforde didn't come, she could very well bear the brunt of Dunstan's revenge. Instead of telling him the reasons Glenforde would never come, she stepped away, assuring Dunstan, 'I will.'

As the ship eased out from the gentle curve, the harbour opened up before them. She blinked at the sight before her.

An entire town seemed to appear from thin air. The harbour was alight with countless torches. People—women, men and children—lined the full docks and streets. Some laughed, some cried, but all waved and shouted their welcomes to those aboard the ship.

Ropes were tossed to men waiting on the nearest dock and the ship swung easily about as it was wrapped and tied around the mooring post. Beyond were numerous, large storage buildings.

From the looks of it, Dunstan did more than kidnap unsuspecting women.

'You look surprised.'

She nodded, admitting, 'I am.'

'Did you think me nothing more than a brigand committed to mayhem on the high seas?'

Isabella couldn't help herself, she ran her gaze down his body. With his overlong near-black hair, dark looks and recent actions, how could she think him anything else? 'Apparently, looks are deceiving.'

He took her elbow and led her towards the ladder. 'This war for the crown makes pirates and thieves of us all. When in truth I am no different than your father or brother.'

But he *was* different. She shivered beneath his touch. So very different than either of them.

Richard easily picked Conal, his man-at-arms, out from the crowd of people on the quay. The big red-haired man looked grim, as if all were not well on Dunstan. Since there was no show of force—neither friend nor foe—crowding the docks, things couldn't be too dire.

Certain that he would find out how Dunstan had fared in his absence soon enough, Richard turned his attention back to Isabella. 'Since you managed to climb up here, I assume you can get down, too?'

She peered over the edge of the deck and then took a step back. 'I can manage on my own, thank you.'

It was on the tip of his tongue to mention her mishap in his cabin a few days ago when she'd *managed* to be tossed to the floor.

Instead he descended to the deck below and waited for her to do the same before escorting her off the ship towards his waiting man-at-arms.

From the countless tears and seemingly overexcited cries of reunion, Isabella could only assume these men had been gone from Dunstan an unusually long time.

Extended absences were a normal way of life—especially for a community involved in sea trade. She'd been at the quay numerous times with her mother and sister when the ships had finally returned to harbour. Never did she remember witnessing such a display as this at any homecoming.

It struck her as odd. Had these men left under some cloud of doom? Had they been headed out to a known, or suspected, danger? Or did Dunstan's shipping schedules keep them from home often enough to cause this level of emotion?

If the size and number of the storage buildings were any indicator, Dunstan prospered well from his chosen method of commerce.

How much of it was legal would be anyone's guess. But then, less-than-legal goods had been stowed and transported on both her father's and brother's ships a time or two. Besides, with this never-ending battle for the crown, many not-so-legal activities occurred on a daily basis.

Her escort came to an abrupt stop. He released her elbow and pulled a flame-haired giant into his embrace.

Once the backslapping and greetings were completed, Dunstan scanned the harbour, asking, 'Has the *Lisette Reynolde* returned?' When his man shook his head, Dunstan frowned, then asked, 'Where is Father Paul?'

Shocked that Dunstan would so quickly seek the services of the priest, Isabella was speechless.

'He awaits you at the keep.' The red-haired man's gaze drifted to her and then back to Dunstan. 'I assume this is your intended?'

'I am *not* his intended.'

She waved off the man's assumption and turned to her captor. 'You plan to wed so quickly?'

'That is the plan, yes.' Dunstan glanced at his man. 'A plan everyone knew before I left.'

'Well, yes, but we hadn't expected it to happen the moment you stepped on land.' The man's voice rose, causing those around them to give the trio a wide berth. 'You don't think that perhaps a little…gentler handling…a bit of ceremony, or celebration might be in order?'

Dunstan grabbed his man's arm and turned him towards half-a-dozen waiting horses. 'Enough. I don't need you to tell me how to behave.' He spared little more than a glance at Isabella, ordering, 'Get over here. You'll ride with me.'

Only yesterday he'd commented on her less-than-brave

behaviour. If he wanted her to thwart him, she'd be more than happy to oblige. 'Like hell I will.'

She grabbed the reins from his hands, tucked the long skirt of her gown into the girdle about her waist and then hauled herself up on to the saddle. Isabella put her heels to the horse's side, suggesting over her shoulder, 'You can walk, or use another beast.'

Catching up with Dunstan's man, who'd set off as soon as he'd mounted his horse, she asked, 'What do I call you and just where do I find this Father Paul?'

'Conal is my name and unless you have a taste for becoming the next Lady of Dunstan this very night, you don't want to find the priest.'

In the end, she might not have a choice in the matter, but she'd prefer not to find herself tied to Dunstan before the moon fully rose. She'd rather swim back to Warehaven.

'Then would you—?'

Conal raised one hand, cutting off the rest of her request. 'Before you even ask, I'll not help you escape, nor will I naysay Lord Dunstan's wishes.' He cast a sidelong look at her. 'Have you considered that he may have had good reasons for what he did?'

'Oh, yes, I'm certain every knave has a good reason to steal a woman away from her home on the eve of her marriage.'

The ensuing bark of laughter didn't come from Conal. Nor did the hand grabbing the reins from her fingers belong to the man-at-arms.

Dunstan looped her reins to his own like lead strings, while saying, 'And I would think that a woman so eager to wed would have been at her betrothed's side instead of wandering around a dark bailey alone.'

'That still gave you no reason to spirit me away.'

He ignored her statement to warn, 'You take off like

that on your own again and I'll make certain you rue the day you were born.'

She gasped at his obvious threat. 'You wouldn't.'

'Behave like a wayward child, my lady, and I'll treat you like one.'

She glared at him. 'You wouldn't dare.'

'I wouldn't dare what?'

Isabella was almost certain that he wouldn't lay a hand on her—damaging her wouldn't be in his best interest. So, what would he do? She felt the heat of her flushed cheeks as she remembered his earlier warning that some injuries couldn't be seen.

He leaned over on his saddle, closer to her, and answered his own question. 'I would lock you away in a tower chamber without much provocation.'

Even though his deep, sensual tone gave her a moment's pause, relief washed over her, making her response nothing more than a simple breathless, 'Oh.'

Dunstan sat upright and shook his head. 'I can only hazard a guess about the direction your mind took, my lady. But let me assure you that I would never force myself on you uninvited.'

Uninvited? 'And you think for one minute that I would ever—' The barely perceptible twitch of his lips told her that she'd once again fallen prey to his mindless prattle.

Chagrined that she'd so easily let herself be led into this absurd conversation, she lifted her chin a notch, gave a good jerk on her horse's reins to free them and urged the beast ahead of the men.

'Stay on this road. You'll end up at the keep.'

Richard watched her ride ahead of them. With the ocean on one side and ever-thickening brush on the other, she had no choice but to stay on the road. Thankfully, since the ship had returned, his men and some of the men from the village saw to it that the path to the keep was lit with torches.

'She is a high-born lady, my lord; you should not tease her so.'

'She is Warehaven's whelp through and through. Trust me, the lady is well able to take my jibes and hand out some of her own.'

'That may be so, but you aren't her father or brother.' Conal's bristling censure was evident in his words.

Richard ignored his man's attitude. Something had been bothering Conal before the ship had docked. 'No. I am not her father or brother. But I am soon to be her husband.'

Conal snorted before asking, 'Were you able to discover how that accursed dog, Glenforde, came to be involved with Warehaven?'

'No, I didn't. I still have no idea why the Lord of Warehaven gave his daughter to Glenforde, but he did.'

'Then it's a good thing you came to her rescue by kidnapping her.'

'She would never agree.'

'No. And from the looks of it, she'll agree with this marriage even less.'

Richard shrugged. 'Does it matter?'

'No. But over time she might be persuaded to change her mind.'

'You, my friend, are a hopeless sot when it comes to women.'

'Perhaps.' Conal nodded towards Isabella riding ahead. 'So, what if Glenforde doesn't come for her?'

That was the second time he'd heard that opinion voiced. 'He stands to lose too much if he doesn't.'

Conal's snort startled the horses. Once the beasts calmed down, he said, 'You'd better hope so. Otherwise you'll end up with a wife for no good reason.'

'I'm sure I can find some use for her.'

Conal laughed softly before commenting, 'Careful, you might find yourself wanting this wife.'

'Perish the thought.' Quickly changing the subject, Richard asked, 'How did you fare while I was away?'

The humour left Conal's face in a rush. He turned a hard glare on Richard. 'Next time, leave someone else in charge.'

'What happened?'

'The master of the inn is keeping company with the baker's wife. So the baker refuses to supply the inn with breads or cakes. The baker's wife tired of the bickering and has taken up residence with Marguerite.'

'That must make your visits…interesting.'

'My visits?'

'Do you think nobody has noticed?'

'I don't know what you're talking about.'

'Please, don't seek to fool me. Everyone on the island is well aware that you and Marguerite have been enjoying each other's company for at least three years now. I keep waiting for her to one day make an honest man of you. Although, I must admit, I am starting to give up hope.'

Conal ignored the jibe about his lady friend. As if Richard hadn't said a word, he added, 'Now the innkeeper is declaring his lover a whore and the baker is seeking restitution for his loss.'

'Ah.' Richard sighed. 'Well, good. Nothing has changed.'

Chapter Seven

Isabella paused before the gated entrance into Dunstan Keep. The men in the twin towers stared down at her a moment before shouting to their approaching lord, 'She yours?'

His? No, she was *not* his. If she belonged to anyone it was her father—her breath caught as she remembered her father's body falling to the beach. No. She would not slip into grief until she was safely back in her family's embrace. If she now belonged to anyone it was to her brother, Jared—or with hope and a trunk full of luck, eventually a husband of her choosing.

But most definitely *not* Dunstan.

However, on rare occasions, she did know when and how to hold her tongue. This seemed to be one of those times, so she waited for Dunstan and his man to join her.

Once they were alongside of her, she unclenched her jaw to say, 'I am *not* yours.'

He ignored her and waved up at the men as he passed beneath the arched gate. 'Yes, she's mine.'

It was all she could do not to scream. But his grin told her that he knew exactly what she felt and had goaded her on purpose. Instead of screaming, she forced a smile to her lips and followed him into the keep.

Once they were in the courtyard, Dunstan dismounted, then came to her side to assist her from the horse. She accepted his help, making certain to curl her fingers tightly into his shoulders—more to bring him pain than for support.

He rewarded her petty action by pulling her hard against his chest. She struggled to free herself from his hold.

'Keep fighting me, Isabella. I love nothing more than a good battle.'

She fell lax against him. 'Let me go.'

'Not until you apologise.'

Snow would douse the fires of hell before she did so. 'I did nothing that requires an apology.'

While keeping one arm securely around her, he grasped her wrist and placed her hand against the wound on his shoulder. The thickness of the padding beneath her palm made her stomach tumble with guilt.

She turned her face away and softly said, 'I am sorry. I didn't mean to irritate your wound.'

'I beg your pardon? I didn't hear you. What did you say?'

Isabella took a breath before repeating herself a little louder, 'I said I was sorry. I didn't mean to irritate your wound.' Glancing up at him, she added, 'But it was no less than what you deserved.'

'Perhaps.' He released her wrist and then grazed her chin with his thumb. 'But it would be wise for you to remember that I am your only protector here.'

He had a valid point. Had she done any serious harm, she would be at the mercy of his men. She had no way of knowing what manner of men inhabited this godforsaken isle.

She turned away from him and looked up at the keep atop the hill. Made of stone, with round towers at each corner, it was every bit as big as Warehaven.

He pushed past her. 'Come. Father Paul should be here soon.'

Good. At least then she would have someone on her side. The priest couldn't very well marry them once she voiced her objections to this union.

Following him up the steps cut into the earthen mound, she was more than a little surprised to find an entrance at the top of the hill. Confused, she asked, 'Isn't this dangerous?'

'Dangerous? How so?'

'A ground-level entrance?' Had this man spent so little time on land that he didn't know the first thing about defending his keep?

'Until the enemy can learn to fly, we are secure.'

If someone wanted possession of Dunstan badly enough, they would find a way. But she wasn't about to argue warfare with him.

He held the metal-studded door open and followed her inside. She'd expected to walk into a storage chamber at the ground level of the keep. Instead, she paused to discover they'd come through what she would consider a postern gate leading through a thick fortified wall that opened to a courtyard running the length of the keep and not directly into the building.

When she turned to ask why the gate was at the front of the keep, Dunstan hitched an eyebrow. 'Rather deceiving at first isn't it?' He glanced up at the wall to order, 'Drop it down.'

The men, who she hadn't seen at first, lowered a portcullis into place behind the studded door, effectively cutting off the entrance from the bailey.

Dunstan stared down at her. 'No one gets in.' Before guiding her to the steps angling up against the wall, he added, 'And no one gets out.'

Isabella took his comment as a veiled threat—a warning that she'd be unable to escape. What would he do, or say, when she proved him wrong?

Although, as she trailed behind him along narrow courtyards, and up even narrower stairs, only to cross over walkways that had surely seen better days, Isabella wondered if his warning had been necessary. Escaping was one thing—simply remembering the way to get back to the outer yard would prove a challenge.

Finally, they entered the keep through a larger, heavily studded door. Her thoughts and concerns of escape vanished as the stale, rancid air of the Great Hall slammed against her face.

Isabella quickly covered her nose and mouth with the sleeve of her gown, but it did little to veil the stench of the ill-kept hall. She blinked as tears welled from her stinging eyes and prayed there wasn't some damp, musty tower cell awaiting her.

Dunstan shot her a dark frown that she couldn't decipher, but she wasn't going to uncover her face to question him.

It was all she could do not to gag when he led her across the filthy hall to a smaller chamber on the far side. While this room was in even worse condition than the Great Hall, at least it had two narrow window openings. Thankfully, he saw fit to open both shutters letting in fresh, albeit cold air.

'Your servants are lax in their duties.' She stated what she thought was obvious while gasping for breath.

'Lax?'

Isabella ran a fingertip across the thick layer of dust on the top of a chest. 'This didn't accumulate overnight.'

He turned his head to glance in her direction, his dark

expression even more stormy. 'I've yet to see anyone perish of dust.'

She kicked at an obnoxious clump of mouldy strewing herbs, sending it rolling across the floor. 'It takes more than a few days for this to grow.'

'And is easily removed with a broom.'

'The lady of this keep should be ashamed.'

'Presently, there is no lady.'

'Then the housekeeper should be severely reprimanded.'

'There is no housekeeper. And before you ask, there are no chambermaids, scullery maids nor a cook.'

She'd assumed he had no wife, since he was so determined to give her that unwanted title. And he'd told her aboard the ship that his mother was deceased. But to do without any women in the keep was something she could barely imagine.

'It is just you and your men?'

He nodded in reply.

'What do you do for food?'

'The same thing men have always done.'

She knew that meant one of the lower-ranked men did the cooking or some of the village women acted as camp followers did during a march to battle and performed the duty.

Isabella looked slowly around the chamber. Besides the dust and mould, there were cobwebs thick enough to suffocate someone should they have the misfortune to walk into them. Sheaths of papers that had tumbled from the small table in the corner on to the floor were half-covered in rotting rushes. She didn't want to think about the vermin living undisturbed in the bedding.

This is what her father's and brother's chambers would have looked like without her mother's oversight. Well, at the very least her father's chambers would have looked the same, if not worse. Her brother Jared was a little more organised.

She doubted that Dunstan Keep had always been in this condition, not when the wharf and village appeared in order and inviting. *So, how had this happened?*

'And none of you see anything wrong with...' she waved an arm to encompass the chamber '...this?'

'We have managed quite well.'

'Yes, I can see that.'

'Enough!' He spun away from the window. 'I have no desire to listen to your complaints.'

His sudden movement, deep threatening tone and fierce scowl forced her back a step. 'Complaints?' The shrillness in her voice made her take a breath. Regardless of how threatened she felt, showing any sign of fear would be a mistake. To regain a semblance of self-control, she glanced pointedly around the chamber, asking in what she hoped was a milder tone, 'The sorry condition of your keep does not bother you?'

Dunstan stormed towards her, his hands clenched at his sides. 'The condition of *my* keep is none of your concern.'

She fought the urge to bolt from the chamber—where would she go? But it was impossible to stand firm in the face of his anger and it would be foolish to remain within arm's length of danger. Moving away quickly, she put the small table between them.

'Where I lay my head at night *is* my concern.'

'If this chamber isn't good enough for you, there is an empty cell available.'

If he was intentionally seeking to frighten her more, he would have to do better than that. Besides, the cell might prove cleaner. Isabella squared her shoulders and stared at him. 'That would suit me fine, my lord.'

'I wonder.' His eyebrows arched. 'How would your bravado fare amongst the rats?'

Actually, if the closeness of the walls didn't take her bravado away and leave her near senseless, she'd be frantic at the first scurry of tiny feet, but he didn't need to know that. So, in an effort to retain her show of bravery, she shrugged in answer to his question.

'Do not tempt me, Isabella.'

He spoke her name slowly, deliberately drawing it out. She hated the way it rolled off his tongue. And she utterly despised the tremors it sent skittering down her spine.

'Lord Dunstan!'

Conal's voice broke through the closed chamber door a mere heartbeat before the man swung it open and entered. To her relief the priest followed in his wake.

Finally. She exhaled with a loud sigh, drawing the attention of all three men.

Dunstan motioned the men further into the chamber. 'Father Paul, is all ready?'

'Just as you requested.' The priest emptied the contents of the satchel he carried on to the table. 'I take it this is your intended bride?' the priest asked Dunstan.

'Yes.'

'No,' Isabella answered at the same time.

Ignoring her, the priest went about his business of unrolling and flattening a document, sharpening a quill and stirring the ink. He moved aside and waved Dunstan to the table. 'Your signature, my lord.'

Dunstan paused, holding the quill less than a breath above the document. The feathered end wavered slightly, a small drop of ink splashed down on to the vellum, spreading like a brackish-coloured droplet of blood.

An ominous omen of the future? Isabella's stomach clenched at the thought.

He scrawled his name at the bottom of the document, then extended the pen towards her, warning, 'Don't make this difficult.'

'No.' She stared at the quill before glaring at him across the table. 'You can't make me do this.'

'Yes, actually, I can and will.'

She gasped at the certainty in his words. Knowing there would be no reasoning with him, she turned to the priest. Surely he could be made to see how unwilling she was to wed Dunstan. 'I am being forced into this unholy alliance. It will not stand.'

The priest ignored her, seemingly content to gaze around the chamber. His unconcerned air splashed an icy cold on the heated rage that had been building in her chest.

'Are you not a man of God? Do you not represent the Church in this matter?' Isabella swallowed hard in a desperate attempt to remain rational. 'I cannot be forced into this union.'

Father Paul looked down on her with the expression of a long-suffering parent dealing with an unreasonable child—the same type of look she'd endured countless times from Warehaven's priest when she'd railed against lessons she had no desire to learn.

'Child, it seems you do not fully understand the direness of your situation.'

The calmness of his voice had the opposite effect of what he'd most likely intended. Instead of soothing her, it set her teeth on edge. 'I am *not* a child.'

Dunstan snorted, before suggesting, 'Then stop acting like one.'

She ignored him, intent on making the priest see her side of this argument—and then agreeing with her. 'There is nothing about this situation that I do not understand. I was taken from my home. Saw an arrow pierce my father's

chest as he came to my defence. I was made to tend my
captor's injuries. And now—' she flicked her shaking fingers at the document on the table '—against everything
that is just and right I am being forced to agree to a marriage that neither I, nor my family, would desire.'

The priest's eyebrows rose. 'I am certain your family
would find it more desirable for you to wed someone you
detest now, than to return to them next spring carrying a
bastard.'

Next spring?

The floor heaved beneath her feet.

Dear Lord, she'd not taken the season, nor the weather,
into consideration. Her brother and Glenforde would be
unable to come to her rescue for months.

And the priest's concern over her carrying a bastard
come spring made her ill. She drew in a long breath, hoping to calm the sudden queasiness of her stomach. There
had to be a way out of this.

'Child.' Father Paul touched her arm. 'Surely now you
see the sense in a marriage.'

'No.' Isabella shook her head. 'There will be no chance
of creating a child.'

'You cannot know the future. You are here on Dunstan without any protection, with no suitable companion.'
The priest shrugged. 'Even if Lord Richard was the most
chivalrous knight of the realm and placed not one finger
upon your person, nobody can say the same of every man
on this island.'

She glared at Dunstan. 'You have so little control over
the men in your command?'

When he said nothing, she crossed her arms against her
chest and turned her attention back to the priest. 'Then
lock me away in a cell.'

'Locks can be picked, cell doors can be broken.'

Would he thwart every idea she suggested? 'But—'

Dunstan cleared his throat, interrupting her. 'Enough. Your fate was sealed before I stepped foot on your father's land.' He tapped the quill beneath his signature on the document. 'Either sign this yourself, or I'll make your mark for you.'

'No!' She slapped both of her hands on the table. 'I will not do this. There has to be another option. One less... distasteful.'

Dunstan swirled the nib of the pen across the document, making a rather elaborate mark below his name. 'You will not do this?' He made a show of staring hard at the vellum on the table, before shrugging. 'It appears to me that you have already signed of your own free will.'

This could not be happening to her. In a hazy blur, Isabella saw Conal drop something into Dunstan's outstretched palm. Before she could make any sense of his intention, he grasped her left hand and slid a gold band on to her ring finger.

Instead of releasing her hand, he engulfed it in his own. 'With this ring, I, Richard of Dunstan, wed Isabella of Warehaven.'

Her throat ached with the need to scream. She jerked free of his hold, asking in a choked whisper, 'What have you done?'

No answer was required, or forthcoming, as she knew exactly what he'd done. He'd planned this every step of the way.

He'd had some document drawn up that took Lord only knew what from her, placed his signature and hers on it with witnesses present who would swear she'd signed of her own free will. Then, he'd sealed the deed by placing his ring on her finger.

As far as anyone was concerned, she was wed to this

knave. There was only one small…task…keeping them from being for ever joined in unholy matrimony.

While he might be able to forge her mark on a document, Dunstan would find bedding her much harder than he might think. Isabella clenched her hands into fists. Harder? No. She would make it impossible.

'My part here seems to be done.' Father Paul snatched the document from the table, rolled it up and tucked it back into his satchel. 'I'll take this. Should you have any desire to read it, you will find it safe in my care.'

He took a step back and paused. 'Lord, Lady Dunstan, if you wish a blessing on your union, you know where to find me.'

After the priest left the chamber, Dunstan crossed the room and pulled the sheet from his bed.

Isabella frowned. What was he doing now?

In the blink of an eye, he slid a dagger across the tip of a finger, splattered the blood on to the sheet and then tossed it to Conal. 'Lock this up somewhere safe.'

She stared in shock at Conal's back as he hastily left the chamber. Everything about this farce of a marriage—from the creation of the document, her forged signature and now to the evidence of the bloodied bedding—had been seen to in advance.

'You pig!' She turned her full attention to Dunstan. 'You dirty, filthy pig. I would like to see you gutted.' She paused to give her tremors a moment to subside before continuing, 'And your entrails slowly pulled from your body and fed to the dogs while you watched in dying agony.'

Dunstan unbuckled his belt and tossed it on to the narrow cot. 'Could we save all that for tomorrow?' He pulled his tunic over his head and dropped it atop his belt. 'Right now I'd rather sleep.'

'You do that.' She pulled his ring from her finger and

threw it at him as she moved from behind the desk to march to the door intent on leaving this chamber, this keep and, if at all possible, somehow this island.

He grabbed her arm as she reached for the latch. 'And just where do you think you're going?'

Isabella tried to pull free of his hold, but he only tightened his grasp. 'Let me go.'

'Oh, my dear wife, you seem a bit upset.'

'Upset!' His mocking manner nearly made her spit with rage. 'I have never been so…so mistreated in my life.' She pried at his fingers. 'And do *not* call me wife.'

'Nobody has mistreated you.' He released his hold long enough to scoop her up in his arms. 'But perhaps someone should have done so once or twice.' He turned around and walked towards the far corner of the chamber.

'Put me down.' Isabella struggled against his overbearing hold.

As if she hadn't said a word, he continued, 'Had they done so, you might know how to deal with disappointment in a less strident manner.'

Disappointment? Is that what he considered these recent events? Nothing but a disappointment?

'Finding water in your goblet instead of wine is a disappointment. This is far more than that.'

She kicked her legs and to her relief, he lowered his arm, letting her feet hit the floor.

'I am certain you'll eventually find a way to come to terms with your future. But for now, it is time for bed.'

She glanced behind them at the narrow cot. 'I am not sleeping in that vermin-infested thing you call a bed.'

'No, you aren't.' While keeping one arm wrapped about her waist, he shoved aside a dusty tapestry hiding a door, which he opened and then pushed her into the darkness beyond. 'But neither am I.'

Chapter Eight

Richard nabbed a lit torch from the wall of the outer chamber before following Isabella into the room.

Standing with his back against the closed door, he held the torch high enough to illuminate the area around him before using it to light a brace of candles. He mounted the torch in a wall sconce, ignoring Isabella's gasp of dismay.

While a layer of dust had settled from weeks of non-use, this small chamber was serviceable and, as far as he was concerned, that was all that should matter. He crossed the room to slightly open one of the shutters just enough to allow in a breeze of fresh air.

He expected her to make some comment, but to his amazement, she held her tongue and simply glared at him.

The bed jutting out from the far wall looked more inviting that he'd imagined it would and he longed for nothing more than to crawl beneath the covers, drop his head on to a pillow and then sink into the overstuffed mattress.

However, he couldn't help but wonder if Isabella would plunge a knife into his heart while he slept.

Before he could formulate any plan to prevent such an undesirable occurrence, she asked, 'Where do you plan to sleep?'

'In my bed.'

Her brows winged over her hazel eyes. Light from the candles flickered in the speckled depths of her stare.

'And where then will I sleep?'

Even though there was little doubt his answer would be acceptable, he forged ahead. 'In my bed.'

'When boars grow teats.'

Richard wanted to laugh at her bald statement, but knew that would only encourage her. Instead, he asked, 'Did you learn your refined speech at Warehaven's docks?'

'My speech is none of your concern.'

'As your husband, it is of great concern to me. I'll not have you bandying coarse talk about the keep. You are well aware of the trouble it invites.'

'Are you once again saying you have no control of your people?'

She'd taken up that familiar arms-crossed-against-her-chest, rigid-spine, chin-up stance that he'd come to recognise as her ready-for-battle pose. He knew that she would refuse to see reason or agree with anything he said.

His patience was in short supply at the moment and suddenly the idea of locking her in a cell seemed a good one.

Richard sighed. Refusing her bait, he sat on the edge of the bed. 'If you want everyone to think you are nothing more than a trollop I pulled from the dregs, so be it.' He tugged at a boot. 'But don't come crying to me the first time one of the men decides to taste your wares.'

He tossed the boot across the room, drowning out her gasp of outrage. She could feign shock all she wanted. Right now he just wanted sleep.

'I do not have to stand here and listen to you.' Isabella headed towards the door.

Richard reached it first and hauled her over his shoulder. 'You are partially correct. You don't have to *stand* here.'

He crossed the room in three strides and dropped her on to the bed. 'However, you will remain in this room, in this bed and listen to whatever I have to say.'

When she tried to get off the bed, he pushed her back on to the mattress. Holding her shoulders to the bed, he leaned closer. 'If you get up from here again, I will tie you to the bed.' Richard waited for her wide-eyed glare to ease into a frowning scowl to ask, 'Do you understand me?'

Oddly, instead of fighting him, arguing or making demands, she nodded. Her easy acquiescence now, along with her silence when he'd first pushed her into this chamber, made him wary. His concern that she might stab him in his sleep grew stronger.

Richard released her and backed off slowly, not certain she'd actually stay put. With one eye on her, he once again sat on the edge of the bed to remove his other boot and stockings, then turned to slide Isabella's shoes off.

'Don't.'

The tremor in her whispered command caught him unaware. Was she frightened, angry or tired like him? 'I was simply going to—'

'I know what you were going to do.' She drew her legs away. 'I can do it myself.'

'Then do so.'

Once she dropped her shoes and stockings to the floor alongside the bed, Richard stood and stared down at her. The look she returned was…timid…no, not quite timid, he doubted if there was a timid bone in her entire body— perhaps more worried or concerned than frightened. Her arrow-straight body, tense, poised for escape most likely, spoke louder than any words she might have said.

He jerked the covers and sheet from beneath her and drew them over her body. Her gaze followed him, he felt it burning a hole into his back, as he walked around the bed to the other side.

Sliding beneath the top cover, leaving the thinner blanket and sheet beneath him, he settled his head on to the pillow, unable to hold back a sigh.

The leather braces supporting the mattress creaked as she sat up. He opened one eye. 'What are you doing?'

'I can't sleep here.'

'You might want to give it a try before crying defeat.' He reached up, seeking to draw her back down. 'Close your eyes.'

She pushed his hold away. 'I can't sleep in this bed with you.'

He didn't need the candlelight to see the tenseness of her body—not when the tightness of her voice gave evidence to the anger roiling just beneath the surface.

'There is no reason we cannot share this bed.' Richard debated for a heartbeat, before reminding her, 'We are married.'

In a flurry of limbs and covers, she was up and out of the bed before he could stop her. From the other side of the chamber, she said, 'In name only and I'd prefer to keep it that way.'

'If you remember correctly, Conal left the chamber with proof that states this marriage is far more than name only.'

'That proof is nothing but a ruse.'

'Agreed. But who will attest to that in your defence?'

'I know the truth and that is enough.'

Richard knew any battle waged with words was lost, she would argue until the sun rose and beyond. 'This has become tiresome.' He sat up and dragged her side of the covers back, then patted the mattress. 'Get back in the bed and go to sleep. You will awaken in the morning as much a virgin as you are now.'

'What does that mean?'

He sighed. Apparently she was in the mood to argue every little thing he said. 'It means that if you do as I suggest, I will not touch a hair on your head…tonight.'

'And if I don't?'

Was she begging him for an all-out battle? He stared at her. 'What are you seeking to do, Isabella? Do you *want* me to force you?'

Ah, and once again her ready-for-battle pose—she stiffened her spine and crossed her arms in front of her against her chest. Why would this woman want to enrage him?

'You couldn't force me.'

'Haven't we already established the fact that I can? And I will?'

'You didn't force me to wed you. You simply forged my name on a document. I meant I would rather die than have you force yourself upon me.'

Force himself upon her? What the hell was she…? He frowned as her meaning dawned on him. They were talking about two different things. He'd only meant that he'd force her to sleep in the bed, nothing else. Yet she obviously thought he was talking about rape.

Outside of battle, he'd never in his life intentionally harmed any man smaller or weaker. He certainly wasn't about to start doing so with a woman now. He gritted his teeth at the ungodly thought, threw the covers off and rose from the bed. Without another word, he crossed the chamber.

Isabella backed away, reaching behind her for the door. 'Don't touch me.'

He again tossed her over his shoulder. 'Too late.'

This time, instead of arranging the covers to separate them, he dropped her on the bed and launched himself behind her. With one arm wrapped about her waist, he pulled her back tight against his chest, hooked a leg over hers and pulled the covers up.

'Now, close your eyes and go to sleep.'

When she struggled against his hold, he simply tightened his arm, hoping that eventually she'd wear herself out.

Once her struggles lessened, Richard closed his own eyes, certain that he'd have little trouble holding on to her if he fell asleep. After all, he'd long ago learned to remain alert even though he slept. Had he not, it was doubtful he'd be alive today.

Just as the hazy relaxing cloud of slumber rolled over him, Isabella reached for the edge of the bed. Her upper body followed her extended arms, while her soft rounded buttocks pressed against his groin, sweeping away any thought of sleep.

With a grumbled curse, Richard opened his eyes. While splaying his fingers low over her belly, he pulled the pillow from beneath her head and curled his arm in its place. He pressed his palm against her forehead, tipping her head back to ask hoarsely, 'Is it your intention to ensure neither of us sleeps this night?'

To lend emphasis to his question, he held her in place and thrust his hips forward. 'If so, you are succeeding.'

She froze immediately, gasping a strangled, 'No.'

The surprise in her voice only sent more blood rushing to his groin, making rational thought difficult. Richard groaned. What was it about this woman that enticed him so? She was nothing more than a means to an end—a pawn—someone to use to his advantage.

So why then did he keep having to remind himself of that simple fact? And why did he ache to touch her, to taste her, to take her and make her his wife in all ways?

Even through the layers of clothing separating them, the heat of her body swirled around him like a warm, beckoning caress. It was all he could do not to accept such a tempting invitation.

She tugged at his wrist, trying to move his arm. 'You need to release me.'

'No.' He snuggled impossibly closer. 'I find this rather comfortable.'

Finally, with an exasperated huff, Isabella fell still. After a few moments of blessed silence, Richard thought—hoped—she'd fallen asleep and he once again closed his eyes.

And once again, just as sleep promised to overtake him, Isabella broke through the fog. 'This will not work.'

Richard swallowed the growl rushing up his throat and asked, 'What will not work?'

She relaxed, easing down into the mattress and against his chest. 'If you think to seduce me with this sudden bout of gentleness, rest assured you cannot.'

Seduce her? The notion hadn't entered his mind—until now. He didn't know whether to laugh at her assumption, or curse at the ideas filling his head.

'I cannot? And why is that?'

'I am immune to your…charms.'

'Charms?'

She tapped his forearm. 'Yes, this holding me close and not attempting to force yourself on me.'

He choked on a laugh, then cleared his throat. 'The only reason I am holding you close is so you can't run a knife through my heart while I sleep.'

'No. I think you lie. If you were truly worried that I might murder you in your sleep, you would have gone elsewhere.'

'You don't think it would appear odd were I to sleep elsewhere on my wedding night?'

She shrugged. 'You gave your man bloodied sheets to

flaunt before the others. As far as everyone is concerned you already…did your duty.'

Richard rolled his eyes. *Did his duty?*

Before he could say anything in response, she continued. 'So, the only reason for this…closeness…is an attempt at seduction. And just so there is no doubt in your mind, let me assure you, it will not succeed.'

Richard withdrew his arm from beneath her head, unhooked his leg from hers and rolled on to his back. He was torn between two immediately clear options—kiss her until she shut up, or lock her up somewhere and conveniently lose the key.

He sat up, grabbed a pillow and the top cover from the bed and tossed them to the far side of the chamber. Leaning over her, he stroked a fingertip along her cheek. 'Because I am too tired to think clearly or battle any further, you win this round, my lady. But to erase any doubt from *your* mind, let me assure *you* of one thing…' He paused until she turned her head and looked up at him. '…I have never in my life backed down from a challenge.'

'But I didn't—'

He cut off her denial by covering her lips with his own. It didn't matter what she'd said, she could lie to herself all she wanted, but her body didn't lie. He knew the truth the instant her mouth softened beneath his.

Chapter Nine

'My lady?'

Before Isabella could fully open her eyes the window shutters creaked open. Sunlight flooded the chamber, near blinding her and stripping away the last vestige of sleep.

She sat up on the bed and squinted at the older woman now bustling about the room while shaking her head and muttering in disapproval.

'What was his lordship thinking?' The woman tossed the linens from the makeshift pallet into a pile. 'Bringing a lady here with the keep in this condition is unforgivable.' She tossed some clothing atop the pile. 'And to keep you in this tiny room—he needs his ears boxed.'

Swooping up the pile, she stood alongside the bed. 'Never you fear, I'll see this set right. If you're hungry, I'm sure the cook has put something together by now.'

Isabella's stomach growled, supplying the answer before her lips could form the words.

'How thoughtless of me, of course you are hungry.' The woman headed towards the door, promising, 'I will return soon with some food.'

Her senses still muddled, Isabella called out, 'Wait. Who are you?'

'Hattie, my lady.' Still at the door, she added, 'His lordship came to the village at sunrise, on his way to the docks. After seeing to some matter at the bakery, he ordered his servants back to the keep and asked if I would see to your needs for a time. Now, with your permission I'll get you something to eat and then we can plan this day's activities.'

'Yes, thank you.' Rising from the bed, Isabella wiped her sleep-tousled hair from her face, wondering just what activities would be in store for her. Obviously a cook had been found—or retrieved—and perhaps a few servants would be on hand to help clean.

Actually, she hoped there were more than a few, because cleaning this keep would require an army just to make it presentable. She shook one of the bed curtains and coughed at the dust flying up into the air. Her mother would be horrified.

To her relief, the items needed for her morning ablution were stacked on top of the chest at the end of the bed. Noticing the ribbons to braid through her hair, she knew these necessities hadn't been provided by Dunstan.

Hattie returned with the promised food just as she finished adjusting her ornate girdle low around her waist.

Two men carrying a small table and benches followed the woman into the chamber. The younger man—little more than a boy—dipped his head, put the benches beside the table and left.

However, the older and much larger man wasn't as quick to take his leave. She'd seen this man before on the ship. He sauntered towards the door, then turned to face her. His bulk dwarfed the small chamber and he raked Isabella with a look that reminded her of a hungry wolf and made her feel somehow dirty. 'It's a shame Dunstan saw fit to leave you…unattended.'

Isabella guessed from his pointed hesitation that he meant defenceless, not unattended. She took a step away from him, noting the width of his shoulders, the size of his meaty arms and his two missing fingers with trepidation.

'I would never leave my *special* woman wanting for my attention.'

Special woman? What had Dunstan told his men? She moved towards the table, intent on arming herself with the knife sticking out of the round loaf of bread. The small weapon wouldn't do much damage against this oversized oaf, but it was all she saw readily available.

He came closer to tower over her. 'Come now, sweeting,' he drawled low and throaty as if that would tempt her to ignore his ale-laden breath and threatening manner. 'Wouldn't you rather have a real man keeping you safe and warm instead of a lad who uses you, then leaves you to fend for yourself?'

She swallowed the sour taste in her mouth as she reached for the knife. Hattie caught her attention and shook her head. For half a heartbeat Isabella feared the woman was working with the man and was silently warning her not to fight what would be a lost cause.

But a heavy thud and the man's gasp right before he dropped to the floor like a boulder at her feet dissolved that fear.

She drew her confused attention from the floor up to Dunstan's angry frown. 'Are you uninjured?'

After she nodded her reply, he shouted for Conal. When his man rushed into the chamber, he pointed at the moaning heap on the floor, ordering, 'Get him out of here. Confine him so I can deal with him later.'

Once Conal and his staggering charge left the chamber, Hattie turned on Dunstan. 'Now will you listen to me instead of being so pig-headed?'

Taken aback by the way the older woman spoke to the lord of this keep, Isabella remained silent.

Dunstan sat down at the table, motioning for Isabella to join him before he answered Hattie, by asking, 'Which chamber would you prefer?'

'She is a lady.'

Isabella sat across from him and watched the byplay between this master and servant with interest.

'I am not opening either of those rooms.'

'Then she will take yours.'

'So be it.' He turned his attention to the food and Isabella. Without preamble, he explained, 'Hattie was my nursemaid and since then has become the island's chief busybody.'

The woman snatched the loaf of bread from his hands and tore it into two chunks—one for each of them. 'It's truly a sad thing that you still need a busybody to keep you from doing yourself harm.'

Isabella swallowed some water in an effort not to choke.

'It's more of a sad thing that you seem to constantly forget your place.'

Hattie's short bark of laughter was punctuated by a deeper frown from Dunstan. To break the tension she feared would escalate, Isabella asked the woman, 'Have you been on Dunstan Island long?'

'From before this one here was born, yes.'

Dunstan briefly pointed his eating knife towards Hattie. 'She came here with my mother and stayed on after I was born.'

'Someone needed to keep an eye on you.'

'I am no longer in need of a wet nurse.'

'And I am still waiting for you to prove that.'

'Enough!'

Isabella leaned back as Dunstan's face reddened. His

eyes blazed. She wished she could somehow slide beneath the table before he completely lost his temper.

However, Hattie showed no signs of fear—or of relenting. Instead of making a quick escape, the woman patted Dunstan's shoulder. 'I tease you overmuch at times and for that I do apologise. It is hard to remember you no longer need or want a mother figure.'

'Remember what you will, it makes no difference to me.'

Isabella cringed. His surly tone made it quite clear that he truly didn't care. However, Hattie's pursed lips and frown made Isabella wonder if Dunstan's current behaviour was out of the ordinary for him.

The older woman shook her head. 'Ack, I wonder how you've managed not to choke on your sour mood these last months.'

Dunstan shrugged in response, but from the smoothing of his brow, it appeared that his ire was fading as quickly as it had first appeared.

Dismayed by this odd exchange, and Dunstan's easy manner with this woman, Isabella tried to focus on her food. Obviously Hattie's relationship with his mother gave her added worth in Dunstan's eyes. While she wasn't quite family, neither did she appear to be a servant.

The older woman made the bed, asking, 'You will not be overwrought if I move Lady Isabella into your old chamber?'

'Aye, it will wound me deeply to have her housed elsewhere. Especially since I so enjoy sleeping with one eye open all night.'

'Warehaven would be a better place to *house* me,' Isabella interrupted his obvious sarcasm.

Dunstan rolled his eyes, but otherwise ignored her. 'I'm sure it will suit.'

'I have no doubts on that.' Hattie looked at Isabella, adding, 'But perhaps the lady would like to have the final say.'

Isabella nearly jumped at the chance to escape this small room. 'The lady would be happy to take a look.'

'No.' Dunstan shook his head. 'The lady and I have other matters to attend.'

After Hattie left the chamber, Isabella curled her fingers around the handle of the eating knife. At Dunstan's raised brow, she drew her hand away from the utensil. Not that the short blade could do much damage, but gripping it would have made her feel safer.

'What matters have we to attend?'

Yawning, he stretched his arms out, over his head and then brought them back down. 'There is still the matter of the bedding.'

'No. We—' Isabella pushed back from the table in a rush, knocking over the bench and choking on her reply.

Dunstan's eyes glimmered. But it was that familiar twitch of his lips that let her know he had once again intentionally led her mind astray.

He rested his elbows on the table. 'It is far too easy to unsettle you.'

She glared at him, wishing she could find words vile enough to describe what she thought of his amusement at her expense. While his action reminded her of Jared, this man was not her brother, he had no right to tease her in such a manner and she wanted to tell him so. But instead, she righted the bench and sat back down at the table. 'After all that has happened to me—at your doing—why would I not be unsettled?'

To her horror, she heard her voice waver. Her hands shook, stomach knotted and her throat grew tight enough to make swallowing difficult. Isabella knew that now, since she was dry, warm, had gained a night's worth of good sleep and had decent food in her belly, she was on the verge of losing the tight grip she'd kept on her grief thus far.

She could no more help it than she could stop the sun from rising. It was her way—she could forge through a crisis with her wits about her for the most part, but once all was calm and back to normal, she became inconsolable, weepy and unreasonable. It was a weakness, a fault her mother had brought to her attention more than once. Like a silly fool she'd actually thought she would be able to hold back the heavy sadness weighing on her heart until she returned to the arms of her family. She sniffed back the threatening tears.

Dunstan reached across the table and placed a hand over hers. 'Isabella, look at me.'

The unusual gentleness of his touch and his voice was nearly her undoing. She drew her lower lip between her teeth to keep it from trembling and lifted her head to stare at him.

'Do you remember when you thought I'd turned the ship around to take you home and you knew we were heading south?'

Unable to reply, she only nodded.

'We did head south, just long enough for one of my men to depart the ship.'

'Why?' Her voice cracked and she wanted nothing more than to find a reason to grow angry and set her coming bout of sadness aside for a little while longer. Unfortunately, Dunstan's calm, easygoing manner, while unfamiliar, wasn't providing her an outlet for rage.

'Everyone knows that Warehaven is Matilda's half-brother and even though the empress is in Normandy, surely word of her brother's condition would have reached her. So, I gave my man orders to quickly find news of your father and to return on the *Lisette Reynolde*.' He stroked his thumb across her hand. 'The ship docked early this morning.'

Oh, no, she didn't want to hear this from his lips. No. It was not his place, not his right to tell her that her father had died at his hands and that she'd been forced to wed her sire's murderer.

She gasped at the pain lancing through her heart and tried desperately to blink away the tears blurring her vision. The rage she'd been seeking should have sprung to life, but it hadn't. Instead, fear—cold and empty—filled her with a dread she'd not known before this moment.

Dunstan's hand tightened over hers, as if offering comfort, and he reached up with his other hand to brush at the tears on her cheeks before cupping the side of her face. 'Isabella, he is not dead. Wounded, yes, and from what I hear, angry as a crazed boar, but your father is not dead.'

A roaring, like a gale-force wind, ripped through her ears, leaving her dizzy and muddling her mind. She shook her head, trying to clear the annoying howl. 'He lives?'

'Yes.'

She drew her hand from beneath his and rose. Quickly, before she lost the ability to speak, she said in a rush, 'I thank you for telling me. But if we're done here...'

As her words trailed off, Isabella felt his stare piercing her back, but she wasn't about to turn around to face him. She stood in front of the narrow window, her hands pressed tightly into her stomach and stared through a gathering of tears out at the windswept sea.

The scrape of the wooden bench moving across the floor let her know that he'd risen from the table. She closed her eyes tightly, praying he would just leave the chamber.

'Are you dismissing me?'

She nodded at his incredulous tone. Apparently it

had been a long time since anyone had sent him away—verbally, or otherwise.

Thankfully, his heavy footsteps headed towards the door, which he slammed closed behind him.

Without waiting for more than half a heartbeat, she turned away from the window to throw herself across the bed, burying her face in her crossed arms. This ordeal was not yet over. So why was she suddenly falling into a such a muddled state now? Dear Lord, she'd not wanted this to happen, not now, not here, not until she was safely home, but she couldn't stop the tears, or the gasping breaths from escaping.

A firm hand on the small of her back surprised her until she realised it belonged to Dunstan. His nearness tore a strangled plea from her. 'Please, just leave me alone.'

Richard sighed and sat on the edge of the bed. 'That's not going to happen.'

Her odd behaviour moments ago had caught him off guard. It wasn't until he'd left the chamber and taken three steps away from the door when he'd realised what she was doing.

He'd heard her gasping sobs before he had come back into the chamber. The twisting of his gut had nearly kept him from pushing the door open, but he managed to swallow his unnerving response to her tears.

What was he supposed to do? Agnes's tears had fallen nearly every day, but he doubted that a single one of them had been anything other than a means of manipulation. However, it had taken him months to figure that out and in the meantime she'd made him suffer the pangs of misery.

For months he'd been left feeling confused, frustrated and consumed by guilt. It was hard to determine which gut-wrenching emotion unmanned him the most. Regardless, he had no intention of going through that again.

Richard drew his hand along Isabella's spine, knowing that whatever he did now would set the stage for their future. He didn't want more endless months of tears and guilt, but Isabella of Warehaven was not the type of woman who easily dissolved into tears for little reason. Quite the opposite, in truth. He'd seen her fight to hold them in more than once.

With a silent curse, and a fervent hope that she wasn't toying with him on purpose, he eased further on to the bed and pulled her up against his chest.

She stiffened, then tried to shove him away. 'What are you doing?'

Her broken words tore at his heart and he had no desire to determine why that should be so. The only thing he wished to determine right this minute was how to make her stop crying.

He held her tightly against him, not permitting her to escape. 'Tell me what has upset you so. I thought word of your father's well-being would make you happy, not sad.'

'Of course I'm gladdened to know he is not dead,' she mumbled.

He stroked her hair, the silken strands curling around his fingers as if they wanted to cling to him, unlike their owner, who was doing all she could to avoid his touch. 'Then what reason have you to cry?'

Her sudden, loud intake of breath should have served as a warning. Instead, it was her shriek of rage that gave him his first clue to her anger.

'What reason do I have to cry?' She pummelled her fists against his chest, ordering, 'Release me this instant!'

Richard hesitated a second too long. She jerked back unexpectedly, slamming her head against his chin.

He loosened his hold and she bolted from the bed, shouting, 'What is wrong?'

Richard glared at her and swung his chin back and forth to make sure she hadn't broken his jaw before saying, 'Obviously something is.'

She returned his hard stare. 'Need I recite the list of crimes committed against me?'

Again? He waved a hand at her. 'Oh, please do.'

'I was kidnapped from my home.'

'Guilty.' An act he was beginning to regret. He nodded. 'Continue.'

'Thrown on to your ship.' She paced the length of his chamber and while her expression remained tight and cold, her emotions were evident by the motions of her hands.

'I was then carried across the sea.' A deaf person could have kept track of the conversation by the way she punctuated each statement with a flurry of hand gestures.

'And I was forced to care for you.' Even she paused long enough to glance at the finger she'd pointed at him before quickly crossing her arms against her chest.

Richard leaned back against the pile of pillows at the head of the bed. 'Anything you forgot?'

She uncrossed her arms and stormed to the end of the bed with her fisted hands held tightly against her side. 'I was forced to marry you.' She took a breath before adding, 'Against my will.'

Oh, she was building a fine fit of rage. At least she wasn't crying any more, which was an improvement. Instead of stopping her, he nodded and agreed with the obvious, 'Yes, well, forced usually does mean against one's will.'

'And then…then you made me sleep in your chamber.'

He shrugged. 'It would be deemed odd if my wife slept anywhere else.'

'Oh!' She turned away from the bed, only to swing back around and again exclaim, 'Oh!'

Apparently, she'd run out of crimes to list. 'Are you finished?'

When she nodded, he swung his legs over the side of the bed and rose. Like a hunter stalking his prey, he followed her as she backed away until the far corner of the chamber stopped her retreat. With both hands against the wall, he trapped her.

'We have had this conversation before, Isabella, and this will be the last time. Yes, I kidnapped you and forced your hand in marriage.'

In response to her mutinous glare, he took another step forward, pressing his thighs against hers. 'Not one hair on your head has been harmed. You are sheltered and fed.'

'Sheltered? In a pigsty.'

'It serves its purpose and, like it or not, this is your home now.' Agnes had hated Dunstan's keep. It was too small, too plain, too far beneath her. He wasn't going to listen to another woman's complaints. 'You'd better get used to it, because this is where you'll live and this is where you'll some day die.'

At her wide-eyed look of horror, he added, 'You are a means to an end and I will do anything to see that Glenforde pays for what he has done.'

Instead of backing down, or cowering in submission like any rational person might, she stared up at him to ask, 'And I am to suffer for his sins?'

'Suffer?' He marvelled at her brashness. 'It does not appear to me that you are suffering. Oh, yes, you are angry that you did not get your way in this. But you are not suffering.'

'Who are you to decide if I am suffering or not? I am away from my family, bereft of all I hold dear—'

'Bereft?' He cut her off with a snort. 'Give over, Isabella. Had I not spirited you away from Warehaven, you would have soon wed Glenforde. It was unlikely that the two of you would reside in your father's keep. You'd have gone to Glenforde's home, alone, without your family to protect you. Trust me when I tell you that then you would have learned the meaning of the word suffer.'

'Oh, so I should be thankful you kidnapped me?'

'Yes, now that you mention it, perhaps you should be.'

'Phhpptt. You are mightily full of yourself, Dunstan. Does your arrogance know any bounds?'

'I may be full of myself. But you, my dear, are my wife and you are sorely trying my patience.'

'I feel so sorry for you.'

Richard closed his eyes for a moment. The urge to rail back at her was strong, but he stopped himself. Many months would pass before Warehaven landed on Dunstan and he had no intention of living in hell until then. Even when her father did come it would change nothing, they would still be married. He needed to somehow come to understand this woman's odd moods.

Why was she trying so hard to anger him? He peered down at her and noticed that her hands resting against his chest trembled slightly. Interesting. So, she did harbour some fear, some realisation of her current situation.

'What is all of this about, Isabella? Why the tears and the rage?'

'I've already told you.'

'No. I think you've led me on a merry chase to avoid whatever is truly bothering you.'

She lowered her hands and looked away, the pink of her cheeks deepening. He bit back a smile at her flush. If nothing else, at least he hadn't been wrong. Something was chafing at her and whatever it was had little to do with the words coming out of her mouth.

To move this along, he stated, 'I have other matters to

attend. I really don't have all day to stand here trying to coax answers from you.'

'Then go.' She tried unsuccessfully to shoulder past him. 'Just leave me alone.'

Richard sighed as he blocked her escape. And just like that, they were right back to where they'd started. 'I am not going to leave you alone.' He stroked her cheek. 'It is true, we are never going to be happy newlyweds, but most married couples aren't. Would it not be easier to at least try to find a way to get along?'

Her cheeks flushed again and he paused, frowning. What the...? Oh, dear Lord above, the woman was nervous in his presence. Her tears might have been from relief to discover her father lived. He could understand that. But her anger had flared far too quickly when he'd done nothing except seek to comfort her.

She *wanted* him to leave the chamber. She was intentionally trying to anger him enough so he'd storm out of here. Why? He studied her face. Her gaze darted everywhere but at him. And when he did finally catch her attention, his lips twitched at the liquid shimmer in her eyes.

'What do you find so amusing now?'

'You.' He slid his hand to the back of her head. 'I'm going to kiss you, Isabella. So don't say you weren't warned.'

She gasped. 'Don't you dare—'

He covered her mouth with his, cutting off her useless threat. When she tried to pull away, he tightened his hold, keeping her in place until she leaned against him, her lips softening, then parting beneath his. And when she hesitantly returned his kiss, he thought he would drown in the sweetness.

She reached up with one hand to caress his neck, while the other one twisted the fabric of his shirt, clinging to it as if she, too, were drowning.

His heart thudded heavy in his chest and he gathered her closer, resisting the urge to sweep her up in his arms and carry her to the bed.

This was nothing more than a stolen moment of discovery. He didn't doubt for one minute that when the spell wore off, she would once again find her anger.

But until then, he would savour the taste of her kiss, the silky slide of her tongue against his. He could wait, because he was certain that one day his fiery bride would want more than just a kiss.

She froze against him, her eyelashes brushing across his as she opened her eyes. Richard sighed with regret. He'd hoped the stolen moment would have lasted a little longer, but knowing it was over, he released her.

Isabella lifted her arm and he grasped her wrist as her opened hand headed towards his cheek. 'No.' He shook his head at her. 'That wouldn't be wise.'

'How dare you!'

'One day soon I'll dare much more.'

'Why you…you…' She stopped mid-sentence, seemingly speechless.

'You enjoyed that kiss as much as I did.' Richard dropped her wrist to place a finger beneath her chin, gently closing her mouth. 'So, don't play the offended maiden, Isabella.'

He stepped back, then turned to head towards the door. Without glancing back at her, he opened the door and said, 'I'll be at the wharf late and will probably remain in town tonight.'

He closed the door behind him and it was all he could do not to laugh when something bounced off the chamber door.

Chapter Ten

In the waning light of the day, Isabella stood beneath the archway of the alcove and surveyed the work they'd completed these last three days. This bedchamber on the upper floor was even larger than the master chamber at Warehaven. She didn't need this much space, but if her choice was this or Dunstan's current chamber, she'd stay here.

A shiver trickled down her spine at the mere thought of him…Dunstan…Richard…her husband. She wondered where he was and what business had kept him from returning for two nights. Not that she was complaining, or pining for his company. Even though, to her shocked dismay, she'd actually enjoyed his kiss, but she also enjoyed dropping into bed, with fresh mattress stuffing and clean covers, then falling into blissful sleep, knowing that she'd not have to lay awake, alert to his movements while worrying about what he intended to do.

Besides, with the lord absent it had been easier to step into being the lady of the keep. He had to have been blind not to realise how badly this place needed someone to take it firmly in hand. At least with him gone, the maids and women from the village didn't need to second guess her orders. Thankfully, only one of the men had seen fit to question her and she'd easily glared him down.

They might consider her young and possibly think her weak, but she'd been taught to command a keep by the best. As far as Isabella was concerned, no stronger woman existed than her mother. None would dare defy an order given by the Lady of Warehaven and come out of the confrontation unscathed. Isabella had no intention of being any less—to do so would only bring dishonour to her mother's teachings.

She shook off the idle thoughts chasing her to look around the bedchamber. Now that the cobwebs had been removed, the rushes replaced, everything scrubbed and the walls freshly whitewashed, this was the most liveable chamber in the entire keep—not counting the kitchens. Once the newly returned cook had taken charge of her kitchen and scullery maids, she'd set them cleaning with a vengeance. Isabella had never seen a fire pit so soot- and ash-free before—even the pots appeared clean enough to be new. The kitchens at Warehaven weren't as spotless as these.

One of the younger women that Hattie had coerced into helping them clean the chamber brushed an imaginary speck of dust from the freshly washed bed curtains. 'There you be, my lady. Is there anything else you'll be needing?'

While she would love to request hot water for a bath, Isabella wasn't about to risk being interrupted by Dunstan if he returned, or one of the guards. She would make do with the cold water and cloths she had on hand.

Besides, she didn't doubt that the woman was just as tired as she. They'd all worked non-stop to set this one chamber to rights. And they still had the rest of the keep to do. 'No, I think we've all done enough today. You should be heading to your home before it gets too dark.'

The woman nodded, then left the chamber. As she pushed open the door, Isabella briefly saw the man standing guard. It had been a different guard each day and night. For whatever reason, the lord of the keep wanted her under constant guard—or supervision, she wasn't certain which—but she wasn't going to question the men about their orders, she'd save that for the lord himself. She was just thankful that the guard on duty was never the man who'd tried to accost her.

However, that little bit of relief didn't stop her from wishing the door opened into the chamber and that there was a locking bar on her side. Whoever had installed the door must have been a drunken sot to have got it so backwards.

Just as she'd done the last two nights, she dragged a heavy bench over and placed it across the doorway. It wouldn't stop anyone from entering, but when they tripped over the bench, at least she'd know she was no longer alone.

Certain her privacy wouldn't be interrupted unexpectedly, Isabella moved the wash basin, bucket of water and cloths into the alcove off to the side of the chamber. She removed her gown, groaning at the damage done to the best piece of clothing she owned.

Isabella laughed at her thought. 'Best? More like only.' She draped it across a small table, hoping that tomorrow she would find time to somehow, at the very least, save some of the embroidery work at the hem.

Once they finished cleaning the keep, perhaps she'd be able to talk Dunstan into loaning her money to buy fabric for a gown or two. She'd see he was repaid when her family arrived in the spring, as they undoubtedly would once the weather cleared.

After washing, she stirred the coals in the brazier, climbed into the oversized bed, blew out the flame on the oil lamp and snuggled down under the covers.

* * *

Richard paused at the bottom of the stairs. It would likely be easier to turn around and seek the bed in his small chamber at the rear of the Great Hall. He hadn't slept above stairs in years—not since his first marriage had turned sour and he'd made avoiding Agnes his life's mission.

He heard the buzz of whispers behind him and felt the undercurrent of unease and curiosity ripple through those still gathered in the hall. If he turned away now all would assume this wife was no better than the last. And while he hadn't decided if that were true or not, he'd no wish for others to make that decision.

Besides, once the gossips on Dunstan Isle got started, there was no stopping them. Their tongues would wag until every last man, woman and child living here knew that Dunstan's lord had little use for his wife.

That was the last thing he wanted to happen. He'd had two long nights to think about it and had come to the conclusion that it was imperative everyone believe he cared for Isabella, and she for him, when Glenforde came to rescue her. He wanted that cur to suffer in every way imaginable and seeing that the man who'd kidnapped his betrothed was a good husband, and she a satisfied wife, would only be the beginning.

He headed up the steps, knowing full well that a battle of words would ensue the moment he walked into the chamber. The one night he'd planned on staying in town had turned into two and he'd not bothered to send word. Then again, she'd probably not even noticed his absence.

The guard at the top of the stairs nodded, then stepped aside, but the one outside the chamber was seated on the floor, his head resting against the wall, snoring. Is this how she'd been *guarded*?

Clearing his throat, Richard startled the guard. 'You're dismissed.'

The shame-faced man jumped to his feet, stuttering, 'My...my lord, I—'

In no mood for excuses, Richard ordered, 'Leave.'

He'd already lost a cherished daughter because he'd been so certain of her safety. That mistake would never be repeated.

Someone on this island was a traitor, they'd helped Glenforde and Richard had no way of knowing if that person was still on Dunstan or not. Until Glenforde was dispatched to his maker, along with his minion, Richard would not foolishly risk Isabella's life.

He was not completely lacking in wits—he knew that if anything happened to her, her father would see to not just his death, but to Dunstan's complete destruction.

Once the guard was gone from his sight, Richard cracked the door open slowly. Faint light from the glowing brazier lit the far corner of the room. The sound of gentle, even breathing coming from the bed assured him that his timing was near perfect—Isabella was sound asleep.

If he was quiet, perhaps he could slip into bed without her becoming aware of his presence. He opened the door as slowly as possible to ensure it didn't creak, then stepped into the room, slamming his kneecap directly into a solid object.

A blistering curse escaped his lips. His knee throbbed in sharp pain. Without thinking, he kicked a bench out of the way. Obviously she had little faith in her guards.

Even though she said nothing, Richard knew she had to have heard his not-so-graceful entrance into the chamber.

He limped over to the bed, unbuckled his sword belt

and propped the weapon alongside the bed before sitting down on the edge to remove his boots.

'What are you doing?'

'Going to bed.' Even to his ears the words sounded curt.

'You might try your own chamber.'

He tossed one boot on to the floor. Suddenly too tired to argue, he said simply, 'I am.' His other boot thudded next to the first.

She rolled on to her side, facing him. 'Oh, no you aren't.'

Richard pulled his tunic and shirt over his head in one swipe and dropped the clothing atop his boots. 'Go to sleep.'

The bed shifted as she sat up. 'Not here I won't.'

'I am in no mood to argue with you tonight. Just go to sleep.' He rose to finish undressing.

She said nothing, but, grabbing a cover from the bed, Isabella carried it to a chair near the brazier.

He stared at her. Unless he took charge of this situation he knew he'd get no sleep. Without giving warning, he crossed the room and pulled her up from the chair. 'You aren't sleeping here.'

'I am certainly not sleeping with you.' Her eyes widened as if she'd just realised his state of undress. 'You're... naked.'

Richard grasped the skirt of her chemise and jerked the undergown over her head. 'And now so are you.' Before she could pull away, he picked her up and carried her over to the bed.

'Put me down.'

'Gladly.' He dropped her on to the mattress and quickly climbed in behind her. Not giving her time to escape, he pulled her tight against his chest while drawing the covers over them.

He wasn't certain what he noticed first—the warmth of her body against his, or the softness of her skin. Either way the combination was as intoxicating as any fine wine.

'Let me go, Dunstan.'

Her voice was low, the tone laced with warning. A warning he chose to ignore. With his lips against her ear, he whispered, 'Richard.'

'Let me go, *Richard.*'

Sadly for her, using his name didn't make any difference, he still wasn't going to release her. Instead, while keeping one arm slung around her, he propped up his head with the other and, to irritate her further, rested his chin on her shoulder.

She tried pulling his arm away from her body. 'Have you been drinking?'

'No, why do you ask?'

'You seem to have confused me with one of your whores.'

Whores? Her statement drew a laugh from him. 'I fear you are mistaken, wife. I don't have any whores, so I suppose…' He paused to trail his mouth along her shoulder before saying, 'You'll have to serve that purpose.'

His attention to the side of her neck made Isabella shiver. She wished she could find the will to be revolted by his actions as much as she was by his words. 'I am not serving as your whore.'

He paused, his chin once again resting on her shoulder. 'Nor would I want you to.'

'So, you don't desire me?' Isabella clamped her mouth shut. What had she been thinking to ask such a question? The whole idea was to somehow get through this entire winter without him turning into a rutting stallion. Otherwise, she'd never be granted an annulment.

'Desire you?' His voice was so deep, so near, that it threatened to take her breath away. 'Any man with half a brain would desire you.'

She rolled her eyes at that statement. Glenforde obviously hadn't.

'I desire you more than you could possibly imagine.'

Isabella tensed. Did that mean she was in imminent danger of losing her virtue?

A soft laugh brushed against her shoulder, a warm rush of air that he chased with his lips. 'Fear not, my dear, you are quite safe this night.'

She relaxed slightly, but remained alert. Even when her eyes were impossibly heavy to hold open, she fought closing them, fearful he would change his mind. What would she do in that case? While she would fight him as hard as she could, she was no match against his strength, so in the end it wasn't as if she could physically stop him. Besides, from the odd warmth building low in her belly, she wasn't all that certain she possessed enough will to fight him for long.

Why did his arm slung across her, resting against her chest, feel so…right? Why did his steady breaths, brushing against the nape of her neck, beckon her to relax and fall asleep? The last two nights in this bed had started out so cold, she'd shivered herself to sleep each night. But now, the warmth along her back and all the way to her toes was welcome.

He shifted slightly in the bed and she was once again awake, tense and on guard. When he moved his arm to reach up and cup her chin, she held her breath.

'Just a kiss goodnight, Isabella. That is all.' His lips briefly met hers before he settled on his side in the bed. 'Go to sleep.'

Before she could determine why she found that kiss so

lacking, the sound of gentle snoring drew her out of her bewilderment. Perhaps he had spoken the truth—she was in no danger this night of attention she did not want.

However, as much as she longed to find sleep herself, she realised that she now shivered from the cold.

The gown she'd been wearing to bed was on the floor on the other side of the chamber. He would most certainly wake up if she rose from the bed. And the blankets, which had been plentiful the last two nights, were now mostly wrapped around him, leaving her with barely enough to cover her body.

A quick tug on the covers gained her nothing. They were tucked so tightly under his body that she wasn't going to get them free without rolling him off the bed. And as much as she'd like to do just that, he'd looked and sounded tired.

He probably was good and tired. Not because he'd spent the nights with some whore. She didn't truly think that was the case. She'd only accused him of doing so to see if it would anger him enough to leave the chamber. Unfortunately for her, it seemed that he found ignoring her barbs far too easy.

If he was anything like her father and brother, he'd likely spent so many long hours going over inventory and inspecting his ships that he hadn't had any ambition left to come back to the keep. She couldn't be certain, but felt fairly safe guessing there was a makeshift pallet in one of the warehouses. So, he probably needed a good night's sleep.

And since that meant she would be able to sleep without trying to keep one eye open, she was more than happy to leave him to his dreams. But she didn't wish to freeze in the meantime.

Isabella frowned, staring at him in the semi-darkness,

and poked his arm, hoping it would irritate him enough that he'd roll over and free some of the covers. She quickly drew her hand back, waiting to see if she'd disturbed his sleep. But he didn't budge and, once again, the sound of his heavy breathing met her ears.

If he could sleep through the poking, then surely he'd not wake up if she moved closer to share the warmth of the covers. Easing closer, she snuggled against him and pulled the blankets over her shoulder.

Before she could made sense of what was happening, he'd rolled on to his back and she found herself resting halfway across his chest, encircled within his arm. Pushing against his chest gained her nothing except a tighter embrace.

'Let me go.'

He groaned softly and draped his other arm across his body so his hand rested on her hip. 'You poked and prodded, tried to jerk the covers from me before seeking warmth. I am tired and obviously you were cold.' He patted her hip. 'Now, you aren't, but I am still tired.'

'I thought you were asleep.'

'I was.'

His voice was rough with sleep and his embrace was warm without being threatening. Yet her heart raced as if she'd been running in fear of losing her life. 'If you were asleep, how do you know what I did?' She was amazed at the breathlessness of her voice.

'Hmmm?'

She parted her lips to repeat her question, but closed them before doing so. Why risk waking him up all the way? Right now she was warm and while her body tingled wherever it touched his and hummed with curiosity, and unexpected anticipation, she too could easily fall asleep.

She snuggled closer against him, until his hand tightened on her hip, making breathing harder still. 'Please, stop.'

It sounded as if he'd spoken through clenched teeth and, unwilling to risk awakening him further, she closed her eyes.

Chapter Eleven

Richard slowly opened his eyes, quickly shutting them against the pounding in his head. He moved to get up from the bed and groaned at the stiff soreness of his limbs and back. What the hell had happened for him to ache so much?

The chamber door opened. 'Ah, you are finally awake, I see.'

He winced at Hattie's lively greeting.

'Where is my wife?'

The older woman answered with a 'tsk' and a shake of her head, before saying, 'Lady Isabella has been up and about for most of the day.'

Most of the day? He sat up slowly, biting back another groan. 'What time is it?'

'Vesper bells have just been rung.'

Vesper? It was nearly nightfall? He arched his back. No wonder he ached from head to toe. 'Why did no one think to wake me?'

'Lady Isabella tried twice. After that she gave orders to leave you asleep.'

'She what?' They'd been married less than a week, weren't even truly man and wife yet, and she was making decisions for his well-being? Richard knew his anger was foolish, there was no justifiable cause for it, but that didn't change the fact he was still outraged.

'Where is she?'

Hattie reared back at his snarling tone. 'Where is who?'

Knowing the woman was intentionally being obtuse, he glared at her. 'Where is Isabella?'

'Below.' She made a show of picking his clothes up from the floor with two fingers, holding them aloft a moment, before tossing them at him. 'Cleaning.'

Of course she was. Since he'd already informed her that the condition of his keep was none of her concern, she would naturally set about making it her concern. Probably just to spite him. He jerked on his clothing.

Hattie suggested, 'You might want to eat something before you go storming below.'

'Why would I eat now?' Richard pulled on his boots and rose. 'The evening meal will be served soon.'

'I was thinking more of your foul mood than your empty stomach.'

Before he could reply to her comment, Hattie left the chamber. Of course he was in a foul mood. After all, he... he... Richard sat back down on the edge of the bed. He felt like a raging bull. For no apparent reason other than his wife had let him sleep.

A weak defence even to his own ears.

No. He was the lord here. He could wake up in a foul mood any time he desired and no one could stop him. Although having a reason for such a foul mood made one appear less unbalanced.

Richard slapped a hand on the bed and rose. God's teeth, he was thinking in circles like an old woman. Out of habit, he started to strap on his sword, then changed his mind and tossed the belt, scabbard and weapon on the bed.

He strode towards the door, then spun about. Perhaps

just a little something to take the edge off his grumbling stomach might be in order. Richard crossed the chamber to the alcove where Hattie had placed bread, cheese, slices of apple and a pitcher of water on the small table.

He frowned, noticing the slick shininess of the old tabletop, then studied the rest of the chamber. Cleaning? Is that what they called this? This chamber had been redone from ceiling to floor. It shone in a way it hadn't since he was a young lad.

Years of soot and grime had been stripped from the walls and they'd been repainted, the bedding and linen washed. He glanced behind him to find that even the old tapestry hanging on the back wall of the alcove had once again come to life. The colours of the threads appeared brilliant instead of dull with age. He'd nearly forgotten the details of the stitched hunting scene.

He intentionally crunched the rushes and strewing herbs beneath his foot, only to have the scents of lavender and rosemary waft up against his nose. The floorboards beneath gleamed as if they'd been freshly scrubbed and oiled.

A tour of the chamber brought other changes to light. The mattress had been restuffed and the covering cleaned, the skins on the narrow windows were obviously new since they were no longer brittle and cracking. The small tables alongside the bed also showed signs of a recent polishing cloth. The candles in the floor sconces were beeswax instead of tallow. Had he paid any attention last night he would have noticed that the telltale stench of rendered animal fat no longer permeated the room.

In a corner, near the alcove, a clothing chest had been placed beneath a row of wall pegs. Richard ran his fingers over the fur lining of his hooded mantle hanging on one of the pegs. From the fresh smell and softness of the fur, it too had found itself put through a rigorous cleaning. He opened the lid of the chest to find that all of his clothes had been washed, dried, folded and neatly stacked inside. Sachets of sandalwood and cedar at the bottom of the chest would keep the moths away while at the same time ensure the clothing retained a fresh scent.

The lid fell with a thud. Yes, she'd been busy these last couple of days. But Isabella couldn't have done all of this alone. She'd obviously had help. And he doubted if that help had come from the few women he'd sent back to the keep.

So not only was she seeing to the condition of the keep, she was ordering his men about to do so?

The door to the chamber opened and the town carpenter stopped in the doorway. He doffed his cap, twisting it in his hand, said, 'Forgive me, my lord, I thought you were elsewhere. I can come back later.'

'Why are you here?'

'The lady wants the door reversed. But I can—'

'No. Go ahead. I was just leaving.'

Even though she'd overstepped her bounds, he wasn't going to take that up with the carpenter. He'd seek out Isabella instead. Although the door should have been fixed years ago. The only reason it was on backwards was because when he was a small boy he'd picked up the habit of locking himself in the chamber and after his father had had to have the door removed to gain entrance more than once, he'd ordered it rehung to swing out into the passageway and lock from the outside.

Richard headed down to the Great Hall. He paused at the bottom of the steps. At least nothing had changed here. The boisterous shouts and laughter of his men scraped across his ears in a familiar manner, irritating him in the usual way.

Conal spied him and approached. 'I see you woke up just in time to eat and go to bed.'

Richard nodded towards the mostly drunken assembly. 'And I see you've made yourself useful in my absence.'

'Since I know the workload ahead of us, I thought we'd take advantage of a workless day.'

'That's rather obvious.' He glanced around the hall—most of these men would be near useless on the morrow. 'Where is my wife?'

'Last I saw her she was headed towards your chambers.'

Richard paused outside the door to his bedchamber. He took a deep breath, preparing himself for what he might find beyond the door. From what he'd gathered from a few of his men during his walk across the hall, she'd so far confined her cleaning to the chamber above.

If he ignored the fact that he'd told her not to concern herself with his keep, then what she'd done wasn't a terrible thing. He didn't like it, but it wasn't a crime worthy of punishment. However, there remained the fact that she'd taken it upon herself to employ the help of his people and men without consulting him first.

While he didn't want the people of Dunstan to hate her, he'd prefer they had nothing, or very little, to do with her until after his confrontation with Glenforde and her father.

Glenforde was going to die by his hand. Richard hadn't come this far to miss that opportunity. Every fibre of his being screamed for Glenforde's blood. The thought of revenge had been the only thing that kept him waking up every morning after the senseless slaughter on Dunstan, it had been the only thing that had dulled the pain. The passing of time had only tempered that thirst, making it stronger, hardening his resolve until it became as dear to him as breathing.

When that day finally arrived, he would not hesitate to kill anyone who physically came to Glenforde's aid. And that is what the people of Dunstan risked should they decide to support Isabella. He didn't doubt for one heartbeat that she would beg and plead for the life of the man she'd once been set to wed.

If, through some misplaced sense of loyalty, any of his people saw fit to answer her plea, he would send them to their grave. No one who stood in his way would be spared. So, it was safer for all if, for now, they kept their distance from her.

Of course he couldn't explain that to her. He didn't trust her not to use it against him. In truth, how could he blame her? She was a pawn, a mouse caught fast between two angry cats, and he'd put her in that position on purpose.

And until this matter was settled, that is where she would stay. Regardless of what he had to do, or how angry it made her.

He pushed open the chamber door. Isabella was hunkered over his open chest, holding something in her hand. A step closer to her brought the item in to view—a wooden doll, meticulously carved and painted by his hands.

Richard's heart seemed to stop. Time reversed itself until one fateful moment froze in his mind with horrifying detail. A single blonde curl rested against a too-pale cheek. Her head bent at a strange angle and blood had dried where it had pooled beneath her open mouth. Blue eyes, open wide as if in horror, stared at nothing. And the doll that never left the crook of her arm lay on the ground just beyond her reaching fingertips, as if, at the very moment of death, she'd still wanted her doll in her arms. But she'd been denied even that slim thread of comfort.

'No!' Without warning, he lunged to tear the doll and its final wrappings from Isabella's grasp. His hands shook as he carefully folded the embroidered scrap of fabric around the doll before placing it back in its fur-lined nest and slamming the lid of the chest closed.

He glared down at Isabella, trying to see her through the haze of rage and loss. 'Do not touch this chest again.'

Isabella's questions stuck in her throat at the look on his face. She scrambled backwards, away from the irrational anger reaching towards her, only to fall on to a pile of linens she'd removed from the chest. Raising her hands to ward off his approach, she choked out, 'I'm sorry. Richard, I'm sorry.'

His expression didn't waver and she wasn't all that certain he saw her. Isabella studied him. His unfocused glare seemed to slice through her, moving past her as if he was somewhere else, seeing someone else. She stayed where she was, not moving, and closed her eyes.

'How dare you touch her things!' He grabbed the front of her gown and lifted her from the pile of linen. 'I will see you dead before allowing Glenforde's beloved to foul her memory.'

His nearly growled threat dried her throat so she could barely swallow. Isabella knew she should be afraid—any person with half their wits would know this was a moment to appear weak and submissive—and she was afraid, but she wasn't yet ready to die.

She reached out and wrapped one hand along the side of his neck, curled the fingers of her other hand over his shoulder, pulled her body against his, hooked her feet around his legs and hung on for all she was worth. Her reaction might appear foolish to another, but wrestling with a brother and sister had taught her to protect the soft parts of her body. If Richard's idea had been to beat her for going through his things, clinging to him would make that a little more difficult for him.

To her amazement, he tore his hands from her gown and when she thought he would pry her body away from him, he drew her harder against him in a tight embrace.

With his face buried in her neck, he hoarsely whispered, 'Forgive me. I...'

His words trailed off as he released her. She loosened her hold on him. Not sure of his state of mind, she stepped out of his reach, but waved towards the bed, suggesting the only thing that came to her mind, 'Richard, you are exhausted. Rest awhile.'

His lack of response worried her. She wanted to get him off his feet before his shaking legs refused to support him any longer, but at the same time, she had no desire to get too close. Going to the opposite side of the bed, she patted the mattress. 'Just lay down awhile.'

He walked to the bed woodenly, like a man caught in the throes of a terrifying nightmare, and dropped on to the edge.

Uncertain what to do for him, she kept her wary gaze on him. His entire body still visibly shook and the hands he lifted to his face trembled so badly that fear for her own safety fled.

Friend or foe, this man was in agony and needed soothing. She would never turn her back on a stranger in need, how could she turn away from Richard?

She sat down near the head of the bed and reached across to place a hand on his shoulder. When he didn't shrug off her touch, she tugged gently, coaxing, 'Please. Rest.'

Slowly, he laid down on the bed, facing away from her on his side. That was fine, at least he hadn't tried to get his hands on her or bolted from the chamber. Isabella slid into the bed behind him and placed an arm across his waist. To her unexpected surprise, he turned over and drew her close.

He said nothing, but with his face buried in the side of her neck, he held on to her like she was a lifeline keeping him from going under. She, too, remained silent, stroking his back, running her fingers through his hair, waiting for the tremors to subside.

Once they finally did and he seemed to relax across her, she rested her cheek against his head. 'Richard, I may hate what you've done to me, what you've forced me to do, and while I might seek to annoy you in payment, I would never intentionally upset you in such a manner as this. Never. Please, tell me what I've done so I do not accidentally do so again.'

After one long, shuddering breath, he turned his head, so he rested on her shoulder, with one arm across her stomach. He shifted the arm beneath her so he could reach up to stroke light circles on the side of her neck. Gentle, teasing movements that suddenly made the muscular thigh resting between her softer ones more…noticeable, in ways that seemed inappropriate and far too welcome at the same time.

Isabella closed her eyes briefly, praying he couldn't feel the swift pounding of her heart.

'You didn't know.'

It took her a moment to make sense of his statement. She didn't know what? Oh, the trunk. 'Who did the doll belong to?'

'Lisette.'

'Who was Lisette?'

'My daughter.'

Isabella frowned. He had once accused Glenforde of killing a child and she hadn't believed him. Her stomach tightened at the thought that he might not have been making up stories to frighten her. Determined to find out what she could, she asked, 'Your daughter?'

'Yes. A daughter born too soon.'

She sighed. This was going to be like picking nails out of a board with her fingers. She reached up to stroke his cheek and he jerked his head away from her touch, but not before her fingertips brushed the dampness on his face.

Isabella held her breath. This was not a man who would shed a tear over something minor or imagined. This was serious and very real. She suspected that he wasn't evading her questions, he was answering her as best he could under the circumstances.

Unsure how to proceed, since she was fairly certain she knew the answer, she chose the direct route. 'Richard, what happened to Lisette?'

The finger stroking circles on her neck stopped. The arm draped across her stomach tightened. 'Your husband-to-be killed her.'

Every muscle in her body stiffened. She curled her toes in an effort to stop her legs from trembling. He hadn't been concocting stories.

'Why? Why would he do such a heinous thing?'

'Do you think I have not asked myself that very same question?'

When he made a motion to move away, Isabella tightened her hold on him. 'No, stay. Talk to me. Help me understand.'

In truth, it didn't matter whether she understood or not, but this ate at him, it was like a poison in his blood and she wanted to somehow lance it and let at least some of the vile humours drain away.

'Why? Your understanding doesn't change anything.'

No, it wouldn't change a thing. His daughter would still be dead and she'd still be here on Dunstan as bait for Glenforde. What would happen to her afterwards was anyone's guess. But right now, this moment, his talking about it might make things more bearable for him. Although she knew that if he were like most men of her acquaintance, his willingness to talk would soon pass. 'No, it'll change nothing. But it's part of your life and you are my husband. I want to know about the man I wed.'

He settled back into her embrace. 'It was all my fault.'

If she hadn't been confused before, she was now. 'What do you mean, your fault?'

'I wasn't here to protect them.'

She rolled her eyes at the ever god-like notions of men. 'Richard, are you not one of Stephen's men? Do you not own more than one merchant ship? Unless you are possessed of some inhuman power, you cannot be everywhere at once.'

'Perhaps not, but I should have been here.'

'Because you knew what was going to happen?' Isabella knew she could, and at some point probably would, cross an invisible line that would turn him from talkative to defensive.

'What? No.' There was a touch more life to his voice. 'Had a hint of what was to come reached me, I would have been here and none of this would have happened.'

'Or, you could be dead, too.'

'You think Glenforde could have beaten me?'

Ah, now his defensiveness was starting to kick in. Since she truly wanted to know what had happened, she needed to disabuse him of that notion. 'Heavens, no, Richard. The man is a weak coward who puffs up his own image by ill treatment of those deemed smaller.'

'Yes, well, he proved that well enough.'

'So, what happened? Did he attack Dunstan while you were away?' When he remained silent for a few moments, Isabella warned, 'If you don't tell me, I'll be forced to make up things in my mind.'

His heavy sigh brushed against her neck. 'He landed in the cove instead of the harbour. Nobody ever anchors a ship there, it isn't always safe. Someone from Dunstan, who knew the tides and currents, had to have told him when it would be safe to anchor there and how long he could stay before he would lose his ship.'

She knew she could be presuming much, but asked, 'The cove isn't patrolled during low tide?'

'Of course it is.'

'Then—'

'How did he make the landing?' He completed her question, then continued. 'That's what I haven't been able to determine. All I'm certain of is that he did and since three of the four men on guard there were also killed, he obviously had help from someone already on the island. The fourth man lived only long enough to identify Glenforde's ship, but didn't see his attacker.'

'Could he not have docked in the harbour to allow a man or two off his ship before leaving to sail into the cove and await some sort of signal?'

'Yes, he could have. But he didn't. The harbour master had no record of Glenforde's arrival at the docks.'

The Dunstans had been a seafaring family longer than her own, so she was certain he employed only the best men for the most important positions. But to make certain he'd considered every option, she had to ask, 'And you trust your harbour master?'

'Yes. Without reservation.'

'Then I'm sure you are right. Glenforde had to have had assistance. So, how did he come across your daughter? Wasn't she in the keep with her nursemaid?'

'That lying she-devil of a whore met him in one of the cottages and took Lisette along with her.'

'The nursemaid?'

'No. My whore wife.'

Stunned into silence, Isabella reminded herself to breathe. He was already married? Finally, after she could catch her breath, she hesitantly asked, 'Where...where is...your...wife?'

'Glenforde slit her throat.'

His short, blunt answer brought an icy fear to Isabella's heart. If Glenforde had treated Richard's wife and daughter so cruelly, and she had no reason to doubt him, what did that mean for her future? She knew she was here as bait, that had never been a secret. But what about afterwards?

Another thought shook her to the core. Dear Lord above, what if Glenforde turned his attention to her sister? For the first time since this all began back at Warehaven's bailey, she hoped Glenforde did come for her—and received all he deserved.

Richard released her and shoved himself off the bed. He stopped halfway to the door and turned back to look at her. 'Do you have what you need from the chamber?' He motioned towards the pile of linens. 'Is there anything else?'

'No, there's nothing else.' She sat up. 'I have no reason to come back here.'

'Good.' He turned back around and headed to the door.

'Richard.' He stopped with his hand on the door latch, but didn't look at her, so she asked, 'What happens to me after Glenforde pays for his crimes?'

'I don't know.' With that, he left the room.

Isabella stared at the door. His abrupt departure and even more abrupt change of mood confused her more than his rage and the aftermath. Since she didn't think he was normally given to such sudden changes, she could only surmise that after his family's deaths he had taken no time to mourn his loss, too intent on seeking revenge that he'd not given his soul time to grieve.

Other than her grandparents, she'd never experienced the loss of a family member. When her mother's mother had died, Isabella remembered being so sad that it physically hurt for days afterwards. And then there would be times when she'd be almost normal…until she remembered what had happened, bringing the sadness and pain back once again. But eventually, even though she'd have moments of near unbearable sadness, the pain started to fade until eventually she could think of her grandmother without feeling as if someone was trying to tear her heart from her chest.

Her mother had reacted in the same manner—only for longer periods of time.

But when King Henry died, her father spared one night for his pain at losing his father and, while he had still been sad for weeks afterwards, that one night had been his only display of grief.

Had Richard spared even one day for his loss? She didn't think so, not since he was still suffering bursts of outrage and utter sadness. His teasing didn't bother her overmuch, even though it did rankle at times. She could find a way to suffer through it until her father came. And his blustering barked orders, or demands, were easy enough to ignore— her brother acted in the same 'I am your lord' manner at times and she ignored him quite well.

But this anger, this blind rage that dragged him back to the horrors and left him shaken, needed to change. He had to somehow get beyond the nightmare and his need for vengeance. Otherwise his narrow focus on revenge might make him foolishly careless.

How? She frowned, wondering how she was going to help him without him realising what she was doing.

A niggling imp in the back of her mind asked, *Why?*

She shrugged. There was no way of knowing what was going to happen to her. Even though she dearly longed to return home to Warehaven and forget this entire kidnapping and marriage had happened, once her father found out she was married to Richard, he might very well make her stay.

A shiver prompted her to get up from the bed. As much as she hated to even think of that possibility, it did exist. After all, her parents were forced to wed and from listening to her aunt's telling of the story, many months passed before her mother and father could be in the same room without wanting to strangle one another.

So, God forbid, if it happened, it would be easier to live with a husband who didn't cringe at the sight of her.

Chapter Twelve

Richard took his seat at the head table and stared down the length of the Great Hall. The men had obviously spent most of the day drinking, they were sloppy, rowdy and loud. Yet they all sat before the table as if waiting for… what?

He leaned his head towards Conal on his left. 'Are we waiting for something?'

'I would guess Lady Isabella.'

Richard turned to look Conal in the eyes. 'Excuse me?'

'I've been with you in town.' Conal shrugged. 'So that's the only thing that makes sense to me. They did the same thing earlier—waited until she was seated before eating.'

'It is a welcome change, is it not, my lord?' Hattie set a pitcher on the table between the two men.

Welcome change? No. This wasn't supposed to be happening. Things were supposed to stay the same as they were. Richard silently cursed himself. He was supposed to discuss this with her, but seeing her with Lisette's doll had unexpectedly overwhelmed him and any thought of setting her straight flew out of his mind.

He held up his goblet for Hattie to fill, then took a much needed swallow of—water? 'What is this?'

Conal snorted and at the same moment Isabella took her seat next to him on the right, asking, 'What is what?'

'This.' He held the goblet to her nose.

'Water?' She dipped her fingers into the small wash-bowl near them on the table. While drying her hands, she asked, 'Do you think anyone here needs more wine or ale?'

'I do.'

'You do what? Need wine for yourself, or think some-one else does?'

Richard narrowed his eyes. She was being difficult on purpose. He could tell by the bland expression on her face and devilish twinkle in her eyes. Fine. She wanted to play? Oh, she could play, but he'd damn well make sure she paid for it.

'May I please have some wine, my dearest wife?'

She shrugged. 'Entirely up to you, my lord. Hattie, wine with dinner, please.'

Hattie motioned the servers into action and retrieved the wine. Richard watched the servers. Their skills seemed newfound, but not one of them dropped a platter, or spilled a drop of food or drink as they placed their loads on the tables. It didn't require any thought to know who had taken them in hand.

Conal leaned over to whisper, 'She's been busy.'

Richard ignored him to put a generous portion of meat and a mix of vegetables on the trencher he shared with Isabella, while she poured wine into both of their goblets.

He finished his off in one long swallow before refilling his goblet. Her glare, had it been an actual flame, would have burned a hole through his head. Richard set the ves-sel down. 'Fear not, Wife, it would take much more than that to turn me into a fool.'

'Don't call me that.'

'What?' He leaned closer. 'Wife? Isn't that what you are?'

'Sometimes I feel more like a prisoner.'

Richard hooked a foot around the leg of her chair and dragged her closer so he could whisper in her ear, 'Do you want to be my prisoner, Isabella?'

A shiver rippled down her arms and a flush covered her cheeks as she stared at him in shock. He kept his smile of success to himself. He'd intentionally deepened his voice and made certain to let her name roll off his tongue because he knew she was unable to resist the seductive tone.

She broke his intent stare with a gasp and looked down at her food. 'No, I don't want to be your prisoner.'

'Pity.' He could envision her chained to a bed in a cell, helpless, and in desperate need of comforting. *From where had that thought come?*

'I just want to go home.'

He sat upright in his chair, more in an attempt to rid his mind of the erotic thoughts threatening to make this the shortest dinner in his life than anything else. 'You are home.'

'Warehaven.'

'That isn't going to happen.' He handed her the untouched goblet. 'Drink. I don't want you sulking.'

'Sulking!' Her voice rose and an odd silence descended down the tables.

Turning to look at her, he suggested, 'You could be louder, then everyone else wouldn't have to strain to hear us.'

The men at the tables turned their attention back to their food.

She lifted the goblet to her lips with a shaking hand and Richard wondered if she'd spill half of it down her gown. The sight of her gown gave him pause. It was the same one she'd been wearing when he'd taken her from Warehaven.

He refilled her empty glass and handed it back to her.

'No. Are you trying to get me inebriated?'

'Yes.' Actually he was, but not for the reason she thought.

She slammed the goblet back on to the table hard enough so some of the contents splashed out on to the white table covering, leaving behind a deep red stain. 'Why? So you can take advantage of me?'

He once again handed it back to her and lifted it to her lips. 'Oh, definitely, because I can't think of anything I'd rather do than have sex with a woman so full of wine that she'll pass out and not remember a thing. That certainly would make for an exciting evening.'

Her eyes narrowed to mere slits. 'You are a pig.'

'And sometimes you are a fool. Now drink.' Once she did as he bid, Richard slipped a hand behind her head and drew her closer. 'Trust me, Wife, the first time we make love, you won't be intoxicated from any drink and you will most definitely remember every touch, stroke and kiss for a very long time to come.'

When her lips parted for the gasp of shocked virginal outrage he fully expected, he covered her mouth with his own and swept his tongue across hers, then just as quickly released her and moved away.

This time the shiver tracing down her body was longer and lingering. He wondered if the deep flush on her cheeks burned.

'Oh! I never.'

Before taking a bite of meat, he agreed, 'I would hope not.'

She sat there for a while and just stared at her food. Richard had to give her credit because a few times he thought she was going to burst out in tears of rage and frustration. But she didn't. Somehow, after a few hard swallows, she managed to check the flow of tears.

He waited until she seemed more calm before pointing out, 'Your food is getting cold.'

'I'm not hungry.'

'Isabella, did your mother never tell you not to bait someone more experienced or stronger?'

'I never baited you.'

'Really?' He waved his eating knife towards the hall. 'What do you call this?'

'What?'

'I told you that my keep doesn't concern you, yet here we are, seated at a relatively polite dining table.' He tapped the pitcher of water still on the table. 'With water as the main drink.'

'But—'

He raised a hand, cutting off her reply. 'I'm not finished. And what about the chamber above? Am I mistaken or has it not been cleaned, painted, rearranged and refurnished?'

'Yes, but—'

Again he raised a hand and she instantly stopped. 'Was that not a carpenter who was sent to reverse the door?'

'Yes.'

This time she didn't even attempt to add anything after her admission. So, he asked, 'You could not have accomplished all this without giving orders to my people. Am I right?'

'Yes.'

'Nobody gave you permission to do so.'

Her eyes widened and she stared at him speechless for about one heartbeat. 'As your wife, am I not the chatelaine of this keep?'

'No.' He fell silent to let that fact settle in her mind. The instant the disbelief filled her eyes, he added, 'Not until I say so.'

She placed her hands against the edge of the table and tried to push her chair away.

'Do you plan to run away now? Hasn't your past experience with that tactic proven a mistake?' Her brows furrowed in question, so he reminded her by asking, 'Isn't that how I captured you to begin with?'

When she didn't answer, he stuck his foot behind the leg of her chair. 'You need to eat something. Then perhaps I'll permit you to leave the table.'

If she clenched her jaw any tighter, Richard was certain she'd break a tooth.

'You are…you are…'

'Yes, a pig. I know. That doesn't change the fact that you need to eat.'

'Fine.' She stabbed at the food in a manner that made him glad he wasn't on the trencher.

After a few mouthfuls, she said, 'This keep is filthy. It needs cleaning.'

He looked around. It didn't matter to him if it was filthy. But then it also didn't matter if it was clean. Either way made no difference to him. Which he found odd, but he just couldn't summon up the need to care. 'If cleaning makes you happy, be my guest.'

'And how am I supposed to do that without help?'

'You could try asking.'

'Who?'

'Me. You could try asking me.'

'Then can I have the use of a couple of your men to start on this hall tomorrow?'

He sighed. 'Surely you can do better than that.'

Again her jaw clenched, then unclenched. 'May I please use a couple of your men, my lord?'

'Oh, so polite and proper.' He set his knife down and turned to face her. 'But that isn't quite what I meant.' He leaned closer to whisper against her ear, 'Ask me nicely, Isabella.'

'Nicely? How nicely?'

He rested an arm along the back of her chair to toy with a lock of her hair. 'Why don't you just try asking and we'll see if it suffices?'

She stared down at her lap for a few moments, before raising her head to look everywhere but at him. 'Please, may I use some of your men tomorrow, Richard?'

He had to admit, she was a fast learner. Her imitation of his husky tone was worthy of any mummer. He stroked her cheek with his knuckle and this time felt her shiver trail along his touch.

It was cruel to play with her so. But Richard couldn't seem to help himself. She didn't dissolve into hysterics and usually handed his glibness right back to him. Verbal sparring with this woman was akin to foreplay, so he teased her on purpose—it seemed a harmless way to end the day.

Besides, he couldn't deny that he enjoyed the play of colour filling her cheeks, but could only imagine how the green specks in her eyes would darken if she looked at him.

Agnes would never succumb to his teasing. As soon as he would try to engage her in this way, she would turn around and leave.

Knowing Isabella waited for his response, yet not wanting this evening to end so early, he brushed his knuckle across her cheek again. 'You could try looking at me when you ask.'

She frowned for a moment, but to his amazement she finally met his gaze, batted her eyelashes, then leaned closer and placed a hand on his chest. 'My Lord Richard, ice will form at Satan's feet before I beg you for anything.'

Her words, spoken in a near breathless whisper, rushed against his chin like a lover's caress. His heart thudded and from the small half-smile playing about her lips—lips he could easily claim again with his own if he leaned forward just the slightest bit—she knew exactly what effect she was having on him.

Then the actual words she'd spoken filtered through the feelings they'd caused. He frowned. By the saints above, the woman excelled at handing him back a good measure of his own teasing.

One of the men cleared his throat. Another slammed a goblet on to the table and, from nearby, Richard heard the distinct sound of a snort that seemed suspiciously like it came from Conal.

He didn't need to look out at the hall to know that everyone in attendance was watching and waiting to see what he would do.

He knew exactly what he wanted to do—pull her into his embrace and kiss that smug sliver of a smile from her lips. But he also knew that he wouldn't stop at a simple kiss. Unfortunately, there were too many prying eyes about for him to give into his urges.

Richard tilted his head down until his forehead nearly rested against hers. 'You play with fire, Isabella.'

'You started it.' She shrugged and leaned away.

'Perhaps. But to issue such a dare could prove to be a mistake on your part.'

'The mistake is yours. I issued no dare.'

He stared at her, slowly trailing his gaze from the top of her head, across her face and then down to her breasts before drawing his attention back to her face. 'You intentionally tempt a man to test your words and then deny it was a dare?'

Richard waited a moment for his meaning to put the flush back on her cheeks, before he mused, 'I wonder just what it would take to hear you beg me.'

The colour on her face deepened as she gasped, shoved back her chair and left the Great Hall.

He watched her until the ribald laughter from his men prompted him into action. However much he might enjoy exchanging quips with her, she would not be allowed to make him look a fool before his men. Richard followed her up the stairs two at a time. Catching up with her on the landing, he swept her up into his arms without missing a step.

She squeaked in surprise and tried pushing away to break free of his hold. 'Put me down.'

'I will.' He hit the latch on the bedchamber door, grateful it'd been reversed, shoved it open, stepped through, then kicked it closed and carried her to the bed where he dropped her on to the mattress.

She scrambled to the other side. 'What do you think you're doing? Get out of here.'

'No. Get undressed.'

Before he realised what she was reaching for, she freed the sword he'd tossed on the bed and grasped it with both hands to point it at him. 'I swear, I'll use this.'

He stared at her for a moment and blinked, not quite believing his wife was threatening him with the weapon. Had she any idea how to use the blade? Doubtful. He proved that by easily batting it out of her hold. 'It would take someone a lot stronger than you to use my own weapon on me.'

Richard grabbed the sword from the foot end of the bed before she could regain possession, slid it back into the sheath and placed it under his side of the bed. 'Now, get undressed.'

With her head bowed and shoulders drooping, she sat on the edge of the bed to remove her slippers and stockings. Over her shoulder she shot him a mutinous glance before sliding beneath the covers to fumble with her gown. Pulling it free, she dropped it on to the floor.

It was all he could do not to sigh at her self-imposed fear. After quickly stoking the coals in the brazier and then undressing in the chilled night air of the chamber, he slid under the covers next to her and, before she could protest, pulled her against him. Her skin was like ice. 'You're cold.'

Isabella only nodded.

He gathered her closer, pulling her part way across his chest, with her head resting against his shoulder. He could feel her choked breaths warm against his neck.

'You can relax, I'm not going to hurt you.'

'I know what you're going to do and, yes, it will hurt.'

Richard stared up at the ceiling. He'd had no way of knowing whether Agnes had been a virgin on their wedding night. He'd been young, too young to have had enough experience with women to be able to tell and like a fool he'd not questioned her claim of virginity.

But the woman in his arms now was so nervous, so inexperienced, and so very certain of what was going to happen, that he knew she'd never slept with a man. From her hesitancy whenever he'd kissed her he doubted if she'd ever been truly kissed by a man before, let alone anything else.

He'd followed her from the hall with every intention of proving to her who was in command. Now that she was in his arms and he could feel her fear, all he wanted to do was to calm her nervousness and banish her worries. He kissed the top of her head. 'Isabella, I should have apologised earlier in my chamber. I am sorry for frightening you so.'

'And what about now?'

He smiled against her head, then reached over to stroke her hip. Ignoring her startled flinch, he asked, 'Should I apologise for wanting to touch the softness of your skin?'

He buried his nose in her hair and breathed in deeply. 'Or for wanting to savour the scent of a beautiful woman?'

She rolled over on her back, claiming, 'Now you should apologise for being so silly.'

Richard shifted on to his side, propping up on his forearm. When she immediately tried to shift away, he put his arm across her and caressed her side, not letting her escape.

Again, he said, 'Relax, Isabella. I am not going to hurt you.'

She wouldn't even look at him. With her eyes tightly closed, she asked, 'Then what are you doing?'

Drowning in your innocence. 'Relishing the feel of a woman next to me.' He splayed his fingers across her belly, feeling the sudden contracting of muscles beneath his hand. He kept his movements slow, barely brushing his fingertips across her smooth flesh.

She grasped his hand. 'I don't think this is going to help me relax.'

Richard captured her hand beneath his and threaded his fingers between her own, then once again lightly stroked across her belly and over her ribs with their hands joined. He leaned his head down to softly ask, 'Do you feel how soft and smooth your skin is? Can you feel the warmth against your fingers?'

Once she nodded, he brought her hand to his stomach and mimicked the same movements, asking, 'Do you find the difference as interesting as I do? Where your skin was soft and pliant, mine is tougher and the muscles beneath hard and less giving.'

'Not so tough.' She adjusted her fingertips to trail along a scar. 'It is smoother than I thought it might be.'

He was surprised to discover she actually thought about it at all. Allowing her to guide the direction of their exploration, he sucked in a breath when she drew their hands up his ribcage and wandered across his chest. She slowed their movement to lightly trace a circle around one now hardening nipple, before trailing her touch down the line of hair to his waist.

But he wasn't at all surprised when she stopped there, her hand trembling lightly beneath his. To take her mind off what she feared to find, he moved their hands back to her stomach, where he then traced the same path she had, up her ribs and between her breasts.

Richard closed his eyes. He longed to tear his hand free to cup her breast, to feel the warmth, the softness and weight against his palm. With an effort he reminded himself that this wasn't about him.

So, he slid their hands to circle along the side, then beneath the fullness. Back and forth, slowly edging a little higher with each pass until she breathlessly gasped. Not wanting her nervous anticipation to get the best of her, he drew his fingertips around, then over her hardening nipple.

'Oh!'

Richard shivered. He couldn't remember ever having heard such a softly issued exclamation before. The obvious surprise and wonder in her hushed voice nearly made him groan with desire.

She turned her face towards his. 'Does it feel like that for you, too?'

'Probably not as much.' He turned his lips to hers, capturing her with a kiss to stop her questions and distract her on purpose.

She opened her lips to accept his kiss and soon followed his lead. When she moaned, he reluctantly drew their hands away from her breasts, stroking down the length of her ribs and stomach, along the curve of her hip and down her leg as far as her arm would reach.

He deepened their kiss, drawing her curiosity and wonder deeper into the play of their lips and tongues. She leaned up towards him, close enough that he could feel the pounding of her heart against his chest.

Isabella was so focused on meeting the demands of his mouth, that she didn't seem to notice he'd skimmed their hands up the inside of her silken thigh. There was no change in her breathing, or her focus, when he lingered over the patch of tight curls to knead the soft flesh beneath.

Richard fought to restrain himself from giving into his urge to roll her on to her back and settle himself between her legs. He couldn't remember the last time he'd so intensely wanted to claim a woman.

Instead, he dipped a finger between the swollen folds of flesh. Surprised and emboldened by the hot, slick dampness already evident, he teased the nub with his fingertip. She curled the fingers of her hand resting against his chest, digging her fingernails into his flesh and angled her hips as if to get closer to his touch.

Richard swallowed a smile. *Oh, not just yet, sweeting.* There was still at least one body part he wanted her to discover before taking this any further. He withdrew his touch to slide their still-clasped hands to his belly.

He once again let her take the lead and without coaxing, she brushed over the thicker thatch of curls covering his groin to draw one fingertip along the length of his erection and around the rim towards the tip. His heart thudded inside his chest.

Richard gave her but a few moments of tantalising exploration before he took back control of their movements to curl her fingers around his shaft and then grasped her wrist to move her hand up and down the length.

As he'd already gathered, she was a fast learner and shook off his hold, giving him the freedom to do some exploring of his own. Which from the pounding of his own heart and the difficulty he was having in keeping his breaths even, he either needed to do quickly or expend more concentration on reining in his lust.

Certain she was intent on discovering his reactions, he focused his attention on teaching her about pleasure.

She didn't reject his touch between her thighs, instead she let her legs go lax, giving him the freedom to cup her, kneading, stroking until she hastily broke their kiss to raggedly question, 'Richard, what—?'

'Shhh.' He soothed her, then coaxed, 'Trust me in this, Isabella.'

She nodded, then buried her face against his chest.

He felt her confusion and uncertainty in the sudden tensing of her legs. Before she could change her mind and pull away, he delved between the padded folds of flesh to once again feel the hot slickness of her more-than-ready body. Teasing, stroking until her breath was nothing but ragged pants and she released her hold on his shaft to curl her fingers into his back.

With ease he slid a finger into her, drawing in a deep shuddering breath at the slick, hot flesh wrapping around him. He could barely imagine what it would feel like to bury himself in that lush warmth.

Her soft gasp of surprise urged him on and he imitated the strokes that he hoped one day soon to make with more than just the touch of his hand.

Richard gritted his teeth at the sound of her building climax. The heavy throbbing in his groin wanted more than just a touch.

No, he silently whispered. It was more important to disabuse her notion of pain and fear than it was to satisfy his needs. Sweat beaded on his forehead from his shaken control over his body.

Soon, her moans of pleasure turned to a frozen gasp as

she arched her back. He felt her toes slide, then curl against his leg. The hot, wet flesh surrounding his touch pulsed as if trying to draw him in further.

Just when he thought he could no longer deny himself, her legs fell lax, the pulsing eased and she withdrew her fingernails from his skin.

Richard withdrew his hand and wrapped his arms around her, pulling her into a tight embrace as he rolled on to his back, bringing her along with him.

Even though his heart still thudded heavy in his chest, hers eased and she pushed up on his chest to gaze down at him with an embarrassing, to him, look of awe. 'I don't think I'll be needing any of your men tomorrow. I have other plans.'

Humour teased at him. 'What might those plans be?'

'I need to gather ice for Satan and learn how to beg.'

He knew exactly what she was saying. At the dinner table she'd sworn that ice would form in hell at Satan's feet before she begged him for anything. And now...she was so willing to beg for more of his touch that she herself would provide the ice for Satan. It was completely inappropriate, but there was no helping it—he burst out in laughter.

Chapter Thirteen

Slowly stretching awake, Isabella sighed. She hadn't felt this well rested since being taken from Warehaven.

She yawned and threw back the covers, only to have her hand come in contact with a solid object. A quick glance brought her wide awake. Richard sat beside her on the bed, fully clothed.

Her cheeks flamed as her mind whirled, remembering last night. She jerked the covers back up over her body and then sank down beneath them.

'I need to go back to the warehouse today.'

His tone was non-committal, flat. *Where had the teasing man from last night gone?* Unwilling to answer, she simply nodded. It wasn't as if she required him for anything. Although she did wonder at the tweak of disappointment building in her heart.

'We need to go over your plans for today.'

Confused, she asked, 'Why?'

'I need to know how many men you'll need and what tasks you wish them to perform, so I can give them their orders.'

So, he had been serious at dinner last night. She was not permitted to perform her duties as the keep's lady. 'I have nothing planned for today. You can keep your men.'

His glare could have lighted the cold charcoals in the brazier, but she didn't care.

'Now you're going to be contrary.'

He hadn't asked a question, so she didn't respond.

'Why? Because you can't get your way?' When she remained stubbornly silent, he continued, 'I am not going to give you control over men you know nothing about.'

Isabella turned her head away from him. She knew she was being petty and that it could possibly come to hurt her in the end, but if she let him take complete charge of what was supposed to be her position, one she had trained for her entire life, where would that leave her?

He grasped her chin and forced her head back to face him. When she closed her eyes, he tightened his hold. 'Look at me.'

She ignored him, afraid of losing her will in the deep blue depths of his gaze.

'God's teeth, woman, I am not giving in on this. You will do as I say.'

At what sounded like a threat, she did look at him. 'Or what?'

He stared at her for a few long heartbeats, then released her chin and with a vile oath rose from the bed. 'You have no need of any men today?'

'No.'

'Have it your way, then.' He strode briskly to the door, pausing to ask, 'Are you certain?'

'Very.'

'Do not leave the keep.'

His unexplained order and the slamming of the door behind him brought her flying from the bed. She was an idiot, a stubborn, witless fool. Perhaps if she gave in to him now, after a while he would relent. She needed to stop him. Her hand on the door latch, she opened her mouth and heard Conal's voice float through the still-closed door, making her pause to listen.

'Did you bother to explain it to her?'

'Explain what? That someone left a missive stating Lady Dunstan is in danger? We don't know who left it, nor do we know what the danger might be. Besides, she was being so contrary that she wouldn't have heard me if I had tried to explain.' The anger in Richard's reply made her cringe.

'Still—'

'No.' Her husband stopped his man from saying anything else on the matter, and then continued. 'She'll wallow in her self-righteous anger for a few days. But as soon as boredom overwhelms her, she'll give in.'

Self-righteous anger? If he wasn't so close to the truth, she'd throw open the door and rage at him.

'And if she doesn't?'

Isabella knew she would likely give in long before he expected her to—the thought of doing nothing for even a single day made her stomach churn.

'She will. But in truth, she's safer sitting in her chamber than anywhere else while I'm not here.'

Conal's snort of reply made her frown. *Safer? Was she in some danger?*

Richard's man asked, 'Have you been able to determine who issued the threat?'

Threat? What threat? As far as she knew the only person who'd ever posed a threat was her husband.

'I've narrowed it down to a few people. We'll discuss it on the way to Marguerite's.'

'And why would we go there?' Conal's voice held a note of surprise.

She heard what sounded like a heavy slap—as if maybe Richard had slapped Conal's shoulder, or back. 'Because you stop there every morning to visit with your lady love before going to the warehouses—why would today be any different?'

Conal's grumbled reply faded beneath their departing footsteps.

Isabella leaned against the door. What was going on? And who was Conal's lady love, Marguerite?

If Richard was seeking to protect her from something, why didn't he just explain that to her? The thought that he was intentionally keeping her in the dark rankled. Why would someone threaten her safety?

She wandered back to the bed and sat on the edge. She hated secrets, just hated them. Mostly because she could never figure out the correct scenario.

Isabella dropped back on to the mattress, her head coming to rest on a pile of soft fur. She sat up and looked behind her. Someone—most likely her husband—had draped a gown, chemise, a pair of plain slippers, soft boots and a fur-lined mantle on the end of the bed.

She ran her fingers through the silken fur and sighed with pleasure at such a wonderful gift. Apparently he truly wasn't as displeased with her as he'd led her to think.

If she couldn't successfully figure out secrets, how would she ever figure out the man she'd been forced to wed?

She picked up the deep forest-green gown and rose to dress. There would be an entire day of nothing to do but devise a plan to coax Richard into telling her what was going on. That way, tonight after dinner, and after they'd climbed into bed, she could set her plan in motion.

Isabella pulled the fur-lined mantle tighter about her in an attempt to shield herself from the biting wind. She stood on the wall surrounding Dunstan and stared out across the stormy windswept sea.

'My lady?' Another one of Richard's ever-present guards braved the weather to try coaxing her back inside.

She turned to glare at him. This one was much younger than the last, perhaps they thought she'd feel sorry for him. If so, they were wrong.

'I am fine. Go back inside.'

'But his lordship—'

A curt wave of her hand stopped his words. 'Is at the wharf and won't know I'm disobeying him if you don't tell him.'

The guard's sigh as he turned to stomp back to the ladder would have been laughable if she wasn't so angry at his lord.

Nearly a month ago Richard had carted her off to her chamber and taught her such a wondrous lesson about being in bed with a man. She still shivered with desire every time she thought about it. But since then he'd been distant and cold, ignoring her whenever possible. She'd never been able to coax him into their bed, let alone get him to explain what was happening. The one time she'd tried had ended with him leaving the chamber, never to return.

A blast of wind pushed the hood of her cloak from her head. She pulled it back up, sinking her fingers into the luxurious lining. She had been quite pleased to find such treasured gifts then, especially after she'd forgotten to ask him for enough gold to purchase fabric to make a gown. But now they felt more like some sort of payment—a compensation.

Which, as far as she was concerned, was fair considering the work she'd accomplished in the Great Hall without the help of his men. While he'd told her she couldn't order his men about, he'd never said she wasn't permitted to put the women to work.

And she had. It hadn't been that difficult, not after she'd stooped low enough to explain the circumstances to the women of Dunstan. Her mother would be horrified to learn she'd used such a sneaky trick, but her mother wasn't here. And while Isabella wasn't going to argue this with Richard any further, she wasn't about to live in a pig's sty.

So, with help from Hattie, the women servants and a dozen more women from the village, the only thing they had left to finish was the floor. Everything else was cleaned, repaired or painted.

She knew full well that Richard had noticed. Every night when he returned from the wharf, he'd paused to look around the Great Hall, his expression growing darker each passing day. Isabella wasn't going to say a word until he asked. Of course, she knew that asking would come with pointed glares and angry accusations.

Right now, though, his shouting would be a welcome change from his one-word answers and silence.

She knew that men could be moody creatures at times, but this... Isabella shook her head. Something was wrong with him. Something she was not at all familiar with. Granted, there was some sort of secret danger that she'd not been able to discover anything about, but why would that make him ignore her? She posed no danger to him, or Dunstan. So, his off-putting manner had to be due to something else.

She leaned her shoulder against the wall and gazed down towards the snow-covered village. Surely there was someone here on Dunstan who could answer her questions. Someone who knew her husband better, on a more personal level that his men did.

Never would she question his men. Not only had he basically forbidden her contact with them, it would be foolish and wrong of her. He needed their respect, needed them to follow his orders, not be his friend, nor a confidant to his wife.

She'd tried asking Hattie, but the woman seemed unwilling to divulge much in the way of useful information. Oh, yes, the older woman had told her stories about when Richard was a babe and young lad. Perhaps if she asked again, explaining why she wanted to know, Hattie might be more forthcoming.

Isabella knew she really didn't have many choices. Maybe a midwife? They were usually privy to every snippet of gossip. Or the priest? She'd not seen him since the evening he'd so willingly helped to seal her fate.

No. Her best source would be Hattie. She just needed to figure out how to gain the woman's trust enough to talk to her.

A movement on the road leading up to the keep caught her attention. She leaned away from the wall. Richard and Conal were returning. And they were closer than she'd like. If she didn't want her jaunts up here to the wall forbidden to her, she needed to get back inside before he saw her.

She grabbed the edge of her mantle, so she wouldn't trip over it as she raced down the ladder to the inner yard. Thankfully, she'd been able to get one of the women to show her an easy way out of the keep and into the bailey. Unfortunately, the quickest way back inside would take her right across the middle of the open bailey where he'd be likely to see her.

A quick glance towards the gates assured her that he wasn't quite yet entering the yard. Still holding on to her garments, she took off at a decidedly unlady-like run, hoping to reach the postern gate before Richard and Conal passed through the main one.

'My lady!'

Isabella cursed, looked over her shoulder to see which guard was now hailing her and tripped, slipping on a patch of ice. Her knees hit the frozen ground hard enough to bring tears to her eyes and she fell forward, landing on one arm.

She wanted to scream in frustration and pain, but before she had time to clear her mind a horse stopped alongside of her. There was no need to look up at the rider, she knew who she'd see. So, she relaxed as best she could, giving in to the throbbing of her knees and burning of her elbow, letting the sharp pains roll over her until she was able to take a deep breath.

'Get up.'

'Richard, the woman is injured.' Conal's tone was filled with censure.

'This is none of your affair.' Isabella winced at Richard's cold, unforgiving voice.

He repeated, 'I said, get up.'

She pushed herself up on to her knees with her good arm and then struggled to her feet. 'I am fine.'

To prove it, she took a step, prepared to return to the warmth of the Great Hall with as much dignity as she could muster, and then cried out in pain as her ankle crumpled beneath her weight, sending her right back down to her knees on the cold ground.

Before she could catch her breath, Richard dismounted and came to her side. He pulled her up from the ground and swung her into his arms, holding her against his chest.

She wrapped her arms around his neck and buried her face in the lining of his mantle. 'I am sorry.'

'Be still.' His voice was gruff and he headed towards the side gate, shouting orders over his shoulder, 'Conal, bring Marguerite. Someone find Mistress Hattie. Now.'

Once inside, he took the stairs to her chamber two at a time as if he held nothing heavier than a tankard of ale. The only sign that he'd exerted himself at all was a slightly faster beating of his heart.

Isabella held back a smile when this time he deposited her on the bed gently instead of dropping her on to the mattress as he had in the past.

He sat next to her and unpinned the brooch holding the front of her cloak together. It fell from her shoulders and he pulled it from beneath her.

To her amazement, instead of tossing it on the floor, he went and hung it on a peg. His own followed before he came back to the bed to push the skirts of her gown and chemise up to her knees.

'What are you doing?'

'Trying to decide how to get your boots off.'

She sat up. 'I can do that.'

He batted her hands away. 'Just lie back.'

Isabella frowned—why in the name of heaven did his voice shake? And why was he acting like a mother hen when she'd expected him to be angry?

Before she could question him, he returned to sit next to her, the boots forgotten, and pulled her tight against his chest. 'When you first fell, I thought someone had killed you.'

Why would he think such a horrible…? Oh, Lord, was that the threat he'd talked to Conal about? Someone had threatened to kill her? And she was out in the open, an easy target, without any hint, or warning, of danger?

She shoved hard against his shoulders, pushing him away. 'That was the threat? Someone plots to kill me?'

At least he had the decency to look sheepish when he nodded and answered, 'Yes.'

'And instead of simply telling me, you thought somehow I'd be able to guess what was going on just because you held a conversation with Conal outside this chamber door where you knew I'd hear?'

'You were smart enough to deduce why the conversation was held within your earshot. I thought—'

'For the love of God, Richard, the only thing you said was that Lady Dunstan was in danger. How was I to make sense of that? I may be able to guess at a few of your moods, but I cannot read your mind.'

His sheepish look vanished. He narrowed his eyes to glare at her. 'Had you done as I ordered, there would never have been any danger.'

'I may concede that point, but still, a better warning was warranted.'

'At least now you understand why you need to stay within the keep.'

'No. I don't understand. Nobody harmed me. I was distracted and fell on some ice. I will not become a prisoner in what should be my own home because of some vague threat. No.' Isabella gaped at him. He couldn't be serious. She shook her head. 'No. What I understand is that you need to find the miscreant and take care of this. You are the lord here. And while I may have been brought to Dunstan as bait, I am now your wife. Your *wife*, Richard, not some unnamed captive. I am not about to suffer further for another person's actions.'

'Oh, so once again you are suffering?'

'And don't you start with that again.' When his lips thinned to a hard line and his eyes seemed to blaze, she shook a finger at him. 'Don't you dare try to avoid this issue by feigning outrage. You know exactly what I meant. Without question, *you* are responsible for me being here. So, you are now responsible for me being in danger.' She lowered her arm. 'You need to see to this, Richard. Immediately.'

He leaned away to stare at her. 'Apparently, fear for your life steals your common sense.'

'And you think that is why? Because I dare take you to task? Did you think I was going to cower and cry? Or that I would hide in a dark corner wringing my hands?'

'I think that because you sound like a shrew.'

'A shrew?' She grasped the front of his tunic in both hands. 'I do not know whether I fear for my life or not. But I do know that I am in pain. And I am so angry with you right now that I could spit.'

He lifted one eyebrow, then shoved her arms away, pushed her down on to the bed and came over her to whisper a warning against her lips. 'Stop talking before you say something you regret.'

She knew exactly what he was going to do. Against all common reason, she urged him on by parting her lips as if to speak. His mouth covered hers and he gathered her into an embrace that he most likely thought harsh. But she found it warm and comforting enough to want to sigh with relief.

His kiss was near ruthless and she welcomed it gladly. He plundered and took, leaving her to do little else than slide her hand up to caress the back of his head, holding him close as he swept her away.

'My lord?'

Richard broke their kiss on a groan and sat up at Hattie's entrance into the chamber, her arms laden with enough supplies to heal an army.

Isabella sighed with regret at the loss of his warmth and touch. She looked at the older woman's array of items and laughed. 'Hattie, I may have twisted my ankle and bruised an elbow, but I assure you that I am not at death's door.'

Hattie sat her goods on the floor near the bed and shrugged. 'Nobody knew what was wrong, they said you were hurt and that I needed to get up here.' She looked at Richard, adding, 'Now.'

At that moment another breathless woman loaded down with more supplies rushed into the chamber. 'Hattie, what happened?'

Isabella rolled her eyes. She pointed at her left foot. 'Twisted ankle.' And then to her right elbow. 'Bruised elbow.'

The new woman joined Hattie in glaring at Richard. 'And *this* is the life-or-death situation I need to attend?'

Richard stood and backed towards the door, holding his hands up before him as if to ward off an attack. 'I know when to retreat. And since I am outnumbered, this seems a good time.'

He lowered his arms and in three long strides returned quickly to the bed, to cup the back of Isabella's head, lean down for a quick, mind-robbing kiss and then whisper, 'I will return, later, after your troops have thinned out.'

Before her lips could cease tingling, he was gone from the room. She blinked twice, then turned her fuzzy attention to the other women. They, of course, had their heads together, twittering behind their hands.

Isabella swallowed hard to banish the heat of embarrassment flooding her cheeks, before addressing the woman she didn't know. 'Obviously I'm Richard's wife, Isabella. And you are?'

'Marguerite, my lady. Dunstan's midwife.'

Sitting up straighter on the bed, Isabella smiled at her sudden stroke of good fortune. 'Oh, it is so nice to meet you, Mistress Marguerite.'

The woman flipped her auburn braids over her shoulders while coming closer to the bed. 'I recognise that tone. What are you looking to discover, Lady Dunstan?'

'Isabella, please. Whatever I can about my husband.'

Marguerite glanced at Hattie, who had started mixing a poultice together on the table near the window. 'You were right, subterfuge is not one of her strengths.'

'If you prefer, I could chatter merrily on about the beauty of the snow and then complain about Richard's lack of manners.'

Marguerite grasped her boot. 'Go on, tell me all about the snow.'

Isabella frowned. 'Is there a reason for distracting me?'

The woman easily stripped the boot and stocking off her right foot, then began tugging on the left boot.

Isabella winced. Naturally her ankle had already begun to swell, making the distraction welcome. 'Yes, well, the snow is white. And cold. Very cold.' She curled her fingers into the covers beneath her as a decidedly painful jolt shot up her leg at Marguerite's not-so-gentle tugging. 'Yes, very cold. And I don't think it'll ever end.'

She paused to take a deep breath. 'And I'm fairly certain—' When Marguerite gave one final jerk, pulling off the boot and stocking at once, Isabella jumped, gasping out, 'Damn, that hurts.'

Marguerite swung the boot on the tip of one finger before tossing it and the stocking next to their mates on the floor. 'Didn't seem fair to prolong the inevitable.'

Isabella glared at her. 'I wager you're a joy during childbirth.'

'And I wager you'll sound like a guttersnipe during the birth of your own child.'

'Yes, well, that's something we have no need to worry about.'

Marguerite's eyes widened in surprise. 'Really now?'

'How odd.' Hattie joined them to hand Marguerite the poultice she'd made. 'Everyone in the keep is already placing wagers on the date of your first child's arrival.'

'When it doesn't happen within the next nine months, do I get the money?' Isabella slapped a hand over her mouth to stop herself from saying anything further on the subject. What was she thinking to be sharing this type of information with these women?

'Blunt and entertaining.' Marguerite spread the poultice over her ankle. 'We'll become fast friends.'

Isabella offered no comment since that remained to be seen. She did ask, 'Comfrey root?'

'Of course. I'll wrap the ankle and, as long as you stay off of it for a day or two, it should be good as new.'

Hattie handed Isabella a goblet of odd-smelling wine. 'I don't think that will be an issue tonight.'

Isabella wrinkled her nose at the warmed, overly sweet-smelling wine. 'What is in this?'

'Never you mind.' Hattie pushed the vessel to Isabella's lips. 'Just drink it.'

Marguerite stayed Hattie's hand with a shake of her head. 'A little lavender, lemon balm and lovage, with just a touch of rosemary for the swelling and honey to make it palatable.'

Sceptical and more than a little leery, Isabella asked, 'Nothing to dull the pain?'

'Pain?' Marguerite made a show of studying Isabella's foot as she wrapped the ankle. 'Did you cut off your foot, or just twist your ankle?' Without waiting for an answer to the obvious, she added, 'I just want you to rest tonight, not addle your wits.'

The thought sounded good. However, she had responsibilities to attend to before the day was done. 'But the evening meal should be just about ready. If someone would assist me down the stairs, I'll be fine.'

Marguerite pulled the covers from beneath her, then drew them up and tucked the ends under Isabella. 'I will stay to assist Hattie with the meal. After all, it will be nice to enjoy a meal I didn't have to make and it will give me a chance to discover why Lord Richard has been so inattentive to his new bride.'

Isabella gasped, horrified at the idea of Marguerite questioning Richard on something so personal. She tugged at the covers encasing her like a cocoon so she could swing her legs off the bed, but the midwife stopped her with a laugh.

'Good heavens, I was but teasing you. Never would I think to so boldly divulge something you said in private. Stay in bed, drink your wine. I'll send your husband up with some food. You, Hattie and I can have a fine chat tomorrow.'

Chapter Fourteen

Richard felt the tick in his cheek twitch faster the third time the midwife asked, 'Yes or no? Are you going to take this food up, or should I find someone else?'

Seated between him and Conal, Mistress Marguerite surveyed those gathered in the Great Hall for the evening meal, settling her gaze on one of the finer-looking younger men at the far end. She nodded towards her selection. 'Perhaps he would be inclined.'

Richard unclenched his jaw long enough to order, 'Enough.'

The woman pointedly turned her attention to Conal. 'Do you not agree that it would be best if Lady Dunstan was offered some food and drink?'

'You need stay out of this, Marguerite.' Conal leaned away from her, shaking his head. 'He's already had his fill of your harping.'

'I am not harping in the least. I am only suggesting what might be best for his *wife*.'

'Concern yourself with her ankle and leave the rest to me.' When the good, albeit oddly intrusive, mistress made a noise that sounded suspiciously like disapproval, Richard tightened his grip on the knife in his hand. This is exactly what he had feared. Once the people of Dunstan started interacting with Isabella they would find themselves defending her at the most inopportune times.

How could they not? It wasn't as if she was an evil or unlikeable person. She possessed a quick wit, cared for others, knew how to control the running of a keep without letting anyone realise she was in fact also controlling them.

He let his narrowed stare roam the Great Hall once again. How had she accomplished so much with no men to help?

Each evening for the last month, he'd return from the warehouse to find more progress completed on the reordering of his keep. And each night he tried to fathom how she'd accomplished such feats.

He could understand the scrubbing of the furniture, fire pit and such. But the tapestries hanging high on the walls had somehow been cleaned, along with the decorated shields belonging to his family that were perched above the tapestries. They had been removed, cleaned and returned to their rightful spots. And the fresh coat of paint on the walls didn't miraculously apply itself.

Someone was helping her. The question was, who? He'd intentionally made certain that every man, excluding whichever three he had left behind to guard her, was put to work in the warehouses or on ship repairs. And the guards swore they'd not lifted a finger to help the women.

He couldn't believe for one heartbeat that the women were doing this alone. The idea of Hattie, or any of the maids, scurrying up and down a ladder was absurd. He should have followed his gut instinct and not hesitated. Instead of waiting until the evening to return to the keep, he should have dragged himself back here some time during the day to catch the culprits acting behind his back.

The only thing that had kept him from doing so was

simple, to him at least. He actually didn't want to catch any of the men in the act of disobeying his orders. He didn't want to have to discipline them for helping the lady of the keep. They wouldn't understand his actions, which would only breed resentment. And in the end, he'd look like a fool for marrying a woman he appeared to despise and not trust.

He should never have married her. He should have taken her as a hostage and held her captive in a cell. It would have been much easier to do so. As long as he didn't take his conscience into consideration.

At the time she'd done nothing to him. Nothing. He'd had no reason to harm her, or treat her poorly. She was never his target for revenge. So, he'd mistakenly believed that marrying her would not only save her reputation, but that it would make controlling her easier, and would also ensure her a measure of safety from the other men on Dunstan.

Granted, it had preserved her reputation. But what had possessed him to believe either of the other two was true?

He could no more control her than he could the falling snow. And there was a poorly written missive in his private chamber that threatened her life.

What bothered him right now more than anything else was the fact that when he'd seen her fall in the bailey and had thought someone had struck her dead, he'd felt as if not just his heart, but his entire world, had stopped.

He'd been angered when he'd found Agnes's body. He hadn't cared for the woman, but she hadn't deserved to die in such a vile manner. And he'd been nearly torn asunder when he'd happened on Lisette's small form. His chest had tightened—and hadn't yet relaxed. He'd seen red—a blood-red rage that did nothing but grow stronger with each passing hour.

But today had been different. When Isabella had fallen

to the ground, he wanted to die with her. His first response had not been anger, or even fear. It had not been a terrible thirst for revenge. Truth be told, he hadn't even looked for the man who had let loose the arrow, or rock, that had taken her life. Instead, it had been all he could do not to throw himself from his horse, race to her side and plunge a knife into his own heart so he'd not be without her.

That dire vision of taking his own life had enraged him. It wasn't as if she was his life, she wasn't even his love. She was nothing more than a means to an end. That was all. His only hope had been that once Glenforde was dead, that he and Isabella could somehow find a way to be... friends. Companions who could work together for the good of Dunstan.

So why then the ungodly urge to take his own life? And why then did he sit here now, in the Great Hall, not touching his food and dreading his return to her chamber?

'Richard.' Conal grasped his wrist and slapped a tankard of ale into his hand. 'Go talk to her. Tell her what is happening, so this doesn't occur again.'

Richard shook the fog from his vision and turned to look at Conal. To his surprise, Mistress Marguerite was no longer sitting between them. He spied her helping Hattie and the other servants to clear the tables.

'So what doesn't occur again?'

Conal snorted. 'You can lie to yourself. You can lie to her. You can even lie to God if you so desire. But you can't lie to me. You care more for that sharp-tongued wife of yours than you'll admit.'

If he couldn't figure out what he felt about Isabella, or why, then how could Conal? 'You are seeing things that aren't there, my friend.'

'Perhaps. But after the way you reacted in the bailey, I

don't think I'm wrong. Never have I witnessed such a look of horror on your face before.'

'Why wouldn't I react with horror? If anything happens to his spawn, Warehaven will descend on Dunstan, sparing nothing in his path.'

'Again, that whole lying to everyone else is fine. But rest assured it is not going to work with me. If Warehaven descends with the intent of waging war, we fight with the advantage of defending our homes and loved ones. In the end, he will return to Warehaven a little worse for wear.'

Richard shoved back from the table and rose. 'Conal. Have I recently told you what an ass you can be at times? Like now?'

'Probably, but I hear it so often that it no longer sinks in.' He tapped the platter of food the women had prepared for Isabella. 'In your haste to escape, don't forget to take this to her.'

Richard set down the ale, grabbed the plate and left.

Isabella picked at the edge of the top cover. Her head spun from the wine, steadily revolving faster with the passing of time.

Apparently she'd been forgotten. That didn't surprise her considering how little she mattered to anyone here at Dunstan.

Her mother wouldn't have forgotten her. Neither would her father or sister. Jared might have, but her brother usually had so many things on his mind that he always ended up forgetting some thing or another. But the others would have brought her food and drink. They'd have come into her chamber more often than she'd liked just to check on her, to see if she wanted or needed anything. They'd have come simply to keep her company.

But she wasn't home at Warehaven. She was here at Dunstan where nobody cared about her.

She sighed, dropped the cover and crossed her arms over it against her chest. Thankfully she had earlier realised this melancholy settling over her was caused by the herb-laced wine, otherwise she knew she'd have dissolved into tears of self-pity and homesickness by now.

The door to the chamber opened and she sat up, eager to see who had come and if they'd brought something to eat. Richard walked through the doorway, with a heavily loaded platter in his hand.

She took one look at his face and leaned back against the pillows she'd piled up at the head of the bed. He didn't look angry, but neither did he look pleased. Actually, if anything, his expression was bland, as if bored. She felt her eagerness fade, knowing he'd be less than cheerful company.

He hooked a foot around the leg of a bench and dragged it over to the bed to use as a table. Setting the platter down, he said, 'I know it's a little much, but they thought you'd want a selection to pick and choose from.'

Even his voice sounded bored.

'It doesn't matter.' She sniffed. 'I'm not hungry.'

He stared down at her. 'Are you in pain?'

'No.' Isabella swiped at her watering eyes and silently cursed.

'Then what are you crying about?'

'I have no idea.'

Richard frowned, then looked around the chamber until he ended his search on the empty goblet tipped on to its side on the table next to the bed. 'What was in that goblet?'

'Wine.'

'And what?'

Unable to remember everything in it, she shrugged. 'Some herbs and stuff.'

'Stuff?'

'Yes, stuff.'

'Oh, well, yes, if they put *stuff* in it, I'd probably be crying, too.' He sat on the edge of the bed and pushed her over. 'Make room.'

She wiggled over far enough so he had enough space to sit beside her.

Richard adjusted the pillows, took off his boots, then swung his legs up on the bed. 'So, what dark thoughts have you in such a morose state?'

Isabella leaned against his arm. 'Everyone forgot about me.'

He hooked his arm across her shoulders and pulled her against him. 'That would be impossible.'

'Everyone left and I was alone.'

'Ah, yes, I know. For almost an entire hour.'

She shook her head. 'No, it was much longer than that.'

'Not really.' He handed her a hunk of bread. 'Eat this.'

She nibbled at a corner, but couldn't swallow past the thick dryness of her throat. 'Can I have something to drink?'

'No. All I brought with me is wine and you don't need any more.'

'But I'm thirsty.'

He took the bread from her. 'How about some broth instead?'

'Fine.' Somewhere in the back of her muddled mind Isabella knew she sounded and was acting like some spoiled child. But at the moment, she was unable to find the will to care. What she wanted most of all was for the bed to stop spinning like a top.

He held the bowl of broth to her mouth. When she reached for it, he said, 'I've got it, just take a sip.'

She did and felt some dribble down the front of her gown. With a shudder, she pushed the bowl away. 'Richard, I think I am intoxicated.'

He wiped a rag across her chest. 'Isabella, I know you are.'

She tried to slide down on to the mattress. 'I need to sleep.'

'No.' He dragged her back up against the pillows. 'You need to eat something first.'

Her stomach lurched at the thought of food. 'I don't think that's a good idea right now.'

'Are you going to be sick?'

'Sick? I am a lady.'

'Ah, yes, how foolish of me to forget that ladies never vomit.'

Isabella wanted to laugh, but the best she could do was to bat at his leg. 'You, Lord Dunstan, are vulgar.'

'I think I've been told that a time or two before.' He eased his arm from her shoulders and swung off the bed. 'I'll find you something to drink.'

'You are leaving me?' To her horror, her lower lip quivered and her eyes welled with tears.

'Isabella, I will be right back.'

'You won't. I will sit here all alone.' She choked on her words. 'For ever.' God's teeth, what was wrong with her? Every time she opened her mouth, something more foolish spewed forth. Isabella waved towards the door as she slid sideways off her pillows on to the bed. 'Go. Leave me.'

She vaguely heard Richard's grumbled curses over the sound of him stomping across the chamber to open the door and shout for Hattie.

Everything seemed to be coming at her through a thick, hazy fog. Her heart pounded so hard and fast that her pulse sounded like roaring waves in her ears. She curled her fingers tightly around the bedcovers. 'Richard?'

He came back to the bed and pulled her upright. 'I am here.'

'Some…thing…something is…wrong… I…'

With a sigh she closed her eyes and sank into the welcoming embrace of a warm, dark void.

'Isabella!'

Richard's shout, followed by a stinging slap across her cheek, jerked her back to the murkiness of her spinning and now oddly bouncing chamber.

He had lifted her into his arms and asked questions she couldn't understand. Unable to form words, she grunted in reply to his undecipherable queries.

People shouting, and what sounded like countless items hitting the floor, made her wonder if Dunstan was under attack.

A hand grasped her chin. Hard, unforgiving fingers pressed into her cheeks, forcing her lips apart. She flailed her arms at the rough treatment, but her pleas to be left alone were cut off when someone poured a foul-tasting liquid in her mouth, clamped her mouth shut and stroked her throat, forcing her to swallow.

The arms holding her placed her on a hard, solid object. It wasn't cold enough to be the floor. But she couldn't imagine what it might be instead because she was trying to focus on what she swore sounded like Richard apologising for something.

Isabella groaned. There were too many things to try making sense of when all she knew for certain was that her head throbbed horribly and her stomach cramped in the most painful manner possible.

Yet, when she tried to curl into a ball to ease the cramping, hands pushed and prodded her on to her stomach and dragged her until her head hung over the edge of this hard, unyielding bed.

She stared down at what appeared to be the floor. Even though it rippled and undulated like a wave, it still looked like a floor.

A hard, dirt-packed floor that made her mouth water profusely and swallowing only made it water more. When her stomach gurgled Isabella gagged and gripped the edge of her uncomfortable bed, realising then that she'd been placed on a table.

Richard combed his fingers through her hair, dragging the mass to the back of her head where he held it in one hand, while he rubbed her back with the other one. His infernal massaging made her feel worse, but before she could tell him to stop, her throat and stomach convulsed at the same time.

After what seemed like hours, her bruised-feeling stomach settled, permitting her to groan in exhaustion and rest her forehead on the table. Her throat felt raw, her face wet and she shivered uncontrollably. But the room had stopped spinning, her heart had slowed its riotous pounding and her head no longer hammered in agony.

She turned her head and opened her eyes to see Richard place a fur-lined bedcover over her before he sat down on a bench, clasping one of her hands in his own. He brushed her hair from her face and cupped her cheek.

He looked terrible and rather pale, making her wonder what had happened to upset him so. The hushed sounds of people talking prompted her to tip her head back far enough to see what had to be half of Dunstan's citizens gathered around them.

Humiliated to be seen in such a state, she swung her focus back to Richard, to hoarsely beg, 'Please, get me out of here.'

She struggled to rise, only to have Richard place a hand on her shoulder blades. 'Stay still, let me.'

He slid his arms beneath her and rolled her into his embrace. Marguerite tucked the hanging edge of the cover around her, and pressed the back of her hand to Isabella's cheek. With a nod, she said, 'Go, I will be right behind you.'

Once in her chamber, the most wondrous sight met her—a huge, oversized tub with rose-scented steam rolling from it had been set up in the alcove. Never had she seen such a large, more inviting-looking bath.

Richard set her down on a small bench facing the tub. When she swayed, he steadied her with a hand on her shoulder.

Isabella sighed. If she couldn't sit upright by herself, how was she going to take advantage of the bath? And she so wanted to soak in that lovely tub. It was calling to her, inviting her to relax in the warmth of the water and let the troubles from this day fade away with the steam.

Her lip trembled and when she couldn't stop it or the cursed tears from building, she closed her eyes and turned her head away to hide her unwarranted distress. She couldn't believe she was going to start crying about nothing again. How could she be any more foolish than she'd already been this evening?

A calloused hand wiped away the tears from her cheek, then rested there. 'It will soon be better, I promise, Isabella.'

She leaned into his caress. 'I am a silly fool.'

'No, you aren't. You are a woman who had a terrible reaction to either the herbs, or the wine.'

'And one who is blessed to be alive,' Marguerite interjected from the doorway. She carried a pitcher, a cup and at least a dozen drying cloths over to the bath before joining them at the bench to pull the cover off Isabella's shoulders. 'Come on, into the bath with you. I want you to sweat the rest of the poison from your body.'

Shivering, Isabella gripped the edge of the bench. 'I can't even sit upright, how am I going to sit in that tub without drowning?'

Deftly untying the laces of her gown, Marguerite nodded towards Richard. 'I am sure your husband will see to it that you don't drown.'

Isabella gasped. That meant he was going to be there for her bath—a thought that made her burst into tears. 'Have I not embarrassed myself enough in his presence today?'

He chucked her lightly under the chin. 'Sweeting, feel free to cry all you want. Hell, if you have the strength, you can scream and fight me. But you'll not win this one.' He leaned over to wrap his hands on either side of her waist and lifted her from the bench far enough for Marguerite to pull her gown and chemise free. Then he lowered her back to the bench, adding, 'You may as well resign yourself to my presence. I'm not going anywhere.'

Her cheeks flamed, making him laugh before he started to remove his own clothing. By the time he was down to nothing but his braies, Marguerite had managed to strip her mostly naked, too. The only part of her body still covered by cloth was her ankle.

Isabella squeezed her eyes closed, hoping when she opened them that all of this would have been nothing but some odd, drugged dream. She peeked out of one eye to see Richard reaching for a bucket of steaming water next to the tub. She inhaled sharply at the play of muscle across his back and arms as he hefted the bucket.

Marguerite's soft laugh made Isabella more self-conscious and nervous than she'd already been at seeing Richard's almost naked and completely healthy body.

'Like I said, I'm sure he'll keep you from drowning.

Come on, up with you.' The woman tugged on Isabella's arms, pulling her from the bench and helping her over to the side of the tub.

Without so much as a by your leave, Richard swooped her off her feet from behind and, holding her against his chest, stepped into the tub, still wearing his undergarment. There was no stool to sit on and she couldn't figure out how this was going to work in the high-rimmed tub until he bent his knees and plopped down into the water, bringing her along to sit on his lap.

Water sloshed out of the tub, flooding on to the floor. Marguerite unfolded and dropped a few of the towels on the floor to soak up the water before attaching a pole to the outside of the tub behind Richard. She then draped a cloth over the pole and fluffed it out to surround them, with the edge of the cloth hanging just past the top rim of the tub. Not only did it provide them privacy, but it kept most of the steam trapped inside with them.

Isabella couldn't see them through the makeshift tent, but she heard heavier footsteps approach and jumped when two more buckets of hot water were poured into the bath at her feet.

Once the footsteps faded out of the chamber, Marguerite stuck her head inside the tent to address Richard. 'I put the bench with cool water and a cup to your right. There will be two guards outside the door. More water is already heating. Call out when you want it added, or need anything, and make sure she drinks all the water in that pitcher.'

'Consider it done,' Richard replied over her head.

Marguerite briefly touched Isabella's shoulder. 'Relax. Let your husband care for you. He owes you that much.'

The chamber door closed and a heavy silence fell over the room. Richard's heart thudded against her back and hers fell into the same rhythm.

Isabella struggled to breathe and leaned forward, only to be stayed by an arm wrapping beneath her breasts and pulling her back. 'There's nothing here you haven't already touched and stroked. Be still, Isabella, be still.'

Would she ever be able to resist that deep gravelly tone? Or not welcome that firm yet gentle hold?

She took a long breath, let it out slowly, then leaned her head back against his shoulder.

Chapter Fifteen

Richard leaned his head back against the rim of the tub. He wasn't tired and didn't fear falling asleep, not with such a soft, curvaceous woman stretched out on top of him. But he did long for a few moments of respite to wipe the memories of the last few hours from his mind.

This wife of his had probably frightened a good ten years off his life. And in return, he'd probably frightened at least that many off the lives of his men. He could only imagine how he'd looked when he had bolted down the stairs, carrying her in his arms, her head lolling about as if she was dead and him shouting at the top of his voice for Marguerite and Hattie.

Conal had never moved so fast in his life, clearing the table of platters, trenchers, goblets, utensils and bowls with one swipe of his giant arm. The rest of his men had instantly jumped into action, Matthew leading half of them to draw their swords and guard the studded double doors at the entrance to the Great Hall, Conal leading the other half to clear Richard's path, shoving benches, stools, people out of the way.

His earlier concern about the people of Dunstan coming to care for his wife was obviously a moot point. Their actions made it plain that they already saw her as their lady and that was something he was never going to be able to change. He wouldn't know where to begin.

The deep lines of fear and worry on Mistress Marguerite's face had nearly caused his heart to stop beating. She'd not expected such a reaction to the herbs she'd given Isabella. For far too many moments, the woman had been convinced she'd killed Dunstan's lady. To be honest, so had he.

Thankfully, they had both been wrong.

'I am sorry.'

'Hmm?' Apparently his stolen moments of respite were over. He nearly laughed at his wish for her to return to normal. It wasn't that long ago when he'd wished she was meeker and much more quiet. Now, he would so much rather she rail at him, than simper and cry. Her anger set his blood boiling, but her tears? He sighed. Her tears raked across his heart like a whip, making it bleed.

'I said I am sorry.'

He dragged his fingers through her hair, trying to free the tangles. 'For what?'

'For acting like such a witless nit.' Her shoulders rose and fell with a huge sigh. 'And for embarrassing you in front of your men.'

Richard wondered which misconception to address first, since one was as incorrect as the other.

'A witless nit for crying?' He placed a palm against her forehead, tipped her head back and looked down at her. 'Had you been sleeping when I came up here, I never would have known anything was wrong with you until it was too late. Your tears and babbling were what warned me that you were in dire trouble. So don't apologise for them. They saved your life.'

'Perhaps, but I did embarrass you along with myself. I don't think anyone other than maybe my father has ever seen my mother be ill. Doing so in public the way I did was shameful.'

'Surely you are jesting?' He shook his head in disbelief. 'Isabella, if you drank overmuch and became ill on a regular basis, that might pose a problem and we would have to consider watering your wine. But this had nothing to do with over-imbibing of your own free will.' He stroked his fingers down her cheek to her chin and turned her head to face him. 'Do you understand that you nearly died tonight?'

'I am sure my parents will be relieved to know I didn't.'

He released her chin and frowned. Was this more senseless babbling or was she regaining a bit of her wayward tongue? It was too soon for her to have regained all of her wits, so this had to be more of the malaise that had affected her earlier.

'Yes, I am sure they will be.' *But so was he.*

A sudden bout of sniffing made him want to cut off his tongue. He shifted her so she was more sideways than straight across his legs. Her liquid gaze gave away her losing battle with yet more tears. 'And so am I, Isabella, so am I.'

She rested her cheek against his shoulder. 'I can't help myself.'

'I know.' He wrapped his arms around her, suggesting, 'We could distract you.'

'I doubt that anything could distract me from this infuriating *oh, poor sad me* mood that has captured me fast in its clutches.'

'Oh, ye of so little faith.'

They were in a tub together and she was naked. Distracting her would take little effort. He lowered the arm he'd draped across her chest and placed his hand on her thigh.

'Well, yes, that might distract me somewhat.'

'Somewhat?' He caressed her leg, stroking a lazy path from knee to hip and down again. 'Just somewhat?'

She shrugged and said nothing. But the quickness of her breaths told him that he'd already surpassed distracting her *somewhat*.

'While you're *somewhat* distracted, you need to drink.' He reached under the tent for the pitcher of water and the cup, which he handed to her. 'Hold this.' After filling it with the water he nudged the bottom of the cup, then waited for her to finish it off before returning the items to the stool.

Settling back against the tub, he casually rested his hand on her stomach, asking, 'Now, where was I?'

Isabella picked up his hand and placed it on her thigh. 'I believe you were here.'

'But I remember being here.' He moved his touch to caress the soft skin covering her ribcage.

'I think your memory is faulty.'

'My mistake. I was here.' He cupped her breast, teasing the pebbled nipple with his thumb and tightening his arm across her shoulder when she jumped in surprise.

'No, you're wrong.' She turned slightly in his arms to breathe against his neck. 'I would have remembered that.'

'Are you certain?' The sound of her quick breaths coaxed him to tease a little more. 'After all, you were drugged. That might have confused your memories.'

'Maybe.' She gripped his shoulder. 'I might have been remembering someone else.'

Richard laughed, knowing she was but teasing him. 'My lady's humour is returning.'

She trailed her hand along the side of his neck, up to his cheek and turned her face up to his. 'Humour is not what I'm feeling.'

He placed a quick kiss on her lips, then reached once again for the water and cup. 'What you're feeling is called thirst.'

Isabella briefly pressed her fingernails into his shoulder before taking the cup. 'What you're feeling is plain mean.'

'Drink.'

When she finished, he once again put the items back on the stool. 'So, I'm feeling mean, am I?'

She squirmed on his lap, making him gasp as his lust leapt from wanting, to clawing need. Richard breathed deeply to calm the riotous pounding of his heart. He wasn't turning this leisurely bath into anything other than what it was—a means of helping her relax and rid her body of the poisons that had made her sick.

'Yes, you are being mean. You tease and tempt, but do nothing to ease my torment.'

He stared at her, wishing there was enough light inside the dark confines of this bathing tent to see her face. Did her eyes shimmer with desire, or were they still glassy from the herbs?

When she started to move around again on his lap, he grasped her hip. 'Stop it.'

'Why, my Lord Dunstan, you sound…distracted.' She ran a hand down his chest, coming to rest low on his belly.

'Cease.'

She inched her fingers lower, sliding them beneath the soaked fabric of his braies.

'Isabella, you need to choose.' He caught her wrist. 'You can either sit here with me in this bath. Or you can sit here alone.'

'But I yearn for you and I'm willing—'

'I'm not.'

She jerked as if he'd slapped her. 'You don't desire me?'

From the waver in her voice he knew she was still at

least partly caught in the drugged fog. 'Not desire you? Have you lost your wits completely?'

Still holding on to her wrist, he pushed her hand to his groin, closing his eyes with a groan when she wrapped her fingers around him through the thin fabric. Before he lost control, he pulled her hand to his chest, placing her palm over his heart. 'Can you feel the pounding of my heart? I don't just desire you. I lust for you.'

'Then—'

He didn't know whether to laugh or rage at himself. He'd started this, so his building frustration, and hers, was his fault for trying to distract her with teasing. 'Woman, you have not the strength to stand on your own two feet, or even sit upright on a bench. I may be a black-hearted knave, but I am not low enough to take advantage of a woman in such a manner. No. Not tonight.'

She sniffled against his chest. 'Now what are you crying about?'

Of course losing his patience only made her sniffle more. Richard released her hand to grip the edge of the tub, fighting to get himself under control. He closed his eyes tightly and breathed.

Once he was certain he could talk, move, think without wanting to either lose his temper, or satisfy baser urges, he wrapped her in a tight embrace. 'I'm sorry. Tell me, what's wrong?'

'Nothing.' She wiped at her nose.

Richard stretched an arm over the edge of the tub, reaching for one of the towels. Using the corner of it, he ran it over her face. 'No. Come on, tell me.'

'You'll think me foolish.'

'Probably.'

'You are not a black-hearted knave.' Her sniffs had

turned to earnest cries. 'You are the kindest, most gentle man I know.'

Richard was…speechless…and not a little bit frightened. Kindest? Gentle? She thought him kind? And gentle? He'd gone too far with this helping her feel better. He should have left her in the capable hands of Marguerite and Hattie.

Now, instead of seeing him as the brute who'd kidnapped her, forced her to wed him and plotted to kill her former betrothed, she saw him as kind and gentle? That did not bode well for the future.

He needed to disabuse her of that notion before she did something truly foolish.

'Isabella…' He cleared his throat and began again, 'Isabella, listen to me. The wine and herbs are making you imagine things are different than what they are. Nothing has changed here. You are still bait to draw Glenforde out and he will still die by my hand. There isn't anything about me or my motives that you could consider kind, or gentle.'

He waited for her to say something—anything to show him that she understood.

She rubbed her fingertips across his shoulder. He felt her mouth working against his chest as if she were mulling over his words and debating how to respond. Finally, she sighed softly, then asked, 'I am never going to have the kind of love my parents share, am I?'

She confirmed his worst fears. This tenderness he had shown her made her long for things that he would never be able to give her. He couldn't lie, he wouldn't lie to her. That would be unfair and would only lead to broken false promises down the road. He knew the type of pain that created and he wasn't going to be the one who caused her to suffer like that. 'I am sorry, but, no.'

She pushed against his chest and sat up to grasp the

edge of the tub. He watched her struggle to rise before she let her arms fall to her sides. 'I want to go to bed.'

Richard swallowed hard against the tightness in his throat. He hadn't wanted this night to end this way, but there was nothing he could say, nothing he could do to ease the disappointment she now felt.

He rose from the water, pulling her up with him. It was better this way. The hurt she felt now was minor compared to what it would feel like later if he had lied and led her to believe there was hope for some grand love in their future. Perhaps eventually she would learn that love was a myth, or something couples envisioned in their minds, and she would come to accept a comfortable companionship as something worthwhile.

For now, however, he didn't want to argue with her or fight over this. She was weak and not herself, it wouldn't be fair.

He stepped out of the water and quickly wrapped her in an oversized drying cloth before sitting her down on the stool next to the tub, so she could hold on to the edge if need be.

Briskly rubbing another towel over her limbs and hair, he dried her off, then unwrapped the cloth strips binding her ankle. Marguerite could replace them shortly.

He took a towel to his own body and once he'd squeezed as much water as possible from his braies, he reached for his clothes.

'What are you doing?'

Confused, Richard left the clothes on the floor and turned to look at her. She leaned against the tub, staring at him.

'I'm going to get dressed, tuck you in bed and leave. I'll send Marguerite or Hattie up to stay with you.'

Isabella shook her head. 'No.'

'What do you mean, no?'

'You are coming to bed with me.'

'I beg your pardon?'

'You heard me.'

Richard rubbed the towel over his head, trying to give himself enough time to figure out what thoughts were running around in her mind. 'Don't you think we've gone beyond repairing this night?'

She pushed herself to her feet, still gripping the tub, and let the towel fall. She closed her eyes for half a heartbeat and then stared at him hard. 'My lord husband, you have sentenced me to a loveless marriage, with no chance of escape. Since you saw fit to wed me and confine me to this island, I have no options before me but to accept that as my life, as my future. But I will not live without someone to love and cherish. And since it will not be you, then you owe me someone as a replacement.'

He dropped his towel to the floor and crossed his arms against his chest. 'A replacement?'

'I want a child.'

'A child?' He studied her face. She was still a little pale, but her gaze seemed totally focused—on him.

'Yes. You owe me at least that much.'

'I owe you?'

Her cheeks blazed with colour. 'You have taken everything from me and now, even my future.' She lifted her chin. 'I demand my marital rights as your wife.'

He clenched his teeth together to keep his jaw from falling open. Not certain he could speak without sputtering, he asked, 'You demand?'

She tilted her head slightly to the side and lifted one finely arched brow. 'Did you lie?' She stroked a hand down the curve of one hip. 'Is my skin not soft and pliable beneath your touch?'

Her hand slowly roamed up over her stomach and ribs to cup a breast. Keeping her stare locked on his, she brushed her thumb across the peaked nipple. 'Do you not find these enticing?'

She stroked a trail to her parted lips to trace them with a fingertip. 'Do you not enjoy my lips against yours, or the taste of my kiss?

'You do not want my heart, or my love. So be it.' Isabella leaned a hip against the tub and spread both arms wide. 'Does that mean you want nothing? Not any part of me?'

He'd thought her a quick learner. She was obviously far more than that. She'd taken his few lessons and created an entire curriculum on seduction.

God forgive him, but in her anger, her hurt, her rage, she was breathtaking. Her boldness captivated him. Her demand stole his mind. Oh, yes, he wanted her. And if she couldn't see the proof of that standing out before him, then she was blind.

He freed his tongue from the roof of his suddenly dry mouth, to warn, 'This will change nothing between us.'

'It will change everything. I will be your wife in more than just name.'

He took one step towards her. 'If I take you to that bed, there will be no turning back.'

'I may hate you at this moment, but, Richard, I burn for your touch.'

That declaration grabbed hold of his lingering reservations about her being weak and tossed them out the window. He peeled the still-damp fabric from his body, cleared the distance between them in two steps, swept her into his arms and, without breaking stride, placed her on the bed.

He released her, intending to stretch out by her side, but she dug her fingernails into his shoulders and pulled him down on top of her. 'Don't try to be nice. Don't think to

make me swoon and forget what is truly happening here.
I don't want your love play, Richard, it's a lie. I just want
your child.'

Oh, no. No. He wasn't going to play this sort of game
with her. She wasn't some cheap whore that he was going
to use to gain his release and then toss aside. Regardless
of anything else, she was his wife and he wasn't about to
spend a lifetime not taking full advantage of what pleasures could be shared with her.

He shrugged out of her grasp and grabbed her hands,
pinning them to the bed. 'I'll give you the child you so
desire, but we're doing this my way, not yours. Do you
understand me?'

When she nodded, he released her hands. He knew she
was nervous, it would have been odd for her not to be. And
he knew just how to distract her from her worries.

His lips against her ear, he whispered, 'I told you once
that you'd have to beg me for this. Are you ready to beg,
Isabella?' He drew out her name intentionally, knowing
how it made her shiver.

'I'm not going to beg.'

'Ah, and there's that challenge again.'

Isabella closed her eyes, wondering if she had made a
mistake—a huge mistake, one that was too late to correct.

He brushed his lips across hers, running his tongue
along the seam before delving inside to sweep her into his
kiss. This is what she'd wanted to avoid, this mind-robbing
wave of pleasure that she was unable to resist.

She raised her arms to wrap him in her embrace, and
he broke their kiss, to sharply order, 'No. Don't.'

When she dropped them back to the bed, he once again
stole her breath with a kiss. The moment she thought she
would drown, he trailed his lips to the soft spot where her

neck met her shoulder, kissing, sucking the sensitive skin until her toes curled.

His low husky laugh should have been a warning, but when he eased down her body to cup a breast, then tease the tip with his tongue before closing his warm mouth around it, her breath caught on a gasp of surprise.

While he gave full attention to one breast with his mouth, his hand sought the other. Isabella clamped her lips tightly together to hold back a moan of pleasure as her pulse quickened and the need he was so artfully building rippled down her stomach. The need grew warmer, hotter, spreading until she swore she could feel her heart beating low in her belly, coaxing her moan to escape.

A deeper laugh made her wonder what pleasure-filled torture he intended to inflict now in his quest to make her beg. She was uncertain she'd be able to withstand much more.

Keeping a hand on one breast, he stroked the other along her side and over her hip as he eased further down her body until he manoeuvred his shoulders beneath her thighs.

She held her breath, her legs hooked over his shoulders trembling, uncertain what to expect.

He caressed her breast one more time before sliding his hand to her stomach, resting his palm flat against her as if to hold her in place. 'Breathe, Isabella.'

She sighed, trying to ignore the rapid beating of her heart, and took a breath. Only to have it catch in her chest at a kiss so intimate she thought at first she was imagining the rush of wonder and unadulterated lust-filled need washing over her.

This is what riding a white-capped wave would feel like. She was certain of it. Weightless, having no control as the strength of the water carried her up, then cresting, pulling away to let her fall breathlessly before once again catching her to push her towards another crest. Isabella curled her fingers into the covers beneath her.

He paused, slowing his onslaught, and she fought to catch her breath. The moment her shaking legs stilled, he renewed his relentless need to break her, to hear her beg as he'd promised she would. Isabella closed her eyes, knowing he was right and that soon she'd not be able to stop herself from crying out mindlessly, begging him to fulfil her.

The exquisite stroking, circling of his tongue against her fevered flesh had her panting, gasping for each breath. Her belly contracted and when the crashing wave carried her higher and higher her body tensed, then pulsed madly around the touch of his finger inside her.

Isabella released the covers and reached for his shoulders, crying out, 'Richard, please, I beg of you.'

Before she could finish her cry, he was over her, angling her hips with one hand beneath her as he eased himself into her.

She moaned at his gentleness, wanting more, needing more, and pushed her hips harder against his.

He cupped her cheek, teasing her lips with his. 'Easy. Take it easy.'

'No.' She curled her fingers into his shoulders. 'It doesn't hurt.'

She gasped as her release beckoned. 'Please, Richard, please.'

He picked up the tempo, quickly finding the pace that made her toes curl. She wrapped her arms around him, holding him tightly, clinging to him as she felt herself fall, spiralling down to claim the release she so desperately needed.

Before her ragged breaths could ease, Richard stiffened, his body shaking as his own ragged groan raced against her cheek.

Isabella ran her fingers through his hair, whispering a teasing dare she hoped he'd not be able to ignore, 'You will never be able to make me beg again.'

His shoulders shook with laughter and he rolled on to his side. 'Wife, you are quite the bawdy temptress, aren't you?'

She snuggled against him, not yet willing to let the inevitable distance come between them just yet.

Richard sighed and patted her hip. 'I should go. You need to sleep.'

'No.' She reached up to place her hand against the side of his head. 'Don't leave me. Stay.'

'But—'

Isabella placed a finger over his lips. 'If this is all we are to share, then can we not share it fully? There is no reason for you to sleep elsewhere.' At his raised brow, she continued, 'I know what this is. I know full well that it is not a sharing of hearts. But, Richard, it is something, it connects us and is that not at least a thing to treasure?'

He clasped her hand and brought it to his lips. 'Isabella, I fear your tender heart is going to suffer mightily for this, but I will stay with you…this night.'

Chapter Sixteen

As the aromatic scent of cinnamon, cloves and nutmeg in the mince pies baking in the kitchen filled the keep Isabella couldn't help but wonder if her family would celebrate Christmas in her absence this year. She hoped they would. And she prayed they'd be merry and thankful in honour of the season.

'What do you think he'll say?' Isabella helped Hattie wrap another garland of pine boughs around one of the support beams in the Great Hall.

The older woman shrugged. 'Once the deed is done, will it matter?'

'I suppose not.'

It wasn't as if he hadn't seen the piles of freshly cut evergreen, ivy and holly stacked in the hall as he'd left this morning. She'd had the men put the piles near the door intentionally so Richard would see them. That way, if he had any complaints, he could voice them before she placed them about the keep. He hadn't said a word, hadn't confronted her about her plans, so surely he'd not been averse to her decking the keep with the greenery.

Marguerite's laughter as she trapped Conal beneath a sprig of mistletoe hanging from ribbons over the archway of a small alcove at the far side of the hall made Isabella smile.

It was nice seeing the two of them so at ease and so obviously enjoying each other's company. She couldn't help the twinge of jealousy over what they shared, especially knowing she would never have the type of marriage she'd longed for. Richard had made that quite clear.

'Child.' Hattie touched her arm. 'It isn't my place, but it needs saying. He has been through much. Give him time.'

Isabella turned her attention back to the evergreens. 'An entire life would not be enough time for him.'

Hattie snorted and shook her head. 'My lady, do not be blind.'

'It has nothing to do with not seeing. He has made it perfectly clear that I am little more than bait.'

'There was a puppy once.'

Uncertain where the older woman was headed with this sudden turn in the conversation, Isabella asked, 'A puppy?'

'Hmm, yes. A deep dark-brown, floppy-eared puppy that the young master so badly wanted as his own. He would sneak out to the stables every chance he had to hold and play with the pup. She was his entire life. To him the sun rose and set on that gangly-legged ball of fur. I don't remember how many times I had to go out there, intending to chase him in for the evening meal, only to find him fast asleep with the puppy in his arms.'

Having had many litters of puppies at Warehaven, Isabella understood the young boy's devotion to the playful animal. There was nothing easier to fall in love with than a soft, warm puppy.

'His father made certain to give that puppy away first.'

'No.' Isabella groaned at the heartlessness of such an action—by his own father no less. 'That was cruel.'

'Yes, it was, but his lordship would not listen to reason.

He was determined to teach the boy a hard lesson about life. The boy cried himself to sleep for countless nights afterwards.'

'The only lesson he could have learned from that was not to care overmuch for something.' Her heart ached for the little boy he'd been.

Hattie stopped, a branch of evergreen clutched in her hands, to stare at her. 'Exactly, my lady.'

Isabella frowned. Could that explain his reluctance to let himself care for her?

'It was a lesson reinforced by his first wife and then again by losing Lisette.'

'But, Hattie, I am going nowhere.'

'You can't be certain of that, can you? What happens when your family comes for you, Lady Isabella?' The woman turned back to hanging the evergreens, adding softly, 'And what happens to him?'

Isabella could not say what her father would do when he arrived. He might consider the marriage binding and be content to leave her at Dunstan. But he might also still be angry enough to take offence to the entire situation—the kidnapping, the marriage—and escort her back to Warehaven.

What *would* happen to Richard then?

She gazed around the Great Hall. Dunstan Keep was by no means a large dwelling. It would fit inside Warehaven with room to spare. There were no decorative paintings on the walls, just a simple limewash. Even the tapestries were worn. The furniture was serviceable, not cushioned for comfort.

But it was a sturdy keep, built to last many generations. When she'd first arrived it had been immediately obvious that it cried out for a caring touch. And now it was a dwelling to be proud of, a safe harbour in which to raise a family.

What would happen to it if she left? Would Richard let it fall into ruin? And if he had no one to argue with him, no one to set his temper flaring, would he let himself fall into ruin, too?

No. She couldn't imagine Richard moping about the keep alone. He would direct his full attention to his ships and warehouses. After all, isn't that what her father did whenever her mother went to visit her family without him?

She frowned, confused by her own questions and her inability to answer them. Even though her father became rather morose during her mother's absence and he spent far too much time at the docks, he had always known that his wife would soon return to him.

'What dark thoughts are swirling round inside your head, Isabella?'

Ice-cold fingers stroked the side of her neck, making her jump. Surprised to see him back at the keep so early, she looked up at Richard to ask, 'What brings you back from the warehouses so soon?'

'The warehouses?' He turned to point towards the doors. 'What good is a pile of greenery without a Yule log?'

She peered around him to see a good-sized oak tree trunk resting alongside her piles. 'Ah. You didn't have to do that.'

'I know I didn't have to, but I am not such a black-hearted knave that I wish to ignore Christmas.'

'Please, Richard, that is not what I meant.' She rested a hand on his chest. 'I didn't think that of you.'

'Even armies pause for Christmas, Isabella. There is no need to be so serious.' He covered her hand with his own. 'I was but teasing you.'

His heart beat steady beneath her palm. The heat of his gaze flowed into her, bringing to life memories of the night three long weeks ago when he'd truly made her his wife. Suddenly shy and embarrassed for no obvious reason other than the visions her mind created, she looked away.

He leaned closer to whisper against her ear, 'Isabella, it is easy to tell where your mind has now flown.'

She shivered with longing from the warmth of his breath and the deep, raspy tone of his voice. Uncertain how to respond, she reluctantly pulled her hand free, took a deep breath and stepped away.

His soft chuckle at her withdrawal only flustered her more.

'My lady, do you think you and your husband can finish this?'

Relieved by Hattie's timely interruption, Isabella took the greenery the older woman held out to her and looked at Richard. 'If he agrees to lend me a hand, I'm sure we can.'

At his nod, Hattie sighed. 'Good. I want to see if they need a hand in the kitchen.'

Isabella knew Hattie was making up an excuse to give her and Richard time together. They didn't require any additional help in the kitchen. She and the cook had spent many hours going over the menus for the holiday feasting. More than enough extra help had been put to work days ago.

But she appreciated the woman's gift of time with her husband and without a word watched her leave the Great Hall.

Richard climbed the ladder to wrap the upper portion of the support beam with the evergreen, while she went and retrieved some more branches and ribbons to hold them in place.

When he finished, he climbed down from the ladder, only to watch as the rope of evergreens slid down the beam.

Isabella laughed and sprinted up the ladder, teasing

him, 'If you only knew how to tie a ribbon, my lord, the decorations might stay in place better.'

He handed her the end of the greenery, shaking his head. 'Well, that answers that question.'

Busy securing some holly into the ribbon, she asked, 'And what question would that be?'

As she reached up as high as she could, he grasped her legs to keep her steady on the ladder. 'Now I know who painted the hall.'

She looked down at him. 'Who did you think did it?'

'I wasn't certain.' He slid his hands beneath the skirt of her gown to wrap his fingers around her thighs. 'But now I know it was someone with soft skin.' He brushed a thumb across the back of her leg, making her gasp, before sliding one hand higher. 'And the most enticing pair of legs I've ever had the pleasure of caressing.'

She lost her balance on the ladder and, with an undecipherable squeak, fell into his waiting arms.

'Richard!' Isabella batted at his shoulder. 'Are you trying to kill me?'

He nuzzled her ear. 'No. Just distracting you.'

She heard the twitters and laughs of amusement from the others in the Great Hall and batted at him again. 'Put me down.'

To her surprise he did so without arguing. Straightening out the skirt of her gown, she reminded him, 'There is much to be done before the Angel's Mass tonight.'

'Yes, there is.' He nodded in agreement. 'We need to eat.'

Of course he would think of that before all else.

'Then I need to find the remains of last year's Yule log so we can light the new one later.'

She was actually a little surprised that he thought of that considering how miserable the months in between had been for him.

He glanced around the hall. 'Tables and benches still need to be arranged for tomorrow's feast. And you will need time to get dressed before we head down to the church.' He paused, then asked, 'Did I forget anything?'

'Richard, catch.' Conal tossed something at him.

Richard caught it and smiled. 'Oh, yes, I see that I did forget something.'

He held a beribboned sprig of mistletoe over her head and graced her with a familiar half-smile that never failed to set her heart fluttering. 'My lady?'

She leaned against him and tipped her head back for his kiss, sighing when his lips covered hers.

When their kiss ended, he kept his arms around her, holding her against his chest. Content to remain in the circle of his embrace, Isabella closed her eyes. She had no mistaken notion that this easiness between them would last beyond the holy season. But she was determined to enjoy it for as long as possible.

His embrace tightened around her and he kissed the top of her head, before releasing her. 'I have a log to find and the men should be here soon, they can help you with the tables and benches.'

While Isabella had found the three holy masses comforting, she was glad they were done traipsing back and forth to the church in the village. The walk at midnight for the Angel's Mass had been cold, but the sky had been clear and myriad stars had twinkled brightly. The warmth of her husband's hand clasped securely around hers had made the frigid air less biting. After being kept awake by Richard's undivided attention most of the night, the dawn trip for the Shepherd's Mass had been exhausting. The church bells had called them to the Mass of the Divine

Word just as she'd been directing the placement of the last trestle table for the Christmas feast.

Everyone on Dunstan had gathered at the keep after the last church service to partake in the Christmas feast. With so many people in the Great Hall, at times the din was near deafening.

But she was pleased that everyone seemed to be enjoying the merriment. The cook and her helpers had outdone themselves. Everything, from the deer, half-a-dozen geese roasted in butter and saffron until golden, partridges and a spitted pig, were done to perfection. To Richard's amusement, Isabella had moaned in pleasure when the meats seemed to melt in her mouth. A perfect blend of shredded meat, fruit and spices, the mince pie had been as near to heaven as she could imagine.

One long side table, laden with other baked goods and sweets, supplied by Dunstan's baker, and wheels of cheese brought up from a warehouse near the wharf, was so overflowing with food that Isabella feared the wooden legs would snap beneath the weight.

Ale and wine flowed freely, but she'd confined her choice of drink to the contents of the wassail bowl. The spiced and sweetened ale was warm and gentled her normal dislike of noisy, crowded places.

At Warehaven she was free to bolt when it seemed the walls were closing in around her. But not here. Not now. As odd as it still sounded to her ears, she was Dunstan's lady and she'd not shame herself, or Richard, by running from her duties.

With the meal now over, the men had helped clear the tables and rearranged them for games now taking place. While some took chances dicing, others played chess and all appeared to be enjoying the company of their friends and neighbours.

She leaned back in her chair, which had been placed near the burning Yule log. After much searching, Richard had found the leftover piece of log from last year's fire buried under the small bed in his private chamber. They'd used it to start this year's fire, which from the size of the current log would easily last until the twelfth night.

A giggle from Marguerite seated nearby, next to Conal, caught Isabella's attention. She smiled softly at the couple. They were lost in each other's company.

Richard leaned closer as he took a seat next to her, to ask, 'What are you smiling about?'

She nodded towards Marguerite and Conal. 'How long have they been together?'

Richard reached over to clasp his hand over hers, laughing softly at her curiosity. 'Ever since Conal was old enough to realise she was a girl.'

'And this arrangement is fine with Marguerite?'

'You don't approve?'

She shook her head. 'I didn't say that. I simply wonder if he knows what a good woman he has.'

'I've never asked.'

'Oh.'

Richard squeezed her hand. 'He's not just my friend. Conal is my right arm on this island. I'm not going to risk that by asking questions that are none of my business.'

She understood his position, because right now, there were many questions she wanted to ask him about Conal, about Richard's father, about her husband's life growing up, but wished not to risk losing his good mood. So she bit her tongue to keep them from spilling forth.

'Go ahead.'

She looked at him. 'Go ahead, what?'

'From the pensive frown on your face, you want to ask me something. So, go ahead.'

'No, it's nothing important.'

His long, drawn-out, exaggerated sigh made her want to laugh. Instead, she explained, 'You have made this day very pleasant for me and I simply wish not to ruin it. My questions will wait.'

'They're that bad that you feel it needful to wait until I haven't made your day a pleasant one?'

'That's not what I meant.'

'Then, ask.'

Obviously he wasn't going to let this go. So, Isabella chose what she hoped would be the least dangerous one to ask. 'Do you think Conal cares enough for Marguerite to marry her?'

'Are you asking me if he loves her?'

Well, yes, she was, but she knew Richard's thoughts on that subject. 'No. Just wondering if he cares for her.'

'Of course he cares for her. Isn't that obvious?'

'To who? Not to me. I wasn't certain they had any relationship until yesterday when they helped me decorate the hall.'

'You haven't heard any of the island's gossip?'

She rolled her eyes. 'In case you've forgotten, I, too, have spent my entire life on an island. I learned long ago not to listen to gossip.'

'Oh, I haven't forgotten. I don't know how it works on Warehaven, but the only way to know what's going on here is through gossip.'

'Are you serious?'

'Quite serious. For example, how much gold will you gain if a child isn't born before summer?'

Isabella felt the burn of embarrassment rush to her cheeks. How had he heard about the off handed wager she'd made with Hattie the day she'd sprained her ankle? It wasn't even a serious one. After hearing about those in the keep placing wagers on how soon a child would be born, she'd simply made a sarcastic comment about winning the wager herself if she proved everyone wrong.

'Or, were you aware—?'

'Enough.' Isabella cut him off. 'I see your point.'

He released her hand, dragged her chair closer and slung his arm across her shoulders. 'Listen to the gossip. Just remember that while most of it is pure fabrication, there might be a grain of truth buried beneath. You'll have to determine what's worth remembering and what's not.'

She groaned. 'I am not very good at that.'

'You'll learn.'

'I suppose I will have to.'

A group of men called out for Richard to join them. 'I am slated to challenge the winner of this round of chess.'

'Go.' She waved him away. 'Enjoy your game.'

He rose and then leaned over to quickly kiss her cheek, whispering, 'I'll be back soon.'

A shiver rippled down her spine at his hushed promise and she watched him take his place at the table, unashamedly hoping his king quickly got checked and checkmated, ensuring a speedy return to her side.

Chapter Seventeen

Christmas, Epiphany and now Candlemas had come and gone. And as she'd expected, so had the comfortable easiness between her and Richard. She watched him from across the Great Hall and fought to ignore the constant longing that burned deep in her belly. While he had shared their bed Christmas Eve and again Christmas night, he'd not returned since then. Nearly six long weeks had passed since she'd felt the warmth of his body next to hers and she wondered if anyone else could see the desperate hunger in her eyes.

She knew what he was doing, or she was fairly certain she did. He had claimed that he feared her tender heart being broken, but she had to wonder if he might also be concerned for his own. Did he believe that he could spare either of them by keeping his distance?

Foolish man.

Little did he realise that he was just fanning the fires for an all-out battle between them.

He turned his head and caught her staring at him. Isabella felt the heat creep up her cheeks as he smiled. That slow, deliciously sensual half-smile that was reserved only for her never failed to make her shiver.

She looked away and then spun back to stare at his hair. His face. His clothes. Who was this clean-cut, freshly shaven, well-dressed courtier who possessed her husband's face? And when had this change taken place? How had she not noticed?

One of the serving girls walked up to the group Richard was standing with, to offer the men wine or ale. She swayed back and forth, playing with her hair while talking, laughing and flirting with one of the younger guards. But it was Richard's gaze that trailed after her when she left.

Isabella frowned. This would not do. She'd often overhead her father's men make off-hand comments about being married, not dead, and she'd seen how her mother dealt with her father when his eyes wandered. She highly doubted that her father had ever taken another woman after marrying her mother, but even after all the years they'd been married, he was not above trying to make her jealous.

And her mother was not above threatening to castrate him with a dull knife.

Although she didn't think that tactic would work well with Richard. He might be tempted to push her just to see how far she would go. Thankfully, she'd never have to test that theory, since she had no liking for that type of game.

The only game she wished to play with her husband involved much less clothing and a bed. However, she needed to find a way to coax him back to her chamber before she could even think of getting him into the bed.

Isabella leaned against one of the support beams on the far side of the hall to study her husband. Even though they'd shared nothing more than a passing word, a brief touch, a meal now and then of late, she'd noticed small changes. He seemed less angry, less willing to burst into unreasonable fits of rage. And on an occasion or two, like now, he'd taken time to talk, jest and even laugh with his men.

She didn't think for one heartbeat that he'd given up his quest for revenge—there were times when an unsettling darkness fell over him and she knew without a doubt the direction his thought had drifted—but it didn't seem to consume his every waking moment.

And there were times, other moments, when she'd catch a glimpse of his face and see such overwhelming sadness that she ached to hold him and to chase away the terrors haunting him.

Oh, Richard, do you not see what is right before you?

Isabella sighed. If she stood here any longer, she would sink into the same depressing malaise that afflicted him at times. She pushed away from the timber to cross the Great Hall.

Her husband had moved away from the group of men to talk with Conal in private. Their conversation ceased when she joined them.

'Are you looking for something?' Richard slid his arm around her as if he hadn't just spent the last endless weeks avoiding her.

Unwilling to lose the warmth of his touch, Isabella bit her tongue. Instead, she leaned against him. 'No. I simply tire of my own company and thought perhaps I'd venture out to visit Mistress Marguerite.'

'Are you sure? It is cold out there.'

'If I wear my fur-lined cloak I will be warm enough.'

'I will see you to her door.'

'Richard, I am well able to make my way down the path alone. It's not as if I will get lost.'

Both men shook their heads at that statement. Her husband lowered his arm. 'No. It has nothing to do with getting lost. Go get your cloak and I will escort you.'

Conal offered, 'I am headed to her cottage in a little while, if you want to wait I would be more than happy to accompany you.'

'Oh, yes, Sir Conal, a man sitting in on women's talk, that's just what I want.' She looked from one to the other. They were both far too willing to keep her company on her short walk outside the keep. 'What are the two of you trying to hide this time?'

They met her stare, but she wasn't backing down. She narrowed her eyes and to her surprise Conal broke the contact first. He shot a rather pleading look at Richard. 'Tell her.'

'Tell me what?'

'Come.' Richard grasped her elbow and guided her towards his private chamber. He said over his shoulder, 'Since this was your idea, Conal, you are of course joining us.'

Once the chamber door closed behind the three of them, Richard retrieved a small wooden chest from beneath his pallet. After shoving aside stacks of documents and maps strewn over the table, he set the chest down to unlock it.

He handed her a rolled missive, asking, 'Can you read?'

'Yes.' She plucked the missive from his fingers. 'And I can sign my own name, too.'

Her veiled reference to the mark he'd made for her on their marriage document drew a strangled snort from Conal and a hiked brow from Richard.

She unrolled the vellum and read the poorly written contents. Her heart seemed to skip a beat. 'This is not the same missive as before?'

Richard shook his head. 'No, this is a second one.'

'The first one wasn't quite as...detailed,' Conal added.

Isabella turned her attention back to the missive. Her eyes followed each word.

Since my attempt to poison Lady Dunstan failed to bring about her death, I fear a more direct approach is in order. After I have torn her still-beating heart from her chest, fed it to the dogs and slit her throat, remember you were warned.

Her hands trembled. Struggling for breath, she dragged her focus from the note to look at Richard.

His non-committal, expressionless look never wavered as he held her stare. To her amazement, his steady emotionless response calmed her wildly drumming pulse.

She blinked, trying to digest that realisation while at the same time letting the knowledge that someone hated her enough to want her dead sink into her mind.

Richard pulled a high-backed chair from behind the table and guided her down on to it. 'Sit.'

Grateful, Isabella offered no resistance. Had the chair not been available, her shaking legs might not have kept her upright for long.

She handed him back his missive. 'Does Marguerite know?'

Conal shook his head. 'No, I haven't told her yet.'

'She still believes her herbs were responsible for my sickness?'

'Yes,' Richard explained, 'Mistress Marguerite was not my first concern.' He rested a hand on her shoulder. 'You were.'

'Why? Because my father will soon arrive?' She truly didn't know what was wrong with her, but the need to lash out at this threat wouldn't be ignored.

At her strident tone, Conal made a hasty exit. Richard

crossed the small chamber to lean against the wall, seemingly undisturbed by her outburst.

She pointed a shaking finger at the note he still held. 'That…man…that monster poisoned my wine, threatened to cut out my still-beating heart and feed it to the dogs, and to slit my throat. Yet, here we are, going on about our day as if nothing is amiss.'

Richard shrugged, but still his expression hadn't changed. Although his eyes seemed to glimmer in an oddly distracting manner. She mentally shook off the distraction.

'I could have been taken, killed at any moment and once again you didn't see it as important enough to warn me.'

Again he briefly lifted one shoulder.

She gasped. 'You truly don't care about me in the slightest.' Her stomach twisted and knowing that she was as worthless to him as a flea made her throat burn. 'What is wrong with me? How many times have you told me that I am nothing more than a means to an end, yet I keep hoping that some day there might be something more. I could be violently murdered and the only thing you would care about is that Glenforde arrived on Dunstan so you could claim vengeance for your first wife and child.'

Isabella stopped to drag in a much-needed breath of air. She wrapped one arm around her now-churning stomach.

'Are you done? Have you spilled all the accusations you can?' While she couldn't read his blank look, his deadly tone was clear. She'd gone too far.

She nodded.

'You are certain there's nothing else you wish to add?'

She shook her head.

When the missive left his fingers to fall to the floor, Isabella knew she should run. But her legs refused to listen to her head. Instead they kept her frozen in place, permitting him to grab a handful of fabric at the front of her gown and jerk her to her feet. And when the chance to struggle presented itself, still her body would not comply. She remained limp and compliant as he marched her to the back of the chamber and through the door to his inner sanctuary.

He pushed her into the room and slammed the door closed behind them. 'Now it is my turn.'

'Richard, I'm sorry.'

Ignoring her, he said, 'Let's take your complaints one by one, shall we?'

He shoved her down on the bed, then paced before her. 'It's true that it would be upsetting for your father to arrive only to find you dead. But is that my main concern? No. I don't fear your father any more than I do anyone else. He's a man, that's all. He can die just like the rest of us.'

She shivered at that thought, but kept her lips pressed tightly together.

'Yes, the man who wrote that threat is a monster. But the only person who has gone about their days as if nothing were amiss is you. You're so observant that you haven't noticed you are watched and guarded every single minute of every single day. You have not been alone for one heartbeat since the day you arrived on this island.' He stopped before her and leaned over so they were nose to nose. 'Not one heartbeat.'

He straightened and resumed pacing. 'As for me not caring about you. Since the day after Christmas, Conal or Matthew have guarded you each day and tried to catch up on their duties each evening. That's why Marguerite hasn't been told anything—Conal has not had the opportunity to see her for longer than a few stolen minutes at a time. At night you are guarded by me. I have sat on the floor outside your chamber door, my sword at hand, ensuring your safety. I have delayed repairs on my ships, rearranged shipping schedules to see to your well-being.

Not my men. Me. To ensure you are not again poisoned, I personally have tasted every bit of food or drink prepared for you and then made certain that food or drink was delivered to you by Hattie or me. That's how much I do not care for you.'

She wanted the floor beneath the bed to part and just swallow her whole. Dear Lord, how could she not have known?

'I can tell you what is wrong with you.' Again he leaned close. 'You are so damned concerned about tomorrow, next week, next month, that you can't see what's right in front of you today, this moment. That's what's wrong with you.'

He walked away. 'I am gladdened to know that what I freely offer is not enough for you.'

Somehow she found a way to swallow her groan. What had she done in her haste to lash out at him from fear? Had she destroyed everything?

He glared at her. She knew he wasn't finished and that the worst was yet to come. She took a deep breath and bowed her head, knowing she deserved every bit of his anger.

'Yes, Glenforde will die. By my hand. I long for the day I shed his blood.'

She flinched when he roughly grasped her shoulders. 'Agnes did not deserve to die in such a horrific manner. Alone. With no one to protect her. Not even the husband who had promised to keep her safe.'

She ached at the anguish in his voice, knowing there was nothing she would ever be able to do to ease the pain he suffered at their deaths. And now relived because of her.

'Lisette was a six-year-old child. She had been loved and cosseted each and every day since her birth. She had no understanding of the pain and agony being inflicted on her the last moments of her short life. *I* kept her safe during the storms that frightened her so. *I* kissed the scrapes and bruises away to make them feel better. *I* protected her when she did something to anger her nursemaid or mother. *I* held her when she was sick. But when she needed me the most, *I* was not there.'

Isabella let the hot tears fall from her eyes. Sorrow and shame that she had pushed him to this state tore at her. How would she ever be able to make this right for him? How could he look at her? How could he bear to be in the same room with her?

He pushed her on to the bed, falling with her to gather her in a tight embrace. 'Isabella, do you not understand?' He shoved his fingers through her hair, forcing her head back and placing his lips near hers. 'I cannot go through that again. Not with you.' His kiss was rough, demanding and far too brief. 'Especially not with you. I would die.'

She raked her fingers through his hair, clasping his head in her hands. 'Richard, I'm sorry, I'm sorry,' she repeated over and over, choking on a sob. She asked, 'What can I do? Please tell me what to do.'

He released her to push up and rest over her on his elbows, his hands cradling her head. 'Trust me. Let me do what I must in my own way. I do not avoid you out of spite, or any lack of desire. There is nothing I want more than to taste you, kiss you, feel you beneath me and hear your cries of fulfilment.'

Her cheeks flared with heat and when he tilted his hips to give her proof of how much he wanted her, she choked back a soft, strangled gasp.

'Conal and I have narrowed the culprit threatening you down to three men. We are certain this is same man who helped Glenforde on to Dunstan. We are so close to snaring him. I am watching you, always watching, waiting for him to make a move.'

Why didn't they just toss the three men into a cell? When she opened her mouth to ask, he shook his head. 'Let me do this on my terms. Mine.'

She closed her mouth.

'I will not tell you who we think it might be, for fear you would do something reckless that would show our hand before we are ready. I promise, it won't be long. I want this taken care of before your family and Glenforde arrive. The weather is breaking early this year. They could be here any day now. Soon, this will all be over with.'

'And then?'

'And then Glenforde dies, Isabella. You need to make a choice before that day arrives. If you want any type of future on Dunstan, do not plead for him.'

'Plead for him? Oh, Richard, I have not been completely honest with you. I care not what you do to Glenforde. I never have, not really. When you kidnapped me, I'd just come from seeing him kiss and fondle his whore in my father's hall. And when he spied me, instead of stopping his betrayal, he kept his stare pinned on me while he lifted her and carted her into an alcove.'

She took a breath, then continued. 'I suffered that humiliation from him just hours after he had knocked me to the ground for disagreeing with him about my sister and what he considered her unseemly infatuation with Charles of Wardham. And this is why I don't think he will come for me, he has no reason, or desire, to do so.'

'Does your father know any of this?'

'No. I was trying to determine how to tell him when you found me.'

'Then rest assured, he will come. Your father will see to it. Glenforde is too much of a coward to admit to your father what he had done. He would not risk your father's retaliation. So as far as Lord Warehaven is concerned, you and Glenforde are nearly betrothed.'

She wasn't convinced he was right. 'I'm not so sure about that.'

'If your father doesn't convince him, then Glenforde will be led here by his greed. You are too wealthy an heiress to let slip through his grasp.'

'We shall see. Besides, my choice was made many weeks ago. Do what you must to banish your ghosts, that is all I care about. Glenforde concerns me not at all.'

'That's what you say now. But you have no way of knowing what choice you will make when that moment arrives.' He rested his forehead against hers. 'But I pray your words prove true. And if they do, when all is said and done, we'll have to get busy working on that child you want.'

She knew that no matter how many times she told him her choice was made, it would only be her actions that convinced him in the end.

'Conal waits for us.' He kissed the end of her nose before standing up and offering her his hand. 'And you wanted a visit with Marguerite.'

Richard pulled her closer to his side and tucked her hand beneath his arm. 'You are freezing.'

'No, actually, I am more than fine. The fresh air feels lovely.'

Conal, walking on the path a little ahead of them, laughed. 'Spoken like a woman who doesn't have to be out in this...*lovely*...weather every day.' He paused, turning to offer her his added assistance crossing a huge puddle. 'See, someone could drown in that.'

She laughed at him as Richard picked her up and handed her across the water to Conal. The man had been complaining since they'd left the warmth of the Great Hall. 'The trees are starting to bud. Soon the buds will swell.'

At the men's sniggers, she bumped Richard with her hip, hastily adding, 'Into leaves. I swear the two of you act like randy youths at times.'

'That's because we're constantly surrounded by beautiful women.'

Conal grunted his agreement at Richard's claim.

Isabella rolled her eyes. 'You mean like the young serving maid?'

'She's not old enough to be beautiful yet.' Richard shrugged. 'Right now, she's just young. A reminder of years long gone.'

'So only old women can be beautiful?'

Conal glanced over his shoulder at Richard. 'Talk your way out of that one.'

'Mature, I meant mature.'

'Isn't that simply another word for old?' Isabella couldn't help tease him. After what she'd put him through he needed a light-hearted moment or two.

'I—uh…I meant…'

Conal laughed. Isabella giggled, asking, 'So, am I old and beautiful, or young?'

Without missing a step Richard reached over, grabbed her and swung her up against his chest. Her breasts pressed against his hard muscles, nose to nose, her feet dangling. She wrapped her arms around his neck and hooked her feet about his thighs.

'No matter how beautiful the serving maid might become, she will never be as lovely, desirable or tempting as you.'

Conal groaned. 'God, I wish the two of you would stop.'

'He has no reason to talk.' Isabella whispered, then added, 'Please, let me.'

At Richard's nod, she said loud enough for Conal to hear, 'You're just jealous, Conal. But it is your own fault, you know.'

'Beg pardon?'

While Richard stopped, to let her slide down the length of his body until her feet hit the ground, she explained, 'There is a beautiful woman who would move the moon and the stars for you if you but asked. And yet she lives alone.'

The man waved his hand in the air as if brushing away flies. 'You, too?'

'You can't expect her to wait for ever.' She raised her voice more as he picked up his pace. 'One day while you're dawdling, someone else will sweep in and steal the prize.'

Richard sighed. 'And if that day comes the man will be miserable.'

'Then I suggest, for his own good, he be prodded a bit more.'

'Is that an order?'

Isabella wrinkled her nose, debating. 'Does his happiness affect Lord Dunstan's?'

'Yes.'

'Well, then, of course it's an order.'

'Very well, I'll take it under advisement.'

She poked him in the ribs. 'I suggest you do a little more than that.'

'Yes, my lady.'

They rounded the last curve on the path leading to the midwife's cottage. Isabella stopped, holding Richard from approaching. She nodded towards Conal and Marguerite standing in the doorway. 'Perhaps we should just let them be.'

'I have some business with Father Paul.'

'Then we'll go to the church.'

As they walked past Marguerite's cottage, Richard briefly explained where they were going to Conal.

Marguerite pulled Isabella aside, to ask, 'I know it has been many weeks, but you've had no lingering effects from the poison in the wine?'

'Ah, Conal told you.'

'That's what he was just explaining when the two of you arrived.'

'No. I seem to have survived. My dignity, on the other hand…'

Marguerite laughed at her. 'I'm sure by now everyone has forgotten, but if not, what's a little sharing of bodily functions amongst friends?'

That made Isabella laugh wryly. 'That's what you're going to call it? A little sharing?'

'Why not? Anything else sounds too vulgar and un-refined.'

'Isabella?' Richard interrupted them and she took her leave of Marguerite, promising to return soon.

He led her away from the cottage, stopping just outside the church door. 'I'll just be a minute or two. Do you want to wait in the narthex or out here?'

'I'll stay out here if you feel I'll be safe.'

He nodded. 'I'm sure of it. But if anything startles you, or gives you pause, scream. You do know how, don't you?'

She pushed him towards the door. 'Go.'

Once he disappeared inside, she pulled her mantle tighter about her, rubbing her cheek against the soft fur and strolled the muddy grounds in front of the church. Spying the small cemetery, she opened the gate and took a seat on a bench.

The headstones in front of her were those of Dunstan's wife and daughter. Isabella shivered. Of course they would be. At times their ghosts hung over Richard like a black cloud, so why wouldn't she choose a spot directly in front of them. As if she needed a reminder of the mental anguish she'd needlessly caused him a short time ago.

She leaned forward to read the carved words. The one for his wife simply said *Agnes of Dunstan* and the date of her death. But the one for his daughter read: *Lisette, Beloved daughter of R. Dunstan.*

Isabella frowned. Something was off with these inscriptions. His daughter was beloved, but his wife wasn't? And why wasn't Lisette the daughter of R. and A. Dunstan?

She reached out to touch the girl's stone, wishing it would give her an answer, but the sound of approaching footsteps made her pull her hand back.

Richard sat down beside her.

'That was quick.'

He nodded and took her hand.

When he threaded his fingers through hers and held on tightly, she silently cursed herself. Why had she come into the cemetery without thinking? He'd told her he'd only be a minute, she should have known that he'd find her here.

'We can go.'

He relaxed his hold. 'No.' He reached beneath his mantle and pulled out a leather scroll. 'Here, this is for you to keep.'

'What is it?'

'We don't know what's going to happen when your father arrives. He or your brother could run a sword through me without warning.'

'No! Richard, they wouldn't do that. I won't let them.'

'If I was your father, I would make certain you weren't anywhere near.' He leaned over and kissed her cheek. 'It's all right. Who knows, I could some day die in my sleep. But either way, you need to know what is yours.' He tapped the scroll. 'This is our marriage contract. Keep it close.'

She slid it beneath her cloak, intending to secure it behind the girdle wrapped low on her waist.

'No. Read it first.'

She opened the end and pulled out three rolled-up sheaves of parchment. The first page was just the who, what, when and where of the ceremony, which she shuffled to the back after a quick glance.

The next page was a list of what he would gain from marrying her. It was brief. And contained one line—simply her. No dowry, no exchange of gold, land or any other material wealth. Just her as his wife. She wasn't too certain this agreement would be considered binding with such an exclusion.

The last page was a list of what she gained from marrying him. It, too, was brief. And contained one line—Dunstan Isle and all of its wealth, warehouses, ships, buildings and land.

'Richard!' She pushed the pages into his hands. 'No.' Flustered, horrified by what he'd done and greatly awestruck, she said, 'Fix this. You will fix this. The minute my father arrives, you will fix this.'

'Everything here is mine. Nothing is entailed to the crown. I am free to do with it as I please.'

'No. You *will* fix this. If not for me, then for any children we might have.' She tapped the pages he still held. 'This makes me responsible for Dunstan. I cannot hold all of this safe. I cannot offer the ships protection once they set sail. If anything were to happen to you, I could lose everything you and your father and his father worked so hard to build. I could leave our children with nothing, not even a place to live.'

When he didn't say anything, she repeated, 'You will fix this. Why on earth did you do such a thing?'

'These were drawn up before I left Dunstan set on kidnapping you. At the time I thought it fair. You would give me the opportunity to avenge my wife and daughter, and in return, I would give you all.'

Isabella was dumbfounded and, for one of the few times in her life, utterly speechless.

'Even now, I still think it a fair exchange. Isabella, you have given much to Dunstan and its people.'

'I cleaned your keep. That is all. Even that act was more for selfish reasons than anything else.'

'Your selfish act made the men remember they were supposed to be civilised and not barbaric animals, made the women more willing to return to the keep.'

'I cannot speak for the men, but the women came to work and were useful.'

'Useful? Is that what you call climbing around on ladders and doing work more fit for men?'

'I had no men to use. So we managed on our own.'

'And whose fault was that?'

'Yours.' She paused, then admitted, 'And mine.'

He patted her hand. 'I willingly share the blame in that. But trust that if need be, Conal and Matthew would keep you safe. You would lose nothing. They will fight for you, Isabella, the men will follow your orders. For the most part, they are good men. A little rough around the edges, but good men.'

'No. You and my father can decide this. Even he would not be so greedy as to permit you to give it all away.'

'Again, it is mine to give.'

She wasn't going to keep arguing this with him. He could do that with her sire, because she wasn't about to step into what was rightfully her father's place in this negotiation.

'Tell me, is this the same type of agreement you signed with Agnes?'

'No.' He looked down at her. 'We are sitting here before all that remains of the woman. Is there anything you wish to know?'

She turned her face away. There were many things she wished to know, but hadn't he had enough this day?

'I would rather get all of this behind us now.'

Sometimes she wondered how he so easily read her thoughts. She leaned her head against his arm. 'These grave markers, they are odd to me.'

'How so?'

'Richard, if I ask you something about your wife, will you answer me honestly?'

'Isabella, you know that if you ask me something, I will tell you the truth. So, if you ask me something, you'd better be ready to hear the answer.'

Was she ready? Probably not, but to put it all behind them, it had to be asked. 'Did you love her?'

'Yes. With all my heart.'

She closed her eyes. He'd warned her not to ask unless she was ready to hear the answer. But she'd gone ahead and asked anyway. So she had no one to blame for this sudden pain in her stomach, or her inability to swallow past the growing lump in her throat but herself.

He draped his arm around her and pulled her closer to his side. 'Until I learned that love is just a myth, a tale devised by troubadours to lure the foolish into believing their stories.'

'What happened to make you think that?'

'She never belonged to me. She belonged to another, but I didn't know that until it was too late. Her father didn't deem the other man worthy of his daughter. His need for fast gold didn't permit him time to consider his daughter's wants or desires.'

'Most people don't get the opportunity to choose their

spouses.' She laughed softly at the irony of her statement. She had been given the chance and she'd let it slip through her fingers, only to end up being forced into a marriage she hadn't wanted and now did.

'No, they don't. But unbeknownst to me, she'd already chosen her lover, months before she ended up in a marriage bed with me.' He nodded towards Lisette's stone. 'She wasn't my daughter.'

Shock froze her tongue for a minute. This was unheard of. Granted, her own father was a bastard, but his sire had been the king. For a woman to give birth to another man's child while that man still lived was more than adultery, it condemned not just the mother, but also the child to an unimaginable life. She'd heard stories of families setting the child aside—literally setting the newborn in the cold to die. 'And yet she bears your name.'

'What else should I have done? She was an innocent child. Nothing of what her mother had done could be placed at her feet. And by the time she was born, I wanted someone to love, someone to cherish.'

He looked down at her. 'Don't for one moment think I don't understand your need, Isabella. I do.'

'And Agnes?'

'Oh, she lied well at first. She was gentle, loving, kind and attentive to my face.'

'So, how did you find out it was lie?'

'Something seemed off, just a little wrong. Nothing major, an odd look, a distracted kiss, a small flinch at my touch, so I started watching and intercepted one of the monthly missives she'd supposedly written to her father.'

'It wasn't to her father, was it?'

'No. It was to her lover, telling him all about his child that she carried, how horrible it was to be in my presence, how sickened it made her whenever I so much as touched her and supplying him with enough information about Dunstan that he could have led an attack and succeeded in taking over my keep.'

How any woman could stoop so low was beyond her understanding. 'Oh, Richard, I am so sorry.'

'Yes, well, not as sorry as I.'

She was beginning to understand why he placed no faith in love. 'What happened after that?'

'Just what one would expect. She cried, swore it was over, promised to be a better wife. I was young and foolish enough to believe her.'

'And you gave her another chance?' Isabella could hardly imagine him doing so.

'Of course. Until right before Lisette was born and a missive from her lover found its way to my office at the warehouse.'

Isabella cringed.

'They had never stopped writing to each other. They made jokes about how gullible I was and how easy it was to lie to me. Worse, she had been sending him gold.'

'Your gold.'

'She had none of her own. He was saving it up to buy a ship and hire men to come kill me, so the two of them could marry and live on Dunstan as the lord and lady.'

'Oh, my.'

'That was nothing. When I confronted her, she turned into a shrew, spewing her hatred for me, my men, my keep. Everything I held dear became a target for her hate.'

'And Lisette?'

'It was worse for her, because I loved her so. Sometimes it would get so bad that I'd take the baby and we'd sleep aboard one of the ships.'

'And yet you flog yourself for not being here when Agnes was murdered. Why?'

'Because I refused to petition for a divorce based on a false claim of kinship, she remained my wife. It was my duty to keep her safe, no matter what.'

Isabella wanted to pull him into her arms and soothe the furrows from his brow. She took his hand and stood up. 'It's turning cold. Come, let's go back to the keep.'

He rose and stared at the gravestones. 'Do you know what the real horror is in all of this?'

The things that had been done to him weren't enough to be considered horrible? She leaned against his chest. 'No. Tell me.'

'The man she claimed to love and who claimed to love her, the man who was Lisette's true father, is the same man who killed them both.'

Isabella's knees buckled. From somewhere outside of her body, she watched as she slowly slipped to the ground at his feet.

Chapter Eighteen

A demon chased her. One with claws and glowing eyes. Blood dripped from his jagged teeth. He lunged at her.

'No!' Isabella awoke from the nightmare.

'Shhh. It's all right.' Gentle hands pulled her back down on to the bed.

She curled into the warmth of his chest, asking, 'How did we get here?'

Richard laughed softly. 'You do realise that you aren't that heavy, don't you?'

'You carried me?'

'Would you rather I'd left you in the mud?'

Snippets of their conversation at the cemetery flooded her mind until they filled in all the blank spaces. She rose up to stare down at him. 'Oh, Richard, I am so sorry. How can you stand the sight of me? How can you not despise me?'

'For what?' He slid his hand up her arm, across her shoulder, to rest against her neck. 'You have done nothing. You are most assuredly not responsible for Glenforde's actions.'

When she shook her head, he eased her down on to his chest, admonishing, 'Don't be foolish, Isabella.'

'Make him die slowly. Cut him into tiny pieces, one slice at a time.'

She felt his sigh before he said, 'You have overheard far too many conversations between the men.'

'It couldn't be helped. You were the one who told me to listen to gossip and who gossips more than the men?'

'I can't argue with that.' He rolled her over on to her back and propped up on his elbow to look at her. 'How are you feeling?'

'Like a fool for swooning like a spineless maiden.'

He curled his finger around a wayward wave resting over her shoulder. 'Other than that.'

She shrugged. 'Fine. I simply fainted. Which is odd considering I never faint.'

'You are certain?'

'Yes. Why?'

'I gave Conal the night to spend with his lady. Matthew needs to be relieved so he can check things at the wharf. So I need to take his place.'

'Can you not guard me just as well from here?'

He laughed. 'No. It would be too…distracting.'

She reached up to stroke his cheek. 'Richard, please.'

He grasped her hand and kissed her palm. 'No. It is best if we wait.'

Frowning in confusion, she asked, 'Wait? For what?'

'Until all of this is over.'

'What on earth for?'

'If anything goes wrong, Isabella, I wish not to leave you with a babe in your belly.'

She tore her hand from his and grabbed the front of his shirt. 'If you have any doubts about your victory, I suggest you wipe them from your mind right now. Otherwise you are just asking for something to go wrong.' She pulled him closer. 'Do you hear me?'

He blinked. Twice. Then peeled her fingers from his shirt. 'I am fairly certain I don't need you telling me how to fight.'

'Obviously someone needs to.'

He shoved himself off the bed. 'Are you seeking to anger me for any particular reason?'

'Anger you? No. I'm angry enough right now for the both of us. I am seeking to force you into getting your mind straight.'

He swiped his sword from the floor. 'I know how to use this.'

'I would hope so.'

He headed for the door. 'Fear not, I do.'

'Good! I am glad!'

He swung the door open and shouted back at her. 'Good!'

Isabella sat up and threw a goblet hard enough to bounce it off the closed door. Only to hear a fist pound on it twice from the other side.

She threw herself back down on the bed, closed her eyes and in the quiet chamber counted out loud, 'One. Two.'

The door slammed against the wall of the chamber. 'And another thing.' He stormed across the room and fell on to the bed atop of her.

She circled her arms around him, asking, 'Which other thing?'

'How did you know I wasn't angry?'

'By the look in your eyes and your shouting. You never shout when you're enraged. But, I could ask you the same thing.'

'And I would give you the same answer.' He trailed his tongue along her lips.

Isabella sighed. 'Do you truly have to go sit in the corridor all by yourself in the cold?'

'No. I could get the serving maid to come sit with me.'

She tugged a lock of his hair. 'Go ahead and try.'

He slipped his tongue between her parted lips, stroking and teasing until she moaned. With a lighter kiss, he said, 'Yes, I do have to go. And I fear I should do it now. Matthew is beside himself with worry over our shouting.'

'Ah, Matthew needs to stop being so serious all the time.'

'I'll be certain to tell him that.'

Isabella released him. 'Go.'

'If you need me, you know where to find me.'

'Goodnight, Richard.'

The sound of Hattie whistling as she moved about the chamber brought Isabella's eyes open. She squinted against the sunlight streaming in.

Hattie placed a gown across the foot of the bed. 'Oh, you are awake.'

Isabella didn't answer since that had been Hattie's reason for whistling in the first place.

'Lord Richard sent up a trunk from the warehouse. I had the men set it just inside the door.'

She swung her legs from beneath the covers and sat up on the edge of the bed. An odd aroma wafted across her nose, making her stomach gurgle suspiciously. 'What is that smell?'

'What smell?' Hattie came closer.

Isabella's stomach rolled and she slapped a hand over her mouth. She couldn't possibly have been poisoned again, she hadn't eaten or drunk anything. The chamber wasn't spinning like a top and her mouth didn't feel as if something furry had crawled around inside of it. She looked around the room and spied food on the small table in the alcove. 'What is that?'

It hit her a second before the woman answered. Moody as a fussy old woman, then fainting yesterday. Now sick to her stomach? No. Impossible. Well, perhaps not impossible since they did make love, but unlikely since they'd only done so a few times—three to be exact—once the night she'd been poisoned, Christmas Eve and Christmas night. Surely it took more times than that? She couldn't be pregnant.

Hattie rattled off the list of items on the table. 'It's just bread, cheese, some porridge and…' She paused to stare at Isabella and then smiled. 'Oh, goodness. Are you going to lose that wager? Will there be a babe before summer arrives?'

Keeping her hand over her mouth, Isabella shook her head, hoping to disabuse the woman of such a notion. If she was correct, the child wouldn't arrive until the end of summer, meaning she would prove those holding the wagers wrong—Richard hadn't taken any liberties before they were wed.

Hattie rushed into the alcove and came back with the crust from the bread and a cup of water. 'Eat this. Slowly. Then lie back down for a few minutes. I'll have Mistress Marguerite get you some ginger root.'

Isabella nibbled on the bread. 'This can't be happening now.'

As Hattie went to the door, Isabella called out, 'Wait. Who is out there on guard duty?'

'Sir Conal.'

'No. No. Don't say anything to him.'

Hattie walked back towards the bed. 'My lady?'

'I want to be the one to tell Richard, later. After…' She trailed off, uncertain how many of the details Hattie knew about Richard's intentions.

'After he deals with Glenforde?'

'Yes.' She sighed with relief at not having to come up with some story that she'd not be able to remember a day from now.

Hattie frowned, making Isabella worry the woman wouldn't see her point, but then the frown disappeared. 'I won't say that I like it, but I do understand your reasoning.'

'Thank you.'

'Well, Lady Isabella, you best hope it happens soon, because you won't be able to keep this a secret very long.'

If she truly was with child, and this wasn't some sort of joke nature was playing on her, the last thing she wanted to do was keep it a secret. She wanted to shout it from the battlements.

Time would tell.

She eyed the domed trunk near the door and quickly dressed, shoving her feet into her stockings and shoes, while Hattie tried to braid her hair at the same time.

Once dressed, Isabella walked over to the trunk. She ran a hand over the travel chest, admiring the workmanship. Domed so any water would run off and wrapped in waxed leather to protect the goods inside.

Unbuckling the leather straps, she lifted the lid, letting it fall backwards as she gasped at her first glance of the contents. She dropped to her knees to slowly pull out one item at a time.

Finely woven linens and wool fabrics were folded inside. Some lengths were sun-bleached, some left natural and a few were dyed the most wonderful shades of blues and greens. There was enough fabric to make clothing for at least five people.

When she'd considered asking to borrow money for cloth, she'd never dreamed of purchasing this much. She brushed the soft linen against her cheek—nor had she dreamed of anything this fine.

Beneath the linen and wool was a separately wrapped package. Isabella laid it on her lap to unfold the soft leather—the wrapper alone was fine enough to use for clothing items. She peeled back the last fold and blinked at the brilliant green, almost emerald, cloth.

'Hattie.' She called the woman over. 'Is this what I think it is?'

Almost afraid to touch the fabric, for fear of ruining it, she wiped her hands on her gown and then ran the tip of one finger along the edge.

Hattie touched the length. Picking up a corner she inspected it, then declared, 'Silk.'

'What am I supposed to do with silk?'

'Make a gown, I'd imagine.'

'With silk?' And then for what event would she wear the gown? She'd never had a garment made of silk before, there'd never been a need. She wasn't certain her parents owned anything made of silk and they'd attended court more than once in her lifetime.

She rose to stretch the length of silk carefully across the bed. It hung over the far side and had she dropped her end, it would have fallen on to the floor. There appeared to be enough fabric for two gowns—or a gown for her and a formal tunic for Richard.

Since the fabric was unadorned, she could embellish it in any manner she desired. Isabella picked at a corner with a fingernail. She was certain the tightly woven threads would ensure whatever she decided to make would last a long time.

'Lady Isabella, look.' Hattie pulled strips of embroidery work from the chest.

Isabella ran her fingers through the embellished strips. As if the silk wasn't enough of a luxury, these pre-embroidered pieces would save immeasurable time.

She looked at the bottom of the chest to find everything she would need—from pins and needles to shears for cutting the cloth, smaller scissors for snipping threads and an array of flaxen threads dyed to match every colour of fabric she'd received.

He'd lavished far too much on her. If his warehouses were anything like those on Warehaven, they were full of costly, precious goods. Goods meant to be sold or bartered at other ports. The value of the silk alone would feed the people in the keep for over a season. She shouldn't accept this, she should make him put it back in his inventory.

Isabella lovingly ran her hand over the silk and brought the soft linen to her cheek once again. Perhaps, if she used everything carefully, making certain to put each inch to proper use, she could make both of them clothes that would last for years, ensuring his inventory hadn't been squandered.

She needed a place to sew. Looking around, she decided that with a chamber the size of this one, it shouldn't be too hard to make space for a workroom.

'Hattie, have a couple of the men bring up a table and bench.' She walked around the chamber, until sunlight fell across her face. 'We'll set it up here, beneath the window opening.'

'That is not necessary.'

Isabella disagreed. 'There is no better place.'

Hattie walked to the door, beckoning. 'Follow me.'

Intrigued and a bit confused, Isabella trailed behind the woman. Instead of turning left outside of the chamber door, Hattie went to the right. She walked past the first door, but swung open the door to the chamber at the end of the hall.

Isabella stopped outside the chamber. 'Richard gave orders not to open these two chambers. What have you done?'

From behind her, Conal said, 'He changed his mind last night. A couple of the women and some of the men worked all night to remove the bed and clean the chamber as best they could. I am surprised their attempt didn't waken you.'

She took a few tentative steps into the room. With an additional window, even more sunlight streamed into the chamber. Between the two far windows there were two padded armchairs with matching footrests, a small round table sat between.

Curtains draped the entrance to the alcove. A long cushioned bench lined the back wall inside.

While the walls of the chamber lacked a fresh wash of paint, they were clean. The floor shined as if it were newly polished.

'Will it suffice?' Conal asked.

'Oh, yes. It is perfect.'

'Good, because that clatter coming from the stairwell is the men bringing up a table and benches.'

It didn't take long for the men to set up a trestle table and to drag the domed chest from her bedchamber into this one. To Isabella's delight, two of the kitchen maids came up to ask if she'd mind letting them help in their spare time. They loved to sew, but rarely got the chance any more.

She welcomed the offer of assistance, knowing that if she was left to do it alone she'd quickly run out of excitement for the task and would still be sewing garments come next winter.

The light had faded before she realised the morning that had given way to afternoon was now turning to night. She'd spent the entire day measuring, cutting, piecing, pinning and sewing.

Pushing away from the table and up from the chair, she

stretched before leaving the sewing chamber to head to the Great Hall and help set up the evening meal.

She stopped in the corridor outside the door to speak to Conal. 'I never said thank you.'

He slowly brought his lumbering frame up from the floor and shook his head, sending the wildly curled mass of red hair flying. 'For what?'

'For helping with this.' She waved towards the door. 'And for seeing to my safety. I do appreciate it.'

'You're Richard's wife, of course I would see to your safety.'

'Even so, I still thank you. It's almost time to eat, so I'll see you below.'

She nearly skipped down the stairs. For the first time in what seemed ages, she felt…happy.

'Lady Isabella?'

Surprised to see Father Paul in the keep, she paused at the bottom of the stairs. He hadn't shown his face here since the Christmas feast, so she found it odd. 'Father Paul, can I help you with something? Would you care to join us for the meal?'

'No, no. I just wanted to ask you if you had a chance to look over your marriage contract?'

'Oh, yes I have.' He'd probably been as shocked by it as she had. 'And I assure you, it will be changing soon.'

'I assumed that would be the case. But there were a few things I wanted to go over with you, it won't take but a minute.'

She waved towards the high table where the chairs were already in place. 'Certainly, why don't we have a seat?'

He looked around and then wrinkled his brow. 'I would prefer somewhere more private. It is a lovely night. Can we not just step outside away from this throng of curious ears?'

Isabella glanced over her shoulder and didn't see Conal behind her. Richard had told her to trust no one other than Conal and Matthew. He hadn't mentioned Father Paul in that short list, so she wasn't certain leaving the keep with him was a wise idea.

'I'm not sure.' She motioned behind her. 'I'm not supposed to leave without Sir Conal and I don't know how Richard would feel about this.'

'I completely understand. But I am certain your guard only stopped to use the privy. Fear not, Lady Isabella. I can put you at ease.' Father Paul called over one of Dunstan's men. 'My good sir. When he comes down, could you tell Sir Conal that I have taken Lady Dunstan just outside into the bailey for a word. We'll be right outside the doors.' He turned back to her. 'Will that ease your worries?'

Something prompted her to say no. But he looked so sincere and with one of Dunstan's men standing by to let Conal know where she was, what would be the harm? Isabella motioned towards the double doors. 'Lead the way.'

She followed him outside, glad that he'd been correct about the mildness of the weather. While there was a slight nip in the air, it wasn't frigid. And while the breeze in the bailey might make it feel colder, here in one of Dunstan's countless small courtyards, they were protected from the ocean wind.

Father Paul didn't slow his stride. Instead of stopping just outside the door as he'd suggested, he kept walking.

'Father Paul, isn't this private enough?'

He stopped and came back to her side. With a pointed nod, he tipped his head towards a small gathering of women. 'I wish them not to overhear business meant for the Lady of Dunstan.'

She rolled her eyes. Now he was worried about how things looked or sounded? 'Fine, let us go.'

She glanced back at the women to see if they'd taken offence at the priest's words and spotted Matthew standing off to the side. He held a finger to his lips, silently telling her not to alert anyone to his presence.

Isabella stumbled, but quickly regained her footing. Dear Lord, not the priest. Father Paul was the man seeking to kill her? A man of God? No. It couldn't be.

'Are you coming?' He'd paused in front of the postern gate. The portcullis was raised.

'Yes. Yes. I stumbled over my feet, a clumsy habit I have.'

'That is understandable as the ground is uneven in these godforsaken courtyards.'

Isabella raised a brow at his insult. She liked these courtyards and had every intention of planting roses along the wall come spring. Some of those trailing ones like Marguerite had along the one wall of her cottage garden.

They would smell wonderful and look beautiful as they climbed up the wall here. Isabella's gaze followed her thoughts and met the frigid sapphire glare of one guard peering over the wall at her.

Even if he was dressed as a guard, she recognised that glare well. And from the complete lack of visible emotion, he was livid and very dangerous.

She quickly lowered her gaze. Someone would die this night at Dunstan. From the resolve etched on her husband's face, she was certain it wouldn't be her.

'Come, my lady. We can talk right out here.' Father Paul took her elbow to lead her under the gate and out into the bailey.

Now her legs trembled. But she wasn't certain if it was from fear of Father Paul, or Richard's anger.

She moved her arm, to free herself from the priest's hold, but he tightened his grasp and whistled.

Instantly a man led two horses to them. Father Paul shoved her towards the now-mounted rider, who easily grabbed hold of her wrist. She recognised him as Father Paul's deacon at the church. Both men of God were involved in this?

'No!' Isabella struggled. 'Release me!' She dragged her feet and hung from his hold, making herself as heavy as possible, so he couldn't pull her up on to the horse.

At her first scream the heavy portcullis to the main gates started to groan as they were lowered to close off the only escape from the inner yard.

The bailey, which a heartbeat ago had seemed empty, now appeared to fill with men. Armed men.

A strangled gasp from the man holding her wrist drew her attention back to him. His hold instantly fell away as he frantically waved his hands at the arrow sticking through his shoulder. She hit the ground, quickly scrambling away from the horse's shod hooves.

Father Paul's shoulders slumped. He dropped the reins to his horse and stood there.

A hard hand grasped her upper arm, dragged her to her feet and shoved her against Conal's chest. 'To your chamber.'

'Richard, I—'

He didn't spare her a glance, instead he turned away to deal with Father Paul.

Conal put his hands on her shoulders to spin her around and pushed her towards the keep. When she dug in her heels, he paused long enough to ask, 'Are you going to walk like a woman, or am I going to toss you over my shoulder like a sack of grain?'

'You would shame me in such a manner before all of Dunstan?'

'In a heartbeat.'

She stormed towards the keep, shouting, 'You're as bad as he is.'

'No. I'm worse.' He caught up to her, to add, 'Because, at the moment, I don't care about your tender heart.'

When they entered the Great Hall, he placed one large hand on the centre of her back and pushed her directly to the stairs. She felt every pair of eyes glued to her. She swore she could hear their curious thoughts wondering what she'd done.

Isabella kept her chin high, refusing to bow beneath the stares and marched up the steps to her chamber.

Conal opened the door and pushed her inside. Before closing the door he suggested, 'Don't grovel, that will only set him off more.'

She stared at the closed door. Grovel? What made him think she'd ever grovelled before anyone?

No, there were no worries on that. She'd not grovel. She would simply explain why she'd left the keep with Father Paul and he would understand the dilemma she had faced.

Doubtful.

To keep her hands and mind busy, she went to the chest of linens in the corner and pulled a bedcover out. She spread the cover on the bed and then refolded it. She repeated her actions until she heard the distinct sound of heavy boots heading up the stairs.

Her pulse quickened, certain from the determined stride it was Richard. She looked down at her hands to reassure herself that she was in complete control of her emotions.

The chamber door banged against the wall, making her jump. Isabella turned around and gasped at the stranger barging into her bedchamber.

His frown was so fierce that it seemed to form a single line above his eyes.

She knew instantly that the crazed berserker stalking

her was her husband, but she backed away from the fiery blaze of his steady stare until her retreat was stopped by a solid wall. All of her calmness fled. 'I had no choice.'

Still intent on explaining, she continued, 'He made everything seem so normal. What else was I going to do?'

He didn't appear to be listening to her. She pointed a wavering finger at him. 'You never told me he was one of the men you were watching, so how was I to know?'

He didn't answer. Instead, he flung his cloak on to the bed, tore the sleeveless tunic bearing Dunstan's colours over his head and dropped it to the floor.

She held her hands up, as if they'd offer any protection and tried once more to reason with him. 'He said we were only going right outside the doors.'

He lunged at her, shoving her arms aside and pinned her against the wall.

Before she could say anything else, before she could even so much as catch her breath, he claimed her mouth in a kiss that curled her toes and set her mind spinning.

His face was cold. His fingers, tearing at the laces of her gown, shoving the fabric off her shoulders, were nearly freezing. But his kiss…his kiss was, oh, so hot.

She shivered when the cool air of the chamber rushed across her naked shoulders. Their tongues tangled and she moaned softly, forgetting her intention to calmly explain herself to him.

He answered her with a throaty growl, roughly pulling her gown and shift down her arms until they slid to pool at her feet. He then picked her up and deposited her naked on the bed.

Before she could complain of the cold, he was on the bed, pushing her legs apart to shatter her thoughts with his mouth.

Isabella tugged at his hair. When he grasped both of

her wrists with one hand she had no choice but to let the out-of-control spiralling quickly take her over the edge.

'Richard!' she cried out. 'Please.' Wanting more than just the wickedly wonderful feel of his mouth, she wanted him to fill her.

He released her wrists and loomed over her. Grasping her chin firmly, he glared down at her.

Startled by the fierce glimmer in his eyes and the hard line of his mouth, she touched his cheek, whispering, 'What?'

'You were perfect.'

She frowned, uncertain what she'd done to be described as perfect.

He released her chin, wrapped his arms tightly about her as he entered her, claiming harshly, 'I have been worried sick that when the moment came, you would give all away.'

She returned his desperate embrace and managed to choke out a strangled, 'Thank you,' before her tears mixed with her laughter.

Laughter of relief at his declaration when she'd been so certain he was angry, and tears because the heart others had declared too tender was shattering from the pain of unreturned love. It was lost. Well and truly lost without any chance of ever saving it from hurt now or in the future.

From the way he made love to her, she wondered if perhaps his heart wasn't as unaffected as he claimed.

Even if that were true, she knew that she would never hear the words from his lips. But perhaps, if she listened closely, she could some day hear the whisperings of his heart.

Richard grumbled something she couldn't quite make out, but she completely understood his growl against her lips. He'd sensed her wandering mind and wanted her full attention.

She curled her legs around his waist, more than willing to give him all the attention he desired.

Through a clouded haze of pure lust, Richard couldn't remember a time when he'd ever wanted a woman as much as he did his wife right now. He knew there was nothing tender, nothing gentle in his touch, or his kiss.

He'd watched the priest closely this day and knew by the man's odd comings and goings that he was planning something. Hours of worry had chased away his ability to be easy. He knew she was safe, and well, but he needed to hear her cry out with abandonment.

From the tightness of her legs wrapped about his waist and the way her body met his, he doubted if his wife was feeling ill used. Still, he forced himself to rein in the unbridled lust, to regain some measure of control.

Chilled to the bone, he shivered. Gathering her closer, he let the heat of her body seep into him, warming him and chasing away his inexplicable concern for her well-being.

Richard groaned in frustration. It wasn't enough to just be skin to skin, he needed to be closer. But the way to accomplish that oneness he craved glimmered just beyond his reach.

Troubled by his inability to fulfil this unnatural need, he focused on the spiralling physical need driving him on.

Isabella curled her fingers into his back and arched her hips, seeking release from her own needs. He let his wavering control slip, quickly bringing them both to completion.

Unable to breathe past the hard pounding of his heart, he rolled off of her, kicking the cloak off the end of the bed.

Isabella placed a hand on his chest and laughed weakly. 'This can't be good for our hearts.'

He lifted her hand to his lips, kissed her palm and then lowered their locked hands back on to his chest. 'If this is the way I must die, at least I will meet my maker with a smile on my face.'

Once he regained his breath, he asked, 'Did you receive the chest of fabric?'

'Yes, I did.' She slipped her hand from beneath his and sat up to look at him. 'Thank you, but you needn't have taken so much from your inventory.'

He guessed from her cocked eyebrow that she was about to berate him. Seeking to stave off an argument, he said, 'I wasn't aware that I suddenly needed someone to manage my inventory.'

'I—'

He grabbed her shoulders to pull her back down against him. 'Not tonight, Isabella. This may well be our last night together.'

She drew lazy circles on his chest with her fingertips. 'And why is that?'

'Your father's ship is anchored off the coast.'

'Ship? As in one?'

'Yes.'

'No.' She sat back up. 'That is not right.'

'I thought the same thing. It made no sense that FitzHenry would come to rescue the granddaughter of a king without an army at his back.'

'Have you checked the cove?'

He stared at her, wondering what had made her decide he was suddenly too dense to protect his own island and people. 'No. I never would have thought to check the one place Dunstan had proven vulnerable in the past.'

'Truce.' She held up a hand. 'I am sorry. Of course the cove is guarded. What will you do now?'

Richard groaned. 'There isn't much I can do until they disembark from the ship.'

Isabella ran a hand down his arm. 'You need not fear

my father.' When he stared at her, she at least had the decency to wince at the foolishness of her claim before adding, 'True, the two of you will most likely exchange blows along with a great many angry words, but once he knows I am safe and well, he will listen to reason. He may not like it, but he'll listen to it.'

'So while he and I argue, his force will seek to lay waste to my ships, warehouses and village. Little comfort there, Isabella.'

'No. His men will not raise a sword until they are ordered to do so. And they will not be given that order until my father knows of my well-being first. I guarantee you that he will not recklessly risk my life in such a manner. My mother would not stand for it.'

Before he could respond, the sounds of battle floated up from outside. Richard rushed to the window to tear back the covering.

He watched as flaming arrows flew across the battlements, setting one of the outbuildings on fire.

A heavy pounding beat on the chamber door. Richard waved at Isabella to cover herself, and called out, 'Enter.'

Conal burst into the room. 'We are under attack.'

'Don't let them burn the place down. Open the damn gates and meet them head on.'

Conal headed back downstairs, shouting orders before he'd hit the stairs.

Richard picked up the clothing he'd tossed on the floor, pulling each piece on as he retrieved it.

'You aren't going to give them entrance?' Isabella held the covers to her neck.

'Yes. Do you think it could be your brother?'

She shook her head. 'No. My father would not risk the sole heir to his shipping empire so foolishly.' She frowned, then said, 'I don't know how it would be possible, my father never would have given him command of a ship willingly, but I suppose it could be Glenforde.'

'We'll know soon enough.' Richard tugged on his boots. At her quickly indrawn breath, he explained, 'There is one ship. It can only hold thirty to maybe forty men.'

'If that many.'

'Most of Dunstan's men are inside the walls. They can easily dispatch them to their maker.'

'They disembarked ready to fight.' She pointedly ran her stare down his body. 'And they are protected by armour.'

'Then I guess I need be more alert. Stay here.' He strapped on his sword as he headed for the door. 'Bolt the door behind me.'

Chapter Nineteen

Isabella scrambled from the bed and hastily dressed. Laces to her gown half-undone, her hair in disarray, she opened the chamber door and slowly stuck her head out to listen.

The sound of clashing swords lessened, as if fewer and fewer men were engaged in combat. She leaned back inside the chamber, turning her attention towards the open window. Gone were the earlier shouts of men.

Unable to bear not knowing the outcome of this brief battle, she stepped into the corridor and paused to listen to the sound of two men arguing—rather, one arguing, the other seemingly goading the first one on.

While she didn't need to see the men to know that the second one, with the deeper and decidedly steadier voice, was her husband, she did want to discover the identity of the other man. With her back against the wall, she side-stepped to the stairs.

'Give me my woman, Dunstan.'

Isabella bit hard on her lower lip to keep from screaming.

Glenforde had arrived, ahead of her father. Something was mostly definitely wrong. As she'd told Richard, her father never would have given an unseasoned sailor command of any of his ships—not even one of the small river barges. Nor did she believe for one heartbeat that her father would not have come to Dunstan in person. It wasn't in his nature to permit someone else to stand in his place.

She needed to go down there. Isabella stepped away from the wall and looked down at her gown. But not like this. Glenforde would think she'd been made a prisoner, or worse, if she appeared at Richard's side looking like a well-used whore.

'Pssst.' From the shadows on the other side of the stairs, Hattie tried to get her attention.

Isabella pointed at the door of her chamber and the maid nodded. They both hurried as quickly and quietly as possible into the bedchamber. Hattie dropped the bar across the door, while Isabella tossed back the lid of her clothes chest.

There wasn't much to choose from: the gown she'd worn when taken from Warehaven had been patched, even the patches had been patched, the one she wore now was torn and filthy from tussling in the bailey, or there was a deep forest-green one that she'd worn at Christmas.

'Too bad you have no court clothes.'

She shook her head at Hattie's lament. 'No. The last thing I want to do is have Glenforde think I dressed for him.'

The tunic Richard had dropped on the floor caught her eyes. She pulled the green gown from the chest and retrieved the tunic. 'These will do nicely.'

'What do you want with a guard's tunic?'

She held it up against the green gown. 'The colours, Hattie. Dunstan's colours.'

'Oh, that'll be sure to get him riled.'

'That is the plan.' Isabella tugged at her gown. 'Help me.'

With Hattie's help she was dressed in short order and

sat on a bench, scrubbing a wet rag across the dirt on her face, while the older woman combed and captured her wild hair into a matronly plait down her back, complete with blue-and-green ribbons giving her hair a splash of Dunstan to help get the point across—she was Dunstan's.

Rising, she pulled the tunic over her head, laughing at the length. The man's short tunic fell to her knees. Hattie draped a girdle made of golden links low around her waist, then reached into the pouch hanging from her side. 'You might want this.' She handed Isabella the wedding band she had thrown at Richard on the night of their marriage.

'Where did you find it?'

'Lord Richard pressed it into my hand on his way down the steps a few moments ago. He said the choice was yours.'

He still thought there was a choice in this? Isabella slid it on to the ring finger of her left hand, then asked, 'Ready?'

'No. But there'll be no putting it off.'

Hattie fell into step behind her, wringing her hands and muttering under her breath.

Isabella did her best to ignore the woman, pausing at the top of the stairs to place a hand over her grumbling belly and take a deep breath before heading down the stairs with as much dignity befitting the Lady of Dunstan and a daughter of Warehaven.

'I'll not tell you again, Warehaven's bitch is mine.'

She arrived at the bottom step in time to say, 'I am sure Cecilia would disagree.'

As calmly as possible, she'd made a reference to her father's breeding bitch. The hunting hound had bit Glenforde twice, drawing blood both times. Obviously, everyone should have taken heed of the dog's warning.

Both men turned to stare at her. Richard's eyelids lowered slightly, his mouth lifted into that come-hither smile that made her want to act a fool.

Glenforde's eyes narrowed in what appeared to Isabella as outrage. He took a step towards her. 'Thank God, we have been so worried about you.'

'We?' She made a show of looking around the Great Hall. 'I don't see anyone here but you. However did you manage to arrive ahead of my father?'

He shrugged. 'The rudder on his ship broke and I wasn't willing to wait while he made repairs, so I came ahead. Oh, Isabella, I was so anxious to get to you.'

The sound of her name coming out of his mouth made her want to gag and she doubted his tale of a broken rudder. Her father's ships were always inspected. A broken rudder didn't just happen unexpectedly. At her prolonged silence, Glenforde took another step closer. She fisted her hands at her side.

Thankfully, Conal got to her first and offered his arm. 'My lady.'

She tried not to roll her eyes at his overly formal manner and asked softly, 'How fare the village and the men?'

'The village is intact. One man lost, one injured. Marguerite is seeing to his wounds.' He handed her off to Richard and took up a position behind them.

Richard squeezed her fingers lightly before placing them on his forearm. 'I told you to stay upstairs,' he said, in a whisper meant only for her.

She placed her left hand atop of his, making certain to thumb the ring so it spun on her finger, drawing his attention. 'My place is here.'

Isabella glanced around at the upturned tables and benches, then asked, 'What have you done to my hall?'

When he didn't answer, Conal replied over her shoulder, 'Bit of a disagreement.'

Glenforde raked her from head to toe with his stare. 'You seem whole.'

'Why would I be otherwise?'

'You were taken captive, kidnapped—how were we to know what treatment you'd endure?'

She saw no point in dancing around the truth. 'Please, spare us your lies. Everyone in this chamber knows full well I was taken as bait to lure you back to Dunstan. And now, here you are.'

'Yes, here I am.' Glenforde eyed her carefully. 'And there you are, dressed in his colours, toying with his ring upon your finger. Tell me, whore, did he make as good a lover as I did?'

She felt Richard's arm tense beneath her touch and wanted to scream at him not to listen to the lies. Instead, she confronted Glenforde directly. 'Since I have never shared your bed, it is impossible to make a comparison.'

'You can do so after we wed.'

'I am already wed.'

Surrounded by men who would gladly see him dead, Glenforde drew his sword, announcing, 'Then it seems I must make you a widow first.'

Richard wanted to laugh in his face, but first he needed to make sure Isabella was under control. When she opened her mouth to respond to Glenforde's threat, Richard said, 'Enough,' and pushed her against Conal's chest, ordering, 'hold her.'

He ignored what sounded like her hiss of displeasure. But he didn't care, this was not her fight. Her part in this was over.

Richard tapped the blade of his sword against his leg. 'Since we have witnesses, yours and mine, gathered, why don't you explain to everyone exactly what this is about?'

He wanted to hear Glenforde's confession, wanted all

to know how vile this man truly was and what harm he had brought to Dunstan, before he ran his sword through Glenforde's black heart.

'You wronged me first, Dunstan.'

'Did I now? Let's bring your brother into this conversation, he had a different story that I'm sure he'd like to share.'

Matthew dragged Father Paul into the Great Hall. Isabella and Hattie gasped in surprise. Richard had been shocked at first, too. But it explained much. He'd been betrayed by the man who had helped him devise this plan to get Glenforde back here, the same man that everyone on the island had trusted since his arrival just under seven years ago—after Agnes had requested a full-time priest take up residence on Dunstan. When she'd offered up the name of a priest she knew and trusted well, Richard had had no reason to think otherwise.

He pointed his weapon at Father Paul. 'Go on, tell everyone how I wronged Glenforde first.'

'You didn't, my lord.' The man had the decency to hang his head. 'You didn't know she was in love with another until it was too late.'

'And who helped Agnes remain in touch with her lover?'

'I did.'

'Who saw to it that they were able to share personal, intimate moments alone while I was at sea?'

'I did.'

'Now, tell us why you would do such a traitorous thing.'

'Because he is my brother.'

'Enough of this.' Glenforde shoved Father Paul aside. 'I can speak for myself.'

Richard smiled. 'And I would welcome your explanation.'

'How many men have you killed, Dunstan?' Glenforde jabbed his weapon towards Richard.

Unwilling to die, or be seriously injured so soon in this fight, Richard stepped back from Glenforde's reach. 'Outside of battle, none have died by my hand.'

'You are a ship owner. I doubt if you have been in so many battles that you cannot remember them.'

Richard shrugged as he and Glenforde circled each other in the centre of the hall. 'I try not to take the memories of battles off the field.'

'There is one I am sure you didn't forget. Northallerton.'

Richard's stomach churned. Yes, he remembered that battle. It had been his first experience at taking another man's life. For nearly two hours they'd fought King David's men hand to hand. Many had fallen that day. 'That was years ago. Why speak of it now?'

Glenforde swung his sword and Richard stepped into the blow, blocking the other man's blade with his own. Their blades slid along the other until the guards met, bringing them nearly nose to nose. 'Do you remember puking after you severed a man's head from his body?'

Richard shoved free. Unfortunately, yes, he did remember that, too. He'd taken his share of lives that day, but that one had been the first.

'No!' Father Paul's shout rang in the Great Hall. 'He killed Alan?'

'Yes.' Glenforde's lip curled in a snarl. 'Our brother died because of this man's lust for blood.'

'Lust for blood? It was a battle. All there followed their commander's orders.'

Glenforde lunged towards him again. 'Alan was but twenty.'

'And I was sixteen.'

'His wife had just had a baby and no returning husband.' Raising his sword over his head, Glenforde brought it down, missing Richard as he spun away. 'While you came home to marry my betrothed, I was tasked with taking my brother, my dead brother who I watched you kill, home to his wife and child.'

While that explained Glenforde's anger, it didn't justify what he'd done to Agnes and Lisette. 'So, instead of coming after me, you took your rage out on an innocent woman and child?'

'Innocent?' Glenforde's high-pitched shout grated against Richard's ears.

The man came at him again, swinging his sword wildly. Thankfully, Richard was quick enough on his feet to keep out of the blade's way. At the rate Glenforde fought, he would wear himself out quickly. 'Did you know she was again with child?'

Surprised by that piece of information, Richard said, 'It wasn't mine.'

'Nor was it mine. She took great delight in telling me so, over and over, even after I had taste of what she thought to keep from me.'

'You were surprised that the whore slept with another man? You found that reason enough to rape her and then take a knife to her?' Richard ducked away from another swing of his opponent's weapon.

'No. She was already dead by the time I carved her up.'

No sane man would have reacted so violently. Respond in anger at that sort of news? Yes. Leave her? Yes. Rape and kill her? Never.

'And had that little brat done as I said and shut her mouth she might still be alive. But, no, she kept screaming for you. Had I not stopped her, the entire island would have heard her.' Glenforde rushed him, aiming the point of his sword at Richard's neck.

Richard sidestepped and swung his fist, making contact with Glenforde's mouth as he came close. 'She was just a baby.'

'What do you care? She wasn't even yours.'

As he expected, Glenforde was now trying to make him angry enough to lose focus. It wouldn't work.

'Just like that one over there isn't yours. At least she won't be once you're dead.' Glenforde laughed. 'I can't wait to teach her how to be a proper, obedient wife.'

Richard narrowed his eyes. He'd see Glenforde in hell before he'd allow the man to touch one hair on Isabella's head. 'Bold talk for a coward.'

'Coward?' Glenforde grasped his sword with both hands. 'I'll show you a coward.'

The man came at him, swinging his weapon in a chopping motion like it was a battleaxe. Richard backed away, leading them in an ever-narrowing circle, making sure the sharp swords were nowhere near the onlookers gathered along the walls.

Glenforde's blade came close enough that Richard felt the whoosh of air as the weapon barely missed the side of his head. He heard Isabella's gasp and the distinct sound of flesh meeting flesh. He could only assume Conal had quickly slapped his hand over her mouth.

When Glenforde screamed in rage at yet again missing his intended target, Richard knew it was time to end this before the man directed his anger towards an innocent bystander. And before he, too, became tired enough to make what could be a fatal mistake.

He planted his feet and beckoned Glenforde to charge him. 'Come, it is time to join your beloved Agnes.'

'Wade, no!' Father Paul rushed forward, trying to stop his brother from walking into what would be his death by putting himself between the two men.

But Glenforde was moving too fast and was unable to stop his momentum in time. His sword sliced through his brother's unprotected chest. Father Paul fell to the floor, dead before his fall was completed.

Without sparing a moment for the brother he'd just killed, Glenforde jerked his weapon free and slashed at Richard.

He held his ground, deflecting the blows until the muscles of his arms and shoulders burned with the effort.

Then Glenforde made a mistake. He turned his gaze from Richard, towards Isabella. The moment he took a step in her direction, Richard rammed his blade home.

Glenforde's weapon fell from his hand. He stared at Richard and whispered, 'She was mine.'

He hung on to the weapon as Glenforde crumpled to the floor, a look of surprise frozen on his face for all eternity.

With a foot on Glenforde's chest, Richard pulled his blade free and tossed it across the room. He stood over the dead man. Why did he feel no satisfaction in Glenforde's death? Why wasn't he consumed by relief now that he'd doled out his revenge?

No, it wasn't relief or satisfaction flooding him. It was guilt.

Guilt for everything he'd done of late. Glenforde's last words echoed in his mind. *'She was mine.'*

Yes, he'd been right. Agnes was his and Richard had no right marrying her. No right keeping her confined to this island once he'd discovered she belonged to another.

'She was mine.'

Yes, she had been his. And so had Isabella.

It didn't matter if in the end Isabella would have wed Glenforde or not, she deserved the choice.

She been forced into a situation not of her making and he'd been the one who had done the forcing.

No, it wasn't relief or satisfaction he felt. It was guilt and shame.

He had to make this right. The only thing left of this thirst for vengeance was Isabella, an innocent in this entire plot. He had to make things right for her. Otherwise, he'd not be able to live himself.

'Richard.' A gentle touch, a soft voice floated through the fog swirling about him. Yet he had no wish to deal with Isabella until he could decide how to do right by her. He shrugged off her touch and searched the hall. Finding Conal, he gritted his teeth a moment and then said, 'Get her out of here.'

'Richard!'

He heard her scream as Conal took her to the stairs.

'Richard, please, I love you.'

He heard her declaration as he slammed his chamber door behind him.

Love. What did she know of love? Nothing. He'd done well in teaching her lust, and desire, but nothing of love.

How could he when he didn't believe in love?

But Isabella did. He knew that and suddenly that fact made all the difference in the world to him. She deserved the chance to find this love she so craved.

Her connections were mighty. She was the granddaughter of a king. Surely Rome would grant her a divorce and permit her to marry someone else.

Richard's chest tightened at that thought. He shook off the regret teasing him. This was the right thing to do. The only fair thing he could do. Some day, Isabella would see that.

Isabella sat on the edge of her bed and waited, just as she had for nearly the entire night. And still he didn't come.

What had she done to anger him so?

She knew that at first he'd most likely been busy clearing the bodies from the hall, and rounding up Glenforde's remaining men, but surely that wouldn't have taken all night?

A knock on the door made her jump. 'Enter.'

Conal and Matthew entered the chamber. Neither looked as if they'd found any rest during the night. But they were more than simply tired, they looked...sad...distraught.

'Lady Isabella.' Conal stepped forward. 'Your father's ships will dock within the hour. You need to meet him at the quay.'

She rose. She'd looked forward to this for so long, yet now that the moment had arrived, she longed for more time. 'Richard will meet me there?'

'No. I will escort you.' Matthew twisted his hat in his hands. 'You need pack what things you want to take with you back to Warehaven. Two of the chamber maids will be along to help.'

Her heart seemed to freeze in her chest. 'The only thing I wish to take is Richard.'

'Isabella, that isn't going to happen.' Conal sighed. 'He wants you gone.'

'And he couldn't be bothered to tell me that himself?' She tried to fight through the pain lashing her. 'Where is he?'

The two men looked at each other. Finally, Conal stepped aside. 'His chamber.'

As she marched by them, Matthew touched her shoulder. 'He will not change his mind.'

She stared up at the man, noticing that her vision was clouded. She hoped it was from rage and not tears. 'I deserve an explanation.'

The two maids met her halfway down the stairs. Isabella paused long enough to say, 'Use the smaller chest to store my clothes and the fabric. That is all.'

She wanted nothing else. Just the things she'd worn here and the fabric he'd taken from his warehouse inventory specifically for her. She would use it for the baby.

Everyone in the Great Hall paused to look at her as she came off the last step. She turned to them to ask, 'You have nothing else to do?'

Thankfully, they all hung their heads and went about their tasks.

Isabella didn't pause to knock on his chamber door, she shoved the door open and crossed the room to the rear door, shoving through that one, too.

He rose from the bed as she entered. Only to be knocked back down on to the mattress when she shoved against his chest, shouting, 'What is wrong with you?'

'I didn't think you would take leaving here this hard. You are going home, isn't that what you've always wanted?'

His sarcastic tone did not fit the anger shimmering from his eyes. She couldn't quite put her finger on it, but the two emotions did not fit. Not with Richard. He could be sarcastic and teasing, or angry. He was never both. 'No. And you know better. We were supposed to start working on a child when all of this was over.'

'I changed my mind.'

'You what?'

He shrugged. 'I changed my mind.'

She put her fisted hands on her hips. 'Richard, what is going on here?'

'Nothing more than what I'd planned all along. You did your part. You lured Glenforde here. He is now dead. So you are free to leave.'

'And if I wish not to leave?'

'I will have Matthew place you aboard your father's ship. You are not staying here.'

She fell to her knees before him. 'What did I do?'

He reached towards her cheek, then drew his hand back. 'You did nothing, Isabella.'

Her name didn't roll off his tongue, he didn't drag it out, as if cherishing each letter. 'Richard, I love you.'

'You don't know what love is.' He rose, pulling her up with him. 'But you will some day.'

She threw herself against his chest. 'Don't make me go.'

He encircled her in his arms and for a moment held her close. Then, holding her at arm's length, he asked, 'Don't you see? This is the only thing I can give to you. The chance to find this love you so desire. Isabella, you will never find it here, you know that.'

'We are married.'

He brushed wayward strands of hair from her face. 'And you know as well as I that your family can see that corrected.' He cupped her cheek. 'One day, this will all be nothing more than a dream, a nightmare better left forgotten.'

'But—'

'No. I'll hear no more.' He released her and walked away, to pause at the door. 'Go. Your father will dock soon.'

She reached a hand towards him. 'Richard, wait, I—'

He had to stay to hear what she had to say. Instead, he walked through the door, out of the chamber and out of her life.

Chapter Twenty

'Lady Isabella, your parents wish a word.'

Isabella turned away from the servant sent to summon her to yet another discussion with her parents. That's all they'd done of late—discuss her future.

She had no future, why couldn't they understand that? She was married to a man who no longer wanted her. She was pregnant with no possibility of being granted a divorce. So, without Richard, there was simply no future.

'Are you coming, my lady?'

Isabella sighed. 'Tell them I'll be down in a few moments.'

None of these discussions did anything to lift the pall that had surrounded her from the moment she'd left Dunstan just over a month ago.

'Isabella!'

She groaned as her mother's shout sped up the stairwell. She took a deep breath and headed for the Great Hall. There was no choice—if she didn't go down there right now, her parents would only come up here.

One of the lookout-tower guards nodded as he walked past her on his way to the doors. Normally the lookout guards only came to the keep when something dangerous, like being under the threat of attack, was about to happen. Otherwise any needed information was shared via riders whose only task was to deliver any messages from, or to, the lookouts. She frowned and joined her parents at the table. 'What was he doing here? Is something wrong?'

'No.' Her father waved off her questions. 'Everything is fine. He was anxious because one of the riders became a little sidetracked this morning and didn't show up at his post on time.'

'Oh.' She took a seat. 'You wanted to see me?'

'Yes.' Her mother tapped a missive that was on the table before her. 'We have heard from Matilda.'

'And what does she say this time, Mother?'

'It seems no divorce or annulment is required. That Father Paul was not a priest. He'd not yet been ordained and had no right to marry you in the first place.'

Isabella wanted to laugh, but knew if she did that she'd only start crying—again. There was no humour in this situation, but it seemed to her that everything had fallen Richard's way, even down to having a false priest marry them. She was certain he didn't know that was the case, she didn't believe him that devious.

She looked at her father. 'Then I suppose you can stop going over that marriage contract.'

'You need to think of the child.' He leaned his forearms on the table. 'I agree with your aunt in this. We feel that your marriage was valid and she intends on taking possession of Dunstan for the child, of course.'

'No.' Isabella jumped up from her chair. 'She can't do that.'

'She can do just about anything she wants. But why would you care?'

'He would have nothing.'

'Who would have nothing?' her father asked.

Her mother explained, 'The child will be set for life, Isabella.'

'Richard. Richard would have nothing.'

'After what he did to you, taking you from your home, getting you with child and then sending you back to us a disgraced woman? Nothing is exactly what he deserves. He should be grateful if he escapes with his life.' Her father's voice deepened to a menacing tone.

She defended Richard. 'He most certainly did not get me with child alone and we thought we were married, so how am I disgraced?'

Her father slapped his palm on the table. 'You defend that pig to me?'

'That pig, as you call him, is the father of my child.'

'Yes, well, thankfully Matilda and your father are seeing that situation is changed as quickly as possible.' Her mother sought to calm the tempers flaring at the table.

Isabella gasped. No, they couldn't be thinking to wed her to someone else. 'I am not going to marry someone else.'

'You are carrying a child, you need to think of his or her future. You most certainly will marry and the quicker the better.'

'Father!'

'Don't you use that tone with me. No, you will listen, Isabella. I know what it is to be a bastard, but at least I was the king's bastard. The child you carry doesn't even have that benefit. How do you think it will be treated if there isn't a strong man around to claim responsibility for it?'

'And who do you think is going to believe I got married and delivered a legitimate child a few months later?'

'It won't matter. As long as the man is powerful and rich enough to stare down the naysayers, all will be fine, you know this.' Her mother reached out and clasped her hand.

'Isabella, what does this man hold over you? Why can you not get him out of your mind? He was evil, a thief who stole my daughter away in the night and nothing more.'

'Mother…' Isabella paused, trying desperately to not sob as she'd done so many endless nights since returning home. She swallowed. 'Mother, he… I…'

Knowing she was losing this battle with her emotions, she slid to the hard floor on her knees before her mother and buried her face in her mother's lap. 'Mama, I love him.'

Her mother combed her fingers through her hair and gently eased her up from her lap. 'Child, why did you say nothing before now?'

'Because it wouldn't have mattered. Nothing would change. You could marry me to a dozen different men and my heart would still belong to the knave who stole me away.'

She heard her father's chair scrape across the floor and his approaching footsteps as he came over and placed a hand on her head. 'Is this man your choice?'

'Yes. Yes, he is. But I'm not his choice.'

Her father and mother exchanged a look she couldn't decipher before he said, 'I need to think about this a little while.'

She bowed her head. 'Father, there's nothing you can do.'

'That might very well be true. Time will tell.'

One of her father's men entered the hall and requested a moment with the Lord of Warehaven.

She couldn't hear their whispered conversation, but knew by the brief exchange that it couldn't have been too important. Her father returned and once again shared an odd look with her mother before whispering something in her ear.

Isabella narrowed her eyes. They were up to something.

It was useless to ask, because she knew from experience they would only deny her charge.

Her mother patted her shoulder. 'Come, give your father some time to think about this and we will talk again later. Right now, you can join me in the kitchen. You've sat in your chamber sulking far too long. It is time you show me what you've learned about running a keep.'

She rose and followed her mother while her father disappeared into his private chamber.

Once they reached the kitchen, her mother studied the herbs hanging over the work table. 'Isabella, run out to the herb shed and bring back some rosemary and perhaps another bunch of lavender.'

Reaching up to touch the rosemary already present, Isabella asked, 'What are you making that will require so much?'

The cook leaned in to say, 'I've a couple of new recipes I wish to try.'

She shook her head and headed for the rear door, only to be stopped by her mother. 'Change your shoes. It is still damp out there and you will only ruin those slippers.'

Isabella spun around to go back up to her chamber to exchange her soft slippers for a pair of sturdier boots.

Isabella tromped through the bailey. It felt good to get out of the keep even if it was just for a few minutes. The air, while still just a little chilly, was fresh and felt good against her cheeks.

She nodded at one of her father's guards, and continued to the small shed alongside the stables.

She wished her sister was here. But Beatrice had been sent north to stay with Jared and Lea right after the kidnapping. Her parents had had no way of knowing if their younger daughter was also in danger, so she'd been banished to safety.

If Beatrice were here, she'd have someone to talk to, someone who would understand how lonely and confused she felt.

Isabella reached to open the door to the shed, only to have a large work-worn hand slapped firmly over her mouth.

She opened her eyes wide in shock as she swallowed the scream she'd been so eager to let fly.

'My, my, what have we here?' the man standing behind her asked softly over her shoulder.

He ignored her struggles to free herself, to ask, 'Why, I wonder, would Warehaven's whelp travel this far from the safety of the keep?'

He leaned closer, his chest hard against her back, his breath hot across her ear. 'Unescorted and unprotected.'

The deepening timbre of his voice acted like a drug-laced wine, soothing her brittle nerves and setting her blood afire.

She went lax in his hold and, as soon as his vice-like grip loosened, she turned around to rest her cheek against his chest, savouring the feel of his arms around her, the familiar scent of his body and the steady drum of his heartbeat.

Then she shoved against his chest, freeing herself from him and from all the things she'd never thought to feel again, demanding to know, 'What are you doing here?'

'There were some things left unsaid.'

'No. I think you made yourself perfectly clear. I'd served my purpose and you had no use for me.' She turned to leave, before she humiliated herself by bursting into tears. She didn't want him to know how badly he'd hurt her.

He grasped her wrist to prevent her escape and tugged her back around. 'We are going to talk, Isabella.'

'Are you kidnapping me again?'

'I can't very well kidnap my own wife.'

'We aren't married, Dunstan. Your priest wasn't ordained.' She leaned closer to peer into his eyes. Even though she knew better, she couldn't resist vexing him. 'But you probably knew that didn't you?'

'What are you accusing me of now?'

'Wouldn't that have been the perfect ploy? Make me think we were wed so I'd come to your bed easier and then, when all was said and done, cast me aside because after all we never were truly married.'

'You have a mighty high opinion of us both, don't you?'

'What do you mean?'

'For one thing, Isabella—' his warm breath against her ear as he rolled her name off his tongue made her shiver '—I doubt I would have had to wed you to coax you to my bed. And if coaxing had failed, you would have been powerless to stop me from taking you any time I so desired.'

Horrified by the truth behind that statement, she stomped her foot. 'Why you…you…low-life scum.'

'And in the second place, I may be low-life scum and a black-hearted knave, but I'm not devious enough to have planned everything quite that thoroughly.'

She curled her upper lip. 'That much is true. You probably don't possess the—'

He placed a finger over her lips. 'Careful. You don't want to say something you'll regret now, do you?'

Isabella shook her head.

He extended his arm and, to her surprise, Matthew handed him a cloak.

She nodded. 'Sir Matthew, 'tis good to see you.'

'You, too, Lady Isabella. How are you?'

'I was fine until a few moments ago.'

Richard cleared his throat. 'If the two of you are done?'

After Matthew stepped back into the shadows, Richard slung the cloak about her shoulders, pinned a brooch in place, then pulled up the hood and tucked her hair inside.

'So, once again you think to disguise me enough to walk through the gates?'

'No. You will walk through the gates, disguised or not. The cloak is to ensure you and the baby stay warm.'

She grabbed his arm. 'You know.'

'Of course I know.'

'Who told you?'

'Conal.'

Ah, Conal had most likely received the news from Marguerite, who'd received it from Hattie, proving the grapevine on Dunstan was alive and well.

'It is yours.'

He jerked back as if her words had threatened to bodily attack him. 'Why would you say such a thing?'

'I didn't want you to think I'd slept with another man.'

'Don't be foolish, Isabella, it doesn't suit you.'

She hadn't been trying to be foolish. She'd been thinking about Agnes and Lisette. It was important to her that he know this child was his. Did that not matter to him?

Richard placed his palm against her cheek and it was all she could do not to lean into his touch. She'd missed him—she'd missed the warmth of his caress so very much.

'Isabella, if I know nothing else about you, I know without a doubt that you are honourable and faithful. I've no fears that you would have taken another to your bed.'

When he dropped his touch, she nearly cried at the loss tightening in her throat. He took her hand. 'Come, we have a great many things to discuss.'

He headed towards the gates, Matthew leading the way. Isabella noticed the decided lack of guards in the gate tower. 'Does my father know you are here?'

'Let's see, this is an island. I sailed around the south-west corner yesterday. Depending on the speed and diligence of his outlooks, I'm fairly certain he knew within hours I had arrived. Obviously, he gave safe passage, because I docked at his wharf unimpeded. So, yes, Isabella, I imagine he does.'

'So this was planned?'

'No. I've not spoken to him yet.'

A terrible thought tripped across her mind. 'He did not send for you, did he?'

Richard's bark of laughter drew the attention of people passing by. 'Send for me? Like one of his paid men? Not hardly, Isabella.'

'Oh.'

'What were you thinking? That your parents sent me a missive telling me what to do? You know better than that. I'm here of my own accord, have no fears on that score.'

Actually, even though she'd never admit it to her parents, just knowing he came here on his own did make her feel better. Although, with the guard from the outlook tower visiting the keep personally, and the obvious lack of gate guards, added to the guard who'd spoken to her father and the looks her parents had exchanged, she wondered if they'd sent her out here on purpose. She wouldn't put it past them. Especially not after she'd so openly declared her love for her husband.

'They have been planning my future.'

'Good for them. I hope you and your new husband will be very happy together.'

Her feet dragged of their own accord. She stared at him. If he wasn't here to apologise and take her home, why was he here?

Her stomach churned until she had to ask, 'Why are you here?'

'To talk, Isabella. Did I not already say that?'

'You sent me away, there is nothing left to discuss.' To her horror she burst into tears. God's teeth, she was tired of these tears, these sudden bouts of sadness so overwhelming that she wanted nothing more than to fall to her knees and sob.

He swung her up into his arms and lowered his lips to her ear. 'There is much to discuss. Now, hush.'

She fell silent and rested her cheek against his shoulder, for now content to do nothing more.

Once they reached the wharf, Richard boarded his ship, docked at the furthest end and carried her to the privacy and protection beneath the covered aft castle. He lowered his arm to permit her feet to land on the deck. 'Stay here.'

She heard him order the men to disembark and telling Matthew to stand guard on the quay, then he returned.

A sudden bout of shyness swept over her. She didn't know what to say, had no clue what to expect. She studied the cabin. Tableware and food were set out on a linen-covered table near the bed. Two high-backed armchairs flanked the table, near dwarfing it in size. Light from the many-armed candle stand in the corner flickered across the table and bed.

Richard pulled a pillow from the bed, placed it on the back of one of the chairs and held out his hand. 'Come. Sit.'

'I'm not hungry.'

He didn't argue. Instead he stepped closer to pick her up and deposit her in the chair before taking the seat across from her. 'I am.'

Calmly, as if he hadn't a care in the world, he snagged an apple from the plate of fruit and idly began to slice it with his small eating knife. He then did the same with a pear, slicing, placing a piece on his plate, slicing again to place a piece on hers. All the while watching her, his expression placid, giving nothing of his thoughts away.

But she knew by his smooth, unlined, unsmiling face that he was angry.

Unable to bear the uncomfortable silence, Isabella asked, 'Are you ever going to tell me exactly what you are angry about now?' Not that he had any reason to be outraged about anything.

He paused to angle the tip of the knife towards her stomach. 'Why wasn't I told you carried my child?'

That's what had him in this mood? 'I tried.'

'When?'

'The day you threw me off Dunstan.'

'I didn't throw you off Dunstan, I sent you home to your parents. And, no, you didn't try to tell me then.'

'Yes, I did. You cut me off.'

'Ah, when you said "but" before I walked out of the bedchamber?'

'Yes.'

'And we both know you are so meek and mild that you never would have thought to scream at me through the door, or follow after me or tried a little harder to tell me.'

She'd give him that much. Perhaps she could have tried harder. 'Would it have made a difference?'

'To your staying on Dunstan? No.'

'Then what difference does it make?'

'I deserved to know.'

Isabella closed her eyes and took a deep breath. She opened them and leaned forward, her elbows resting on the table. 'Richard, what is this about?'

'I need to decide what to do about my child.'

'Your child?' Shocked and dismayed, she leaned back in the chair. 'Your child?'

'Yes, my child. The heir to Dunstan.'

'This is our child, not yours.'

'You are the granddaughter of a king. Your future is secure. The child's future is Dunstan and it needs to be raised knowing what his or her place is in this world.'

'I am the child's mother.' She leaned forward again. 'And your wife.'

'Isabella, you deserve more than I could ever give you.'

So that's what this was about? He thought her above him? This needed to be put to rest now.

'Don't you see? Your father can secure you a husband who will be able to provide you with everything I can't. But I will not permit my child to be a part of that agreement.'

She watched him closely and asked, 'So it bothers you not if I wed another as long as you possess the baby?'

He hesitated slightly before saying, 'You need do what you must for your future.'

Isabella's heart leapt. There, there it was, she nearly swooned with relief. She easily ignored his words, they were meaningless. His hesitation and that brief shimmer deep behind his sapphire gaze told her everything she needed to know.

The question now was if he would ever permit himself a long enough moment of weakness to realise it. She had to take the risk no matter how much pain it might cause to him, or her.

Isabella rose. 'Perhaps you are right. I do need to see to my future, since it is plain you care not.'

She clasped her hands before her so she would do nothing foolish like reach out to him and walked purposely towards the doorway.

Something behind her fell heavily to the floor. 'Isabella, please understand.'

Without turning around, she said, 'Oh, I fully understand, Richard, once you sated your thirst for revenge you had no room left in your heart for me. You made that clear.'

'No. You are wrong.' The heavy sadness in his tone nearly caused her to turn around, but she stayed in place, waiting for him to say what they both needed to hear.

'When I stared down at Glenforde's dead body I felt no satisfaction. None of the relief I'd expected came from his death. I realised in that moment that revenge no longer filled my heart, it was too full of you to permit something as vile as vengeance any room.'

She gripped the beam of the doorway, to keep from turning around and throwing herself in his arms too soon. 'Yet you sent me away.'

'I ruin everyone I touch. I couldn't let that befall you, too. Not at my hands.'

'Self-pity does not suit you.' She needed more than his explanations and self-accusations, they would not suffice. She wanted his apology for the hell he'd put her through. She turned around to continue her confrontation, only to gasp at the sight before her.

'Richard?'

The sound of something heavy hitting the floor a few moments ago had been him. He was on his knees, on the cold hard deck, staring at her. His eyes glimmered, creases cut across his forehead and the tick in his cheek beat rapidly. 'Isabella, I am sorry. So sorry for all I have done to you. I never should have used you in such a manner. Please, tell me you understand that I need to make up for the wrongs I have committed against you. I only care about what is best for you.'

He hadn't said 'I love you,' but he had apologised and she was certain that one day his heart would prod him to say the words she'd waited a lifetime to hear. For now, it was enough that her heart melted at the honesty of his reply.

But she groaned at his misplaced reasoning and walked back to him. 'Richard, the only thing that is best for me is you. That is all I need, all I'll ever want. Do my needs not matter to you? Do you think another husband will make me not long for the lust I feel at your touch? Do you think he will appreciate me desiring another in our marriage bed? Do you truly believe that a huge keep, filled with servants, men and gold will begin to make up for the love I hold for those at Dunstan?'

He wrapped his arms around her. Resting his head against her belly, he whispered, 'I may never be able to give you all your parents can.'

'Oh, you mean like their lectures on how I should comport myself, what I should or shouldn't do? Trust me, my love, you excel at that. Or did you mean the keep? Warehaven is under my mother's command, not mine. Now that I've had a taste of it, I would rather have command of my own abode, thank you very much. Or were you referring to my father's temper tantrums?' She threaded her hands through his hair and held him tightly to her. 'Yours are so much more enjoyable.'

'Does this mean you will forgive me? Will you come home?'

'Richard, I would like to see anyone stop me.'

The sound of boots hitting the deck outside the cabin and the jingle of amour prompted her to add, 'I believe we have company.'

Richard rose and gathered her into his arms. 'I care not.'

'You had better care, young man.'

Isabella laughed at her father's growl. 'Father, I'd like you to meet my husband, Richard of Dunstan.' She turned to Richard. 'This grousing warrior is my father, Randall FitzHenry of Warehaven.'

Her father glared from one of them to the other. Finally, he asked, 'Ah, so this is the knave who despoiled my daughter and left her dishonoured?'

Richard bowed his head. 'Yes, sir.'

'What have you to say for yourself?'

Richard squeezed her fingers, and raised his head. 'I would do it all over again, sir, without a second thought.'

Her father tried his best to look angry. When that didn't work, he tried to look shocked, which only made Isabella lean her head against Richard's arm. 'Give him but a moment, he'll settle on one or the other.'

Finally her father motioned Richard to join him. 'Come along, it seems we need to revise that farce of a marriage contract you drew up and find a real priest.'

Chapter Twenty-One

Isabella stared out of the window of her chamber at the rising sun. Richard had spent the last two days ensconced with her father, working out the details of their marriage contract. They'd start early in the morning and end late in the evening.

Her parents had assigned him to a chamber at the other side of the keep with orders not to even consider visiting this one.

She had barely got the chance to see him, let alone talk to him.

The ceremony was slated for today. Since there were so many here from Dunstan to attend the wedding, her mother had decided to use the church in the village instead of the family's private chapel in the keep. Richard, Conal and the others would gather outside the church soon, if they weren't already there.

She'd been thrilled to discover that Marguerite, Hattie, some of the maids and others from Dunstan had made the journey to Warehaven. It pleased her to know Richard had been confident enough of her love for him that he'd come prepared for another wedding.

And she'd been delighted to learn that once they returned to Dunstan another marriage would take place. Marguerite was finally going to make an honest man out of Conal—at least that had been his explanation. Isabella was happy that they'd decided to wait until her return before exchanging their vows.

'Looking for someone?' her mother asked from the doorway.

'Is Father Bartholomew ready?'

'I'm sure he is.' She draped her cloak over a bench. 'Come, let's get you dressed.'

Her mother helped her into her gown, then drew her into an embrace. 'I will miss you so.'

'Mother, I will be closer at Dunstan than Jared is at Montreau.'

'It is different with you. You are my daughter, Isabella.'

'You are planning to come to me at the end of summer, aren't you?'

'Child, I wouldn't miss this birthing for anything in the world.'

Whether it was having Richard so close and not being able to talk to him these last couple of days, or carrying a child, or once again leaving Warehaven, or just the simple fact it was again her wedding day, Isabella burst into tears. 'Mama, I am so scared.'

Her mother laughed softly. 'I would be concerned if you weren't.' She stood back and smoothed one of Isabella's braids. 'You are strong and healthy. Richard will be there. Your father and I will be there. All will be well, Isabella, I promise you.'

She sniffed and wiped at her eyes. 'I'm sorry. I just… I don't know. I just feel so…weepy.'

'I hadn't noticed.' Her mother chucked her under the chin. 'Dry your eyes. Don't let your father, or husband, think I've been tormenting you.'

Isabella laughed. 'I'm fine.'

'Good. I need to make sure your father is ready before I leave for the church. He will meet you below.'

Isabella smoothed the skirt of her green-silk gown. She, Marguerite, Hattie and her mother had worked tirelessly to turn the length of silk into a gown for her and a tunic for Richard. They'd trimmed both garments with slivers of blue ribbon.

Slipping on her grandmother's torque, the best piece of jewellery she owned, she took one last look around her chamber and smiled. It would be the last time she'd have to sleep alone.

Isabella met her father at the foot of the steps. He took her hand. 'Are you ready?'

'Yes.' She was more than ready.

'Your mother has already left for the church.'

'Then we should join her.'

He led her out to the courtyard and a waiting horse. 'Do we really have to do this?' she asked.

'Your mother and I were wed in rush with very little ceremony. We weren't present when your brother wed Lea. So, yes, Isabella, we are doing this as properly as we can in the time allowed.'

With the assistance of her father and a guard, she mounted the ribbon-bedecked horse without further argument.

On foot, her father took the reins and led the way to the village church. There, he helped her down, led her to the door of the church, placing her at Richard's left side and stood between them, stepping back only after assuring Father Bartholomew that there was no reason they should not be wed and that he was freely giving her to Richard.

This time, when she said her vows, nobody had to force her hand, or say the words for her.

Richard handed the priest their two gold bands, which Father Bartholomew blessed and handed back.

He slipped the ring on to her finger, saying, 'With this ring, I thee wed.'

His hands were steady, his voice strong, while her hands shook visibly as she slid the band on to his finger and her voice was little more than a hushed whisper, when she repeated, 'With this ring, I thee wed.'

And when they knelt inside at the altar for the priest's blessing it was all she could do not to cry. She wondered if she would always be this weepy. Or if, eventually, she would regain control of her emotions.

A nudge from Richard drew her out of her musings, reminding her where they were.

When the ceremony ended, and they left the church, she noticed that all of Richard's men had green-and-blue silk ribbons tied around their arm.

She glanced at him, realising that she hadn't seen his ribbon because it was made of the same fabric as his tunic.

She reached over and touched the ragged scraps of fabric. 'And where did you find the scraps?'

'I have my ways.' He shrugged. 'I can't tell you all of my secrets, Wife.'

She rolled her eyes. 'Fine. Keep your secrets, then.'

Later, after the meal, Isabella slowly walked around the perimeter of the Great Hall. Between those from Warehaven and Dunstan, the hall was crowded. Much to her mother's delight—and her dismay as the walls seemed to close around her.

'Come.' Richard hooked his arm through hers. 'We're going upstairs.'

She slipped her arm free. 'No. Our friends and people are here from Dunstan. We'll stay.'

'Isabella, I can see that you're ill. Besides, your mother just ordered me to take you from the hall. Who am I to disobey a direct order?'

'I can manage on my own.'

'I never said you couldn't. But I've no wish to let you sneak off without me.'

'I wasn't going to sneak off.'

He leaned close and whispered against her ear, 'Ah, but I was. See, perhaps you weren't aware, but this is my wedding night and I've every intention of wickedly seducing my bride if she'll let me.'

She laughed softly at his teasing. 'Oh? And what exactly did you plan to do?'

'Well, first I thought I'd kiss her senseless until her toes curled and she needed to hold on tightly to keep from falling.'

Isabella shivered. 'And then?'

He put his arms around her, pulling her into his embrace and started backing her slowly towards the stairs. 'Then I planned to remove her stockings. One at a time so I could slowly trail my hands over her shapely legs. Stopping only to kiss her ankles, then her knees and her luscious thighs.'

'Mmm, that sounds wickedly lovely—and then?'

'I'd loosen the ties of her gown and slide my hands ever so slowly up her body, feeling the warmth of her flesh all the while pushing her clothing up until I could pull it over her head.'

'Oh, my. Then she'd be naked.' Isabella's heart raced at the images his words created in her mind.

'Yes, she would. She'd be naked, hot and needy. Better still, she'd be completely and totally at my mercy.'

Breathless, she asked, 'And then what would you do with her?'

'I would stroke and taste her most intimate flesh until

she repeatedly cried out my name in wild abandonment. I would make certain she begged until she could withstand no more.'

Isabella thought she'd faint with need right then and there. But she wasn't yet willing to cry surrender. 'And then?'

In a deep, husky whisper he answered, 'And then, that very moment before I claimed her as my own, I would tell her that I have finally found the one thing that I thought would for ever elude me, the one thing that makes me complete.'

'And what might that be?'

'Love, Isabella. I would tell her how very much I loved her and how I couldn't imagine ever living without her at my side.'

Knowing that everything she'd ever wanted, ever desired, ever dreamed of, was now within her reach, Isabella looked up at him.

His shimmering brilliant blue eyes met hers without wavering.

She placed a hand against his cheek and whispered back, 'And she would vow to hold your heart gently and for ever close.'

* * * * *

Give a 12 month subscription to a friend today!

Call Customer Services
0844 844 1358*

or visit
millsandboon.co.uk/subscriptions

The World of
MILLS & BOON®

HISTORICAL

*Awaken the romance
of the past*
6 new stories every month

*The ultimate in romantic
medical drama*
6 new stories every month

MODERN™

*Power, passion and
irresistible temptation*
8 new stories every month

By Request

*Relive the romance with the
best of the best*
12 stories every month

Have you tried eBooks?

With eBook exclusive series and titles from just **£1.99**,
there's even more reason to try our eBooks today

Visit www.millsandboon.co.uk/eBooks
for more details